VAMPIRE METROPOLIS

by

ROBIN BROWN

A Wild Ink Publishing Original
wild-ink-publishing.com

Copyright © 2025
Edited by Nicole DeVincentis and Claire Godden
Design by Abigail Wild
Layout by Laura A. Wackwitz

ISBN: 978-1-964885-08-7

If you enjoy this book, please recommend it to your friends and leave a review wherever you're allowed.

If you don't enjoy this book, please recommend it to your enemies. Why should you be the only one who suffers?

For Pumpkin, for being a good writing companion and an even better cat.

ACKNOWLEDGMENTS

First and foremost, thank you to everyone at Wild Ink Publishing. The indic publishing scene is a goldmine of stories, original thinking and welcoming communities, and Wild Ink is a fantastic example of this. In particular, I'd like to thank Abigail Wild, Brittany McMunn, Abigail Taylor, Claire Godden and Nicole Devincentis. I sincerely appreciate your trust, advice and enthusiasm.

I'd also like to thank everyone in my family and assure them that they will be receiving a certain book for every birthday and Christmas henceforth.

Lastly, I thank the reader who reviews and recommends. So, thanks! I hope you enjoy my weird little story.

PART 1

"Happy trails!" the military man shouts at me, laughing over the screaming wind and the massive roaring engines. Then he kicks me out of the plane.

I'm not surprised by this—actually I've been expecting it for quite some time, ever since they caught me, in fact— and yet the force of the freezing night wind still catches me off guard. The rushing air surrounds me and tosses me like I'm a rag doll in a hurricane. It doesn't help either that my arms are bound in military-grade cord, but at least my legs are free to flail about uselessly. Yes, they are useless, kicking air and spinning me about aimlessly, but at least they are free to be useless, unlike my arms.

So, this is what it feels like to fall from up high. Arms bound, legs useless, and completely deafened by the buffeting wind. I must admit, I had always wondered. But then again, anyone who is like me wonders about this. And fears it too, I suppose.

I turn midair, and I see the metropolis below me. It is everything I imagined it would be. Dark windows, tall skyscrapers, the occasional fire dotted about the place, and most terrifying of all, the whole place is alive with activity. It's like an ant's nest down there (if ants needed high streets and big, pointy buildings… and a giant wall surrounding it to keep anything from getting out).

All this I catch in the sporadic few moments where my eyes are pointing to the ground. I am, unfortunately, still being spun around by a vicious wind and, yes, I am still falling at what must surely now be terminal velocity. Those small buildings are getting bigger alarmingly quickly, and those narrow streets are looking thicker by the second. It won't be long before I say "hello" to Mr. Ground.

But before that can happen, I'm lucky enough to bounce off the side of one of those tall skyscrapers I noticed earlier. And by bounce, what I really mean is I slam into it, shatter the windows around me, pulverise almost every bone in my body, crack my head on something hard, and then rebound from the sheer force of how hard I hit it in the first place, to then continue on my way down, down, down to the ground.

When I land, I land hard.

Every bone in my body now resembles fine sand, each of my limbs now has several new joints and, despite the fact I am definitely not moving, my head still feels like it's spinning in a hurricane.

I've landed on hard, flat concrete. This was always likely to be the case, but I can't help thinking how nice it would have been to land in a green park area or into a nice, cool pond of water. The ideal scenario would have been falling through a roof and landing in a nice stranger's living room. Of course, even if I had gotten that lucky, I would still be very much broken, but at least I would have been broken somewhere inside and warm. Out here though, I am helpless to the elements, as it were. And it's a cold, dark night.

I'm not sure how long I lie here for. As it turns out, it is quite difficult to contemplate the passage of time when my brain is in the process of knitting itself back together. It was dark when I dropped in, so to speak, that much I know for sure, and for a while it wasn't dark at all, but when someone takes hold of my foot and starts dragging me away the sky has turned dark once again.

I probably should be worried, but half my body is still mush whilst the other half of me has done just enough mending, fixing, and knitting back together to realise how much pain I should be in right now. It is a lot, unfortunately. But I won't die, because I can't die. After all, you can't kill that which is already dead.

***

We vampires don't like light. It's got nothing to do with sunlight being pure and burning away sin or anything like that. We simply don't like it (although it does itch and this is annoying, but not skin-meltingly, body-explodingly agonising).

You know how humans don't like the darkness because they can't see what might be hiding in the shadows. Well, we're the ones hiding in those shadows, with emphasis here on hiding. The darkness, where no one can see us, is our safe space and we've learnt that when humans can't see you, they don't bother you.

I suppose there is also the underlying feeling that the isolating darkness makes us feel better about who we are, because deep down we don't like ourselves, but that's some therapist mumbo-jumbo and a rabbit hole without end.

Regardless of whether the light is too bright, or the dark is too dark, or the contempt for one's own existence runs too deep, it really doesn't matter because it all adds up to the same thing anyway. Vampires don't like the light. So, when I'm finally propped up and some inconsiderate arsehole decides to shine a bright light bulb right in my face, I tell him where he can go stick it.

"That's not very nice," a gruff and deep voice replies. "Specially as we're the ones who saved you."

"Should be more grateful, eh?" someone else says, their voice tinny and cracked.

Wherever we are, we're inside. I can tell from the way their voices bounce off the walls and the ceiling. It's the way the stuffy air presses down on me, though, that tells me we're probably underground. A basement, maybe? Yes, I think so. I can't be sure though because my brain is still a little bit raw (literally) and the light in my face casts everything else in complete darkness. Truth be told, I can barely keep myself on the chair they propped me up on.

I can't see anything, but I can still sense the one with the gruff, deep voice is the one holding the light in front of me. Whoever he is—whatever he is—he's big. Very big.

"You're patching yourself up alright," he comments, and I get the unsettling feeling that he's looking really hard at me, using the bright light to focus on all the damage I've sustained. "Definitely one of the lucky ones."

I know I shouldn't say what I'm about to say. In fact, there are two very good reasons why I should definitely not say what I am absolutely about to say.

The first reason is Scenario One, in which these two people, whoever or whatever they are, have taken me in from the cold. They don't intend any harm upon me, and they are, in fact, helping me. If this is the case, I should be grateful to them.

The second reason, which is Scenario Two, concerns the opposite being true. These two people intend much harm upon me and I'm completely at their mercy right now, so maybe saying what I am about to say will only turn an already bad situation into a far worse situation.

So, I know I definitely shouldn't say what I am about to say. But I say it anyway because I'm an idiot, and because I've got a chip on my shoulder, and because I'm scared of being vulnerable, and because I'm angry at the idea of being indebted to someone, but mostly it's the idiot thing.

"Drink your own piss and die, lughead."

For a second, nothing happens, and I actually feel pretty good about myself. I know I shouldn't feel good about saying what I said, but in my weakened state I can't deny how pleasurable it is to make something else feel small and bad.

In the next second, though, a fist the size of my head slams into my temple. The force sends me flying off the chair, which clatters noisily to the ground, and I'm left in complete darkness. A small and treacherous part of me misses the shiny light bulb.

***

Vampires don't have the luxury of losing consciousness and we also can't fall asleep. There are upsides to this, like no bedtime, no missing anything, and no waking up feeling all groggy. The downsides, however, include no sleeping even when we're tired, missing everything because we're so tired all the time, and spending every hour of every day feeling really groggy because we are always so very tired.

This is why I've been awake and conscious this whole time. From being kicked out of a plane, to plummeting down to the ground, to hitting the city hard, to finally being dragged away and propped up (only to end up getting punched in the side of the head).

I'm still awake when the big one picks me up and chucks me over his shoulder. They clearly don't care for me; they haven't even asked what my name is. Climbing some stairs we leave what apparently was a basement and now we're outside and walking, and so I get my first close-up look at the streets of Vampire City—albeit an upside-down close-up look, but still a close-up.

Imagine a normal city. Lots of concrete, everything's a bit old, there's too much to keep clean and there's never enough space for all the lights, shop windows and advertising boards. Got that? Okay, good. Now add a couple decades of complete and total neglect, then consider cripplingly low resources and factor in a new population that is angry, frustrated and quite literally *hemmed in*. Welcome to Vampire City. It's clearly a shithole. A rough one too and it really does look it. Incidentally, as vampires go, you can never trust the way they look.

Take myself, for example. I look like a nineteen-year-old English country boy, with annoyingly blond hair and irritatingly blue eyes (someone else's words, not mine). I look like dads would approve of me, mums would fawn over me, but more importantly I look like girls would fall for me and other boys would wish they were me.

What I actually am though is a nearly two-hundred-year-old predator, and as of only a few nights ago, I spent my nights skulking in alleyways or behind poor warehouses looking for my next fix. You see, the dads who approved of me are now hunting me, the mums that fawned over me are double-locking their doors at night because of the likes of me, the girls who fell for me ended up drained of blood, and the boys who wished they were me ended up the same way or dead, or as good as. But I don't want to think about that right now. The point is, we vampires are never what we appear to be.

My captor is carrying me through the streets of Vampire City in the middle of the night, and soon we are passing through what appears to be social spot for the vampire community.

Here they are. My brethren. My kin. My future? I wonder who these city vampires really are, underneath what they appear to be. Some of them watch me with curious and hungry looks but most simply ignore me. Are they like me? Did they once prowl the back streets of the world, desperate for ignorant prey? All I know for sure is one thing. Every vampire here arrived in this forsaken dead-end city the same way I did. They were caught, tied up, and kicked out of a plane… by humans. Humans are bastards.

It's a long and bright street. Electric neon lights banish the crushing darkness as heavy electronic beats cry out from the surrounding nightclubs merging together to drown out the cold silence of this rain-spattered night. Seems like a nice enough place.

The vampires in attendance are dressed to impress. Leather get-ups, pristine boots, some with grinning masks and others with long hoods, and it all screams excess, drama, and danger. I used to have a therapist many years ago, and these were exactly the sort of people she loved to warn me about.

We stop moving, there's some conversation between the big, gruff guy carrying me, the one with the tinny and cracked voice, and some others who I don't recognize but sound angry, mean, and menacing. Whatever their conversation is about, it is a short one and it leads to a door being opened and the three of us going inside somewhere, with me still being carried fireman-style over the shoulder of the big guy. It is my rotten luck however that the moment my regenerating neck muscles feel strong enough to lift my head, I'm carried through a doorway, and I end up cracking the back of my skull on the top of the door frame.

I curse loudly and I get a swift smack for my trouble. This is when I finally see an actual face, and it is the one belonging to the tinny and cracked voice. He holds my face to his own and growls angrily at me. It turns out he's a goblin.

His own small face is wrinkly and knobbly, his eyes are big and bulbous, and his hair is dry and weedy. His attire isn't much better, consisting of a sodden coat, rank trousers, and old, worn-out boots. He's definitely an ugly fellow, but then all goblins are ugly (at least they are from where I'm standing, or rather, from where I currently am being carried over a shoulder, hanging upside-down).

"Keep your mouth shut in here, you hear me?!" he spits angrily in my face, but all I can think of is how he has to stand on tippy-toes just to be eye-to-eye with me. Goblins are short in stature, short on patience, and short for brains. For the sake of spite, I tell him this now and I get another whack round my ear. It was worth it though.

Then my world spins and my view changes from the ugly, upside-down face of a goblin and the backside of the large chap who has been carrying me this whole time to a world that is at least the right way up, if not entirely improved.

The large lughead, who appears to be a companion to the goblin, looks down at me. And he really does have to look quite far down. He's huge. Easily nine feet. Tall enough so that the top of his bald head skims the ceiling. Imagine a giant baby with big eyes and a dull face and this is what you'd get.

"You're a half-troll, aren't you?" I ask him.

"I'm Needl," the half-troll growls, his voice a deep and echoing drone, and it's immediately obvious that this particular half-troll doesn't have two brain cells to rub together in that massive bald head of his.

"Shut up, Needl." The goblin elbows the half-troll angrily, though he only connects with Needl's kneecap. "And you too. What'd I tell ya?"

"I think you told me to keep talking, no matter what you say to the contrary," I reply.

"Proper smart-arse, ain't ya!" But before the goblin can give me a good old-fashioned hiding with one of his tiny craggy hands, someone stops him. Someone with such an oily and meticulous voice that I not only hear it inside my ears, but I feel it run up my spine and chill my thoughts.

"Not in here, Gawk."

Gawk the goblin deflates, and even looks a little sheepish, but he soon gathers what anger he has left to shoot me a final menacing glance. He then storms out of the room, dragging Needl along with him, but before he slams the door shut, Gawk says something that piques my interest.

"We got you a good one, we did," Gawk says to someone, probably the owner of the oily voice. "So that's us paid up for the week."

And then the door is slammed shut and I am left in this room. This room. A wide, open room in which, unlike the streets and the clubs, the only light is the moonlight entering through the large, archway windows.

There are expensive-looking furniture pieces everywhere, on one side there is an unattended bar, and in a corner a small stage. And here I sit on a long luxurious sofa, barely able to turn my head let alone explore this private lounge or pour myself a drink from the bar. I can just about look to the side though, and when I do, I immediately wish I hadn't.

Sitting next to me is someone like me. As in, someone who also looks like they've recently been kicked out of a plane and fallen six-and-a-half-thousand feet to land on some especially hard concrete. Beyond this unfortunate individual is another unfortunate, and another, and another. There are several of us sitting here. Some with bones still solidifying, some with parts still growing back, and others that look more like humanoid bags of jelly. Upon seeing these others, I think back to the first thing Needl the dimwitted half-troll said to me, back in that dark basement when he flashed that bright light in my face. I really am one of the lucky ones.

"We keep you here," the mysterious oily voice tells me, "until you've healed. Sometimes it takes days, sometimes weeks, but by the look of you, you'll probably be ready in a few hours."

"Lucky me," I croak weakly.

"Look at that." The oily voice livens up. "You've even got your voice back. You're practically a picture of health."

I turn my head back so that I'm not looking at the others, and I now notice someone is in fact sitting at the bar. Not quite so unattended, then. He is tall and dressed in a smart black suit, with black slicked-back hair. Other than this, I can't make out any more because he has his back to me. He does look like he's nursing a small drink though, one of the stronger varieties.

"Ready for what?" I ask, and what I get for an answer is a mirthless chuckle and a question.

"What do you know…" He gets up from the bar and walks towards me, leaving his drink at the bar. As he steps into the pale moonlight I get a good look at him, and in this moment a fly that had been resting on his cheek flits away. "…of Vampire City?"

He's a snake. Not an actual snake, of course. But if Needl the half-troll looks like a baby, and Gawk the goblin resembles a street urchin, then this man has the feeling of a snake. No. Not a man. I can tell—call it a kindred sense—that this snake is a vampire, just like me, and just like all the others outside on those loud streets.

He has a long face, small eyes, and dry pale skin. He looks older than me by a good dozen years, but we're vampires so how old we look is almost definitely not our real age. He could be thirty, he could be a hundred. Hell, I've known vampires pushing a thousand.

"All I heard is that this place is a dead end. There's no getting out." I say this trying to keep my voice tough and bullish, though alas I am betrayed by an unintentional squeak right as I hit the dead-end bit of my snark.

He nods, thoughtful, then comes at me with another question. "Where did they pick you up?"

For a moment, I'm confused. "Oh. You mean those two?"

"Who? Needl and Gawk?" He shakes his head. "They're only the scum of this city. No. I'm talking about the humans who dropped you in this place."

"Oh," I realise, sombrely. "Them."

"You look European." His watchful eyes pass over me, taking me in, leaving me feeling like I'm on display, which, I suppose, I am. "Maybe American. But you don't have an accent."

"Grew out of it a while ago."

"Ah, got a few years under you, then." He nods, just as thoughtful as before, and he keeps looking over me. It's unsettling to say the least, especially when another fly crawls across his cheek and passes over his lips before eventually flying away. "I was picked up in San Francisco, oh, nearly seventeen years ago now. So, where was it they caught you?"

"London," I tell him.

"London?" He raises an eyebrow. "Dangerous place for our kind. Lots of guards, with guns too, and cameras on every corner, and sixty thousand humans that hate our kind."

"Yep. Sounds like home," I say.

"Why London?"

"One back-alley is like any other," I tell him, hoping he won't pry.

"A back-alley bloodsucker," he grimaces, obviously unimpressed with my recent (undead) life choices. "So many of our kind are reduced to such a pitiful existence. Out there, anyway. In Vampire City, you can be so much more."

"I can't wait," I say with as little enthusiasm as possible, and then I try for even less. "I've always loved the idea of being trapped in one city for the rest of eternity, cut off from humanity's pulse, with nothing else to do but waste away and wonder what might have been if I hadn't been caught, if I hadn't found myself tied up, and if some arsehole human hadn't decided to kick me out of a plane only to then forget about me forever."

"You misunderstand." The oily-voiced vampire smiles, and he moves a chair so as to sit across from me. Once seated, he stares at me, and he now looks like a hunter eyeing their captured prey. I shudder, which is still quite a painful thing to do in my still very broken body. "You will be more here," he continues, "but this does not mean you will be better. For example, you could be more afraid, or you could be more content. You could find yourself under more pressure, or you could be more docile. Whatever you were out there, you will be that and tenfold in this city."

"Oh… goody?" I want to annoy him, but so far, he seems unmoved by my childish teasing.

"You can change, of course," he says, still eyeing me the way a hawk eyes a mouse stuck on the end of its talon. "But only if you learn to play by the rules."

"We're vampires." I try to laugh derisively, but it comes out as more of a weak sigh. "We don't have rules."

He stands up, looks down at me one last time, and smiles once again.

"There are always rules."

✳✳✳

The oily-voiced creepy guy with the slick-backed hair has a name. It's Serat. That's what the other vampires call him, and they all sound like sycophantic bed-wetters when they do talk to him. There are others who come to the lounge bar too. Others who are like Gawk and Needl and, like those two, they come to drop off others like me.

Goblins, half-trolls, dwarves, and even a band of tiny pixies each visit Serat's lounge bar throughout the night, and each bring with them an unfortunate individual they've happened upon. Some of these unfortunates are a little less broken than others, but most of them are pretty bad. The one dragged in by the tiny pixies is basically a beanbag with body bits washing around inside.

I can tell there is a real mix of sub-mortals in this city—a sub-mortal being what humans call anything that isn't human, be it elf or dwarf, pixie or troll, rat-man or treeman—but in this instance, all of the unfortunates are vampires, because only a vampire is truly unkillable.

Oh sure, you can dust us with a stake through the heart, chop off our heads, blow us up or drown us at the bottom of the ocean, but we always come back. The dust eventually comes back together and *undustifies*, the head will eventually regrow a body (or the body will eventually regrow a head, it's always one or the other), if close enough the little smoking body bits will find each other and put themselves back together like a messy puzzle, and if we're stuck anywhere, like at the bottom of the ocean, we'll wait. Sure, it might take a long time; in fact, it might take a very, very long time, but it's not like we need to breathe—that's something only the living have to contend with. Of course, it still hurts. It hurts exactly as much as getting your head ripped off would hurt, or being blown apart, or being crushed under the pressure of the water at the bottom of the ocean. And because we're vampires we're conscious for the whole thing, but like I said, we don't have any choice in the matter but, you know, we eventually get better. So, that's cool. Right?

When it comes down to it, vampires can't die because vampires are already dead.

Back to the here and now, and time is passing on by in this dimly-lit lounge bar. Every so often, a fly skitters over me. At one point, one of the blighters passes across my vision.

It's not too long though before my body starts to wake up. It starts with a finger here, and then a toe, then a twitch, and then I get more movement in my neck, and soon I'm shifting uncomfortably and groaning painfully.

"You look ready enough, took a little longer than I thought, but you'll do now." Serat nods at me. "Before I do this, I want you to know that I'm special. Very special." What the hell is he going on about? "Here. This is for you."

He offers me a square white napkin. I barely manage to lift my arm, open my hand, and grasp it feebly with my fingers. I stare down at it, wondering what the hell I'm supposed to do with it. I'm battered, bruised, and bloodied. Every part of my body is in such tremendous pain that my mind is almost numb to it by now. And this snobby jerk has just handed me a small tissue, as if my only problem is a bit of food around my mouth.

I look up at him with angry eyes, ready to unleash a very snarky and witty remark, but when I do look up at him words fail me for the first time in a very, very long time.

Serat's fangs grow larger, his jaw stretches open, his eyes burn red and fixate on my neck, and he lunges down with a ravenous screech. The pain is indescribable, but I'll give it my best shot.

It's like everything inside of me is being pulled out of me. My blood, my bones, my guts, and my nerves are all being sucked through two tiny holes in my neck. I can't move, I only spasm; I can't breathe, I only gasp airless breaths; I can't blink, my eyes are stuck open; and I can't scream, I can't find my voice.

I can see my hand, rigid and immobile, as it becomes not the hand of a nineteen-year-old English country boy but the hand of a withered old man, and then it becomes even thinner, feebler, and finally it is the hand of a corpse. And I can feel the same thing happening all over my body. My face sinks into itself, my torso shrinks and pulls tight, my mind is screaming.

And then it's over. Serat pushes himself off me and shakes a little with new energy, and I am left here, as limp and helpless as I was when I landed with a thump the previous night.

The vampirism in me brings me back quickly enough. I regenerate. It hurts like hell, and it leaves me exhausted and drained, but within a few seconds I am back. My face is restored, my hand is my hand again, and I can just about scramble to my feet.

"Now," Serat says in a dismissive, but energetic voice. "Get lost."

He's back at the bar, turned away from me, and I don't even have to think about my next move, I just do it. I charge at him. I'm going to tear him limb from limb —

He's quicker than me. I am a tired snail to his primal panther. Of course this is the case, because he drank my blood. He has the energy that was once mine. He catches my wrist, he grips my neck, squeezing painfully on the two holes he was moments ago drinking from, and then he throws me. I fly across the entire lounge and smash into a wall. It hurts but I'm so used to pain right now I barely notice.

I go again. Serat swipes me aside as if I'm nothing but an irritating fly yet still I don't learn my lesson. I pick myself up and try for a third time. He kicks me back down. I want to go again but my body gives up on me. I suppose my body has more sense than I do.

"Get lost," Serat repeats. "And get used to this."

He crouches over me, peering down on me with an almost idle curiosity, and he sighs. There is stolen energy behind his eyes, betrayed by the erratic twitch that always comes after a feeding, but he doesn't look happy. He doesn't look like anything actually. He's as lifeless as the humans say we are.

"You've got spunk, I'll give you that," he says. "You got a name?"

"Caiden," I splutter, too tired to lie and too drained to resist. "My name is Caiden."

Serat nods slowly. "Welcome to Vampire City, Caiden." And he tosses me a fresh white napkin. But I don't even notice because, for the first time since becoming a vampire almost two hundred years ago, I do something I thought was impossible. I pass out and lose consciousness.

***

I wake up. It's a weird experience to wake up for the first time in two centuries. At first, I have no idea who I am, what I am, or where I am, and I don't even have an inkling for the concepts of the *whys*, the *hows*, and the *what fors*.

My hearing is distant, my touch isn't registering, and my nose feels blocked up, but I can just about see. And what I see is old graffiti on a weathered brick wall. In no uncertain terms, the graffiti tells the internet where it can go, and where it can go is nowhere good.

Ah, yes. The internet. Human technology! Connectivity! The ire of the vampire, the end times made real, the fall of a bygone age. Before the internet, before video-sharing was so easy, and before everyone and their kid had one of those cursed camera phones, there was ignorance. Blissful, blissful ignorance. A vampire was nothing but a folktale and a fairy tale, and even if any truth could be countenanced it was a truth that could be ignored, dismissed, and forgotten about. Vampires weren't real, and even if they were, they happened to other people and did not concern any human who had a sense of decency, propriety, and civilization.

But then the internet happened, and suddenly the existence of vampires, and other such demonic and devilish creatures, could not be denied. And so, the humans did what the humans do so well. Everything they didn't like they rounded up and dropped into a city with a big wall surrounding it, all so they could forget about us, free to carry on with their own lives pretending vampires and such like don't exist. As for us, we're left here, in a metropolis called Vampire City, to do what? I don't know. Nothing, I suppose. This really is the dead end.

I'm Caiden, I'm a recently-arrived vampire in Vampire City, and I've woken up for the first time in two hundred years in a dank and rubbish-strewn back alley, no doubt dumped here by one of Serat's cronies, far away from him and his lounge bar. In my cheap dark coat, grubby jeans, plain shirt, and worn-out trainers, I feel a million miles away from the devilish master of the night we vamps are supposed to be.

I rather wish I could go back a few seconds, back to when I couldn't recall who I am, what I am, and where I find myself. Ah, those were the good times.

Huddled behind the dumpster opposite is something that looks like a girl. She sits among the garbage, unmoved by the stench that has me grinding my teeth. Her hair is so dirty it's difficult to tell that, underneath the grime, it is light and fair. The hoodie she is wearing is too big for her, her knees are pulled up inside it, and all I can see of her skin are her fingers and her toes, both as filthy as cobblestones. Then she glances up at me, and I see her eyes: white iris, white pupil. Pale as the shroud and I scramble back. It's a banshee.

"Piss off!"

I scramble to my feet (no small feat considering my body feels like it's been through a meat grinder) and, as she watches me with blank eyes, I turn my back on her and hasten onto the most depressing street I've ever had the misfortune to step out on.

Last night, I had seen bright lights, heard loud music, and everyone had been overcompensating with their fashion choices. Now though, all I see is the deprivation of modern society. The skyscrapers are dirt-ridden, paths are strewn with rubbish, and there are ungainly homeless types that sit anywhere there is space. These poor creatures have nothing but thick layers of old, previously cast-off clothes. Some huddle together whilst others sit apart. I make sure not to look any of them in the eye as I walk on by.

There is lots of graffiti. Most of it is terrible, some of it is quite original, much of it is morosely depressing, but all of it is hateful. There are no cars, no buses, and not even a bicycle, and so this road I walk along is eventually taken up with shabby stalls selling suspicious odds and unnerving ends.

Further along the street, there are also rancid shacks, cobbled together with whatever metal sheets and wooden planks could be found, and they line the streets, forcing the homeless types to squeeze into even smaller spaces, or more likely, return the way they have come.

Finally, as I keep walking, there are oil barrels every so often that burn a pathetically feeble amount, warming only those who have pushed their way to the front (and pushed everyone else out the way).

I try to look inconspicuous, which is actually not that difficult because of the small early-morning crowd populating this street; everyone has something that makes them stand out.

There's a lizard-skinned drake passing by wearing a shabby coat and looking thoroughly bedraggled. A nymph splutters unhealthily as I spot her sitting on the street curb, her dire and weak aesthetic reflecting her surroundings. A few down-trodden elves, in hoodies and dirty jeans, have clustered together outside what must be their shack, and they talk in hushed whispers, nervously looking over their shoulders every so often. They look strange in this harsh environment that is a world away from their wild forests and their woven robes.

There is a goblin, even shorter than Gawk, peddling their wares from a rickety cart. Some stalls sell rancid meats, others hawk suspicious-looking produce, and there are many selling clothing fit for a dumpster. Most of these enterprises are run by gruff dwarves, but I also see a dryad, her skin like bark and earth, who sits in the corner of a tiny stall selling bizarre-looking potions in stained jars, and then there is a beautiful half-naked woman with bulbous brown eyes manning a stall stacked with thin, sickly fish.

The shuffling crowd makes this tumbledown, ramshackle market a fairly busy one, though the sun is still low in the sky, so I get the impression it will get much busier as the day wears on. Even so, amongst the mish-mash there are mist-form sylphs, undines of the sea (or as a layman would put it, fish people), flaming dogs that scrabble around and leave behind burn marks wherever their claws touch, gnomes that come up to my knee, goblins that come up to my waist, dwarves that come up to my chest, elves that could look me in the eye, trolls twice the size of me, and a tree person as tall as a… well, a tree. None of them were kicked out of a plane like vampires are, but they all found themselves here, nonetheless. I tell you, looking at them, I don't know why the humans didn't just do them in. But then, of course, that would make the humans murderers, and like every child's book says… killing is wrong.

Relocation though? As in, putting them somewhere where they won't be able to bother humanity ever again? That's not wrong. That's even for their own benefit. At least, that's how the humans market it.

Killing might be bad, but so is this place. They are all poor, dirty, sullen, and wary. They go about their business, either bartering for goods or trading their own, with a nervousness that comes from finding themselves at the bottom of life's barrel.

I still keep to myself, I don't make eye contact, I don't step in anyone's way, and I keep my head low and my hands in my pockets. In one of my pockets, I find the square white napkin Serat gave me.

I take it out and press it against the bite wounds on my neck. The wound stings and I feel fresh, thick ooze sticking to the napkin. It's because a vampire bit me as to why these little marks remain. Something left over from his fangs is resisting my own healing. I need a scarf. Surely one of these stalls will have a scarf.

At first, I'm not sure why I thought of a scarf, but when I take another look around the market, I immediately realise why I did. Everyone has something around their necks. Lots of scarves and high-necked tops, and just as many keep their hoods up.

Everyone has been bitten.

"Well, well." A tinny, crackling voice speaks up behind me. "Look who it ain't."

I turn and see Gawk and Needl. The goblin and the half-troll who dragged me off the street two nights ago, punched me in the head, and then sold me to a vampire who fed on me.

I should hate these guys, and I probably will, eventually, but right now I haven't got the energy.

"Who ain't it?" Needl drones. The big half-troll is standing behind Gawk and is carrying a rucksack over his shoulder.

"It ain't nobody worth our time, not anymore." Gawk grins, and I get a good look at dozens of broken jagged teeth in his wide mouth.

"You?" I exclaim. "What are you two doing here?"

"Making a living, anyways we can," Gawk replies. "We don't get it easy, unlike you fang boys." He spits at my feet before pushing by me (although it's Needl who does the actual pushing). "Outta our way, greenhorn!"

"Wait, no," I try, but I stumble backwards, and I bump into a grumpy dog man who shoves me back with a snarl and a bark. I'm bustled by the crowd, I completely lose my bearings and were it not for Needl's large stature and rucksack over his shoulder, I would have lost them in a matter of seconds.

Instead of losing them though, I move after them. I'm not sure why. Maybe it's because they know me (though they don't really know me) or maybe it's because I want to tear them limb from limb (not right now though—still too tired) but all I really know for sure is that I don't know anything, whereas they at least know something. Maybe I can tear them apart after they've helped me learn more about Vampire City. That's the vampire in me thinking.

I make my way through the crowd, pushing through the little cluster of elves keeping to themselves, then accidentally knocking into the back of a dwarf as she angrily barters with the stall owner. Apart from an expletive from a disgruntled dwarf, no one pays me any attention, no one gets out of my way, and no one much cares beyond a grumble or a shove when I have to push past them. It's a crowd of individuals, most everyone keeping their heads low and their eyes downcast.

Up ahead, I can see Needl turning off the market and going down another street, narrower and somehow danker but one that is mostly empty. There are only a few homeless down here, crouching to the side, shivering and feeble, but I ignore them and instead catch up to Needl and Gawk.

"Hey!"

They stop, then turn round with confused, quizzical expressions, and they see me. And after they've seen me, they turn back around and continue walking.

"Hey?" I try again.

"We're not your babysitters, fang boy," Gawk calls back. "Go find your own way."

I'm a vampire. We're top of the food chain. I should be too proud to do what I'm about to do. I should have enough self-respect to retain what dignity I'm about to give up. And I should definitely have the confidence to go it alone in a strange new place. After all, I am the shadow in the darkness, the nightmare to a dream, a walker between life and death. But it turns out I'm not too proud, I don't have enough self-respect, and I definitely do not have the confidence to go it alone. Not now. Not after last night. Not after what Serat did to me.

"I'll do anything!" I whine, and how I wish I had not squeaked. I hate my voice.

But it works. Sort of. Gawk stops and Needl eventually stops too, but only after realising his little companion is no longer half-jogging along at his side. They both turn back and face me, one with a grievous, sorry look about him and the other with a dumb and confused expression.

"Look, fang boy," Gawk sighs. "I get it. We've all been there. The rest of us might not have been dropped out a plane, like what happens to you, fangs, but we get trucked in all the same and marched through the gate. We all have our first days. This is yours. You just gotta work it out."

"Help me." I come forward. "I… I would normally be fine… but… something happened last night, and this morning I… I did something I've not done in…"

"You got bit," Gawk sums it up with an almost tired sigh. "And you got knocked out."

"Yes… Yes!" I nod desperately. "But I'm a vampire and we can't—"

"Listen!" Gawk turns on me and points a long, thin, knobbly finger in my face. "Everyone gets bit. Take a look." The goblin pulls down the collar of his scruffy coat to show me the side of his neck and I see two bite wounds, older than mine but fresh enough. "You too, Needl," Gawk says to his friend.

"Don't wanna," Needl moans, shaking his head reluctantly.

"Go on," Gawk hisses impatiently. "Show him!"

The half-troll pulls at the giant jerkin he's wearing and reveals his neck to me, and sure enough I see two pinprick bite wounds. They might look smaller on Needl's thick neck but they're definitely there, and they're definitely the same as Gawk's and my own.

"First thing to know about Vampire City," Gawk says, pushing his collar back up as Needl also hides his own neck under his garment, "is everyone gets bit."

"But it shouldn't happen to me," I reply, and I know I sound petulant and selfish, but I can't help it. It's who I am right now.

"It does in this place."

"Everyone get bits," Needl reiterates.

"But I'm a vampire!" I insist, stepping backwards, swaying, and struggling to accept everything what the goblin is telling me. I nearly trip over a crushed can and then I stick my foot in something squishy and sticky. I'd rather not know what it is though, so I make a point of not looking down.

"It don't happen too often to the rest of us, but when it does, we get a little woozy afterwards," Gawk continues. "Sometimes though, Serat takes too much, and then we're flotsam in the lake, understand? Swimming with the fishes! But when you fangs get it, you get it hard, cos you lot don't die. He can take and take but you can't get offed. Serat can do what he likes but you'll never be flotsam."

"But vampires don't drink from other vampires. They can't! Can they?"

"Apparently, there's something special about being a lord of a borough. That's what Serat says, anyhow. The lord can take whatever he wants, and he does."

"But I'm the one who takes!" I snap angrily at the goblin. I'm losing it. Losing my mind, losing my composure, losing my temper. I want to feed on something. I *have* to feed on something—no, *someone.*

A hospital blood pack I've snuck out into some back alley won't do it. Not when I'm like this. Not when I'm this desperate and this scared. I need fresh blood. I need someone's neck. "I'm the one who takes!" I cry out and I lunge at Gawk's neck.

My fangs are out, my eyes have turned a fiery-red and I am nothing but a predator moving in for the kill. Until I get punched in the side of my head (for the second time in as many days) and I am sent flying into the very hard and very uneven brick wall of an old building on this sparse and desolate street.

"Pick him up, Needl," I hear the goblin say beneath the ringing in my ears. "This one's gonna learn the hard way."

***

How the hell am I back here?

And by back here, I mean staring upside-down at Needl's arse. I'm being carried over one shoulder, whilst the large rucksack is over the opposite shoulder, and I occasionally bump against it as they take me… somewhere. I'm too groggy to ask, Needl's too simple to think of anything to say, and Gawk apparently wants me to learn the hard way.

It's a long walk. At some point, Needl drops the rucksack, and Gawk argues over a price; then we're off again, leaving the rucksack behind. We pass over cracked pavements, overgrown weeds between street slabs, uneven steps, and rubbish. So much rubbish. If there's one thing I'm certain of about this city, it is that it hasn't been cleaned in decades.

Finally, after my body feels more like a lump of heavy jelly, I am carried inside and dropped unceremoniously onto the hard floor.

And the place explodes.

Not in fire but in cheer. And not in jovial, supportive cheer but in mean-spirited, blood-thirsty, hates-my-guts kind of cheer.

I look at my surroundings. It's a large warehouse but it feels small. It feels small because there are so many crammed into it. They stand around me, they sit on high shelves, and some even perch on the ceiling beams, looking down at me and hollering with the rest of them. But I am alone in where I stand, and where I stand is in a crudely dug ditch, circular in shape and a whole man's height lower than the warehouse floor.

"Erm," I start awkwardly, unsure of what I'm supposed to do. "Hello?"

But no one's talking to me. They're only laughing, booing, cursing, and pointing. Needl is standing at the front of the baying crowd and he's the only one who doesn't look like a mad hooligan, although whether this is because he doesn't approve or because he's too simple to join in, I don't know. Gawk's clambered up to someone sitting on a high stool and he's arguing… no, he's bartering… pointing at me? No, wait, not bartering… that little craggy bugger is placing a bet!

I see the betting board and then I notice how everyone is holding paper slips. But are they betting on me or against me? Actually, the most pressing question is what do they expect me to do?

I hear a tremendous thud behind me. Someone—or something—has jumped into the ditch to join me. I get a sinking feeling. Oh. It's that kind of bet. I turn round and I see the biggest, most deranged-looking faun imaginable.

She has scary-looking tattoos up both her arms, each one professing her love for either her mother or for extreme violence. Her goat legs have more muscles than I have in my whole body and each black hoof has been spiked. Quite literally spiked. There are tiny metal spikes protruding in every direction, because apparently getting kicked isn't painful enough.

Her extremely long, dark hair is plaited and is also sporting several sharp metal spikes throughout. With goat-like ears that stick out sideways and eyes with horizontally elongated pupils, this faun looks more wild than anything you'd find in a city. In fact, the only thing about her that places her as a city dweller is the T-shirt she's wearing. It says *My Other Shirt Is In The Wash* although, by the look of it, this shirt is long overdue for one.

"Oh no," I whimper. I really don't want to do this. I haven't the energy. I haven't the will. "Can we not—"

But I don't get to finish my pathetic plea before the faun roars and charges at me, much to the delight of the crazed crowd. I leap to the side and just about scramble away from her wild and haphazard swings.

Right now, it's important to note one very simple fact about me. I'm a vampire, not a fighter. Actually, no vampires are fighters because, crucially, we don't have to fight. We slink about in the shadows, we creep up on our victims, we beguile our prey, and we scarper when the deed is done. We are not naturally strong creatures. Any strength we do have comes from whoever we're drinking. We steal energy, we leech it, we take what we cannot create for ourselves. Sure, we can turn ravenous, but that's only when we're about to feed. Or to be more precise, that's only when our victim is already beaten.

This faun is not beaten. In fact, this faun gives the clear impression that she's never been beaten. If I could have drunk her blood beforehand, well, I'd be as strong as she is now. More so, in fact, because that's just how it works. But face-to-face, I haven't a chance of sneaking in a little nibble. And any energy reserves I once had were drunk up by Serat last night. All this amounts to one very simple fact: I am screwed.

I get to my feet, run to the side, and try to jump up. I don't manage it, and everyone laughs at me. They hoot and wail at my struggle to pull myself up and out of the ditch. I could probably do it with a few tries and no one kicking me or pushing me back down. But the bastards at the front of the crowd are doing just that. Big feet, little feet, craggy feet, hairy feet, and the occasional painful hoof step on my fingers, stopping me from gaining any purchase. I don't stand a chance. Falling back down, I land hard on my back, only to then stare upwards and see the upside-down face of the faun looking down at me. I'm at her mercy.

Before I get a chance to whimper and beg, she grabs my face with one huge hand, pulls me up and throws me against the far side of the ditch. Everyone roars in appreciation.

"Look, I don't think this is fair—"

She punches me hard in the stomach, knocking the air out of my lungs and causing me to wheeze terribly.

"…if you could just… give me a moment to—"

She drives an uppercut into my jaw, sending me rag-dolling into the air only to come back down hard on my back again.

"I don't even know what I'm supposed to be—"

I sit up and this is a mistake because I get a spiked hoof that smacks painfully into the side of my head. It sends me sprawling across the cracked mud floor. I stay down, which is probably the smartest decision I've made since I landed in this city.

I feel it under my hair. A trickle. A warm trickle that's too heavy to be water. I put a hand up to my head and bring it away and there are dark red specks of blood on my fingers.

Everyone goes silent. The faun stops and stares at me. I have no idea why. In front of them all is a blond-haired vampire lying on the ground, who has just taken a tremendous beating, which they have been cheering on, and now this vampire is bleeding. Bleeding. It's a strange thing indeed to see one's own blood, especially when I'm so used to seeing everyone else's. For this brief moment, I ignore the throbbing pain of my bruises and the dizziness in my head. All that stuff will be fixed in a quiet moment anyway. I'm looking at my own blood and it's like I'm seeing a hard and terrible truth. Here, I am the one who bleeds.

The moment of silence is over. Everyone sees my blood and they all cheer louder than ever, and so the faun raises her arms in victory and jumps out of the ditch. I have evidently lost. If my battered and bloodied body isn't enough of a clue to this fact, then Gawk being the only one in the crowd groaning with frustration clearly indicates that, for the goblin at least, I have failed in whatever it was I was supposed to do. I don't care though. I'm just thankful for the few moments of peace, where everybody is too busy cheering and no longer interested in beating me up. These few moments allow my vampiric regenerative abilities to kick in. Within another few seconds, the bleeding has stopped, the bruises have healed, and I return to my original, nineteen-year-old country boy appearance.

I clamber to my feet and am at least glad the whole ordeal is over. At which point, naturally, I hear a tremendous thud behind me. Someone else—or something else—has jumped into the ditch.

I turn round and am faced this time with a sylph. The crowd begins baying for blood once more (quite literally) and the sylph comes forward, advancing on me with an unnerving calmness. It is an air spirit. I think. Spirits are difficult to categorize because they don't have any labels. There is no gender to speak of, no features to describe, and even the voice of a spirit will be unlike any other. The sylph in front of me is condensed swirling air, resembling several hurricane clouds that have come together and concentrated their wide mass into roughly a humanoid shape. It is as if a mad scientist gave life to the air particles inside a compressed air can. Heavy, thunderous, and mean-looking. This cloud looks like it's going to burst.

But who cares? I don't. All I see in front of me is a lot of wind. All bluster, no muster. A muscled, spikey-hoofed faun is physically far superior to me, but I reckon even in my bloodless state I can handle a sentient breeze.

I am wrong.

The sylph comes at me faster than my eyes can see. It rushes through me, sending me slamming to the ground, and then it comes back again, picking me up and throwing me. And it comes again, and again, and again. Each time it is like a strong morning breeze hitting my face, only this breeze travels at twice the speed of sound, and it hates me.

Every few seconds I am being hit by several miniature hurricanes focusing all its strength entirely on me and me alone. Crumbling to the ground, I hold up my hand as if I have any hope at all of protecting myself. The sylph stops, the crowd roars in delight, and I see on the hand I am holding up a sliver of dark blood running down my finger.

"The sylph beats the faun!" someone with a speaking horn declares. "One minute thirty-seven seconds!" I sigh, stand up, and stretch my newly regenerated body. I have already hastily wiped the blood off my finger. "Bring on the next challenger! One minute thirty-seven seconds to beat!"

I sigh. There is a tremendous thud behind me. Yet another someone—or yet another something—has jumped into the ditch to join me. Same deal, I suppose. Just a different bastard.

***

When the game finally ends, a faun, a sylph, a minotaur, a gremlin, a horde of gnomes, a tree-dwarf, and a centycore have been some of the more notable contestants to take on the challenge of "beat the vampire to a pulp until he bleeds". I'm not sure who won the day, but I know for sure I did not.

Dusk comes. Is this it, then? Is this what I have to look forward to for the rest of eternity? I'm a vampire, I'm going to live forever, and there's no escaping Vampire City. On the outside, this place is talked about as the end of the road. It literally is the jailer locking you up and throwing away the key. This is it. This is life now. So, I guess this must be it.

But surely something will happen. Someone will take me by the hand and tell me I'm special. The equivalent of giving me a quest, putting me on a journey, fastening a cape around my neck and telling me to be a superhero. Not that I want any of that stuff. I just don't want what I've ended up with.

Right now, I could really do with a giant, terrifying, mysterious, crossbow-wielding stranger forcing their way in whilst I'm sleeping to tell me I'm a wizard and probably the greatest wizard at that. But none of that is happening. This feels horribly real and if you don't like that then that makes two of us. This isn't a fairy tale, and it isn't a dream come true. This is the city, this is the world as it is, and there's no convenient design that will lift me up. So, hi, I am in the real world, and dusk has come.

Still in the ditch, it doesn't matter that I can't see outside. I know dusk is here. I feel it in my bones, in my chest and in my blood. I wouldn't be much of a vampire if I didn't know when night was falling. As today has proven though, I'm not much of a vampire anyway.

I've been beaten black and blue all day, and dark red too. I've been beaten for the dark red of my blood and I feel humiliated, small, and defeated. I shouldn't be feeling like this. Vampires are at the top of the food chain. Always have been. Always will be. *The others* should be the ones who feel like this. Not me. And I should be the one making them feel like this.

I'll get even with them all someday, I promise myself petulantly. Not now, though. Right now, I'm propped up against a rusty metal column in the warehouse. Every part of my body hurts, though I look as fresh and fine as ever. Regenerative powers make me look good and get me going again, but they don't do anything for the actual pain. Now that's a raw deal if ever there was one.

I'm alone in this massive and dilapidated warehouse, which is somewhere in this massive, dilapidated city. Once the game finally finished, everyone filed out, chatting amiably enough or grumbling loudly enough, some collecting their winnings and far more paying out what they owed. And they forgot about me. So here I am. Alone in this warehouse.

"Thought you'd last a bit longer," a familiar tinny voice chides me. "You fang boys ain't all that, specially when push comes to shove."

I turn my head, which is inordinately painful, and I see Gawk approaching and Needl shuffling along behind him. For a half-troll, the big lug sure can sneak.

"What was the point of all that?" I wheeze.

"Just something we do round our way," Gawk shrugs, sitting across from me. "Passes the time. Can make a few dog-ends too with some smart bets on a pitch fight. Still, we never had a vampire to play with. Usually it's a dumblings match or good old-fashioned fisticuffs."

"You lost your dog-ends, didn't you, Gawk," Needl guffaws.

"Yeah, I did," the goblin sighs, and he shoots me an accusing glance. "Like I said, thought you'd last a big longer."

"Well, I'm so very sorry to disappoint you," I say, rolling my eyes.

"I'm not disappointed, am I, Gawk?" Needl beams like a puppy in a butcher shop. "Made a killing on the fang boy, I did!"

"Needl cleaned up proper," Gawk grumbles. "But I thought you'd last at least five minutes. Didn't even make it to two! And on your first round!"

"Could you both kindly... piss off." I try to turn my head away, but it only ends up rolling back. I haven't even the energy to sulk off.

"That vixen had him in half a minute, didn't she, Gawk!"

"She did, but she's a hot one." Gawk whistles with a begrudging appreciation. "Flame demons! Something else, they are."

I can barely recall the flame demon Gawk is speaking of. I can barely lift my arms, I can't move my legs, everything still hurts, and I have a headache. A really big headache. The kind of headache that weighs a lot and won't go away.

I hate it here. I've been in this city for nearly three days now and there's nothing about it I like. From spending my first day broken and unable to move, to being sold off on my second night and fed upon by another vampire (something I didn't even know was possible), and finally today, my third day, where I've been beaten up and bloodied, all for the perverse pleasures of the lowlifes and nobodies of this city.

"I hate it here," I say, interrupting whatever Gawk and Needl were talking about.

"Course you do," Gawk laughs. "Everyone does. But you're lucky, you are. You're what we call…" Gawk leans in closer, conspiratorially. "…privileged."

Privileged? Lucky? I'd fling my arms up in exasperation if I wasn't worried they might snap off with such a motion. I'm sitting in a rubbish warehouse, propped up like a bendy vegetable, unable to wiggle my toes and internally screaming in agony. And this goblin thinks I'm privileged!

"I don't think you know what that means," I say to the goblin, and the goblin slaps me across the face. It stings, it jerks my head to the side, and I need to summon effort I don't have to turn my head back to where it was.

"You're privileged!" he tells me, almost spitting. "Because you got these!" And he pushes his fingers into my mouth and grips my fangs. As short as my fangs are currently, Gawk still manages to pull at them painfully. Then he takes his hand back and continues, "Everyone gets bit, remember?"

"Everyone gets bit," Needl echoes, rather glumly.

"But not everyone can bite," Gawk bemoans. "We ain't got what you got. We've only got whatever gets left, so what we get ain't hardly a thing worth getting. Follow?"

"Not really," I groan.

"Look, fang boy, listen up and listen good." Gawk stands up and paces slowly around me. "This city works real simple-like. That vampire we gave you to last night—"

"Serat?" I remember his snake-like face, his voice that sounded like oil down my spine, and I also remember the horror of him biting and feeding on me, and how helpless I felt when it was happening. "Bastard."

"That's him, alright. Serat the bastard. But he's our bastard!" Gawk says. "He owns this borough. Duke's Borough, we call it. Every street, every building, every shack and stall, from the market to the slums, and that includes every sorry one of us who scratches out a living here too." Gawk makes a point to show me his own bite wounds, dry and scabby unlike my own, but still as prevalent. "He owns us. Serat owns everyone in Duke's Borough. Because he's the one who does the biting!"

"Everyone gets bit," I say, starting to understand.

"There are other boroughs, and each one's controlled by a different vampire, who do their own biting, but this borough here… this one belongs to Serat," Gawk tells me.

"Just tell me what I've got to do," I say, breathing deeply, "to get the hell out of here."

"Well, that's it," Gawk smiles. "You're a vampire. This is Vampire City. You've got everything you need to make it in this place. You got fangs and you can't die. Basically, you can bite back, and no matter how much you get bit, you'll always get back up… eventually."

"Lucky me?"

"Lucky you." Gawk nods.

"So, if I bite Serat, do I get this borough?" I ask, hoping it could be as simple as this, but knowing it almost certainly is not.

"Pretty much, yeah." Gawk surprises me. "It's simple. Bite the bastard who bit you. But just cos it's simple don't make it easy. See, this is how it works. Every vampire that drops in Serat's borough gets picked up and delivered to him."

"Delivered by you," I interject, accusingly.

"By the likes of us, yeah," Gawk says, smiling appreciatively, like a tradesmen being reminded of a good job. "Keeps Serat from picking on us, see? For the most parts, anyway."

"He's too busy drinking his vampires," Needl contributes, sitting cross-legged on the hard cold floor. "That's how it is, ain't it, Gawk?"

"That's how it is," Gawk responds, but his watchful eyes stay on me. "Do you know why Serat feeds on his own kind? They all do it. All the vampire lords, each with their own borough or district, they all drink their vampires. They feed on their own flesh and blood. Do you know why?"

"Because they're insane," I manage to say, suddenly feeling revulsion swell up within me. "Never happens on the outside," I spit angrily. "Vampires don't drink other vampires! It's disgusting. It's sloppy seconds. It's dirty!" My mind is racing, my body still feels raw after the beatings it's endured, like new skin over a deep wound, and I desperately don't want any of this to be true. Everything Gawk is telling me, everything about this city in which I now find myself, makes me feel small, powerless, and hunted. This sucks.

"They do in Vampire City," Gawk chuckles, getting to his feet and pacing around me, like a schoolteacher circling their latest victim. "Oh, it ain't pretty. And none of them likes it as such, but they want all the power for themselves. Look at you! You're weaker than a bedevilled halfling! But you know what's really funny, what the real punchline is… you lot take it. You get just enough energy to go out at night, to lose yourself for a few hours, but then you got no energy at the end of it, so you slink back to him."

"You're so full of it," I say, petulantly.

"You got no energy right now," Gawk points out. "You ain't the big fish here, mate. You got no choice."

"I'll bite you," I say, angrily. "I'll feed on all of you. And when I'm stronger, I'll crush Serat's head and—"

Gawk turns on me fast. Suddenly he's in front of me, towering over me in fact, and he grips my face in one of his craggy hands and forces me to look up at him. "Do you really think every vampire that's dropped into this city hasn't said the exact same thing?" He drops my face and steps away. "Hell, some of 'em have even done it in the other boroughs, and they take over that borough and then they're the one who gets to feed on everyone else. Circle of life, or whatever you lot are. But Serat won't ever let that happen to him. He keeps a close eye on his vampires. If you start feeding, he'll sense it and he'll come feed on you. He'll keep you weak, and you'll fall into line because it's easier than the alternative."

"What's the alternative?"

Gawk spits on the floor. "Living with the likes of us, the piss-poor scum and the no-hope losers of this city, the arse-end of the world as we calls it. So, yeah, welcome to Vampire City, and welcome to how the world really works."

***

It didn't happen. That thing you think will eventually happen, even though nothing else seems to be happening right now… well, it didn't happen. No hairy half-giant barged in to tell me I'm actually the chosen one. It's been three weeks since I landed in Vampire City, and nothing's happened. The gods closed the door on me, but they forgot to open a window. My train hasn't come in. Fortune hath not turned in my favour. Take your pick.

I spent the first few days getting beaten up, and I spent the next few days recovering, but I've spent the last few weeks doing next to nothing.

I have nothing to my name, no one wants to know me, and I have no idea where to start.

During the day, I do nothing. I don't need to sleep, I don't need a home, I don't even need to drink, despite how much I want to. I wander. That's all there is to do. And at

night, I stick to the darkness and hide, keeping to myself…
I don't want the other vampires to see me.

The other vampires. I've watched them from afar.

They spend their nights in loud clubs and under bright
lights. And then when day comes, they disappear inside.
I'm not sure what happens to them, but I can tell they're
running on empty, even at the beginning of the night.
They're spent. It's exactly as Gawk told me, they haven't
the energy to do anything but move under bright lights and
let the music take over.

Bloody hell.

In all my years as a vampire, I've never come across a
vampire that feeds on other vampires. I never imagined it
was even possible, although now I think about it, I had no
reason to think this. It just feels wrong, let alone something
a vampire would seriously consider doing.

But it is real, it happened to me, and it knocked me out,
and that's something else I didn't think could happen.
After two hundred years, it turns out I don't know half as
much as I thought I did. Apparently, spending two
hundred years doing the same thing is as good as spending
an afternoon doing the same thing.

Serat keeps to himself, isolated in his private lounge bar
and happy to let the plebs of his borough eke out a living,

so long as they do not disturb the status quo that has him seated at the top.

I'll kill him one day. I spend most of my time wandering and daydreaming about what I'll do to that bastard. I'll tear him limb from limb, and when he comes back together, I'll tear him limb from limb all over again. I might even feed on him. No. No, I won't do that. It still feels perverse to feed on another vampire.

Maybe I should feed on some easy prey. A banshee? No, they have tainted energy. They're not real in the same way you and I are real. A faun? No, they'd easily beat me up. Gawk? I haven't seen him or Needl in weeks.

There is a problem though with me feeding on someone. Gawk explained it to me with his parting words back in the warehouse.

"You can't feed on anyone," he told me. "Serat won't let you."

"How will he know?"

"He's fed on all of us, remember?" Gawk reminds me. "He'll sense any other vampire who feeds on one of his stock." Gawk spits again. "You feed on someone, and you'll have Serat on your back in seconds, ready to take back what he claims as his own. It's how he keeps control."

"Bastard," I say, for the umpteenth time.

"Bastard." Gawk agrees with me.

So, here I am. Sitting on the edge of a narrow, inner-city canal. A canal that is more sludge than water, more detritus and rubbish than earth and plants. And it didn't happen.

That thing you always imagine will happen when you have no idea what you should do next. An opportunity bound to come a-knocking? Nope. Nada. Not a dicky bird. That bloody, good-for-nothing, non-existent, hairy, crossbow-wielding giant.

And yet I keep telling myself, even now, something will happen. It can't stay like this forever. Something will happen to take me from this place. But it hasn't. Not yet, I keep telling myself as I throw an aimless stone into the sludge of the canal, watching it sink slowly into the mud.

I lied before. It hasn't been three weeks.

It's been three years.

Three years and three weeks.

Three years and three weeks and another three months.

Okay. Four years.

And eight months.

And three weeks.

It's been a long time. Nearly five bloody years.

It may as well have been three weeks though because nothing's changed, apart from I'm shabbier than I've ever been, my clothes are dirt-ridden and patchy, and I spend my time wandering, beating up the occasional weakling for their dog-ends, running the odd errand for a few more dog-ends, and hiding from everyone else.

Maybe I really should join Serat. Maybe I should let him feed on me like the other vampires do. At least then, I'll be part of the herd. I'll spend my days inside, probably waiting to be fed on, and at night I'll join them in the clubs, in the bars, in all the places where it's too loud to talk and too bright to think. At least then I won't have to mix in the downtrodden markets, alongside the other poverty-stricken wretches of this city.

No. No! I won't ever do that. I feel such temptation in my darkest moments, but I won't ever fall into line. I won't ever be part of that creep's system. I hate him. I hate him more than I've ever hated anyone. I hate him more than I ever thought I could hate someone. He took something from me. My blood, my freedom, my sense of who I was, and then he forgot about me. He tossed me aside as if I were just another nobody. I suppose I am. I hate him for this too.

I stand up and—Ow! Someone's stabbed me through my stomach. There's a long, thin metal pole protruding from my gut, having been pushed through my back with some considerable force, and the only reason I'm not screaming in agony is because I'm just too bloody tired to bother.

I turn round—with the aforementioned metal pole still sticking out of me—and I see before me a very angry, but rather small, young woman. A very young woman, actually. She looks far too young to be stabbing vampires, at least she does to me anyway, although at this moment I'm probably unfairly biased against her.

"What the hell do you think you're doing?" I demand of her, irritably.

"Bastard!" she spits at me and then I notice how she's looking at me. Wow. I don't think anyone's ever looked at me with such hatred, such detestable rage, and such ferocity. This really is saying a lot, because I've done some terrible things to a lot of people over my two centuries of being a vampire (after all, it comes with the territory) and a lot of people have been none too pleased about those terrible things and they certainly made their feelings known.

"Me?" I wince. "You're the one who just… argh, wait…"

I can't ignore the pain anymore. I grip the pole. I twist and turn it and pull it forwards through me… and I also try not to cry. It really hurts. It really, really hurts. Finally—and with only a discreet teardrop that I manage to wipe away—I drop the pole and take a moment to let my body regenerate.

"Okay, now, where were we… oh, yes—OOOOMMMPPH!" The little she-devil's kicked me hard in the stomach and sent me falling backwards into the sludge of the canal. Disgusting mud soaks my clothes, and I can't breathe. Not that I need to breathe, of course, but it's funny what you notice when it's taken from you.

Wait… no… not a she-devil… a vampire. My instincts aren't what they were four years ago (nearly five), but they catch up eventually. She's a vampire.

I look up and there she is, standing on the bank of the canal, looking down on me and looking for all the world as if she's about to rip me apart. She has big brown eyes, dirty blonde hair, and a fierce determined face with a small button nose in the middle of it. She's wearing raggedy jeans, a zip-up hoodie two sizes too big for her, and a T-shirt with a cartoon cat on it. The cartoon cat is saying something which is probably witty and charming, but I can't read it because I'm getting punched in the face over and over again.

I gather up some energy—energy I can barely afford—and I spend it on kicking this tiny, furious vampire off me. She rolls in the mud, growling with frustration, but I don't stop to see what she does next. Scrambling up to my feet, I try to make my escape. Slipping a few times, looking like a baby deer on ice, I finally get to the edge of the canal. With an almighty effort, I haul myself up the vertical, man-made bank. Eventually, I get my head over and I swing my leg up, using what energy I have left to drag myself out of the canal and back onto the edge I was only moments ago lounging on.

She's already here. She looks… embarrassed. Huh. Not angry anymore. Not blinded by rage nor driven mad by violence. Just embarrassed. But not for herself. She's embarrassed for me. Urgh. Seeing how she looks at me now, with an awkward distaste in her eyes, makes more of an impact on me than all the metal poles, kicks to the stomach and punches to the face combined.

"You're not who I thought you were," she tells me, her voice actually quite soft now she's not spitting at me.

I sigh, I groan, I look up at the sky and, for the umpteenth time, I wish I was any place but here and anyone but me. "Yeah," I reply. "I know how you feel."

"I'm sorry." She offers what sounds like a genuine apology, if not exactly heartfelt.

"Don't bother," I say as I get unsteadily to my feet. "After all, I don't." I smile weakly and she shifts awkwardly. "Out of curiosity though, who did you think I was?"

"The vampire who did this to me." And she pulls her hoodie down just enough to show me her neck. There are the bite marks, right where they are on everyone else, but these ones are fresh. Fresh enough that her dark vampire blood still oozes slowly out. My own marks have been scabbed for years now.

"Oh." I nod, understanding. "I see you're new here."

"I'm getting out of here."

"No, you're not." I start walking, and for some reason, she starts walking in the same direction.

"I'm going to kill that son-of-a-bitch first!"

"No. You're not."

"And I don't care if it kills me."

"No." I almost laugh at the cruelty of it all. Repeating itself over and over again. A horrible cycle that happens to all who arrive here. "It won't and you do."

"Whatever," she seethes. "I don't care what you think."

"Nobody does," I sigh. "But let me guess, not too long ago, the humans snatched you and signed you up for a never-ending stay in this here metropolis. They unceremoniously kicked you out of a plane and last night you were delivered to another vampire—a total bastard of a vampire, I might add—who bit you, fed on you, and made you feel like you were dying, at which point you lost consciousness, only to wake up in some back alley this morning. Am I right?"

"Nearly," she says, warily.

"Nearly?" I raise a curious eyebrow. "I'm usually bang on. After all, it's what happens to the rest of us. Why only nearly?"

"I'm not a vampire."

I look down at her. I only notice now what the cartoon cat on her T-shirt is saying: *I don't do mornings… or afternoons… or evenings.*

That's kind of funny.

✳✳✳

Two vampires. One is shabby, dirt-ridden, and tired. The other is not shabby, not dirt-ridden, and not tired. One looks to be nineteen, tall(ish), with bright blond hair, blue eyes, and natural good looks. The other one looks fourteen, small (very small), with dark blonde hair, big brown eyes, and a button nose on a stern face.

I wonder what Gawk makes of us.

"Caiden? Haven't seen you in ages," he says, looking up.

This is Gawk's place. It's a crap hole. A tiny office space, hidden away in a dilapidated building in one of the many forgotten corners of the borough. He has shelves piled high with folders, and boxes upon boxes filled with whatever Gawk manages to get his grubby little fingers on.

"Miss me?"

"No." He shrugs. "Yer a waste of space."

"Missed you too."

"Who's this?"

I'm about to tell Gawk the young girl's name… but then I realise I don't know her name, so I turn to her and ask, "Well, what's your name?"

"Alma," she whispers, eyeing Gawk nervously.

"This is Alma." I turn back to Gawk. "She beat the crap out of me a little while ago."

"Good for Alma," Gawk says with earnest approval.

The grubby little goblin works behind a desk that makes him look even smaller than he already is. Right now, he's feverishly jotting down notes and filing papers away. I have no idea why he does this, and I really don't care. Needl's dead, by the way, about two years ago now. I think it was two years anyway, but I'm not going to ask Gawk to clarify. It's a touchy subject. After all, I was there when it happened.

"So?" Gawk huffs. "What do you want?"

"I've come to introduce you to Alma," I tell him, and my voice is unusually upbeat. I'm enjoying this. It's not often I'm the one with the information. And with what Alma's told me—after we introduced ourselves through violence and apologies—is information worth killing for. "She's new here."

"I know," Gawk says dismissively. I immediately wobble, worried Gawk already knows what I'm about to tell him.

"How do you know?" I ask, hesitantly.

"Your neck is bleeding," he says to Alma. She blushes red, realising her hoodie has slipped down to show off the fresh bite marks on her neck. Alma quickly pulls it back up.

"Well, yes." I nod, relieved. "But there's something you'll want to—"

"Look, Caiden," Gawk sighs, tired. "I haven't the time for strays. Look at all this! I'm busy! Serat's got me doing all this and if I don't get it done…" He trails off, not wanting to say it out loud. He doesn't need to say it though. I can tell from the way Gawk keeps his scarf pulled extra tight around his neck.

"Got in too deep with the boss, huh? I seem to remember telling you it was a bad idea."

"Caiden, don't—"

"Actually, this concerns our bastard of an overlord himself," I say, trying to sound snarky and confident. I think I get the snarky bit, at least.

"You hate him." Gawk shakes his head, looking about as weary as I feel. "I hate him. Your new friend hates him. We all hate him. Same old story. And just because there's two of you who want to rip him apart, it doesn't make a difference. You and your new friend are no match for him."

"Well, not right now, we're not," I say, and I say it so teasingly Gawk can't help but look up from his paperwork.

"What are you on about, Caiden?"

"Here's the thing about our new friend Alma." I sit across from Gawk. I put my feet up and I take my time to make myself feel at home. Alma stays standing, looking nervous and out of place. "She doesn't think she's a vampire."

"I'm not a vampire!" Alma blurts out, vehement in her conviction.

"Great," Gawk groans, holding his arms up as if welcoming a miracle. "You've brought me a moron! Guess what?" The arms come down. "I don't care."

"Oh, she's obviously in denial," I admit.

"I'm not in denial!" Alma stamps her foot. No. It's more than something so petulant as stamping her foot. Her face is fit to burst, her eyes are wide and desperate, as desperate as eyes can be, and there's a vein that's threatening to pop. It's as if her whole body is hell-bent on believing she isn't a vampire.

"Were you kicked out of a plane flying over the city?" Gawk asks her.

"…Yes."

"And you're still kicking?" I note.

"Yes."

"Then you're a vampire." I turn back to Gawk. "But that's not the point… Are you paying attention?" He wasn't, he was looking at Alma with curiousity, but now he turns back to me. "Good," I continue. "Now, our new friend here arrives in a manner such as all us bloodsuckers arrive in this unfair city."

"Humans kicked her out of a plane." Gawk nods, much to Alma's muted chagrin.

"And she landed… somewhere in the borough… and a dwarf picked her up and dragged her to Serat's place."

"So far, so normal."

"So far, so normal," I smile. "But now we're getting to the good bit. Serat does his usual thing. He starts feeding on Alma."

I'm not looking at Alma. Gawk's not looking at Alma. But we are both well aware that she can't stand still, she's fighting back tears, and her mind is obviously racing. She wants to punch something, she wants to scream, to cry, to get away. The fight or flight instinct in her is kicking in and pushing hard.

"And then he stops."

Gawk stops. His thoughts cease, his impatient tapping of his pen becomes still and silent, and where he was only putting up with me before, now he is fixed on me.

"He stops?" Gawk whispers. "Why? What are you on about, Caiden!?"

"He starts, and then he stops," I tell him again, enjoying how much of an annoying, smug prick I'm being keeping my answers so vague and mysterious.

"What do you mean, Caiden?" He slams his craggy fist on the desk and leans forward.

"I mean exactly that, Gawk." I take my feet off his desk, and I too lean forward. "He started but he never finished, never even got close to finishing—"

"How do you know?"

I look over my shoulder at Alma. "Did your body change when he started feeding on you? Did you wither away as he sucked the blood out of your neck? Did your skin dry up? Did your face shrivel? Did you look at your hands and the fingers of a corpse?" I shudder as my own memory comes back to me.

"No," she manages to get out. "Of course not."

"See?" I look back at Gawk, putting the smile back on my face. "He didn't even get to the proper bit of feeding."

"Why? How?"

"Tell Gawk what happened, Alma." I don't take my eyes off Gawk, and I certainly can't keep the smile off my face.

"He…" Alma mumbles at first, then gathers herself and finishes. "Well, he… he sort of… coughed. He coughed."

"Coughed?" Gawk scrunches up his face. "Coughed?!"

"He coughed," I confirm.

"Like…" Gawk is struggling with this. "…Like he got a hair in his throat?"

"Nope." I smile, and I glance at Alma.

"It was a lot," Alma says. "It was painful for him."

"Painful?" Gawk repeats and I nod. "A lot?" he says again, and I nod again.

He sits back in his chair, looking winded and confused. Things like this don't happen. There's the big guy and there's the rest of us. That's how it is. The rest of us have to be content dancing to the big guy's tune because our lives are attached to his fingers, like puppets are to strings. But this… this isn't that.

"He didn't like your blood?" Gawk asks after a while.

"It was more than that," I insist, and with an excited fist I rap the desk. "Tell him, Alma!"

"It was… It was like he couldn't drink it," Alma remembers, her voice soft and frail. "It was like it was poison to him… like *I* was poison."

"And then what happened?" Gawk needs to know more, but Alma appears distressed enough, so I gallantly take over.

"He knocks her about, gets angry, gets really angry," I say, and I can't help the excited grin on my face, despite what I'm recounting. "And then he chucks her out."

"And then what?" Gawk demands, pushing all his papers away and leaning over his desk. "Tell me everything!"

"She walks around a bit," I say. "It's early morning, no one's about, and she hides. She stays awhile down by the canal, hiding from the morning crowds, until she senses me."

"You?"

"I go to the canal every now and then, for a bit of peace and quiet," I explain. "And she sensed me, or rather, she sensed a vampire, and she thought…"

"She thought you were the vampire who attacked her. She thought you were Serat."

"Exactly." I nod. "So she goes a bit mental, sticks a pole through me, knocks me about a bit, before she realizes I'm not the vampire she thought I was."

"Then what?"

"She tells me everything and we come here, and now I've told you everything." I finish, I lean back, I put my feet back on his desk, and I shoot Gawk a very satisfied, very smug grin.

"Right, I see." Gawk rubs his pointy chin in thought, taking his time before pulling his papers back in. "Now, as you so often say to me, Caiden… piss off."

***

"*You* piss off."

After the long and awkward silence that followed Gawk telling us to piss off, I suppose I can admit my response isn't exactly up there with the wittiest of them all. Give me a break, though. After all, it was the last thing I expected the craggy goblin to say.

"This is my place." Gawk scowls at me. "You're the ones who have got to go. And you both have to go right now. Right. Now."

"But… but…" I look round to Alma for support, but she looks deathly afraid, so I round back on Gawk, but he looks fixed and immovable. "…but?…" I try a third time, and then I get desperate. "…Gawk, come on, this is all we've wanted… This is our chance!"

"Don't speak to me about *rubbish like that!*" In his anger, Gawk jumps to his feet, although this doesn't have the intended effect as he is actually now a lot shorter than when he was sitting down. It was all those musty cushions piled on his chair. Now standing, his nose barely breaks over the large, domineering desk. I can still see his eyes though. They're burning into me with a vicious determination.

I know his mind is made up. I can see I can't persuade him—one of my few acquaintances in this city—with either logic or dreams. So, because I'm a vampire and therefore a terrible person at heart, I try playing dirty.

"If Needl were still here—" I stop though. I stop because a double-barrelled shotgun has been raised and is aiming squarely at yours truly.

"Get out," Gawk tells me, his anger barely staying in control.

I can't die. Alma can't die. This is obviously true and means no shotgun in the world can end my sorry existence. This is a good thing, but there's also the problem of, when getting shot by said shotgun, the pain. It's a dirty, messy, and primitive weapon and it causes more damage than one squeeze of a trigger should. I step back, not able to look Gawk in the eye after my mentioning of Needl, and I pull Alma with me. The fact that Gawk was prepared to fire a gun, losing precious bullets, is enough to push me out the door.

✳✳✳

"What now?"

We're both back at the canal. I'm not sure why. It's familiar, I suppose. We were here earlier, and it feels as good a place as any. It's also still pretty deserted, although soon the markets will be up and running and there'll be all sorts coming and going across the borough (doing what, I have no idea, but apparently lots of things need doing in a city that does the same thing every day and night). Until then though, we sit on the bank, feeling lost.

"I don't know," I sigh. Gawk's usually the ideas man, the guy with a plan, the schemer and the one in the know. Needl was the muscle and I… I was the vampire, whenever they needed one.

"Your friend didn't want to know me," Alma says, her voice quiet.

"He's not my friend," I say quickly. "No one has friends in this place. It's kill or be killed."

"But you can't be killed," she points out.

"No, *we* can't."

After a short silence, she speaks up again. "You still think I'm a vampire, don't you?"

I can't help it. I can't help the tired sigh. I can't stop myself from rounding on her. I can't help my harsh voice from taking over.

"You *are* a vampire, Alma," I say right in her face. "Here's why you're a vampire! You have the teeth of a vampire, I can see you don't like direct sunlight, if we had a mirror you wouldn't be able to see yourself in it, you fell out of a plane and your body fixed itself, and if all of that wasn't enough to convince you, I—a vampire of nearly two hundred years—can sense you and you can sense me too! Otherwise, why ram a pole through the back of me?" I stab a finger at her neck. "That's why you thought I was Serat earlier, despite the fact we look nothing alike. You are a vampire, Alma, and I am a vampire and, because I'm a vampire, I know you're a vampire. It's that simple."

For the second time today, I am told with conviction and much anger to piss off. Only this time, I also get shoved so hard that I fly off the wall and land back in the sludge and mud of the canal. I groan, I hear the pitter-patter of footsteps running away, and I give up.

✳✳✳

When night comes, there's another drop.

Usually, I don't even notice the occasional sky-high droning engines of the plane anymore, and I certainly don't bother looking up to see the tiny little figures falling from the sky. They're new vampires for a city with enough of them already. Who cares?

But tonight, I listen, and I wait, and I watch. I hear the plane before I see it, and I know they've been kicked out before I see them falling, so now all I have to do is wait to see where each one lands.

Ah. Here's the first one. The unfortunate individual is sliced in two by a metal wire stretching from one side of a street to another. That'll be a long heal, no good for what I need. Here's another. They hit their head rather hard and spin out at a funny angle, but I reckon they land mostly in one piece. A third follows and slams straight down. This is commonly known as a "straight shot," and it usually means there's more mush than body to clean up.

That'll be no good either then. A fourth, a fifth, and a few others follow; most of them look to be worth checking out. They hit something on the way down, sometimes they hit a few things, and that can be enough to keep all the bits roughly where they're supposed to be. I don't have time for long healing tonight.

Luckily, a few come down in Duke's Borough. I can't be crossing territories tonight. It's never worth the hassle and I'd only get beaten up and chucked back here. Besides, I need to stay here for what I have planned, and for what I want to see.

I jump off the edge of the building, fall fifty feet, and land on the flat roof of another, slightly shorter, building. My ankles break, my toe bones shatter, and I tear nearly every muscle in my legs doing it. But after two hundred years, I'm used to the sudden hit of pain, especially because within a second or two it's gone anyway. My body really can put up with a lot. The tears sew themselves up, my toe bones grow back almost instantly, and my ankles un-break. There are a few perks to being a vampire after all.

I keep running, heading as the crow flies, so to speak, for what I reckon is the closest landing site. I have to beat the others, and by the others I mean every poverty-stricken scum in this sorry city (or rather, every poverty-stricken scum in this sorry borough). I jump again, I fall again, and this time I land in a forward roll. It looks cool, it feels cool, and it hurts like hell and damages more of my body doing it. I'm moving fast. Faster than most of the others who are out tonight, but this is a game more about chance than speed. More luck than any actual skill. It's all about where you are, not who you are, nor what you can do.

I'm doing what Gawk and Needl did four years ago with my own mushy body. I'm joining in with all the body hunters and sycophants. And all for one reason and one reason alone… I need to see Serat. I need to see what state Alma left him in. Tonight, I find out how fucked the enemy is. And a newly-arrived, broken vampire's body is my way in.

I come across the first body in a small open square. The vampire isn't moving but they're in one piece at least, so that's good, but there's a fight over who gets to deliver the new arrival to Serat. Three goblins are squaring up against a winged demon. Blimey, times must be tough. The demon is a shade taller than me, and so she towers over the little goblins. She's as bulky as an orc and also a little bit on fire. Her flaming wings beat down hard, she screeches an ear-piercing cry at her attackers, and when one goblin makes a foolhardy attempt to stick her with a spear, the demon raises one of her sharpened claws and easily swats the weapon away.

The goblin falls backwards and crawls away, but it was all a ploy as the second goblin strikes from the opposite side. The demon cries out more in anger than anguish and swings the full might of her wing against the second goblin. The first was lucky, he got to crawl away, but the second not so much. The poor bugger is sent spinning through the air to crunch awkwardly against a wall. He's not crawling. He's not even moving. He's now a crumpled, limp body lying in the corner of the square. The third and final goblin runs off. Smart. Very smart.

I could take this demon on. I reckon if I really went for it and used what vampiric speed, agility, and strength I have at my disposal, limited as they are, I could probably take a single demon down. I'm not the shell-shocked newbie I was four years ago. I can use my little reserves of energy, if I get the chance to psych myself up, even without drinking blood. But neither am I a force to be reckoned with, and I'm nowhere near Serat's power (until tonight, perhaps).

But I don't want to spend the energy, I don't really have the time, and I'd rather not endure getting hit over and over again.

I move on. The demon has me beaten and she didn't even know I was there. I run fast, flitting through the alleyways and darting across the night streets. I know where I'm going… roughly, anyway. It takes longer to find the second fallen vampire though, and when I find them, I also find an ogre wrestling with a band of elves.

It's a real street alley scrap. No pretences, no nimble precision, and not a woodland bow or elven arrow in sight. These elves have knives and heavy sticks. They jump on the back of the ogre and stab quickly and repeatedly, shouting with pent-up energy and desperation. The ogre is barely harmed by the weak attacks, but it's slow and it can't keep all the elves off him. It lumbers about haphazardly, growling in frustration, and then it crushes one elf against a brick wall.

The other elves don't even notice their fallen companion. Instead, they keep leaping up at the ogre, stabbing and cutting and getting nowhere fast. The ugly ogre, its belly overhanging and its straw hair rancid, throws itself to the ground and I can hear the crunch of bones breaking, followed by muffled screams, yet the elves that are still in the fight keep fighting.

One brave elf charges the ogre, ducks under a clumsy swinging arm, and hops up to grab onto his hair. Then the elf stabs, again and again and again, causing the ogre to scream out in pain. Clever elf. She's going for the neck, but not just anywhere on the ogre's neck… she's going for the bite wounds, Serat's stamp of ownership for everyone in the borough, and the elf maiden is exploiting it for her own needs.

It's not enough though and, upon seeing their latest fallen brethren, the other elves scatter. In the ogre's pain-fuelled desperation, it grabs the last elf maiden and squeezes her torso, shaking her violently before hurling her out of the alleyway… and that's when the unsightly ogre sights me. Bugger.

All this for a half-destroyed vampire body lying in the middle of a rancid alleyway? Not exactly. Not only that, anyway. There's also the other stuff. All this for Serat's favour and good graces. All this for relative peace and quiet. All this to avoid the threat of overwhelming wrath and the fragile ego of a vampire lord. Ah well. I stumble backwards as the ogre stamps angrily towards me.

"Mine!" it growls loudly and clumsily, in half-learned words. "Vampire-slushy-body mine!"

I'm going to get my head kicked in, or punched in, or stoved in; whichever it is, it's not going to be good for my head. So I make sure to stay out of reach. The lumbering brute tries to catch me, but I step back, roll to the side, crouch and duck and it's easy enough. As long as I'm not attacking, I can stay out the way. But I have to deal with this ogre sooner or later, though it actually has to be sooner or someone else might beat me to it.

I clamber up the fire escape of one of the buildings lining the alleyway. It's a quick jump and a hasty climb but I'm soon above the ogre, who spits and roars in anger and jumps uselessly to try and catch me.

I keep climbing; I've got an idea, and I ignore the worrying vibrations in the bricks and the juddering of the old, rusty fire escape. The ogre's punching the wall down below and seemingly trying to bring the whole building down. With every meaty punch, I hear him growl with a growing infantile frustration.

Not long now though, just another level, maybe two, to get just that little bit higher. I can't beat this ogre. The great lumbering brute is too strong for me, even with my sharp teeth and agile moves. So I'm being smart. Well, smarter than a pea-brained ogre anyway. The one thing I have over this ogre—the one thing I have over every lowly soul in this city—is that I'm a vampire. And vampires can't die.

This will do. This is high enough. Just shy of the rooftop. I don't think much on what I'm about to do. Doubts are no good this high up. I grip the shaky handrail, I kick off, leap over, and I fall. Knee-first but from this high up it doesn't really matter. Ogre heads are as fragile as the next. I hope.

As I'm falling, I've enough time to see the ogre watching me with a dumbfounded expression as I come closer, closer, and splat. Bullseye! My knee hits exactly where I wanted it to, right in the middle of the ogre's dumb forehead. Also, my knee completely eviscerates on impact, my leg is completely shattered, every bone in my body shakes and, worst of all, the lower half of my body tries to move into my upper half. But it's fine because the ogre gets the worst of it… and the ogre can't heal itself.

I roll over on the ground painfully. My body takes a few moments to heal the damage. Okay, maybe a few more moments. Taking a bit longer than I thought. Okay, the pain is sticking around, and I want to cry. Ah, there it is, that's better. The leg finishes putting my bones back together and my organs return from whence they came. It wasn't that bad really. It just hurt like it was that bad.

As for the ogre, well, its head is gone, and its body is covered in what used to be its head. It's definitely dead, then.

I rise unsteadily to my feet and wobble a bit before turning my attention to the half-flattened vampire lying in the middle of the alleyway. Maybe I should have brought a shovel and a bag.

Never mind. I steal a tarpaulin sheet from one of the elves (who certainly won't be missing it) and I try to scoop the various bits and the odds and ends into a general pile that will eventually re-congeal. The part of the vampire still recognizable doesn't do much. There's a blink every now and then and an occasional gurgling noise, but nothing more and I don't think on who this vampire might be. I can't even tell whether they are a boy or a girl. It doesn't matter though.

After a few minutes of tiring work, I'm finished. I've had to work quickly, breathlessly even, because I know any minute now something else might come along, searching for this bag of bones or rather, this wrapped-up tarpaulin of bones and body bits and slushy stuff.

I swing my prize over my shoulder and, looking like a terrible Father Christmas impersonator, I make my jolly way out of the alleyway and head off to deliver a very special present.

***

The night life of the vampires carries on as it always has. It's almost a ritual. Something between a dance and a ceremony (or between a yearning and an obligation).

My kin dress up, all black and tight and luxurious and uniformed, and one might wonder where they get all these shiny clothes and smart get-ups from. Well, the humans left a lot behind when they moved out of whatever this city was called before it became Vampire City, and I suppose one of the kickbacks of being an obedient little vampire is you get to pick out the nicer bits from the left-behind hoard. No doubt Serat and all the other vampire lords have got a big old mountain of useless goodies to sit on, like dragons under mountains.

These obedient little vampires go to loud clubs, attracted by bright lights, to congregate together and lose themselves in the deafening music and the pastiche of neon.

Perhaps it is my imagination, but they do look smaller. Granted, I haven't been this close in years, so perhaps it is my memory that has painted them as taller than they really were, but even so… Maybe I'm just in a better mood than back then.

As I walk down the neon-lit street, surrounded by cliques and flanked by gaudy bars, the other vampires watch me with suspicion and distaste, but predominantly apathy. No doubt some of them are talking critically about me as I pass—to them I must seem like a shabby loner, a dejected loser, and an embarrassing failure—but if they are talking then I don't hear them. The music from the nearby clubs is too loud and they're all stepping well clear of me anyway, eager to avoid this shabby, dejected embarrassment of a vampire.

I ignore them. I keep walking, carrying my wrapped-up tarpaulin of body bits and mush over my shoulder, and I head straight for the one place I swore I'd never return to. I knock at the thick steel door and Serat's doorman answers gruffly.

"Piss off!"

And the door is slammed shut in my face. Hmm. Over the last twenty-four hours, I've reached out on two separate occasions to two people (Gawk and now Serat, each on opposite ends of my social spectrum) and they've both told me to piss off. Why is that? After all these years, am I starting to rub off on this place?

I drop the tarpaulin. It's too heavy, but I guess I don't need it now anyway, and my arm still hurts from being broken several times during the night thus far. I think I hear a very muffled, very feeble "ow" but it's not my problem anymore. It occurs to me though that maybe the doorman didn't realise what was inside the tarpaulin.

I pick up the bag of bones and knock on the door again. It opens once more and before it is slammed shut again by the angry doorman—who is far bigger than me and definitely unhinged (it's the violent tattoos, copious piercings and murderous eyes that give it away)—I speak up first.

"Delivery for Serat!" I spit out in a frantic hurry. "A nice fresh one. Won't take longer than a few hours to heal."

The doorman eyes the tarpaulin and nods at me to open it up, which I do. He leans forward to take a look inside. I'm not sure what exactly he sees but he does seem impressed.

"Any other night," he muses wistfully, but then he fixes me a stern gaze. "But not tonight, so—"

"I know, I know," I sigh, defeated. "I'll piss off."

"Good!"

And the door is slammed in my face once again.

So… Serat's not taking deliveries… This has taken another interesting turn into the unexpected. Last night, he's drinking young Alma's blood only to end up choking on it, and tonight he's not taking in new arrivals. Surely, he would want to stamp his ownership on the newbies, thus anchoring them to his borough and keeping them tied to him forever… but, no. He's not interested.

With no other use for it, I leave the tarpaulin in a secluded corner. Out of sight and out of the way. Whoever's inside should be undisturbed as they put themselves back together. It's the best I can do for them. Well, no, that's a lie. It's the best I *will* do for them. I could probably do a lot more but, as the saying goes, I have bigger fish to fry.

Serat's building is a big, dark brick of a building. It dominates the inner street it looks down on, as well as being ugly as sin. Every entrance is locked up tight and even if I could get inside somehow, they'll be a few of Serat's closest vampires only too willing to kick out a wandering stray like me, and I'm sure they'll throw in a thorough beating to give the whole thing that extra special, personal touch.

But still…

I don't know why I'm doing this—circling the building, looking for a way in, watching for anyone going in or out—because it's useless. All the windows are sealed shut and it's clear by now that no one is coming or going tonight. The place really is locked up tight. What the hell am I doing?

Kicking the hornet's nest, that's what I'm doing, or trying to, anyway. And what happens when you kick a hornet's nest? You get stung. A lot. But still… maybe it's worth it. I might be a castaway, a good-for-nothing, a loser, but I know what I also am… angry. I'm down and out and it's the bastard inside this big, dark building who keeps me down.

I want to get him back for what he's done to me and for what he has taken. Perhaps I am being petty, arrogant even, and probably ignorant, but I don't care. I'll never be like the others. I'll never sit inside his building, letting him drink from me during the day, and I'll never pretend to enjoy myself in loud clubs at night. I want to hurt him. I want to take back what I once had. I want to be a hunter again. I want to be confident and in control, I want to be hopeful and assured, and I want to be cool as shit and sexy as hell.

That's the dream anyway. And I also want Serat to feel as small and as lost as I've felt these past years. I want him to hurt. And Alma's given me hope, so maybe tonight Serat is vulnerable.

Yeah. I'm going to kick the crap out of this hornet's nest. But not if I can't get in first.

There is one way inside though. The worst kind of way. It's about as far from "cool as shit" or "sexy as hell" as it is possible to be. Rather, it is embarrassing and difficult. Ah well. I'll just have to hope no one sees me.

I'm around the back of the building, in a rubbish-strewn back alley, and I'm standing on top of a closed dumpster to reach a tiny square window. Old and disused and forgotten about. And because of this, no one's bothered to secure it against a sneaky so-and-so like me. I snap the decades-old, feeble lock with ease and lift the window up. It's one of those windows with tinted glass you often see in the top corner of a public toilet.

As *my* luck would have it, it does in fact lead into a toilet in dire need of cleaning. As I said, not cool as shit, not sexy as hell, rather smelly as shit and looking like hell.

I take a deep breath. I hop up and twist around so my feet go in first. After all, diving headfirst into a toilet with the kind of stench this one's giving off does not strike me as the best idea. My legs follow my feet and then my waist… doesn't.

Bugger. The window might be a tad smaller than I had reckoned. Or maybe, only maybe, I'm not quite as lean as I once was. Is it even possible for an undead abomination such as myself to "let myself go"? Either way, it doesn't really matter now, because I'm stuck horizontally, literally half in and half out. I really, really hope no one—

"Caiden?" Oh no. I recognize the voice, and I know instantly who has found me, but I know her quite well and so, all things considered, it could be worse.

A young vampire has found me—her name is Helisha— and when I say young, I mean she's not yet a hundred.

"Is that you, Caiden?"

"No," I reply, rather lamely and completely pointlessly. After all, from the waist up I'm stuck hanging horizontally out of a toilet window. To be fair, there's not much I can say that will help.

"It is you, Caiden!" a different voice chortles, sounding like a smug squeak, and I groan because it just got worse.

Munstone. Another young vampire, a little over a hundred years old, and probably the biggest tool this side of the sun.

I lean back, ignoring the creeping pain in my spine, and I come face to face with both of them.

They both look about my age (although we are vampires, so don't trust the looks) but this is where the similarities end. Helisha is small, round-faced, wears her shiny black hair in little buns, and has painted her face with silver sparkles in pretty patterns. Munstone meanwhile has meticulously designed his appearance to be as typical as possible. Short black hair, plain white face, buttoned-up shirt and a simple dark suit. Helisha is also wearing black, but she and Munstone are part of a vampire clan so black is pretty much a given. I'm told it's called fashion. At least Helisha has a few frills though, a cool belt too, and fishnet tights and some heavy-duty boots to make the look her own.

"What are you doing, Caiden?" Helisha asks with an intrigued grin on her face and giddy (although the giddy bit might just be me, seeing as my head is now hanging upside down).

"Nothing," I say. "Nothing at all… No, really… I'm being serious… I'm not doing anything… I'm really not." I think I'm turning a little light-headed.

"Come now, Caiden," Munstone smirks, somehow talking down to me even though I'm above him (albeit stuck in a window upside-down). "Tell us the truth. We can still be your friends, you know."

"I'm fine, thanks," I say to him, ignoring this increasing uncomfortable throbbing inside my brain.

"Oh, come on, Caiden!" Helisha whines. "Tell us what Serat's little black sheep is up to."

"Am I the black sheep?"

"You're the only one not playing with the rest of us," Munstone points out. "Or have you finally come to your senses? Grown tired of scraping by with the dung hampers and bottom feeders, have you?"

"*Nope.* Fresh as a daisy, that's me."

"Don't be facetious, Caiden," Helisha sighs, becoming bored with me. "We're all tired."

"The difference is," Munstone puts in, "we're tired together, but you're tired alone."

"Just the way I like it."

"Bloody hell, would you stop being so annoying, Caiden," Helisha snaps. "Just tell us what you're doing! You know Serat won't like you sneaking around his place."

"Perhaps Serat isn't all that fearsome anymore," I reply, being irritatingly vague. "You probably haven't heard, but your shepherd isn't feeling too well. Something he drank disagreed with him, you might say."

The air turns a little. It's subtle and small, but it's as clear as day (so it really stands out in the middle of the night). Helisha goes quiet, her boredom turning into cautious intrigue, and then Munstone steps forward, letting his frustration rise to the forefront. He grabs my hair and pulls. I try not to show how much it hurts, but I don't think I do a very good job.

"You have no idea what you're talking about, you witless fool!" He smoulders. "If you think the new girl's blood made Serat sick, then you're an even bigger fool than we took you for."

"Serat's… not sick?" I wince, suddenly feeling rather foolish.

"He couldn't drink the new girl's blood," Helisha tells me, crossing her arms. "No one's supposed to know. But everyone's talking about it."

"Why?" I gasp, relieved when Munstone lets me go. "I never even knew that was a thing."

"None of us did," Helisha says.

"So…" I ask them both, and my precarious, horizontal, upside-down position is currently forgotten because I need to know. "…What happened next?"

"Serat took extra…" Munstone tells me through gritted teeth, "…from the rest of us."

Munstone pulls his collar down, and I see his bite marks but they're not like mine, or like Gawk's, or anyone else's in the scum-ridden, poverty-stricken parts of the borough. Hell, they're not even like Alma's, which were as fresh as a blood-soaked daisy.

Munstone's bite marks are like gouges into his neck. I can see the inside of his body, the dark pulsing and the fleshy red bits. Helisha moves her scarf, and she has the same ferocious wounds on her own neck. She puts back the scarf and Munstone replaces his collar, but what I've seen cannot be unseen.

"He had to keep you low," I whisper thoughtfully. "Couldn't have any of you getting ideas above your station. I really don't know why you let him do it."

"Because the alternative is living like you," Munstone spits back at me. "He takes from us every day, but today he took more than he's ever taken before. All because that little bitch weakened him."

"But if he can be weakened, then we might yet be able to get rid of him—"

Munstone strikes me across the face and my whole body feels like it's going to crack in two. Thankfully, I'm still stuck so I spring back quickly enough.

"This isn't a revolution," Munstone tells me, his face close to mine. "This isn't your little fairy tale. This is how the city works. Either you're stronger than him or you're weaker. You're weak, Caiden, like the rest of us, and that's what you'll always be. You can't change it, so get used to it."

"I swore I'd rip that bastard to pieces for what he did to me. For what he did to all of us!"

"Give it up," Helisha says. "Can't you just enjoy what little we have?'

"No," I say, pointedly. "I can't."

"Then go back to the grubby little corner you came from." Munstone turns and starts walking away. "And spend the rest of time wallowing in your own sorrow!"

For a moment, Helisha stays with me though I can barely bring myself to look at her, and not just because my head has been upside-down for several minutes now.

"He's a real bastard."

"Who?" she asks. "Serat or Munstone?"

"Both," I huff.

"Come on." Helisha puts a tired smile on her face. "I'll help you down."

***

It doesn't take long for Helisha to wriggle me out of the window, and she even walks with me to the edge of the vampire-populated inner streets where we bid our farewells and go our separate ways. Her way is towards the electric lights and congregated masses, and mine is to the dark, cold, and faraway corners, where broken souls huddle together for warmth.

"He's tearing people to pieces in there," Helisha told me, right before we parted ways. "He's really angry about what happened."

I choked back a laugh, but I also felt my gut twist nervously. "And I thought I'd catch him as a weakened shell of himself." I glanced at Helisha. "You and Munstone probably saved me a lot of trouble tonight."

"You're welcome." She smiled at me then. I knew I liked her. I barely know her, in truth, but she's always been kind enough to me, and that's more than can be said for every other vampire in this city.

But then, as we reached the end of the street, she had to go and remind me that, while I might like her, we are definitely not on the same team. "So, you must have found out about the girl somehow… You don't… know where she is, do you?"

I don't say anything for a little while, instead letting an icy silence fall between us. "Why?" I eventually asked, keeping my voice as neutral as possible.

"…Just curious." But it was the pause that gave her away.

"Thought you were happy with what you have?" I said to her, staring straight ahead, unable to bring myself to look at her.

"Wouldn't hurt to earn a little favour, though."

"You'd hand the girl over? Just like that? To *him*?" I stopped walking then and finally faced her.

"It is what it is, Caiden." She shrugged. "Same for us all."

I left her at that, and I didn't even say goodbye. I know. Pathetic and childish, but after the night I've had I need whatever tiny win I can get.

***

It is dark here, and cold too, and it feels especially dark and especially cold after the street of bright lights and pounding music with all those vampires dressed in black. There aren't any lights up here though. I'm lying on the roof's edge of an old, forgotten building about 25 floors up.

It's nice up here. It's peaceful (if you can ignore the roaring wind) and it's calm (if you don't mind the freezing temperatures). I come up here when I need to get away from everything on ground level, which is most nights.

Alma. Maybe she's a nobody. Maybe she amounts to nothing. Maybe she really is no one special. But I don't want to accept that. Not yet. Instead, I want to believe there's something there, that there's some way she can hurt Serat, that she can change this place. If I can find her… if we can maybe find a way…

By the gods, I wish they'd shut up. I usually can't hear the city at all up here, especially at this time of night, but tonight is different. Typical. Somewhere down below there's an awfully loud ruckus. I can't tell what it is that's going on, but I reckon it's either a hundred voices being horribly tortured, or a hundred voices in jubilant celebration. One of the two.

I sigh. I groan. I give up on my train of thought and jump off. Well, I kick off, really. I make sure to crash into the neighbouring building, then I push off to send myself flying into the side of the building I just jumped off. I kick off cement walls, crash into windows, and bounce off balconies, pushing with my arms when I need to and so, like a game of ping-pong, I descend leaving behind a wake of damaged walls, smashed windows and bent piping. I also break pretty much every bone in my body and twist all my muscles, but you know the deal with flesh wounds and vampires.

After a breathless few moments (quite literally, as it turns out), I'm back on my feet and venturing in search of whatever is going on. And it's entirely anti-climactic.

It's just a fight. A warehouse fight. The very same kind of fight in which I found myself involed in four years, eight months and three weeks ago. The warehouse itself is a battered piece of junk; it might even be the same warehouse I fought in all those years ago, and the crowd is packed inside just the same. From the sound of it, the fighting is well underway. There's raucous cheering, loud betting, angry shouting, and the occasional thump and bump.

Whoever the unfortunate vampire is, they now find themselves playing the role of the mouse in a game where the cats see who can make the mouse bleed quickest. Another thump. Another bump. And another adrenaline-fuelled cheer from the crowd.

No.

Not a cheer. Certainly not appreciative, anyway. More like anger, or maybe surprise. And there's more shouting, more forceful and aggressive than I've heard before. Maybe not quite so anti-climactic. It would appear whoever the unfortunate new arrival is, they are a vampire with uncommon fight in them… oh no.

I push my way into the warehouse, which is quite difficult because the warehouse is jam-packed with everything from little gnomes to hulking half-trolls, and there's even a treeman in the corner who is growling angrily and shaking a betting slip it's holding between two twigs on the end of a long branch.

As difficult as the going is, I finally get to the edge of the fighting pit. I look down into the shallow arena, and I see exactly who I expected to see.

Young Alma. Alma the vampire who vehemently claims she is not a vampire. Alma with the blood that made a vampire choke half to death. Alma… who has just beaten a centaur half to death.

The poor horse person is dragged up and out of the pit, accompanied by angry heckling and booed by sore losers, though no one seems eager to take the next go.

"Come on!" Alma roars her challenge. She's sweating, she's angry, and she looks like she could take on the world. But the world isn't here right now, so a warehouse full of scum and bottom-feeders will have to do. "Who wants next?' she asks the crowd. And no one steps forward.

After a few moments, someone is shoved forward and basically peer-pressured into jumping into the pit. It's quite funny actually. Here is a small girl, looking about fourteen, with brown eyes and dark blonde hair and a button nose, and yet it is the seven-foot-tall orc with rippling muscles, scarred tattoos, and teeth bigger than the girl's hands who is quivering with fear.

There's more shouting now. Desperate, animalistic shouting. It is the baying of gamblers who need to win back what they've already lost. They urge the orc forward, urge him to rip the girl in two, and he does come forward. He's nervous, but then he sees his situation, he sees the eyes on him, the expectation weighing him down, and so he sets himself to play the part of the savage orc. He charges forward.

Alma charges too.

There's no fancy footwork and no sneaky sidestepping. The two of them just clash. Head on. It looks like it hurts. And the crowd goes mental for it. More. They want more. They want blood.

The orc swings his clumsy fists, grabs her hair, pulls and twists, and throws his whole weight into every lunge. And Alma does the same. She's swinging in fury, grabbing at him, pulling and twisting and throwing herself into the fight without pause. The orc is terribly bloodied already but Alma, being a vampire, can take a lot of punishment before blood spills. She's horribly bruised though, and her constant screaming must be both her wild anger and the bone-jarring agony she's enduring. It's a hell of a fight, that's for sure.

Someone grabs me, twists me around, and pulls me down to a lower eye level. A wild-eyed Gawk is staring me in the face.

"She's ruining me!" The knobbly goblin panics.

"Who?" I ask, rather slow on the uptake, I admit.

"Your new friend Alma, of course!" Gawk squeaks. "I put all my dog-ends on her, thinking she'd get bled inside a minute, but she hasn't bled once—and that poor bugger in there with her is the twelfth challenger tonight!"

Blimey. Eleven fights and Alma's beat them all (and by the sound of a certain orc squealing like a stuck pig behind me, she's currently beating the twelfth). She's powerful; not quite as powerful as a blooded-up vampire with the stolen energy of their last victim running through their veins, but she's still powerful. Stronger certainly than the drained vampires Serat keeps close by, and stronger too than my own bloodless self. Maybe it's just that Serat didn't finish drinking her blood, or maybe she really is special.

"*All* your dog-ends?" I ask Gawk, being about as unhelpful as it is possible to be.

"Yes!"

"Why'd you put all your dog-ends on her?" I ask, still being about as helpful as a handrail in a hurricane.

"Because I'm the one who brought her here and put her in the pit!" he screeches, practically shaking with anger. "I thought she'd lose in record time!"

"Ah."

"I mean, she's only a little thing," the goblin wheezes, exhausted by his own anger and now close to collapsing from exhaustion and severely frayed nerves. "All frightened and shy, she was, barely spoke a word, didn't have nowhere to go, so she came back to my office, and…"

"…and you threw her in the pit," I say, shaking my head and really laying on the guilt. "Just like how you threw me in."

"Hey! Cut that mightier-than-thou rubbish out!" Gawk wags a craggy finger in my face. "If a newbie's struggling, the best thing for 'em is the pit. Toughens 'em up, teaches 'em a lesson and—"

"And earns you a few extra dog-ends," I interject quickly. "Dog-ends for the liquor stalls, no doubt. Come on, Gawk, you know that stuff is only troll pee mixed with rainwater."

"*Who's next?*" Alma shouts. Clearly the savage orc has just been savaged.

"Shove it, Caiden!" Gawk spits venomously. "You always were a useless piece of—"

But I don't hear what it is I am a useless piece of, because I've jumped backwards and landed (with only a bit of a stumble) in the pit. I'm next.

***

Dog-ends are the currency we bottom feeders use. Each one is a little chunk of worthless scrap metal that one of the craftsmen from the market has bashed into a flat, sort-of coin shape and stamped with a symbol of something (nobody knows what, believe me, I've asked). We use them at the market stalls to buy things we need, and however much we have left we spend on cheap liquor and cheaper pleasures, like betting on the occasional warehouse pit fights. Wait. No. I got that the wrong way round. We use our dog-ends on cheap liquor and cheaper pleasures, like betting on the fights, and however much we have left we spend at the market to buy things we actually need. Yeah. That's how it is.

Right now, I know two things. One, a lot of dog-ends have been lost by punters and therefore won by the warehouse organizers thus far, and two, a lot of dog-ends are hurriedly being bet on the small girl who so far has decked twelve contenders and is presumably about to deck lucky number thirteen, i.e. me. Actually, I know three things, and the third thing I know is this: whoever does manage to make the vampire bleed gets a small cut of the warehouse winnings at the end of the night. Otherwise, what would be in it for the challengers?

With these three things that I know, I can surmise two further things (now stay with me on this). Firstly, the warehouse has made an absolute killing tonight. The rat-men who organize these fights will have made more dog-ends tonight than they ever imagined possible. And secondly, that small cut reserved for the fighters who actually make the vampire bleed is looking a lot like a big cut right now, and if only one fighter gets any blood from this small girl, then that one fighter will get that big cut all to themselves.

I chortle sneakily. I love it when a plan comes tog—

Ow. Alma's drop-kicked me into the side of the pit and one side of my body suddenly feels like a very fragile puzzle.

"What the hell are you doing here!?" she barks at me. She's terrifying and tense and snarling and *oh my God she's going to tear me to pieces*. Holy crap. I can't beat her. What was I thinking? I need to get her on my side.

"Wait!" I say quickly. "I've got an idea, a good one!" I pant desperately, trying to ignore the pain. "And my idea will help you!" I hurriedly add as she cracks her knuckles and comes in close to me, and then I rather foolishly say, conspiratorially, "But first, we have to fight, and we have to make it look convincing."

"Okay." She nods and then roundhouse kicks me across my jaw, sending me fully up into the air where I spin around before landing hard on the rough ground. I hear a collective "ooooohhh!" from the crowd.

I roll over in time to see Alma grab me by my shirt collar and slam my head back down on the ground. She's really good at this. She punches me once, twice, but compared to the dropkick and the roundhouse kick and the slamming my head on the ground, the punches are barely more than a tickle.

"What… are you… talking… about?" Alma asks me between punches. I bring my hand up and grab her wrist. We make a show of a power struggle, although it's more like I'm holding onto her as if she's a life raft and I'm about to go under.

"I can help you," I tell her, through gritted teeth. "You and I want the same thing."

"You have no idea what I want," she hisses back at me.

"Alright, fair enough," I concede. "But I know neither of us want this."

"This fight?"

"This fight, this warehouse, this city, the other vampires, Serat, the whole bloody place," I tell her. "I don't want it. You don't want it. City living? It's not for us."

She hits me, a little harder this time, and then throws me against the side of the pit. I struggle for breath and then I struggle some more when she puts her hands around my neck.

"I hate this place," Alma admits. "I want out. I want to go home." And I suddenly see beneath the splatters of blood on her face, and between the vengeful scowl and snarling mouth, small tears creeping out the side of her eyes. "I want to go home."

"I'll help you with that," I tell her, trying to imbue as much sympathy and sincerity into my offer as possible. I have to try really hard though because, of course, I'm lying.

"How?" she demands.

"We can't talk about it now," I plead, and she looks sideways with wide eyes at the baying crowd, as if she had forgotten they were there. "But let me draw some blood—"

"My blood!"

"Your blood." I nod. "And then these fights will be over. And we can talk."

She thinks for a moment, unsure amid her confusion, but then she releases her hold on me. It's enough for me to free one hand, which I clench into a fist and bring around in a wide swing. The punch sends her sprawling to the ground, much to the shock of the boisterous crowd, and I move in to finish this.

I step behind her, open my mouth, lean into her arm… and I grow my fangs for the first time in years. I touch them to her flesh. I have no idea what's about to happen. I've never drunk from a vampire before, least of all from a vampire whose blood made another vampire choke uncontrollably. Come to think of it though, I haven't drunk fresh blood in decades. What am I getting myself into? But I have no intention of drinking her blood, I remind myself, I only have to puncture her skin. I only have to hurt her a little.

I touch my fangs to her flesh, I bite down, and she screams. She screams so loud it hurts my ears. She screams like a terrified fourteen-year-old girl. And then she hits me. Really hard. As hard as she can hit me. I crash against the side of the pit, everything between my bones and the walls of the warehouse seem to shake, and I even feel the stone behind me crack and break apart. Ow. Very much… ow.

✱✱✱

The warehouse is still standing and I… eventually… managed to stand as well. But no one cared, certainly not about me anyway, because my fangs had done enough. Blood dribbled down from some embarrassingly pathetic bite marks on Alma's arm and that meant, technically, I won, despite the fact Alma was still standing whilst my spine needed a whole minute to fix all the pieces of itself back together. As I said before… very much ow. The bloodening of the *mouse* though means the game is over (this is a recent addition to the rules, and one that I really could have done with four years ago, when I had been the one tossed into the arena).

"What now?" Alma asks me. She's been sitting next to me ever since the fights came to an end. We've both been sitting here, in the pit, waiting for someone to come and see to us. It's not too bad, actually. While we've been waiting, we've listened to everyone grumbling as they pay up, and we listened too to some of them get beaten up before they finally relented and also paid what they had gambled away. And one by one, the poor souls (and some of them are far poorer now) filed out of the warehouse, entering the cold and dark night, heading back to whatever they call their home, be it a shack or an alley or a desolate room in a decrepit building.

It's nice to sit here though, ignored for now, and listen to the rest of the world grumble on by.

"I don't know," I sigh in response.

"You said you could help me!" Alma exclaims, sitting up and shooting me a look.

"Oh, yes, that." I stumble a bit. "I can. I mean, I will help you, but not now. Right now, we don't have to do anything."

She relaxes a little, or at least she leans back against the side of the pit, and for a short while we don't say anything to each other.

"I don't know what happened to me." Honestly, I'm not sure if she's really talking to me because she's whispering as if to herself. "Your goblin friend told me to go in the pit. And then it just… happened."

"They didn't tell me what it was all about either." I nudge her, and I remember how Needl had dropped me into this very same arena. Poor Needl. He didn't deserve much from life, but neither did he deserve how it eventually ended for him. Poor Gawk too, come to think of it. I wonder where the grubby little goblin has got to now, and I also wonder how much he lost on his mischievous scheme tonight. He probably deserved to lose though for tricking Alma into the fights.

"I had never been in a fight before." Her knees are up with her arms wrapped around her legs. "I didn't know I… I didn't think I was that kind of person…"

"It's the vampire in you—" I start to say, without thinking, and I get another shooting glance of pure venom from Alma. When I meet her gaze though, I get the impression it's more hurt than anger. More desperation than wrath.

"*I am not a vampire!*" She says every word with as fierce and warped a conviction as when she demanded yet another challenger for the next fight. I would have to be a real idiot, and a terribly insensitive fool, to stubbornly contradict her. So that is, of course, what I immediately do.

"You are a vampire, Alma," I groan. "Either that or you're something entirely new that also happens to have all the qualities and traits of a vampire."

"I'm just a girl," she insists, holding the tears back this time. "I'm a normal girl. I'm fourteen. I've got school on

Monday. My mum will be wondering where I… where I am…" Oh, never mind, the tears are coming now.

"What are you blithering on about?" I ask her inconsiderately, because apparently my capacity for sympathy couldn't fill a teaspoon. In fairness, I am tired. But then I'm always tired so maybe I should have learnt by now.

"I'm really not a vampire," Alma cries loudly between big, ugly tears. She's obviously distressed, very upset, and going through a whirlwind of emotions right now. So why do I get so angry when she raises her voice at me? Am I that selfish? Am I that much of an arsehole? Apparently, I am, because I feel the anger shoot through me, and I can't help but snap back at her. She's wrong. I'm right. Why can't she see that?

"You *are* a vampire, Alma!" I growl at her. "Accept it. And if you think you're not a vampire, then tell yourself you're wrong! It's that simple! You. Are. A. Vampire."

She loses her cool, but that's okay because I've already lost mine. She's up and she takes a swing at me. I'm also standing, and I bat her arm away. She hisses at me, her fangs grow, her eyes turn red, and I respond in kind. We're about to tear each other to pieces, or rather she's about to tear me to pieces and I'm about to throw myself into the meat grinder. She's still got most of her blood, remember.

"Fight's over, children."

That voice.

That voice. My anger vanishes in a puff of smoke and out of that same smoke strides fear. My fangs shrink, my mouth goes dry, and my eyes turn from narrow and red to wide open. That voice. Made of oil it is, so meticulous and precise it sounds, sending shivers up my spine and chilling my brain. By the look of her own wide eyes, Alma feels it too. Some tiny flies dart across my vision, like little black comets.

He's here. Serat's standing above the pit, standing on the very edge, and looking down at us both. He's wearing a smart black coat, with his slicked-back black hair, and with a smirk on his face that scares me.

"Caiden?" He looks at me. "What a surprise to see you here."

Why can't I say anything? Why don't I say anything? I feel weak. As weak as I felt on the night I met him, when he drank from me and took… everything.

"The more the merrier." He smiles. "Only for us vampires though."

With that, he kicks a dirty, hairy brown ball into the pit. It rolls across the hard ground, bumping haphazardly as it goes, and finally comes to rest in front of my feet. It's not a ball, of course. It is the rat-man's head. The same rat-man who organizes the warehouse fights and who would have owed me a considerable cut of this night's winnings. Bugger.

"Come on up," he tells us both. "I'd like to have a little chat."

"No," I spit out, and even this word trembles out of my lips. Gods! Why can't I get it together? Why am I so useless at this? Why can't I do this the way I've always imagined doing it… charging at the bastard and ripping him apart, limb from limb?

"Well, to be honest, I'm not here for you, Caiden," Serat shrugs. "It's really only *you* who I want to talk to." And he's looking at Alma, and Alma is staring wide-eyed back at him, looking very much like the rabbit staring down the headlights.

Other vampires are here too. As I clamber out of the pit, followed closely by Alma, I see them standing around us, standing apart, all in black pristine attire and all looking like obedient guard dogs, waiting for their master to click or whistle. One of them is Munstone. Seeing him is enough to give my hatred the kick it needs.

There is the body too. The rat-man's body, covered in bite marks. I look closer and I see Serat's obedient guard dogs are also eager, twitching guard dogs, some of them still with rat blood on their lips. He's let them drink. Just a little. Just enough. Nowhere near his level, but more than enough to...

"What's the matter?" I turn to Serat, my voice a little shaky, my legs a little wobbly, but my conviction somewhat recovered from the initial shock and emboldened by the sorry sight of the rat-man's corpse. Gods help me but I feel sorry for the hairy rodent. His was not a good death. "Couldn't come down here without your bodyguards?"

Serat fixes on me, and his long, snake-like face is as dry and pale as I remember it. His eyes are as distant too, but also a little... bloodshot. Hmm, that's new. I barely notice the occasional fly crawling over his body.

"My followers... my tribe... my kin..." Serat turns from me to gaze upon his vampires. "I brought them here tonight because we do things together. We're like a family."

"And I suppose it'll help remind them who the head of that family is..." I say, sounding braver than I feel—not that I sound particularly brave though, but this only highlights how very not brave I am currently feeling.

"Excuse me?" Serat puts on a perplexed look.

"Whatever you came here to do to her," I say. "I'm not going to let you do it."

Who the hell am I? And when did Alma step behind me? Or did I step in front of her? I have no idea. This is insane. Alma's nothing to me. She made the guy I hate puke his guts out. That's all she is. She's also fourteen and terrified and alone and surrounded by vampires, including me, but I shouldn't care about any of that. It's not my problem. Right? Then why the hell am I doing any of—

Wait.

"You're fourteen!" I spin round and stare at Alma in astonishment.

"Yes." She nods, confused. "I told you."

"But… you're actually fourteen!"

"Yes!"

"But… I'm nearly two hundred years old." Forget the fear, forget the anger, even forget Serat for now, I'll just let pure shock and surprise take the wheel for this one. "And she's three hundred!" I point to one of the vampires, and then another, and another, and another. "He's nearly a hundred, that one's a hundred and fifty, she's five hundred, he's six hundred, and Serat… well, he's got to be a few hundred, at least." And then I turn back to Alma, and all the vampires, even Serat, are staring at her too with expressions of shock and curiosity. "But you…" I say to Alma, "you're fourteen."

"Yes," Alma nods, quieter this time.

"Fourteen years old?"

"Yes!"

"So… when were you… you know… made into one of… you know…" I tap my own neck.

"Tuesday," she eventually tells me, nervous of all the eyes staring at her.

I can't believe it.

"And you've got school on Monday," I remember.

I can barely comprehend this. She's so young. Too young.

"Well, that explains it!" The snake-faced bastard whoops with laughter. "Your blood is still… mixing. That's all it was!" He's talking to his vampires now, and he's sounding quite relieved. "Only a mix-up. Nothing more! She's not properly done yet."

"Is that why you puked after drinking from her?" I challenge him. Could it really be that simple? Is Alma not special after all? Perhaps there was never any real hope after all. No secret weapon to be used against the all-powerful bastard. She's too fresh, like a meal that hasn't spent long enough in the oven. A concoction that hasn't yet settled.

"Apparently so." He nods, relieved and a bit giddy. "And I didn't puke. I didn't! But when her blood has settled down a bit, I'll get her then. Don't you worry. But wow… wow! I don't mind telling you this is a relief. I thought… No, you know what, I'm not going to do this to myself. Self-care first. It doesn't matter what I thought, because all's well that ends well. Am I right, guys?"

The other vampires nod uncertainly. Some of them look disappointed and were no doubt secretly hoping along the same lines I was. We vampires are ever the opportunists.

Serat doesn't bother hiding his relief though. Or maybe he can't. He's dressed so smartly, so elegant and smooth, yet he acts now like a kid who has wriggled out of a punishment. Such a serious and evil face, and such black and shiny hair, and he's taller than me too, but for the first time ever… I don't feel intimidated by him. So, I kick him.

It's funny. A minute ago, I could barely speak words in front of him. All I wanted to do was run, or freeze, or curl up in a ball and rock back and forth for a while. But now I'm not like that. What's changed? Nothing. Everything. I think I must have replayed that night from four years ago in my head so many times that, in my head, Serat became something that he isn't. He's not a monster. He's a loser. And a bastard. So, I kick him again.

And it all spills out of me. The fear, the stress, the loss, the pain, the dread. All of it. Everything I've wanted to say to him and do to him explodes out of me now that the nightmare fear is gone. I don't actually say anything because there's too much I want to say, so instead I end up shouting incoherently and very loudly.

And everything I want to do to him is also too much—especially because in a moment or two, several vampires are going to jump on me—so I'm just kicking him. And I keep kicking him. And then he grabs my leg, looks up at me with angry eyes, and I know I've messed up big time. The other vampires haven't moved. He never needed them. My sudden outburst is over in a matter of seconds. And now Serat's going to make me pay for surprising him and kicking him to the ground. Oh dear. Poor me.

That's what I'm thinking as I fly backwards and shatter my spine (for the second time tonight) against one of the metal pillars of the warehouse. I hit the thing so hard that it actually bends. The giant, thick, metal pillar bends. I fall to the ground, little more than a lifeless puppet as my spine begins the arduous task of putting together what feels like a ten-thousand-piece puzzle. I don't spare a thought for Alma, but I do hear her scream as the vampires grab her.

"Keep hold of her!" Serat orders his cronies. "She's coming with us, but first, you Caiden… Why? Why? Why? Why? Why do you want to change the way things are?" He picks me up, which is inordinately painful, and holds me by my throat.

"It's so simple," he says to me. "You stay in your lane, you do what you were put in this forsaken city to do, and you don't cause a fuss. That's it. That's all you have to do. That's how it works. But you don't seem to get that, do you?"

It takes all my courage and all my effort to move my lips together and make a tortured sound that just about resembles the only two words I have left for Serat. "Piss off."

He laughs. I'm nothing to him. I'm not a threat, not an enemy, I'm not even an inconvenience. He drops me, then kneels in front of me. My spine might be feeling like a spine again, but for now I'm still moving like a puppet on one string, otherwise I would have gone for him. Yeah, I would have taken him on, I tell myself. Sure, it wouldn't have ended well for me, but it's not like it can get any worse.

"I like this place the way it is," Serat tells me as it is, as it really is. "Me on top, my followers terrified of me, and everyone else—all you scum—exhausted from the effort of just getting by. That's how it is and that's how I'm keeping it. You're a black sheep, Caiden. A nobody. This new one is a lost little lamb. So, I'll keep her penned up for a while, until she's ready to be just another sheep in my flock. This is Vampire City. You should be used to it by now… or do you need a reminder?"

"What more can you do to me?" I choke back at him, angry at his insurmountable position. "I'm still a vampire, Serat. Just like you. You can hurt me, but you can't get rid of me."

"True." He nods, and he rubs his chin in thought, and then smiles. "But I don't have to get rid of you. I only have to squeeze you. I have to drown you, surround you in pain and suffering, and thus make you small." He stands up, satisfied. A fly buzzes out of his mouth. "It is not you who will pay for your insubordination, Caiden, it'll be everyone around you." He turns to his vampires. "I've let you share the rat-man's blood, so tonight, you can be predators!"

***

The night is cold and dark. Everyone has shelter of sorts; some call their shelter a home, others only think of them as temporary, make-shift, only necessary for the time being. But everyone has a place where they go when the day is done, and the night outside is cold and dark.

Into these places, the vampires come.

Elves are dragged out of their shacks. Dwarves are beaten in the streets. A treeman is set alight. Pixies flee into the cold night sky, and a nymph is carried up the side of a building and then dropped. A drake is set upon. The potions of the dryad's stall are thrown to the ground where their glass bottles smash into little pieces. They explode, and sparking flames land on other stalls, shacks, and all such detritus left upon these desperate streets.

The fire spreads quickly. The night is no longer cold or dark. Instead, the flames dance and the searing heat presses down. The borough is burning, the markets are ruined, the occupants—the big and the small and the groups and the loners—are being put in their place.

"I don't really mind the gambling, the extortion, the cheating," Serat says with a blithe wave of his hand. "Or the beatings, the gangs, the suffering and the murdering. I don't mind any of it at all, in fact." Now he turns to me, and his eyes are cold, and his words are like stone. "But I can't have people thinking I'm weak, not even a little bit."

We're up high, on top of the same building I was on earlier this very night, and we're watching the chaos unfold below. Me, Serat, Alma, and Helisha. Helisha hadn't been in the warehouse, but she's here now, gripping Alma's arm.

I'm on my knees on the very edge, watching the billowing fires and the little figures below run for their lives. Serat comes to sit beside me, dangling his legs over the side.

"After I drank from Alma," Serat tells me, sounding far too casual, "I was incoherent and weak and pathetic. Her blood made me sick. Now though, I know why… a newly-turned vampire is a mess, inside and out. Of course, I'm back to my full strength now. A day of drinking from my followers has rejuvenated me."

I glance at Helisha. Her eyes turn downwards, her face expressionless, but her scarf is wrapped extra tight around her neck.

"And yet, the damage was done, wasn't it?" Serat taps me on my shoulder. "You are proof of this, Caiden."

"What the hell are you talking about?" I moan, tired and defeated.

"Your little rebellious conversation with your goblin friend, your little venture into my domain, your little attempt to break into my palace, no doubt hoping to find me weak and helpless, and finally, your little friend here." I can practically hear him smirking. Is there nothing Serat doesn't know? "Little, little, little," he says whimsically. "Nothing of consequence and easily dealt with but… out of little acorns grow burning trees." Far below us, a treeman runs through the destroyed market. It is covered in flames and roaring so loudly we can hear it above all the other screams and crashing destruction.

"I have no intention of being usurped," Serat says. "But, between you and me, every vampire has the potential to usurp me. Truthfully, there's nothing special about me. By fortune alone, I get to be the one who drinks everyone else. So, with this in mind, I have to keep a heavy hand on all of you. Keep you all in your places."

"But they're not vampires down there!" I snap, and I'm surprised to feel tears behind my eyes. "They can't do anything to you."

"I know, but tonight isn't for them," Serat looks into my near-tear-stricken eyes, and I see his own eyes are plain and dark. "Tonight is for you."

As quick as lightning, Serat grips my neck. The fear is back. It fills me completely and I replay the night from four years ago in my head again. It's like I'm in Serat's private lounge once more. Helpless. Completely at his mercy.

Serat crouches on the edge of the building and, still holding me by my neck, he dangles me over the edge. My legs kick air uselessly. My fingers claw at the hand around my neck, but they are just as useless.

"Either join my flock," Serat whispers above the wind, bringing me in close, "or stay low and insignificant, I really don't care." Then he hisses in my ear, his rage suddenly seething and his contempt for me all too apparent. *"But don't ever think you can beat me!"*

His fangs are growing, I start to panic. His eyes burn red, I have to get away. His mouth opens, I can't, not again, but he bites into me. It is as it was. It is like everything inside of me is being pulled out. I become a skeletal thing. Weak and feeble. I feel less than nothing. A void where I once existed.

And then he drops me. I fall. I hear Alma scream.

On the plus side though, I pass out before I hit the very hard ground. The very hard ground which is also on fire.

Silver linings and all that.

PART 2

I'm dreaming.

It's a good dream, which is lucky because I haven't had a dream since before some arsehole turned me into a vampire. It's wonderful, fantastic, and best of all, I have no idea it's a dream. As far as I can tell, this fantasy is my reality.

But it's only half a fantasy, really. It's one-half fantasy and one-half memory.

There he is. He's small, wiry, and his hair is a dark cloudy white. He looks like what he is, an honest and hard-working farmer. Well-respected and friendly. And there she is. As small as him, with a cheerful face and an endearing smile, she is the farmer's wife. They're good people, a good couple, married all their long lives. They're good people from the village I grew up in. The village in which I spent my first nineteen years… when I was human.

And there she is. The farmer's daughter. She has nice eyes and a warm smile. I see her sometimes putting out the milk or tending to the farm animals, and once I passed her in the village, and I smiled, and she smiled. But that's as far as the memory goes. I'm here for the fantasy.

We're together, searching for the right home, and we're going up and down through every hut and hovel in the village. Finally, we find a small place, far too small really and more 21st century than 19th century, but this is a dream, so logic and anachronisms don't matter at all.

I've known this place all my young life and, though I have never been back even once, I feel I know it as well now as I knew it then. We're together here. Together forever and we have it all ahead of us. Me, the nineteen-year-old country boy, and her, the farmer's daughter, who put out the milk and once smiled at me.

I wake up. The dream is over. Reality is restored. The fantasy is only a fantasy, and the memory dogs me for everything it never got a chance to be. And I'm crying. I can't stop it. I can't restrain myself, no matter how much it hurts my scorched voice or my charred body. I'm exhausted, I'm devastated, and I'm longing for what I feel

I've lost, which is totally bizarre because I know I never had it in the first place.

I want to go back. I want to go back to the dream. I don't want… this.

My body is struggling to fix itself. It not only took quite a tumble, but I suspect it spent the rest of the night on fire, burning to a blackened crispy shell of its former self. I fear I am like the little piece of bread that falls into the toaster and becomes impossible to retrieve, destined to be burnt over and over again.

It's daylight now. Maybe it's the morning, maybe the afternoon, or maybe a hundred years have passed. I have absolutely no idea and I'm not sure I care. Right now, lying here with my broken body and somehow-still-working tear ducts, the only thing I care about is her. The farmer's daughter. It's funny, though. I can barely remember her face.

As I think about her, and about everything I should have said and everything I might have missed out on, a worrying realisation dawns on me.

There isn't going to be a happy ending.

This is not the latest superhero movie, there is no prophecy conveniently pointing me in the direction of a good finale, and there is no magic alien piano that, when played correctly, will solve all my problems for me.

It truly is horrible to realise this is how it will end and that nothing is going to save you, or take your hand, or offer you a way out. This is it. You're going to stay like this, and this is how it will be for you from this point on. All your dreams? They won't happen. All your mistakes? They're cast in stone now. The person you wanted to become? He missed the last train and he's not coming.

This is it.

Ow.

No. Really. Ow. Very much ow. Very, very much ow. I want to complain, moan, and say something annoyingly sarky, but my selfish voice box hasn't grown back yet. I try to growl, but nothing happens, so I have to be content with staring angrily at the sky above me. The moving sky. How is the sky moving? And the tops of the buildings too! And ow, again. Ow. The ground is moving too, in the same direction as the sky and the tops of the buildings, and it's hurting me. A lot. Freshly-made skin is peeling away, tender muscles are being twisted out of position, and bits of bone are knocking painfully against concrete roads and jagged bits of stone.

Oh. Wait. Someone's dragging me. That explains everything. Still hurts though.

***

Her hair is a moody silver. His hair is a bright scarlet. There are others here too, sitting in the background and watching us, all with strangely-coloured hair. With a sigh, I realise who I've found myself with, and I haven't even registered their ears.

Their colours might change between them, but always they wear their hair long and often plaited in intricate and beautiful patterns, though some here have simply tied it back. With their long, arrow-like faces and their striking ears that point upwards like sharp daggers, I find myself feeling groggy, half-conscious, aching all over, and surrounded by elves.

I'm lying down inside a small, dark place. Metal sheeting for walls, dirty mattresses for flooring, and a rather shaky-looking ceiling. A shack then, but an elven shack, so there are also hanging charms made of woven plant stems and chiselled stones, and painted wards of a strange and alien design on almost every surface.

"What happened?" I whisper painfully. My voice is weak and croaky. New voice boxes can be a pain to break in.

"Last night happened," the elf with the moody silver hair says. She doesn't sound too pleased with me. The scarlet-haired one pats her on the arm, nods sympathetically, and leaves. I rather wish he would stay. Left alone with the moody elf, I feel like a little boy caught red-handed and facing up to the belt.

"Why?" She fixes her eyes, with silver-circled irises, on me. They really are beautiful eyes, on a hard and cutting face though.

"Why... what?" I ask lamely.

"Why did last night happen?" she insists, just about keeping her patience with me. She speaks with authority, her voice stern and her general manner austere. From the way the other elves hang on her every word, she's clearly a leader to them. It fits her well.

"Oh," I sigh. "Last night, you say. Well... what makes you think I know—"

She grabs me by the throat and squeezes hard. I would scream but my voice box, being less than a few hours old, means I can only squeak like a strangled rat. I don't know if this elf knows what she's doing, but her fingers are digging into a very painful and very tender bite wound on my neck. I wonder how much she might already know.

"You are like them." She labels me with such derision in her voice.

"I… am…" I struggle against her grip and eventually she relents a little and so I manage to speak again, albeit petulantly and bad-temperedly. "I am not… one of them!"

"But you *are* like them," she persists. "So, tell me, what happened last night and why?"

I shrug her away, turn onto my side, and push myself upwards. I'm now sitting up and I wish for all the world I had stayed horizontal. But I'm not going to flop back down. Not in front of these dozen or so elves anyway, who are all now watching me with guarded and even hostile eyes.

Many of them are sporting fresh bruises whilst some have suffered more serious wounds covered in bandaging. They all look tired, stretched, and forlorn. "I think you know what happened last night better than me," I say to them all.

"But why?" The moody, silver-haired elf rounds on me. Her eyes stare into mine, and where they are determined and still, I feel mine are quivering and wet.

"Serat and his vampires have never come to us like they did last night. Why now?"

Should I tell them the truth? Should I tell them last night only happened because Serat wanted to teach me a lesson and keep me, a foolish black sheep, in line?

"I don't know," I say to her, but I can tell she is unsure whether to believe me. "Whatever the reason, it doesn't matter now," I say glumly. "It's over."

"Will they come again? Tonight?" one of the watching elves asks, nervous and afraid.

"No," I say, sounding more sure than I feel, but then I think on it for a moment, and I know I'm right. "They don't need to." Lesson learned, I suppose.

This place looks like hell. It really does. Okay, even on a normal day this place looks like a rubbish heap, but at least then it only feels like hell. Today, though, it literally looks like hell.

The market stalls have all burned down. Many of the shacks are in tattered ruins. Last night's fires have left behind a desert of blackened surfaces. There's dirty smoke everywhere, and there are shrivelled bodies, some big and some not so big.

Looking sombre and empty, the people set about doing everything that needs to be done. Things are being cleared, corpses are being covered and moved, and stuff is being thrown away. Many of the elves, quiet and sullen, help with the clean-up. The dryad who owned the potions stall is trying in vain to salvage anything he can. A small band of pixies are working together to lift a cracked cinder block off one of their kin. The treeman is resting in a corner of the street, looking like a giant twiglet.

I feel responsible. I am responsible. I tell myself I don't know them, they're strangers, and that Serat's the real bastard. But somewhere deep inside of me, I still feel responsible. A crying child is a crying child, even if I don't know them and even if the crying child is actually a giant, grown-up twiglet. But I wanted to live a life alone. I chose the path of the black sheep. But seeing this… I don't know… I shouldn't care, I don't know them…

Across the street from where I'm standing, a banshee is looking at me. I've only just noticed her, but I get the impression she's been watching me ever since I stepped out of the elf's shack.

There's something familiar about this small, slender banshee girl, but I can't quite pinpoint what it is. I can feel her creamy white eyes staring at me. Her long, fair hair is sodden, and her oversized grey hoodie, which is more like a gown that whips around her thin frame, is filthy.

I don't like banshees. Banshees are weird. They don't quite fit in to what normal should look like. They're not people. They're not things. They're… odd. Also, I hate how this one is staring so intently at me. If I had more energy, I'd cross the street and tell her to piss off. As I am though, I turn away and tell myself she's not there, though I still feel her gaze on me even as I walk slowly away.

"You can help," someone says behind me. I turn back and it's the silver-haired elf catching up with me.

"I'd only get in the way," I lie. The truth is I can't stand to be here. All of this—this devastation and loss—is all on me. And if they knew…

"I wasn't asking," the silver-haired elf tells me. "You got a name?"

"Caiden," I say despondently.

"I'm Amirah," she introduces herself. "Now help me with this." Yes. Definitely a leader. If she had been human, she'd have been a big-time CEO or a successful politician. She's tough, self-assured, attractive, and she's not here to coddle anyone, least of all me. I do what she says.

The day drags on and it takes far too long to do something I didn't even want to do in the first place. I help move the things, I avoid the corpses, and I throw the stuff away. Any stuff. All the stuff. I don't know. It's like a fever dream, and I've mentally checked out. I'm not thinking. I know this isn't very noble of me, but it's easier than dealing with what's in front of me.

"So, tell me." Amirah interrupts my non-thinking thoughts. We're at the canal of sludge and mud (the same canal Alma beat me up in only yesterday morning, though it feels longer—ah, good times), it's early in the evening and the two of us, with a few others, are chucking unsalvageable detritus away. "Why does a vampire choose to live apart from his own kind?" silver-haired Amirah asks me.

"Because they're not my own kind," I reply, rather brusquely. "I don't want to be like them."

"You don't like being a vampire?"

"I do," I say, although I'm surprised to find I'm not sure if I believe my own words. I quickly move on, burying this newfound and rather worrying self-doubt. "It's just that I don't want to be *their* vampire," I add, with venom in my tone.

"Ah, a rogue." Amirah nods. "You belong with misfits and inbetweeners, is that right? You're one of us? Do you feel at home in such a mixed community of society's losers?"

"No." I shake my head. "I don't want to be here either."

"Oh. But you are here."

"Yes," I concede glumly, picking up something so twisted and burned I can't even tell what it is before chucking it into the canal. "But it's not where I want to be. This... this isn't how I imagined it would go."

"And how did you imagine your life in Vampire City would go?" I get the unnerving impression she's testing me, like a teacher asking casual, probing questions about a topic the school children should definitely know everything about because it was in last night's homework.

"I... I don't know," I admit. "I guess I thought it would all figure itself out. It always did before."

"Outside the city, you mean?"

"In the real world, yes," I clarify.

"That's not the real world out there," Amirah tells me. "For sub-mortals like you and me, the human world is hiding, running, and pretending. That is not real."

"And this city is real?" I ask her, dropping what I was holding and not bothering to hide my pessimism.

"Yes." She nods, unperturbed, and turning to face me. "This city is real. It is hard and it is unfair, and it is broken. And that is real. We cannot hide from it, there is nowhere to run, and so there is no point in pretending."

"Amirah," I sigh, picking the thing I dropped and tossing it away. "You're not exactly cheering me up here."

"I'm not trying to cheer you up," Amirah says. "I am trying to understand why you are not like the other vampires. It would be an easier life for you, surely. Why do you not want to be with them?"

"Because I hate them," I say, keeping my eyes downcast. "I hate him."

"You mean Serat?"

I nod. I then do something I haven't done in a very long while. I pull down my collar and show off my bite marks. Amirah moves her scarf to show me her own.

"Serat bites us all." I nod, replacing my collar. "And the other vampires… they just… I don't know…"

"They hide from what he did to them, and they run from facing what he still does to them every day, and eventually they end up pretending it never happened at all and will never happen again." And just like that, Amirah explains to me exactly how I feel.

"Yes, yes, you're right," I say, standing on the edge, looking down at all the carnage. Another armful is chucked down and crashes in the heap, becoming lost in the mass almost instantly. "But I can't do any of that. I can't let it go. I won't. One day… one day, I'll get him."

"So, it's revenge you seek?" she asks me.

"I suppose so," I sigh. "Not very noble of me, I know."

"That depends," Amirah says, putting a hand on my arm and turning me round to look her straight in the eye. "Are you angry with Serat because what he did to you was wrong… or are you angry because he did the wrong thing to you?"

"…I don't know," I shrug uselessly. I suddenly realise how incredibly tired I am. Even more so than usual.

***

The sun is falling. Soon, night will come and darkness will cover the city. I welcome it. I want nothing more than this day to end. But there's something I have to do first. Something I probably should have done several hours ago. More specifically, there's someone I should have probably checked up on after last night's chaos.

Gawk's office has been left in ruins. Everything has been trashed and broken. And Gawk is lying in a corner, bloodied and broken, barely able to open his eyes even as I kneel down in front of him.

"Oh, it's you," the arsehole sighs.

"You look… terrible," I tell him, horribly unsure of what to say.

"Well, ain't that a coincidence," he winces, spitting up blood, "because I feel like it too."

"What the hell happened?"

Gawk scoffs and then wheezes with the pain that follows. "I took a little tumble, you see," he manages eventually. "Stubbed my toe on the end of my desk, bumped my shoulder on the shelf there, then one thing followed the other, and it finished with the whole place coming down on top of my head."

I manage a smile. This is harder than I thought it would be. I don't even particularly like Gawk. He's a shifty, untrustworthy scoundrel. But he's also the closest thing I've had to a friend these past four years. We hardly saw one another, we would often try to get one over each other, and so neither of us particularly trusted the other one. But we were friends. And now I'm watching him slowly succumb to one of the harshest beatings I've ever come across. His jaw is swollen, one of his eyes is closed up, dried blood stains his clothes, there's a mean-looking gash on the top of his head, and his arms and legs have been broken. My closest-thing-to-a-friend is dying. Yeah. This kinda sucks.

"Came for you, did they?" I say.

"Yeah," Gawk sighs, the fight in him completely spent. "I guess Serat's cronies didn't much like the idea of a goblin getting in good with the boss…" He trails off, unwilling to finish what he was about to say. There's an awkward silence between us. And then Gawk sighs deeply.

"A soul should go unburdened into the next life," the goblin whispers, his voice sad and forlorn. "So listen, Caiden, because I'm not going to say this twice, I don't think I'd be able to." He coughs up a bit more blood. "I'm the one who told them where the girl would be."

"Alma?"

Gawk nods. "I told them she'd be at the warehouse, but I told them a later time because I wanted to make a few dog-ends before they came for her." He laughs, and this causes him another shot of pain. "Didn't think they'd do all this to their own neighbourhood though."

"You told Serat where he could find Alma?"

"As good as." The goblin looks me in the eye. "I told one of his cronies who came to my office yesterday. Snooping around she was, asking about the girl, and I'd already convinced Alma to be at the warehouse at sun fall, and I figured my info would get me in good with the boss."

"Who was snooping around?" I ask, but I suspect I already know.

"Your old mate, Helisha." Bingo. "Very keen, she was. That one'll be in Serat's inner circle for a good while after last night."

"I suppose so." I nod, and then I sigh, disappointed. "She really is living the dream."

I can't bring myself to get too close, so I stay kneeling in front of him, watching my friend slowly succumb.

"What's so special about her anyway?" Gawk asks, and for a moment I think he's talking about Helisha, but then I realise he's asking about Alma.

"Nothing," I tell him. "As it turns out, nothing at all."

"Then why did Serat struggle when he bit her?"

"She's a freshly-turned vampire," I explain. "That's all. A newbie, a greenhorn, a blank page. A mixed-up vintage, you might say. She hasn't settled yet."

"Oh." And I can hear the disappointment in his voice. "So, it really was a great big goose chase, then? Bloody hell." He's getting weaker and slower by the minute. "Why did Serat have to torch the borough though?"

The devastated neighbourhood, the burned bodies, the destroyed office, and the beaten-to-death goblin… well, that's all on me. All to show me who's in charge and how things work around here, and how nothing will ever change. Is Gawk lying here because he got too close with the boss, or was it me he got too close with? "Because he's a bastard," I respond. "No other reason."

Gawk manages a wry smile. I draw back, unsure. Does he know? He can't. But it doesn't matter anyway. I can hear his heart struggling and I can sense the blood in his veins weakening. He doesn't have long left.

"Do you forgive me?"

The question catches me off guard. Me forgive him? For what? Oh, right. The whole snitching on Alma thing and indirectly bringing Serat's terrible vengeance down on the borough.

"Of course," I say, too quickly. "You couldn't have known what he would do."

Gawk nods, but he doesn't look entirely satisfied. "That's it, then. Nothing more to say." He sighs deeply, his body starting to shut down. 'Wonder what's waiting for me on the other side… ha… maybe I'll see Needl again. Would be good to talk with him after all this time."

I shift uncomfortably. I don't want to say what I'm about to say. It'll help neither of us and very likely ruin the last few moments this small and rather pathetic goblin has on this earth. I shouldn't say it. It doesn't need to be said. But I'm going to say it anyway.

"Gawk… I'm the one who killed Needl."

✱✱✱

About two years ago…

What am I doing here? Needl's a pain to be around at the best of times. And it's raining. I hate the rain. It's cold and it's wet, and it gets everywhere. And by the look of those heavy grey storm clouds in the sky, it's only going to get worse.

I'm standing on the corner of the street, huddled against the wall and trying to shelter in an alcove. It doesn't help at all though because the wind is whipping the rain right up into my face. My shabby coat is already drenched. I am this close to turning around and giving up on this whole thing. I doubt Needl would even notice if I left.

He's sitting on the curb. The great big half-troll looking like a great big baby. A very ugly baby, mind. He doesn't look bothered by the rain though. He's wearing a poncho, which is actually a large tarpaulin sheet with a hole for his head, and he's staring expectantly at the giant iron gates.

We're at the wall. The wall that circles the city. The wall that keeps us in. It's taller than any skyscraper, both above ground and below ground, and thicker than one too, and it's made out of the heaviest metal and hardest stone. It looks terrifying and indomitable. With the wall as a backdrop, Needl only looks like a tiny baby—but still a very ugly one, of course.

This was Gawk's idea, but he's not here because this sort of dangerous work is what Needl's for and the grubby goblin doesn't want to risk his own neck. I've come along because I'm bored and Gawk offered me some dog-ends (also I secretly think it's a rather good idea). New arrivals are always the most vulnerable, and as Gawk excitedly explained, they'll never be richer than they are right now. It's all downhill from here, folks.

The gate groans. It's a deep and melancholic sound that reverberates along the wall for miles. Titanic cogs are turning, massive chains are pulling, and a building-sized gate is slowly grinding open.

This is what the half-troll and I have been waiting for. Soon, the latest batch of sub-mortal refugees—be they elf or dwarf, pixie or troll, rat-man or treeman, and everything in between—will walk through the open gate, the gate will then close, and that'll be it. And we're here to help the new arrivals. Help them get accustomed to how this city works. We'll take anything they don't need anymore, and if we see anything else we like, we'll probably have that too.

I know I'm being a bastard, but I've been in this city two years now and I've had far worse done to me, so get off my back about it.

So, Needl and I are going to mug a few fresh faces. That's it. Where's the danger, then? Well, the wall itself is the danger. Get too close and the guns start firing. Big guns. Big, metal guns. Big, metal, automatic guns that are so big the humans firing them don't even bother aiming. They'll blow anyone apart in seconds. Now, I'm invincible but I'm not a loony. Stray too close and I'd get blown apart too… and after re-congealing myself over a matter of weeks, I'd wake up and find myself in the exact same spot in which I was blown apart earlier… so I'd get blown apart again. I knew a vampire who tried it once. I think the silly sod is still out there somewhere, getting blown apart every few weeks.

Just inside the wall, there is only flattened ground—courtesy of those big guns—and it's about a half mile inwards where Vampire City actually starts to look like a city. This is where we are now. This is where we wait. To pass the time, I make stilted conversation.

"You know, I once saw a sylph charge the wall."

"What happened?" Needl asks, sitting thoughtlessly on the edge of the curb.

"Humans fired a barrage, like they normally do, and it didn't work."

"Air bloke got out?" Needl lifts his head, suddenly hopeful.

"No. The humans pulled out a weird gun," I say. "It's like a giant air cannon that aimed right on the sylph. Blew the poor guy apart, quite literally actually. It's amazing how creative humans can be when they have the right incentive."

"If I was fairy," Needl says, looking up at the grey sky as his simple drawl struggles with this rare venture into his own imagination, "I'd fly over walls. Humans don't clip fairy wings, eh."

"Fairy wings are like insect wings, mate," I point out. "Fragile things. There's an air screen, kind of like a hair dryer, that runs along the top of the wall. If any fairy managed to get high enough, the humans could blow it right back. They can shoot it over the whole of Vampire City."

"Hate humans." His head slumps back down.

"I do too." As stilted conversations go, that wasn't too bad.

And here they come.

There are a few hundred of them. A few large figures, which we'll have to avoid, and some other dangerous-looking fellows. A clawed afanc hops along but isn't worth our time; I think I spot a finfolk, which looks promising although they'll be difficult to keep track of; and there's a squonk, and we'd have to be very quick with that bag of emotions.

Elves huddle together, so they're not a viable target; dwarves would put up too much of a fight; and ghouls are as worthless as they are scrawny and scary looking. Finally, I spot a good one: a young harpy.

With the wings, claws, tail, and lower half of a bird, the chest and head are the only humanoid features the harpy has. There's no doubting how beautiful the wings are or how impressive the claws look, and the tail looks very nice too. Meanwhile, the human face of the harpy is just as beautiful. Her long wild hair flows down her back. But there's no getting around it, these features combined look ridiculous. A little taller than myself but probably weighing a tenth of what I weigh, harpies are too big to be agile and too weak to be strong. Target acquired.

Don't get me wrong, I don't feel good about how Needl and I are about to rough up an easy target. On the other hand, harpies don't last very long in Vampire City anyway, so…yeah.

"Follow me, Needl."

"I'll follow you," Needl pouts. "But only cos Gawk says I got to do what you say tonight, not because yer my new boss, cos you ain't."

"I know," I chide him, irritated by his slurring speech and infantile brain. "Now, follow me."

The new arrivals trudge nervously across the dead land between the wall and the city proper. They're like a flock of sheep moving as one to pastures new. But, like they do every time, once they start getting close to the buildings and the alleyways with all their nooks and crannies, they start to break apart. The faster ones dart down the alleys, the larger ones stomp on through, the smallest find cover, and the slowest dally nervously. All of them have their own ways of dealing with being completely clueless and hopelessly lost.

I hop down and peek around a corner, keeping my eye on the harpy, who is definitely one of the slower ones, and I wait to see which direction the poor soul will eventually end up heading. As I watch her, Needl sneaks up behind me. I can't just hear his low, guttural breathing, I can also feel it on the back of my neck.

"Do you mind taking a step back?" I moan at him. He pouts some more and makes an ugly grunting noise, but he does take a small step backwards.

The harpy disappears into an abandoned garage, all on her own and doubtless feeling very scared right now, which is fantastic for us. Oh yes, this is all going very well, as far as Needl and I are concerned.

There are gaping holes in the garage walls. Everything of value or use was scavenged long ago, and the large puddles on the weed-infested floor suggest several leaks in the ceiling. The harpy looks rather pathetic amongst it all. She's standing inside, pawing at the ground with her claws and looking around nervously. She bats her wings a bit, but there's nothing useful she can do with them now. Not anymore. She's been clipped, as all the larger flying sub-mortals are when the humans process them into Vampire City. She'll never fly again.

"Hello there." I step into the garage alone. The harpy spins round, her eyes wide and frightened, and she wraps her mutilated wings around herself. "Don't be scared!" I hold up my hands in a placating gesture. That's all it is, of course. A gesture. Not a promise. Funny how often it works though.

"Who are you?" the harpy asks me, her voice coarse and rough, sounding alien to me, though I can still hear the terror in her speech.

"I'm no one. A nobody," I say, smiling. "I'm no threat to you."

"What do you want?" she shouts at me. "Stay back!"

I stop moving towards her, but that's okay. I've already got her undivided attention.

"I just wanted…" I speak slowly, carefully, playing for time. "…to welcome you… to Vampire City…" The words send shivers down my spine, but I pay them no attention because Needl chooses now to make his move.

Needl bops the harpy on the head, and she drops instantly. That's a very nice way of putting it. What actually happens is, growling with the effort, he swings his two meaty fists into the side of her head. She cries out from the sudden pain, collapses, and the other side of her head smashes off a countertop. Then she hits the floor. Either way you look at it, it all adds up to the same end though.

"Come on." I close in on the unconscious harpy and lean over her docile body. "Quickly!"

Needl grumbles at my snapping orders, but he does as he's told. He pulls out a large, smelly sack and holds it open for me. As for me, I start plucking.

With such a varied and wild populace, Vampire City's black market (which is only the seedier side of the normal market) is rife with many interesting and exciting items. One of them is the feather of a harpy, which fetches a reasonable price and can be used in simple spells, potions, rituals and… other activities. Crush it, grind it, boil it, smoke it, burn it, or tickle with it, whatever you want to do with it you can, as long as you've got the dog-ends to pay for it.

I bend over and take a tail feather, and another, and another. They are long and sturdy feathers, so I have to get right to the skin, take a firm grip, and pull quite hard to free each one. They prove stubborn things to dislodge, but I don't mind. No one will be bothering us because the other newbies will have moved further inside the city by now, or they've already been nabbed by vampire cronies working for their respective borough bosses. Also, no seasoned citizen of Vampire City would ever come this far out. I think it's the massive guns that put them off, but it might also be the frequent fights that break out over the latest batches of refugees. It can get a bit intense.

Which is all fine by me, because it means Needl and I have all the time in the world to pluck as many feathers as we can. That is as long as the harpy doesn't wake up. Right on cue, the harpy wakes up.

She wakes with a terrible screech, one filled with agony and hatred, and she thrashes wildly in her fear and desperation to get away. For my troubles, I get a wing right in my face, and my chest, and every other part of me. The single beat of her wing sends me crashing across the garage floor. But Needl gets the worst of it.

A swinging claw scythes across his bulbous belly and opens it. Understandably, it's not a pretty sight. The harpy kicks herself up and scrambles out of the garage. She's gone and for now at least she's free from danger, because Needl's in no state to run after her and I'm certainly not going to.

Instead, I stand lamely in front of Needl, who has slumped to his knees and is holding his belly closed as best he can. He looks up at me. His eyes are welling up. Along with everything else, including the horror of what I'm seeing and the disappointment of losing out on our score, I suddenly feel extremely awkward at the big boy's tears. Why does he have to cry?

"Hurts bad," Needl croaks.

"…It would," I say. Well, what the hell else am I supposed to say? *"Don't worry"? "You'll be fine"? "It's only a flesh wound"? "Goodbye"?* …Hmm, maybe the last one.

"Hurts real bad…" The big lug sobs, choking a bit and looking very wobbly.

I go to his side. I don't want to but eventually I take a look at what's happened to him. It is bad. Real bad. Despite Needl's big arms holding tight, they can't stop the flow, or the seeping, or the weight of what is coming out. He's a goner. This much is obvious to me and, if Needl had a few more brain cells, he'd know it too. As he is lacking in the brain department though, he still looks up at me with a hopeful, doe-eyed expression.

"Fix me up?" It sounds like a question. Not a question asking whether or not I can help him, but a question asking whether I'm going to fix him now or later.

I can't find the courage to say out loud I won't be helping him. Vampires regenerate themselves, not others. As for any medical knowledge I might have, I've spent the last two centuries enjoying the ability of unlimited healing… what would I need medical knowledge for?

But it's far too late now anyway. He looks up at me again. His tear-stricken cheeks and his painful grimace tells me it's getting worse. I really feel like I should do something. Anything. But the only thing… no. Not that. It wouldn't even work, anyway. Would it?

"I could…" I begin, but I lose my voice, and I trail off into silence. Even so the damage is done and hope kindles anew in his doe eyes.

"Help me!" Needl whimpers. He falls sideways. Still holding his stomach, he lands hard on his shoulder. He spurts loudly before bursting into all-out crying now. And he's losing his grip. Bits of him that should really stay on the inside are now spilling over to the outside, joining the already rather large puddle of blood that surrounds him. "Pleases!" the dying half-troll begs me.

"It wouldn't be helping," I try to reason with him. "What I can do for you… It would make you… different." How do I explain this to a dumb-as-they-come half-troll who is currently watching his guts pour out of him? It's a toughie, that's for sure. "You would be like me."

"Hurts!" Needl's voice is weakening. He's trying to shout, trying to cry, but he's fading. Breaking down. "Help… help me… hurts… Gawk… Gawk…"

The only thing I could do for him is this: I could feed on him. I could drink his blood and then I could make him drink mine and then, maybe, he would turn into a vampire. I can't see any reason why a half-troll couldn't become a vampire, but not everyone who starts the turning process finishes it and the troll community aren't exactly known for their mental fortitude. Going through the turning, be you troll or not, will often kill you straight out.

But it could save him. I could still try. So, I stand up and I tower over the blubbering oaf… and I turn from him, and I walk away. I'm not even going to try.

There are so many reasons to justify what I'm doing. One more vampire in the world is probably one too many, so I'm doing the world a favour. And being a vampire is its own strange and upside-down hell, so I'm also doing Needl a favour. And turning someone into a vampire is a big no-no as far as the borough rules are concerned. Serat would come down on me hard, so I'm also doing me a favour.

The truth is, everyone's better off if I just let Needl go. Except Gawk, maybe.

But that's not why I'm walking away. I'm walking away because I know I can't do it. I physically could, but mentally I'm simply not there. I knew it from the moment I thought of turning Needl into a vampire. I knew I was never going to do it. I knew I wouldn't even try. My voice failed. My idea never became anything real. To put myself out there like that… to open up… to try and turn someone… it's too much… too much… I can't. So, I walk away.

I guess what I'm trying to say (in far too many words) is that I am a coward.

I sit down in the doorway of the half-collapsed garage. The rain is coming down harder now, hitting the city with an anger that feels personal. I can't see the harpy. I can't see anyone. The rain is loud and angry. I don't want to step out into the deluge, but the alternative is staying here. No matter how loud the rain or how hard the raindrops hit, they pale in comparison to the dying sounds behind me of a friend-who-wasn't-a-friend, of someone who was nothing more than an acquaintance by chance, only a colleague by selfish design, and a lug who scraped me off the concrete two years ago.

I feel rotten, weak, and cowardly. I am the lowest of the low. And now there is no more blubbering, no more crying, no more wheezing, and no more movement. Just the rain. All around me and on me. Loud, terrible, and intrusive, feeling like strangers on my skin. Dripping down my back, soaking my clothes, and even coming down my cheeks.

****

Back to the now…

Gawk stares at me. I can't read his face. Is he mad? Is he sad? Is he devastated beyond comprehension? Will he summon what strength he has left and lunge at me in a rage-fuelled attack? No. He won't do any of that. He's dead. He must have bled out at some point during my confession. I wonder if he even heard the important bit. Probably not because it was at the end.

All that for nothing.

Still, I wasn't to know, and even if Gawk did die halfway through, I still feel like I've gotten something off my chest. It feels as if a small weight has been lifted. And in a weird way, sitting here in this destroyed office belonging to my little goblin friend, opposite the lifeless body of that same little goblin friend, I do feel a bit better about myself.

I am sad Gawk is dead. He wasn't the best, not even of his own lowly species, but we worked together a few times and, for what it was worth, we both found ourselves at the same arse-end of this forsaken city. That has to count for something.

"I didn't think he'd do all this," someone says. I look up and see Helisha standing in the doorway. She looks over the remains of the office, all the broken bits and the general carnage, and from Gawk's broken body to me sitting on the floor opposite.

"What did you think they'd do?" I ask her sharply, my brow furrowed. "Break out a six-pack and play a round of *cards?*"

She huffs loudly and steps around me. The young vampire kneels down to inspect Gawk's body closely. I can't see her face, but she's keeping very still.

"Helisha," I say, breaking the silence. "Why were you looking for Alma?"

"Because he was looking for her," she replies, not turning to face me. "And he is the boss."

"Serat's a bastard."

"He is." She finally stands up, wipes something from her face, then goes to the desk. "But he's also still the boss."

"What are you looking for now?" I snap at her.

"The goblin did a lot of work for Serat," she replies. "He wants it."

"What kind of work?"

"Just work, nothing interesting."

"You mean snitching?"

"Nothing so dramatic." She rolls her eyes at me, momentarily looking up from rifling through the bent and broken drawers. "It's only boring stuff," she continues, "like counting people, making notes on comings and goings, checking up on what you lot are getting up to."

"Sounds a lot like snitching," I grumble. Still on the floor. Still too tired to do anything more than grumble.

"Call it whatever you like," she sighs. "I just hope it hasn't all been lost."

"Maybe you should have scooped it up before you burnt the borough down."

"That is what Serat wanted," she tells me. "But it looks like someone got side-tracked."

"When you say *side-tracked*," I snarl, finally standing up, "what you mean is someone had too much fun beating my friend to death and then forgot about whatever they were supposed to pick up."

She stops searching. She lifts her head up. Looks me dead in the eye. "You don't have any friends."

I hesitate. Bloody hell. Embarrassed and angry, I try out my own huffing. I do a rather good job, but I don't think Helisha notices because she's gone back to searching through the chaotic filing system that Gawk put all his papers in.

"Besides, Serat should have seen it coming," she says in an idle tone. "Munstone always gets carried away."

"Munstone did this?" I sputter, thinking of that weasel-faced, sycophantic, bootlicking phony.

"This was Munstone, alright. Ah! Here's something that looks important." She begins flicking through a folder of papers and I go back to sitting on the floor. I'm stewing.

"Why'd you do it, Helisha?"

"Do what?"

"Snitch on me and the girl."

"Oh. That." She sighs, forgetting the folder for now. "It's the job, Caiden. You should try it sometime."

"Why?" I retort. "So I can play at being happy every night only to sell my soul to an absolute bastard during the day?"

"Oh, fuck off. It's so you don't have to eke out a rubbish existence in this cesspool!" she snaps back at me.

I sigh. "Worth it, is it?"

"It's better than what you've got now," she stubbornly says.

"Better than what I've got?" I think about this. "Maybe… But the way I see it… The closest thing you've got to a friend is the sadistic sociopath who spent last night butchering the closest thing I had to a friend."

"The closest thing you had to a friend…" Helisha lifts one of the papers out from the folder, turns it to me to show off a blurry, amateurish photo of myself walking away down a street, and next to me is Alma, walking by my side. "…was ready to sell you out for a few extra dog-ends a month."

"Bitch," I say, because there's nothing more to say.

"Loser." Ah. She's got me there.

✳✳✳

The days roll on by. I'm not sure what day it is today or how much time has passed since the night when everything went up in flames. It's not been too long though. I'm almost positive we're still in the same season anyway.

No one ever talks about this part… the low part. The sense that you aren't the main character of a story waiting to take you somewhere cool. The sense that you are, actually, just another shmuck, eking out a living, and going nowhere in particular. Harry Potter never felt like this. That little git literally had a scar on his forehead constantly reminding him he's special. I wonder how those movies turned out, by the way.

Amirah has me working most of the time. I don't like it very much, but the dull, monotonous tasks help keep my mind occupied and my hands busy. I'm not sure why Amirah started telling me what to do and I'm definitely unclear as to why I keep listening to her. I don't even like elves.

The funny thing is though, I'm not the only one. Amirah's telling everyone what to do—everyone who's left, that is. And everyone complies. No. That's wrong. They're not complying and they're not falling into line. They actually *want* to do whatever Amirah tells them. Is it something about her silver hair? Or her stern face? I don't know. She doesn't shout, bark, threaten, or cajole anyone though. She tells us what to do and we agree to do it.

She's a leader and a good one too, so maybe that's all it takes. It helps that she seems to know what she's talking about, and everyone always sees the sense in what she wants us to do, and she's strong too. Strong enough for those of us who aren't strong ourselves.

Before, we lived side-by-side, traded with each other, sometimes talked, and often worked together, but we never really got to know each other. Hell, I'd known Gawk for four years and I didn't know a dickybird about him. I don't even know what a dickybird is.

Everyone had their own little cliques. The elves stayed in their shacks, the dwarves resided in basements, the tree people stood in the park, pixies gathered in little nooks, and so on and so forth. Everyone had somewhere where everyone else wasn't welcome.

But now that's changed, arguably through necessity but it's still there, even if it is probably only temporary. Everyone from tree people to pixies, from dryads to swamp-people, and even from elves to dwarves, have kind of… well… come together.

We're rebuilding the market, putting up new shacks, clearing out the rubbish, and cleaning up the borough.

We're helping each other, comforting each other, and coming together and forming a community of support, security and togetherness… I hate it. Of course I hate it. It's just the way I think. I am who I am. I'm a vampire. I'm a predator. This *niceness* goes against everything I feel comfortable with. Don't get me wrong, I feel the support and the security and that lovely warm, fuzzy feeling you get from coming together as a community. I even like it. But I hate that I like it, and I hate that everyone else is clicking with it and becoming… more. More than what they were when they were alone, when they were… prey.

"Where are you?"

The night is young, the air is cold, and the slum is dark and overcrowded. We group together under what used to be a part of the freeway. The long-ago abandoned buildings might provide some shelter from the wind, but they are almost all skeletons of their former selves, as liable to collapse as they are to provide refuge.

So, we come together under this part of the freeway, somewhat protected from the wind, and we huddle around one of several oil barrel fires. It's not actual fire, though. We don't have the fuel to spare for actual fire, so Amirah convinced some fire dogs to each sit in an oil barrel and let themselves burn. It's Amirah who asked me the question, by the way.

I look up, weary-eyed.

"I'm right here," I answer cluelessly.

"I meant in here." She taps her own temple, her hood folding under her finger. "I watch you, Caiden. You're always in your own little world."

"Oh, yeah," I sigh. "It's easier in there."

"It would be." Amirah nods. "I also like to let my mind wander, let my thoughts drift away from this place… but wander too far, or drift for too long, and you risk getting lost."

"Good," I huff. Amirah chooses not to press the issue. That's probably a wise decision, seeing as I'm not in the mood to be reasoned with. Insightful wisdom would have only annoyed me, irrefutable proof would have entrenched me on the opposite side, and a comforting hand on my shoulder would have imminently suffered broken fingers. Sometimes, there is no talking with someone, and I am that someone right now.

"What will they do with your friend?" Amirah eventually asks me.

"My friend?" I have no idea who she's talking about. Helisha's right. I don't have any friends.

"The young girl?" Amirah persists. "The vampire from the warehouse fights."

"Oh," I realise. My brain is slow when my mood is low. "As far as I can tell, they've locked her up in Serat's building. And her name is Alma."

"What will become of her?" Amirah asks, her curiosity playing a dangerous game with my volatile mood. Most of the others have been avoiding me precisely because of my mood, while the rest simply tolerate me, but Amirah has decided to ask questions. Good leader she might be, but right now she's pushing it with me.

"They'll make her like the rest of them," I say brusquely, glumly staring at the bright flickering of a fire dog's bald head. "Or she'll end up like me."

"A black sheep?"

"A loser."

Silence. I was rather hoping she'd disagree with me and then explain why everything wrong with me isn't actually my fault at all. I suppose silence is still better than her agreeing emphatically with how much of a loser I am. Got to look on the bright side.

A large, bear-like creature sits to the other side of me. Its fur is a dark red which glows ominously in the firelight of the oil barrels. Despite how large the beast is, I didn't even hear it coming before it sat alongside me, but I sure as hell smelled it. The animal stinks as if it's been rolling around in sewage all day. And there's something else to the stench. Something that hits at the back of my throat and makes my little arm hairs stand on end.

"A mapinguari," Amirah tells me the name of the beast. "A wild one would have torn you to pieces by now, but when they come here, they're mostly docile, thanks to the human procedures."

"Oh, right," I say. "Lucky me."

So, I guess this is it. This is all I have left with no hope of anything more. This adopted and ramshackle community, this dirty and downtrodden slum. A smelly mapinguari sits on one side and a hard-faced, silver-haired elf who tells me what to do is sitting on my other side. This is it.

"He hasn't beaten us." Amirah speaks up, talking to me but also loud enough for those close by to hear. "We've come together, haven't we? We're stronger now than we've ever been—"

"You don't get it, do you?" I butt in, and I can't help but laugh. It's the hopelessness of it all that tickles me so. "We're nothing to him. He's in charge and he has the power. He's the top one percent. And whatever we do, or however we come together, it doesn't make a difference to him. He drank our blood, remember? It's that simple. It's how the real world works."

Garlic. That's what is hitting the back of my throat. My little arm hairs are still on edge and my spine feels unnerved. Garlic. Mapinguaris apparently have a hint of garlic to their odour.

Why'd it have to be garlic?

***

Time is a funny thing. Seconds tend to drag on and on, minutes will stretch into the ether, and hours have a tendency to stand still and watch you back. But days slip away, weeks fall on by, and months become years in the blink of an eye.

It's been over a year since Serat's cronies torched the neighbourhood, and I haven't done anything new or different in that time. (This isn't exactly true, but I'm not facing up to that yet. I just make sure my grubby coat covers my forearm at all times, and I look around to ensure I'm alone before I… No. Not now. Not yet. You'll find out later, I suppose.)

Amirah's rebuilt the borough (our rubbish corner of it, anyway) and Helisha swans about as Serat's new right-hand vampire, not that I see either of them very much anymore. Serat keeps to himself, as he always did, and he spends his days drinking from his own vampires and the nights drinking from any new arrivals his cronies bring him or his subjects deliver in exchange for his favour and a few extra dog-ends.

As for Alma, I have no idea. Haven't seen her. I'm not sure I want to, either. It would really suck if she turned out like all the rest. Just as soulless, directionless, lost, and unhappy as all the black-laced vampires in this city.

This is why I'm not exactly thrilled when Alma kicks me on my shoulder.

I was slumped on the side of a street, with nothing to do and nowhere to go, watching the world grow older around me. There's a small, ramshackle market nearby and there are others like me, who sit alone and stare into their mind's abyss, but none of them paid any attention to this grubby, blond-haired, blue-eyed vampire slumped on the edge, or the black-clad and smartly-dressed, pristine, and professional young vampire with big brown eyes, dark blonde hair (tied back and combed within an inch of its life) with a small button nose on her impatient and stern face.

"Get up."

"Erm," I manage, and then I manage another word. "No?" It's definitely a question. I don't want to get up, I don't want to move, and if things were up to me this is how I would remain.

I am stuck in a rut.

But for a fourteen-year-old girl (who has an extra year as a newly-inducted vampire), Alma has a surprisingly commanding aura. It rivals that of Amirah's, though Alma's has added bite. Pun intended.

"I'm going to show you something," she tells me, then starts walking. I begrudgingly get to my feet and stumble after her.

It's a long way up, wherever she's leading me. The stairway is one of those standard, boring stairways you get in standard, boring buildings. You climb a set of stairs, then you turn in a half-circle and have to climb another set of stairs. And so on and so on. Like I said, it's a long way up. The building we're climbing is another disused office block. I think we're near the edge of Serat's territory though, on the border of Duke's Borough, but I could be totally off… I'm barely paying attention.

Finally, and mercifully, Alma leads me out onto the rooftop of this skyscraper, overlooking much of the borough and quite a bit of the city beyond. It's a blustery day, and it only gets bluster-rier when you're this high up.

"You're not going to chuck me off, are you?" I ask, trying to sound jokey but I am genuinely a little bit worried. There's an art to jumping off buildings, after all. It takes technique and awareness to tactically bounce off the buildings on your way down, only breaking bones and tearing the odd muscle. If Alma were to grab me and throw me off now, all I'd manage is a painful splat, which would take a day or so to heal.

"First things first." She turns to me, all business and serious. "How were you going to help me?"

I'm caught off guard, which isn't an unusual thing to happen to me these days, so it takes me a few moments to work out what she's on about. And a few moments later, I give up and ask her what she's on about.

"That night in the warehouse, when we were fighting," she explains. "You told me you had an idea. You told me we both wanted the same thing. You promised you'd help me. You gave me hope. So, how? How could you have helped me?"

"Oh, yes," I remember, feeling a resurgence of guilt. "Well, that was a long time ago, and Serat and his vampires did what they did—"

"How would you have helped me?" she insists, cutting through my stumbling excuses. "Or was it all a lie?"

"I…" I think about trying to lie to her. Maybe I could fob her off with a half-baked plan. Maybe the two of us could have ambushed a weakened Serat after he had fed on Alma's freshly-turned blood. But I'm not going to lie. What would be the point? "I have no idea," I admit. "I thought we might have had something, if your blood had turned out to be Serat's kryptonite, but it didn't turn out to be anything." This is evident by the fashionable scarf Alma wears tightly around her neck. "But, if I'm going to be honest, I had no idea what we would have done after that. I was only thinking of getting at Serat…"

I hate the way she's looking at me, her eyes just watching me, taking me in. I can't read her at all. "You're pretty useless," she eventually tells me.

"Yeah," I agree, resigned to the truth of it.

"There's no beating him." She gazes out over the city, finally turning her eyes away from me.

"I know," I say, downcast.

"This is the system."

"I know."

"It's designed to keep the one percent in charge," she continues, "and the ninety-nine percent low."

"I know."

"It's how the real world works. Don't you know?"

I choose not to respond.

For a short time, neither of us says anything at all. I do glance at her though and take a good look at her for the first time in over a year.

I've been here five years, and I look forlorn, bedraggled, and spent. She's been here a year and, not only does she look the part, but she gives off all the right signals too. Calm, assured, composed, and smart. Strong too. She's everything I'm not. To my shame, I have to suppress a sudden dislike rising within me, a dislike directed towards her. I have to remind myself it's not her fault I'm the city's biggest loser (and therefore, also the world's).

"What happened to you?" I eventually ask her.

"I could ask the same of you," she shoots back at me, and then she sits on the very edge of the roof with her feet dangling over a very high drop. She taps the space next to her and I eventually sit down (though I keep my feet underneath me and not dangling over the abyss).

"Nothing happened to me," I shrug. "And I haven't done anything since that night." I try not to think about my forearm, although I do check that it is safely covered up underneath my coat. "Your turn."

"Well, not much happened to me," she says. "But I haven't changed either and I haven't stopped. I want to get out of here. I want to go home."

"Do you still think you're not a vampire?" I ask and she laughs, surprising me.

"I know what you see," she eventually says. "I'm not crazy. I know what I look like, and I know what…" She struggles for the right words. "…I know what's happened to me, and to my body. I know what my body is on the outside. But I also know what I am, Caiden. I'm me and I'm not a vampire. On the inside, I don't feel it. Can you understand that?"

"…So… you are crazy," I say, teasing her because the truth is I don't understand, and because I don't understand, I quickly change the subject. "What's the last year been like then, living in the belly of the beast?"

"Lifeless," she says, with the word coming quickly to her lips. "And boring. We spend all day inside, mostly waiting in small rooms, passing the time until we're called…"

"Called for what?"

Alma turns her head towards me, gives me a toothy smile and shows off her fangs.

"Do you feed?" I ask her.

"No, none of us do." Alma turns away and picks up a little handful of tiny stones. One by one, she drops them over the edge and watches them fall. "Only Serat feeds. He's the boss. And he feeds on us. He claims it's to keep him strong, strong enough to defend the borough from the other boroughs, but I don't believe him."

"What do you believe, then?"

"I do think he feeds on us to make himself strong, but it's only to keep the rest of us weak," she says. With a single swipe she clears the last stones from her hand, and they fall like shrapnel. "Ensuring none of us will ever be strong enough to take him on."

"Makes sense." I nod. "And what do you do at night?"

"At first, I went outside," Alma goes on. "To the clubs and the bars, but I didn't like it. Honestly, I don't think the others like it either. They tell themselves they do, but I don't see it."

"Fakers and shakers," I grumble.

"Some of them, maybe," she says, "but I think a lot of them feel sad, only they don't really know how to feel sad. Does that make sense?" I look at her with what must be a dumb face, and she shakes her head. "Now I spend my nights on rooftops," she continues, and then she does something that surprises me. She smiles. "I like being this high up."

"Why?" I blurt out, suddenly feeling a little defensive for some reason. "You like the wind?"

"Yes, actually." She swings her legs back and forth playfully. "I like the wind, I even like the cold, but I especially like looking down."

"But all you can see is the city," I sigh.

"I know, but it looks beautiful from up here."

I laugh out loud. I can't help it. It just spills out of me. Gods, I think this might be the first time I've laughed in years. It actually hurts a bit. "If there's one thing Vampire City is not," I eventually protest, "it is beautiful."

"I know that too," Alma sighs. "But from up here, it looks like it could be beautiful. The tall buildings, the labyrinth of roads, people moving like water in soil, and the little twinkling fires on street corners. I think it looks beautiful."

"Wow." I raise my eyebrows. "You really are crazy."

"Being this high up helps me think, and I like being alone with my thoughts, don't you?"

I shrug dismissively, but Alma doesn't notice. She's too busy staring at the cityscape below us.

"I still dream of getting out of here, but now I also dream of changing this place, of making it better, of getting of rid of Serat and making this a place where we can come and go as we please, where no one is less than anyone else. I'm trying to work out how I can do it."

"Vampires don't dream," I say, morosely. "No sleep, remember."

She ignores me. Truth be told, it all sounds uncomfortably familiar. Well, the getting rid of Serat part anyway. And the not knowing how to actually do it.

Before the night of flames, before Alma was taken, and before Serat drank my blood for the second time, I used to do everything Alma is describing. I used to think on rooftops, I used to like being alone with my thoughts, and yes, I used to dream of getting rid of Serat and even getting out of this city completely. I never got around to figuring out exactly how I'd do it, but that's by-the-by. I honestly thought I was close when Alma turned up, but all of that went to hell before I'd worked out the nitty-gritty details. Those nitty-gritty details being the whats, the whos, the wheres, the hows and the everything-in-betweens.

I don't go on rooftops anymore. This is the first one I've been on since Serat dropped me off the last one. It's not that I'm scared of them, or that I'm scared of falling, but more that I just don't see the point anymore. No more dreaming for me.

"What are we doing up here?" I ask Alma. She takes a while to respond, her gaze still looking out over the city. I notice her fingers have started fidgeting though.

"It's a rat race down there," she tells me, as if I don't already know. "But it can't be a real race, because there's never a winner."

"Serat looks like a winner to me," I respond, sardonically.

"No, you're wrong," she says, speaking so earnestly and without any hatred. My attention is thoroughly rapt. "There are others above Serat, and around him, just like Serat's above us."

"Well, I've never seen any of the other lords, and I've certainly never heard of anything above them—"

"You only ever see the world you inhabit," Alma interrupts me. "Never the whole world."

"Who out there could Serat be afraid of?" I scoff, though I'm putting it on a bit. Alma sounds very convincing which is why I've become more than a little nervous.

"I don't know," she admits. "But I suppose we might find out."

"We?" I wish I could have asked the question without a traitorous squeak slipping into my voice.

"Do you want to get out of here?" Silly question. Getting out is impossible. "Do you want to change this place for the better?" Again, it's impossible, so I've never thought about it. "Or do you just want to get back at Serat?" She looks at me, her eyes as big as they've ever been.

"I don't want things to stay the way they are," I reply, avoiding the fact that I don't believe we can get out, that I don't think this place can change, and that all I want, all I've ever wanted, is to make Serat hurt as he has made me hurt. Does that make me shallow?

"Good," she smiles. And then Serat's building explodes, and Alma barely flinches before she says, "I was hoping you'd help me."

***

It's not a normal explosion.

Where the flames would normally be yellow, they are instead red. Where there would normally be black smoke, there is a strange darkness that bends the air around it. And where the red fire meets the warped darkness, there are forks of lightning that crackle violently and throw tangled flames sideways.

The building itself—Serat's big, square, boring building—is reduced to a million tiny pieces, ranging in size from as big as a small van to as small as a big grain of sand. All of it is lifted up into the air by the initial huge and deafening eruption, and it is not long before it all comes raining back down to the ground. Some of it smashes onto nearby buildings, but most of it falls straight down, and all of it eventually comes to a rest.

The after-explosion is like a storm cloud. An enormous, deep red, warping storm cloud. It hangs over the borough. It blocks out the rest of the city and also the light of the sun. It reverberates with energy and spits lightning like an angry god.

"Bloody hell!" I exclaim, leaping to my feet and staring in awe at what has happened to the place, the same place I've called home for the past five years. Alma also stands up as I turn to her. She looks like a doe-eyed puppy standing next to a perfect little pile of poo. "You did this." I state the obvious.

"I had to!"

"Why?" I squeak in anger now. Anger and shock. "Did you want to piss off every vampire in the borough? Every vampire in the city? And Serat's going to go mental! That won't kill him! We're vampires, Alma! Nothing kills us!"

"I'm not—"

"If you say you're not a vampire—after all this time!—I am going to lose my freaking mind!" I screech, currently in the middle of losing my freaking mind.

"*I'M NOT A VAMPIRE!*" Alma bellows in my face. The storm cloud rolls over itself like a writhing mass of flesh, producing crackling thunder in the background. We are doused in red light, we have to shout over the dull booming and electric cracking, and we're both on the edge (of the roof and of our sanity, it seems).

"You *are* a vampire!" I'm almost pulling my hair out. "You are! You are! You are! And blowing up Serat's place doesn't change anything! We're still stuck in this place, we still can't get over the big wall surrounding the city, and now—because of that!" I point at the expanding explosion. "— Serat is going to… is going to…" I have to remember to breathe. Technically, I don't have to breathe (one of the perks of being an undead, soulless abomination of nature), but breathing still helps to keep the mind in one piece. Feet on the ground mentality, that kind of thing.

"I'm not afraid of Serat!" Alma claims, and she's so convincing I almost find myself believing her.

"Then you're a bloody fool!" I spit in despairing anger. "You saw what he did a year ago. I had only been poking around, thinking I might have a chance of beating him. Do you remember that night?!" I challenge Alma, and I grab her by her shoulders, not letting her turn away from me.

"Of course I remember," she admits.

"Look at that!" I point again at the spider-like cloud. And it is spider-like. A couple of minutes after detonation and the cloud is starting to drift apart, but it's still very much solid and its expansion has given it red-laced tendrils that resemble the legs of a spider, stretching over everything. "Do you have any idea what Serat is going to do after this?"

"Serat's in a million pieces!" Alma shouts back at me, pulling free from my grip. "He's always in his building during the day!"

"But he's a strong vampire, Alma!" I cry. "That's why he drinks incessantly! That's why all the vampire lords drink like they're the town drunk on St. Patrick's Day! Because it makes them strong! So when something like this happens, they'll be ready to bite back harder!"

"I had to do it," she snaps at me, a fearful desperation in her words.

"But how in the hell did you even manage—"

"I had to do it, Caiden!" She's breaking out in tears, her voice is cracking, and her button nose is as red as Rudolph's.

"Why!?" I demand of her.

"Because you weren't coming to save me!" She hits me with a stinging left hook, both in conversation and in reality. Both hurt, but one hurts rather more than the other. And as I lie on my back, nursing a bruised cheek and reeling from the other left hook, all I want is to curl up in a corner, lift the forearm of my coat, and… No. Can't. Not with Alma here.

We have to run. We have to get away from here. Whatever's happening… it's happening now.

***

"What the hell's happening?"

"Nothing. Everything. I have no idea. Maybe something." From her face, I can tell these are clearly not the answers Amirah wanted.

All across the borough, a red haze has descended. It is a dense fog with only a person's immediate vicinity visible to them. Very handy for sneaking, the vampire part of my brain offers.

It's not been too long since Serat's building was turned from a big square into a billion tiny odd-shaped bits and, understandably, everyone is rather on edge. Not least of all the de facto leader of us bottom feeders, our silver-haired elf, Amirah.

The street is packed with gawkers, worriers, followers, and sneaky opportunists making sure more than a few dog-end purses get filched in the fog.

Amirah is out on the street with everyone else and has grabbed my collar and pinned me up against a brick wall. She must be awfully mad because my tippy toes are no longer able to touch the ground.

"If anyone knows, you'll know!" she growls menacingly. She's got a point too. I might be a black sheep amongst vampires, but I'm still a vampire. I've lived their world. I am, by association, the go-to guy for anything involving vampires. So, when the big vampire building mysteriously blows up in a strange, otherworldly explosion, everyone down here looks to me, expecting me to have all the answers.

"Let him go." Alma comes forward, all composed and serious, and Amirah fixes this fifteen-year-old fourteen-year-old girl with a brutal gaze. A young, brave girl is going up against a strong and wise woman, and I'm in the background, struggling with my tippy toes and squeaking like a strangled mouse. And I'm the one who everyone looks to for answers? I don't understand it either.

"Who the hell are you?" Amirah demands of Alma.

"I'm with him." Alma nods in my direction and Amirah glances at me quizzically before returning her iron gaze to Alma. If either of them noticed how pathetic I look right now, then neither of them let on.

"Caiden," Amirah says, keeping her eyes on Alma. "Who's your friend?"

"Not really a friend," I squeak. "More an acquaintance… an old contact… someone I ran into a while ago—"

"Caiden!"

"She's a vampire, Amirah. This is Alma. And we need to hide her. I told her you'd help."

"Why would you tell her that?" Amirah turns her fearsome eyes on me now, and I wilt even as I'm held up by her hands.

"Because you help everyone." I panic. "It's what you do. Isn't it?"

She drops me. I wobble on my feet for a moment or two before straightening myself out and acting as if the last minute hadn't happened at all. Total denial, blank it all out, move on and try to act cool, and keep telling yourself no one noticed.

"You in trouble?" Amirah asks Alma, and the young vampire darts her eyes up at the dark centre of the fog left behind by the explosion. Amirah follows Alma's darting eyes and puts two and two together, coming up with four… cked, as in *we are fu—*

"Oh, my stars," Amirah sighs, finally realising she may have landed into the very dangerous middle of whatever the hell is going on. "Caiden?"

"I'm sorry," I say instinctively, then I apologize again for saying the wrong thing. "Erm, I mean… what?"

"Can we trust her?" And I'm a little flummoxed by Amirah's question. I look from Amirah—who looks deadly serious—to Alma—who also looks deadly serious, but with deadly big brown eyes and a serious button nose.

Here's the thing—and try to follow me on this. I know we can trust Alma. I know we can trust her because she is here, and her being here is proof she doesn't want to be anywhere else, and there can only be one reason for someone wanting to be here rather than anywhere else, and that reason means we can trust her.

Let me try to put it another way. She's a vampire and she should be with other vampires. But she's not with the vampires. Instead, she came to find me. She confided in me. And she's here now, on the streets with us bottom feeders and with the fog descending on top of us all. She shouldn't be here, doesn't have to be here, and wouldn't be here if she didn't want to be here in the first place, and yet here she is, standing alongside myself and Amirah.

So, yes, I trust Alma. Just as she apparently trusts me.

What has temporarily left me a little flawed and quite speechless though, is the fact that Amirah wants my opinion. The silver-haired, stern-faced elf, whom everyone looks to for leadership, is looking to me for help. I feel a horrible weight of responsibility. I don't like it one bit.

"Yes." I eventually gather myself. "We can trust her."

"Right, okay. Iliaior!" A small elf runs over to Amirah's side, ready for the instructions he knows he is about to receive. "We have to move," Amirah tells him. "Everyone has to move. Now."

"But this fog." The elf called Iliaior gestures around himself. "We can barely see the streets, we should wait—"

"By then these streets will be swarming with vampires!" Amirah insists. "Everyone! Move! Now! To the underground!" She looks from Alma to me, concern etched across her hard face. "We go underground."

Going underground is exactly what it sounds like. Alma and I follow Amirah as she leads us off the fog-covered streets, through a dingy alleyway, down a narrow stairway, and into a basement. It's more like a chamber though. A hollowed-out chamber with several crudely dug-out passageways each leading away in different directions. There are racks of shovels and pickaxes as well as stacks of buckets, wheelbarrows lined up together, and oil lamps on shelves.

"What is all this?" Alma exclaims in total surprise.

"What we've been working on for the last year," Amirah tells her, and there is pride in her voice even now in these strenuous circumstances. "Come on. All of you!"

There are others with us. The elves act as Amirah's marshals, shepherding and guiding the others down the passageways. Dwarfs, dryads, nymphs, pixies, fauns, drakes, selkies, goblins, sylphs, and more alike. And I couldn't care about any of them.

I don't mean this in a vicious or cruel or hateful way, of course, even though I suppose it is a cruel and horrible way to feel. Rather, I mean it as a statement of fact. I suddenly don't care about any of them. I don't care about Amirah. I don't care about Alma. I don't care about Serat, or myself, or the explosion or the fog or even the threat of an angry horde of vampires descending upon Duke's Borough.

All I care about is this sudden feeling that has rushed through me. It is a wave of longing, of need, and of desire.

It happens like this.

It actually didn't happen at all when I first started under a year ago, and even later it only happened very rarely, but recently it is becoming more frequent. Far more frequent.

It's the thing I don't want to think about. It's the reason I keep my forearm covered at all times. But here now, in this cavernous basement, it starts to take over. I suddenly feel strung out, stretched, and unbearably tired. I'm weak and I need to get away. Get away from everything that's happening. Get away from me.

I drop back. Amirah is busy directing other sub-mortals down specific passageways. She's got it all worked out. She knows what she's doing. Alma is standing out of the way. She's taking everything in, watching carefully and even notices a sprite in need of aid whom she moves to rescue. The little winged fellow, no bigger than my shin, nearly got himself trampled under the chaos of everyone trying to find safety.

The point is no one's paying attention to me. I drop further back. I'm in the corner, hidden in shadow. I feel how natural it is to be here. I feel at home here. This is where vampires belong, in the shadows, hiding from the real-world problems.

I can do it here. No one will notice. But to be honest, I don't care if they notice anymore. The feeling is too strong, and I am too weak. I want to go back. Gods, how I want it!

I pull up the sleeve of my coat. My arm is pale and thin… and there they are. There they are. They sicken me and shame me, but they're going to give me what I want. They're going to get me away from here. They're going to take me back. One bite. That's all it takes.

I open my mouth, extend my fangs, and drop my head down to my forearm as if curling into myself. I bite into the bite marks on my forearm—my own bite marks—and I drink. I only drink a little, not too much, but I always end up taking more than I intend.

I release myself and I sit back, staying hidden in the shadows, and here it comes. Here it comes to pull me away from here and to take me back. My eyelids are heavy, my body relaxes, and I slip into unconsciousness. Five years ago, I didn't think this was possible. Now, it's my only reprieve.

✳✳✳

It isn't the same every time. I don't know how dreams work.

Most of the time, I dream. When the dreams are good, I dream of her, the young milkmaid, and me, the country boy, in the village where I lived and where one day I would die, but only after a happy lifetime spent with her, my milkmaid.

When the dreams are bad though, I dream of times gone by. Real times. Things that actually happened. But they're always a little mixed up, somewhat foggy and nonsensical. I might be waiting for a train in a place without a station, or I could be working a job even though I have no need for money. I'm not afraid in these dreams. I'm not angry or lost. I'm stressed, pulled thin, and trapped.

I'd rather be terrified or furious, or anything at all, anything other than this. It weighs me down. It's a hill I'm climbing, but the hill is too steep, and it keeps getting bigger and I feel so tired.

This particular dream is a good dream though. I think. She's here, anyway. My milkmaid. Lying next to me in a nice comfy bed. I'm happy. I think. She's not looking at me though. Instead, she gets up and walks away and suddenly we're not in a bedroom anymore. This is a lounge. A private bar at the dead of night, and it all feels horribly familiar.

Serat's bar. And he's here too. She's with him. She's talking with him and smiling at him and laughing with him. It's all in her eyes, her smile, and the way she touches his arm. I hate them both. I hate this place. I hate that I can't move. I'm lifeless sitting on this luxurious sofa, blood draining from my neck, and she's with Serat at the bar and I hate them so much it twists my insides.

No. I don't want to think about her. I don't want to think about this. Forget it. Pretend it never happened. It's just too fucking hard.

***

I'm pulled out of my dream. I don't immediately know how I've been pulled out, but when my cheek and my jawline start feeling three sizes bigger than normal, I can take a guess.

Amirah and Alma are both standing over me, Alma still with her tightly clenched fist and Amirah looking down at me with sombre eyes. One of them looks like she hates me, and the other one looks severely disappointed. I'll leave it up to you to figure out which one is which.

We're still in the basement, which is now more like the first chamber of an underground mine, but now there are far fewer sub-mortals here. In fact, it's only the three of us.

"What happened?" I ask, lamely.

"We found you slumped in the corner," Amirah tells me. "I didn't think vampires could black out."

"There's an exception to the rule," I admit, my eyes dropping away from them.

"When another vampire drinks your blood," Alma explains to Amirah for me. "Or, as it turns out, when a vampire drinks their own blood." I can tell she wants to spit on me. I wouldn't blame her if she did, and I don't think I'd react.

Amirah's eyes pass over my bare forearm, which is still dribbling fresh blood. "Why, Caiden? Why?"

"Because he's pathetic!" Alma blazes. "So, this is what you've been doing all year, is it? Knocking yourself out? Getting a blood high?"

"Not *all* year," I say, and even I can hear how utterly pathetic this sounds. "It just helps me relax, that's all."

"It's not helping you, Caiden," Alma growls. "It's just another lie. How can you be so stupid?"

"Because maybe it's all I've got," I say, turning resentful. Backed into a corner, I look up at Alma and now we're both shooting daggers at each other.

"Okay. Both of you. Stop." Amirah, taking the lead, stands between us. "Whatever you're doing to yourself, Caiden, now's not the time for us to get into it. We will get into it, mind you. You can trust me on that. But right now, we have more pressing problems."

"Oh, really? Gosh, Alma, would *you* know anything about these *more pressing problems*?" Here's me, still crouched on the floor in the corner, dirt on my bum, with a bruised jaw and a leaking forearm, and I'm the one bringing the snark. I really am a waste of space sometimes, and what's more, I never know when to stop. "Like, off the top of my head, erm, how about the big red fiery explosion, hmm? Or the borough-wide fog said explosion has left us under? Or maybe Amirah's talking about the ravenous vampires who are putting themselves back together as we speak and getting ready to tear us all new ars—"

"That's enough, Caiden!" Amirah shouts at me, her voice loud, commanding, iron-willed, and more than enough to leave me thoroughly cowed; yet her shouting is nothing compared to what I'm sure Alma was about to do to me. Thankfully, Amirah placed a firm hand on the little vamp before she reached me. "I know how much you love playing the smart-arse misfit, Caiden, but when you were blacked out and the rest of us were working, Alma told me more than she's told you."

I'm annoyed by this. I've very annoyed by this. Like a pedantic and petulant five-year-old, I wanted to be the one to tell Amirah about the bad thing Alma's done. I huff and I puff, but I do both very quickly so as not to inflame the ire of the elf or the wrath of the young vampire in front of me.

"We can't do anything about it now," Amirah continues, "but we will." And when she says this, she glances at Alma with a meaningful expression. I have no idea what the meaning is, but they both look very serious and earnest about whatever it might be. "Right now, that bastard will be in a million pieces, which is no good for any of us, but soon he'll be in one piece, and that's when you and Caiden can… decide what to do next." Amirah now looks to us both. "I suppose, before too long, we'll have a new lord… or lady. But right now, we need to run the streets."

"Run the streets?" Alma asks, confused.

"Oh no," I groan.

"These are our tunnels," Amirah explains to Alma. "We dug them so we can move and hide if ever what happened a year ago repeated itself, but some of us can't fit in the tunnels. Treepeople, trolls, ogres, and others."

"I'm sure they'll all be fine," I try, but with no conviction.

"They have places they're supposed to go." Amirah nods. "Places where they can hide as best they can, but I'm going to run the streets all the same just to make sure everyone is as safe as possible."

"I'll go with you," Alma says, quickly and firmly. "Of course, I will."

They nod to each other and then, rather worryingly, they both look down at me expectantly.

"…I'd rather not," I sigh.

"Okay, I'll take that into consideration," Amirah says, then holds her hand out for me to take. "Now, come on. Let's go."

***

The world is red. The city is fog. The air is ash. It's quiet, though. Quiet can be nice. For a short while anyway. Unfortunately, it is not long before the quiet becomes the worst part of all of this. A city can be anything… except quiet.

There's no epicentre of the explosion anymore. There's only this red fog that crackles occasionally and hangs over everything. It's as if the sky turned to fire and covered the earth.

"What exact concoction did you use, Alma?" I ask her. The three of us are undertaking a cautious sweep of the local streets, the common haunts, and anywhere else Amirah leads us. Sometimes we crouch low, scope out the red fog in front of us, then decide *to hell with it* and so rush forward, often when crossing a wide-open space or long open road. We're halfway across a narrow side road, where the rubbish and detritus smother the concrete path, when I ask Alma my question.

"I'm not sure, exactly," Alma answers from behind me. I'm sandwiched between the two of them. Amirah is leading, I feel stuck in the middle, and Alma is keeping keen at the rear.

"You're not sure?" I exclaim. "You brewed a bomb that blew a building to pieces, and you're not sure what was in it?"

"There were a lot of ingredients! Really weird ingredients," Alma defends herself stubbornly. "And lots of steps to mixing it, and everything had to be done exactly how she told me—"

"How *who* told you?"

"The witch, of course," Alma tells me. And at this even Amirah stops and turns to stare at Alma. For my part, I stop, turn, stare, and my jaw makes a serious effort to literally hit the floor.

"You met with a witch?!" I cry out in alarm and fear.

"You didn't tell me that earlier." Amirah frowns, her stern expression more than enough to reprove Alma.

"So?" Alma says, suddenly wary of our reactions. "Is it a problem?"

"Is it a problem? Is it a problem?" I choke loudly, trying to hide my suddenly very shaky legs. "You've been in this city a whole year, Alma. You should know better than to go to a witch!"

"I've spent most of it in that ruddy building actually!" Alma growls back at me, glaring at both of us. "The one I happily blew sky high, thanks to the witch and no thanks to you!" She stabs my chest with an accusatory finger.

"You can't have found a witch in the borough," Amirah thinks aloud. "There hasn't been a witch here in years. So, you must have…"

"…Yes." Alma shrugs again. "I snuck out to another borough."

"*You-!*" I squeak very loudly and one of my legs actually gives way for half a second.

"Alma." Amirah shakes her head. "No one crosses between boroughs."

"Well, I did. I did it several times, actually," Alma says, putting her hands on her hips.

"Oh, is that all?" I Tut, making sure the other two can clearly hear the capitalisation of my tutting.

"When I found the witch, it did take a while for her to teach me the recipe," Alma goes on. "Once everything was ready though, all I had to do was wait for the opportune moment. She helped me. What's the big deal?"

"Witches are dangerous, Alma," Amirah tells her. "Very dangerous."

"More dangerous than Serat?" Alma asks.

"Yes!" I snap.

"How?"

"Because vampires are bound by the rules of what a vampire can and cannot do!" I snap again. "We have limitations!"

"And witches don't?" Alma snaps back at me.

Amirah speaks up before I can snap again. "Witches, and other magic-wielders, have few, if any, limits. Magic is dangerous, tempestuous, and limitless."

I put it simply. "A witch can do whatever they like. Ergo, they're all mad, mischievous, and malevolent."

"They can't all be mad," Alma claims. "This one seemed fine."

"Of course they're all mad!" I scoff.

"Wouldn't you be mad," Amirah explains calmly, stepping between Alma and myself, "if you had limitless power, but found yourself stuck in a reality with nothing but limits?"

"But if magic-wielders can do whatever they want, why are they stuck in this place with us?"

I stride forward and put one finger up, silencing Alma, and I gesture for both of them to sit down on the grubby floor. I sit with them. We form an odd little circle, surrounded by garbage.

"I'm going to make this as clear as possible, Alma." I speak plainly and clearly because this is important. "Witches, wizards, warlocks, and the rest of them, all of them who can cast magic, are *not* stuck in this place with us. If that witch wanted to, she could have clicked her fingers and magicked you back to your home. If she wanted to, she could take away the vampire curse. If she wanted to, she could have us all living in a gumdrop forest with candy cane trees and chocolate rivers."

"…I don't believe you," Alma says, but she does. I can tell. "Why would they do nothing with all that power? Why did she give me a recipe for a bomb when she could have saved me so easily?"

"Because they are not like you and me," I insist. "It's so important for you to understand this, Alma. They are fourth-dimensional beings in a three-dimensional reality. Your suffering does not exist to them, our world is like a game on a piece of paper to them."

"I still don't—"

"They're billionaires, Alma!" I snap (that's a third snap in as many minutes; I should probably stop because it's starting to hurt my jaw). "You and I and Amirah get by on meagre dog-ends and Serat lords himself over us, but witches and the rest of them have everything! They're not like you and me. They're not like Amirah. They're not even like Serat. They are above it all. They are beyond the system. Outside it."

"But why don't they do anything?" Alma tries desperately.

"It's a good question," I sympathise. "Why aren't the people with all the power doing anything to help everyone else? Maybe they're mad. Maybe they like things the way they are. Or maybe they don't care, and they simply get a kick out of prodding our anthill every now and then. Bastards."

"Regardless, it changes nothing," Amirah interjects, pulling both Alma and me back up to our feet. "Time is pressing. Come on."

Amirah hurries us on down the side street. "What's done is done. We're nearly finished running the streets anyway, so we can decide what our next steps will be once we're back in the tunnels."

"No need to wait that long," I say, following Amirah. "Regarding Serat, we find his body *after* it's put itself back together but *before* the bastard wakes up, and then I torture him for eternity. No more lord, no more big bully, Amirah gets the borough, Alma gets to look for a way out of Vampire City, and I get what I want."

"Is that all you want?" Alma chides me.

"Yes, alright, I remember, I'll help you look," I say dismissively. Truth be told, I haven't the foggiest idea what I'll do to help Alma. Beating the bastard at the top has always been my only goal. I haven't given much thought to what happens next.

"And regarding the witch?" Amirah reminds me.

"Easy," I say, trying to sound calm and unbothered. "Between your new borough, Amirah, and your searching, Alma, and my, erm, revenge and torture for eternity, we hunker down and hope with everything we've got that Alma's witch has completely forgotten we exist. Simple."

"You're making this up as you go along," Amirah says.

"It's more interesting that way." I shrug.

If only.

We have nearly finished running the streets. We've checked abandoned garages, empty storehouses, and backyards overgrown with weeds and other shrubbery. Basically anywhere in which a troll, twice my size, or an ogre, three times my size, can hide away for a while. We've also checked the local park where the tree people have huddled together near the back, hiding in plain sight amongst their rooted kin.

There's one last place we're going to check, and it's a big one. An underground car park, with cracked stone walls and empty parking spots (empty of cars, at least). With so much space there will be many trolls, ogres, and even a few minotaurs probably. So we have slow-thinking trolls; grumpy, half-witted ogres; and quick-to-anger half bull humanoids; all packed into an underground space for the immediate future. A teddy bear picnic, this ain't gonna be. Expect squabbles of the violent variety.

It'll be a minor miracle if when we arrive, we don't have to skip over puddles of blood and avoid the occasional spillage of guts. Amirah assures me everyone's promised to behave in times of emergency, such as now, and to be fair the places we've checked on so far have been reluctantly peaceful. But even so, I'm not confident and I can tell Amirah is a little nervous as well.

We cross a road, walk down an alleyway, and then turn into a side road and finally follow the road down into the car park. It's a precarious and dangerous place to hide, but then the likes of trolls, ogres, and minotaurs have precarious personalities and are certainly more than dangerous, so I reckon it balances itself out.

As we reach the floor of the car park, Amirah's nerves and my lack of confidence are thoroughly justified… and then some. Blood covers the floor. There are spilled guts floating lazily and bumping against one another. Big, hulking bodies lie in this shallow lake of blood, most of them not moving, some of them groaning, and all of them looking a fair bit worse for wear. This is a lot worse than even I feared, and I'm intentionally overly pessimistic about everything (I even doubt the sun will appear over the horizon sometimes).

"What happened here?" Amirah gasps.

"You put a hundred or so very strong, very grumpy, and not very bright lug heads in a very confined space with no colouring books to hand," I respond, unhelpfully.

"But this…" Amirah ignores my petulance, too overwhelmed by the literal bloodbath we've stepped into. "…this is so much worse than…"

"Than what?" I sigh, wanting to leave and seeing no reason why we should stay a moment longer. "Worse than putting two hundred of the half-wits down here? It all adds up to the same thing, Amirah. Except the blood would be up to our knees and not just our socks."

"I thought they'd be better than this," Amirah says; her voice is fragile, and her eyes are wet. I've never seen her like this before.

"Yeah, well," I say, awkward and uncomfortable. "Half-wits disappoint you, and bastards try to eat you. Welcome to Vampire City."

"They didn't do this," Alma tells us, looking beyond both Amirah and me. The silver-haired elf and I follow her gaze and, somehow, I know exactly who I'm going to see. Overly pessimistic, remember?

Walking out from behind a particularly large ogre, and now slowly coming towards us, is a humanoid that can only be described as *assembly required*. A skeleton mostly covered with the usual fleshy bits and with organs on display that wiggle and thump is casually and calmly walking towards us. It's the eyes though that give the bastard away. As I see him now, I can scarcely believe it. He regenerated himself so fast...

"Haven't you ever wondered," Serat says with a smile, although it's more of a half-smile due to his lack of skin, "why we keep you lower sorts around at all?"

Two others step out as well and they stand on either side of Serat. With a sigh, I recognize both of them. Helisha and Munstone. Neither of them is as far along in the regenerative process as Serat though. Helisha hobbles along, her legs only bone and her face half done, and while Munstone has stronger legs, he's missing most of his torso and his arms look very thin indeed.

Serat stops and Helisha and Munstone stop too, staying one step behind him. The red raw bastard makes a showing of cleaning one of his blood-stained fangs with a fleshy finger.

"It's because you're a wonderful resource to squeeze on," Serat tells the three of us, "when times get tough." And he gestures to his growing body.

I look sideways at the bodies, and I curse myself for missing the telltale signs of a body drunk dry of its blood. The sunken eyes, the shrivelled skin, the gaunt expressions. I should have been paying closer attention, and if I had looked closer maybe we wouldn't have walked right into this. The shallow lake of blood around our feet is nothing but the crumbs, the crusts, the turkey bones, and the untouched salad of what was a five-course meal.

I can't believe it. It's so obvious. Alma's wrong. The ogres, the trolls, the minotaurs, they *did* do this. They couldn't hold themselves back. They got angry, they got territorial, or maybe they were simply too bored, and so they turned on each other and killed one another, or at the very least they beat each other witless… and all Serat had to do was come in afterwards and drink them.

Bad guys like Serat don't have to do anything. They only have to wait for us to do it to ourselves, and afterwards they can take all they want from us.

The three of us face the three of them. What with being in such ungainly states, they are not as strong as they usually are after a feeding, but we're not strong full stop, so it really is a bit of an awkward stand-off. And what is abundantly clear is that none of us want to be here. Well, that's not entirely true. One of us wants to be here.

I can practically hear Alma grinding her teeth at the thought of tearing them to pieces. Her fists are clenched, her eyes have taken on a rather crazed look, and she's not blinking.

Amirah doesn't want to fight at all. By her own clenched fists and resolute posture, I know she'll fight if she has to, but it's not in her to want to fight, and that's why they'll beat her if it comes down to an all-out brawl. But what's saving us right now is they don't want an all-out brawl either. Not yet.

Helisha and Munstone are so terribly fragile that, were Serat not here, I'm sure they would have scarpered at the first possible opportunity. They're scavengers. Leeches. And right now they're nervous and skittish. They are neither leaders nor fighters.

Finally, Serat doesn't want to be here because, despite all his bravado and cockiness, he's a half-baked corpse hunched in on himself, who was not so long ago blown up into a billion pieces. It's incredibly impressive how quickly his power is restoring him, but his nakedness and vulnerability are on full display here.

And he doesn't trust himself.

It hits me as quickly as that. Serat is full of doubts. His eyes flit between me, Alma, and Amirah. His fingers are at his side, and they can't stay still. He's standing on the balls of his feet. He's nervous, afraid, and unsure. Without his big building, without his fancy clothes, without his overwhelming strength, he is just another vampire. Which all means one thing… he can lose.

"Do you have any idea," Serat begins, "what torture I'm going to wreak on every single one of you?"

"What makes you think we had anything to do with this?" I try lamely.

"Unleash whatever you like," Alma butts in. "I'd happily do it again. I'll blow you all back to hell!" I close my eyes and let out a sad sigh. Well, there goes my bluff.

"This doesn't have to end like this, Serat," Amirah tries, completely pointlessly, and I wonder if Serat even knows who this silver-haired elf is. "We can find a way to get past today."

"No, no, little elf." Serat shakes his head. "Time is nigh for a reckoning. Perhaps it's overdue, in fact. See, it's the law of the jungle. When the weeds grow too wild, when the trees grow too strong and the undergrowth becomes too dense, Mother Nature provides a solution."

"She scoots down the shop to pick up some weed-killer and garden shears?" I ask.

"She burns the forest down." Serat grins… somehow. "And starts again.'

✳✳✳

The fight starts as most fights do. A chaotic rush resulting in a fumbled clash.

Alma charges at Serat and Serat reciprocates. They smash together, producing a great rippling wave of blood around them, and they get down to throwing fists. Through their rage and their fury, neither of them seems to be particularly affected by the other's attacks, but eventually Serat, the taller of the two, gains an advantage. He manages to grab the back of Alma's head and, with a great roar, lifts her up and brings her slamming down onto the ground.

The shallow lake erupts in a volcanic-like explosion of red blood and little gooey bits. Alma's covered in the stuff.

There are glistening red streaks in her hair, her face is splattered and angry, her eyes are manic and vengeful, and her smart attire is now torn, bedraggled, and very bloodstained. Also, her ponytail has come out.

Munstone can't get near to Amirah though. The silver-haired elf moves like a cat, darting to her sides, turning on the spot, and leaping around Munstone's clumsy and heavy swings. He groans and snarls and hurls meaty punch after meaty punch, but all he hits is empty air and, at one point, his own foot.

I can't help but wonder why Amirah doesn't strike him down. She could so easily do it. Munstone is leaving himself open to crippling jabs and ruinous pokes. Elves, as nimble as they appear, have faster reflexes than most and what strength they have they can be channelled into sharp and ruthless attacks. But she resists. Instead she evades, deflects, and contains every attack that Munstone throws her way. Munstone is tiring, so maybe Amirah simply wishes to outlast him, but all it would take is one slip, one miscalculation, or one false step to allow a clumsy attack from this half-made vampire to crush the silver-haired elf. I want her to attack, to take away the risk, but she steadfastly keeps to her methods.

Maybe she's right to do this, because I went straight in on the attack and all I got was a kick to my nether regions. As it is, Helisha may be *weakened* but I am *weak*. She's a single-minded, brutal, and efficient fighter, whereas I am a daydreaming, beggarly layabout with tatty clothes and an aversion to hard work. I think this is why I get another kick to my nether regions. Thankfully, her legs are mostly bone so there isn't a lot of muscle power behind each kick; however, her legs are mostly bone so when they make contact it is hard and unyielding. My poor, poor nether regions.

My first instinct is to lash out in anger, and I try to do this, but Helisha has the advantage in that she is not bent over double, nursing her particulars, and holding back very real tears. She gargles an insult that I don't quite catch, then punches me hard in my chest to send my flying backwards.

I crash through a large, mostly blood-drained body. Yes. That's right. I go through a big, dead body and then out the other side, falling to the floor with an unceremonious wet splat. As I travelled through the corpse, though, I got a rather nasty tang of something. It made me shiver uncontrollably. Something I can't quite put my finger on.

I sit up, which is pain enough by itself, and look back the way I've come. Beyond the messy hole in which I flew through, Helisha is coming. I could stay and fight, but I know despite whatever contest I offer her she will finish me in seconds. I really don't want to get hurt. I want to get away from here, I want to run away, and for a fleeting moment I think of my forearm, of the dream I could fall into, and of the milkmaid who is long gone.

No. I can't get away with that now. So instead, I start to panic. There has to be something, anything! But Amirah's occupied with keeping Munstone at bay, and Alma's so hell-bent on fighting Serat she can't notice my plight. All I have is me, a messy hole, and Helisha coming for me with hatred and disgust in her bloodshot eyes.

The messy hole! What is *around* the messy hole? Not a troll, not an ogre, and not a minotaur. A mapinguari! The big, red-furred beast as silent as the grave and as smelly as an open one. And what do they smell of? Crap! Yes, mostly. But what do they also smell of? The something I couldn't quite put my finger on, of course. Garlic.

I jump to my feet, suddenly renewed and as desperate as ever. Helisha hesitates, surprised to see me actually doing something, and then she's confused because I'm not heading for her. Not exactly, anyway.

I put my arms around the neck of the very dead mapinguari and lock my hands together. Then I squeeze, twist, and pull. It takes a few seconds. A few agonizing seconds in which I hear Helisha's rickety bones splish-splashing towards me. But then mercifully, after the squeezing, the twisting, and the pulling, I hear a deadpan pop, and the head of the mapinguari drops into my arms and I fall backwards.

Helisha is over me, screeching in anger, and she's about to swing at me so I move, more out of instinct than anything else. I roll away, scramble to my feet, and then jam the large, dismembered head of the mapinguari right on top of Helisha's own half-formed head.

She makes three distinct noises, one after the other. Firstly, she gasps in confusion. Following this, she growls in anger. And finally, she starts screaming. It's not awful screaming though, and not even that desperate really. It's confused enough and certainly angry, but there's something more. There's the nasty tang of garlic, only instead of a fleeting encounter like I had, Helisha is getting a full whack right to her noggin.

I can only imagine how intensely uncomfortable this must be for her. Perhaps it is like the sound of fingernails on chalkboards, or brush bristles on stone slabs, or cracking finger bones, or the terrible spine-tingling squeaking of balloons coming into contact with one another. Whatever it is like, it is enough to make Helisha lose her balance and stumble backwards. She desperately tries to push the beast's head off, but I seem to have lodged it firmly into place, and besides, the effect of the garlic odour is leaving Helisha vulnerable and stumbling… so I take my chance and tackle her to the ground. Dazed and hurt, she lets out a long groan and goes limp. Ha! Victory.

With Helisha out of the action, I look up and see Alma on the floor some distance away. Serat is on top of her, and their struggle is looking more and more one-sided with every punch. Amirah is going strong keeping Munstone busy, but I suspect even if this weren't the case, I would still go for Alma first. Maybe it's because she's a vampire, or maybe it's because Amirah's an elf. I don't know. All I know is, I find I cannot bear looking at Serat on top of Alma, whaling on her and beating her down.

I charge for Serat. He's not paying attention and doesn't see me coming, so I barrel into him. An astute observer might wonder why I didn't scoop up some of the mapinguari's garlic blood… to this I say: oh yeah. Bugger. What can I say? Emotions are high, thought processing is slow, and I've never been one for coming up with sensible solutions.

We roll over each other in the shallow pool of blood. I'm swinging my fists like a possessed maniac and kicking out like a thrashing toddler, so it takes me awhile before I notice Serat isn't responding in kind.

I look down and I'm so stunned at what I see that I forget to keep punching him. Not that my punches and kicks were doing anything anyway. He's a corpse. A terribly dry, horribly pale, shrunken, and ugly corpse. His eyeballs have sunken into his skull and the skin around his eye sockets has turned as black as coal. His yellow, rotten teeth are all showing because what he had of his gums have pulled away from his mouth. Stick thin limbs, an empty torso, a bony chest, and wisps of hair are all that's left of the rest of him.

He's still alive, of course. Dribbling, moaning, trying to move. After all, he is a vampire. No death for the wicked, no matter how wicked. But he's nothing of his former self. Everything Serat once had has been taken from him, which only begs the question… who did the taking? There aren't any bite marks on Serat's neck. So, how did she even… wait… his hand. Serat's hand is shrivelled and mangled, and there they are—bite marks! I saw it wrong. Serat hadn't been beating down on Alma as part of their fight. He had been desperately trying to stop her drinking his blood. Alma's just fed on Serat.

I forget Serat. He's nothing now. Everything he represented is gone from him (although I'll probably take out my own personal revenge on him later, and I add a subconscious mental note to do just that). I scramble to my feet and stumble over to see Alma still lying where she was when Serat was on top of her. There is vampire blood all around her mouth, and the dark red stuff is caked all over her extended fangs. She's not moving though.

Her eyes are staring blankly up at the ceiling. Her chest is completely still. The only movements around her are the little waves of the shallow blood lake in which she lies, sloshing up against her as if she were an island of rock and earth. She's dead. I know it in my heart, I feel it in my senses; everything this girl once was is lost and Alma no longer lives to fight for it. Alma's not here anymore.

Is this what happens when a vampire drinks from another vampire? How could Serat feed on his own kind and yet it's done this to Alma? And then like a cheesy, '90s sci-fi movie, my brain throws me a flashback.

"Before I do this, I want you to know that I'm special. Very special." Serat said this to me, on my second night in Vampire City, and then later, Gawk mentioned, "Apparently, there's something special about being a lord of a borough. That's what Serat says, anyhow."

But what could be so special about Serat?

"Amirah!" I scream without ever deciding to. "Amirah! Now!"

Amirah whips her head round, shocked to hear me cry out her name in such a desperate tone, and in the heartbeat when she's not paying attention, Munstone strikes. He hits the elf so hard that her head whips back sharply and her body turns with it. It looks a killing blow, and it sends me over the edge.

I burst at Munstone. Throwing myself at him, we land together but now I'm the one on top. I'm the one beating down on him. His chunky, fleshy arms can do nothing against my rabid attacks. I'm literally grabbing chunks of him and pulling him apart. Alma's dead. Amirah's probably dead. Gawk's dead. Needl's dead. Serat's gone. Without the spark of hope that was Alma, or the comforting leadership that was Amirah, or even the hate that Serat filled me with,

I have nothing. Nothing. Everything's changed. All I'm left with is tearing chunks out of someone who I couldn't care less about. It doesn't make me feel good. It doesn't make me feel anything. But it's somewhere to channel this overwhelming feeling of terror. The unbearable terror of having nothing at all.

***

As it turns out, I saved Amirah's life. Admittedly, I needed Amirah to return the favour immediately afterwards, but even so… it feels good.

She puts her arms around me and pulls me off Munstone, who is now a mess of big bits, small bits, hard bits, and gooey bits. As soon as she's dragged me back, I'm thankful. I'm also exhausted and completely drained, but still thankful.

"Come on," Amirah urges me. "We have to get out of here."

The cracks in the walls are starting to look very ominous indeed, growing bigger and bigger, and the few pillars still standing are starting to make their very own cracks, which are all equally ominous.

"Alma?" I gasp in response, breathless and barely able to stand on my own two feet.

"We'll carry her," Amirah decides. "Now, come on."

In true dramatic fashion, Amirah and I carry Alma out onto the street with barely a moment to spare before the underground car park collapses. Perhaps it's dumb luck or maybe it's simply how these things work out.

I also collapse but I do it on the road alongside Alma's body. And it is just a body now. There's nothing alive about her anymore. This fifteen-year-old fourteen-year-old is now a dead fifteen-year-old fourteen-year-old. Her smart clothes are blood-stained and ruined. The thought occurs to me that she dressed older than she is, and this thought makes me sad.

Her eyes aren't moving, her mouth is like stone, her body is dead weight, and I can't believe any of it. She's a vampire. Vampires don't die. Vampires *can't* die! In fact, she should have all of Serat's strength. So why does she now look so pale? So weak?   "Come on," I hear Amirah say to me. It feels like the one-hundredth time she's said those words to me. "We need to get back to the tunnels."

With a heave, Amirah picks up Alma's body. I can't bear to look at it. It's the way Alma's arms drop down uselessly, or the way her feet wobble without direction every time Amirah takes a step.

I follow along behind them but I'm already lagging. The red fog is starting to dissipate though. I can see far enough in front of me to recognize the same old abandoned, dilapidated, ugly buildings that line these dirty, weed-infested roads. So, yeah… hooray. The air is still thick and warm, and there's a red taint that touches everything, but it doesn't feel as claustrophobic as earlier.

I hate this feeling. It's not this creeping feeling of loss, which I'm intentionally ignoring, or the bewildering confusion that leaves me feeling dog-tired and without hope. It's this feeling that I've been stretched. Stretched beyond myself.

What happens now? Does this borough even have a boss anymore? Is Serat like the rest of us now, weak and feeble? And what of Alma? She's gone, her body an empty shell, I can feel it. I can't sense her vampiric kindred spirit anymore.

Will her demise mean anything? Would she have been the new lord of Duke's Borough? Or is that lady? Will things actually change around here, even after everything that's happened? The explosion that rocked the borough, the brawl under the city, the vampire who lost everything, and the other vampire who died. A dead vampire! All of a sudden, I feel very vulnerable.

So, here we are. The three of us walking through what feels like a dead city. A dusty shade of red hangs in the air, broken buildings form a guard of honour for us, yet the silver-haired elf walks strong. She's carrying a dead vampire, which is an impossible thing, but then Alma always insisted on the impossible.

I'm far behind them, bringing up the rear and holding my forearm. Every part of my body hurts, I feel sick to my stomach and tired in my mind, and my poor and shabby clothes hang heavy on me.

I don't think I've ever felt lower than I feel right now. Alma had something—call it a spark, call it a calling, call it whatever you like. She was reckless, naïve, and she had a long way to go yet, but she still had something. Something Amirah could never have (a chance) and something I never had in the first place (a real hope).

I'm completely resigned to what I know I'm going to do, just as soon as I get the first glimmer of an opportunity to do it. I'm holding my forearm ever so tightly.

***

When I was human, the world was a different place to the one it is now. For a start, it was simpler back then, a lot simpler. The village where I grew up was small, homely, and nestled away. It had a single, lonely dirt road that ran through it. There was a cow in a field, some pigs in a pen, and sheep for as far as the eye could see. At some point during my childhood, one of the villagers found a second cow. This was probably the most exciting thing that had ever happened there.

The villagers were simple too, but I don't mean that in a disparaging way. We simply all had our place, we all had things for us to do, and we all had places waiting for us to go to and come back from. It was as if our lives were laid out before us, with everything neatly ordered and expected.

It was my destiny to work the farm, marry the girl, raise some kids, and eventually die in my sleep after years of hard work and a long marriage with the next generation waiting in the wings, ready to do it all again.

I worked the farm, or at least I started to, and I had the girl. No. Wait. I didn't have the girl. That's the dream talking, confusing me, making me believe in something that was never there. I am one hundred percent sure about there being no kids though. It might all have happened two hundred years ago, but I don't need to worry about that. And as for the dying bit, well… you can't kill what's already dead inside. Old vampire proverb, that is.

Oh dear. This dream is getting away from me. Reality is starting to seep in.

I hated the farm. I never really fit in, was never much good at anything, and I had no hope of making something of myself. I didn't know the girl. She was the milkmaid, and I was completely in love, struck dumb and speechless by the mere sight of her. But that doesn't mean I knew her. I didn't know her. She fit in easily, and she was good to have around, and I could see she'd go far in life. Perhaps even to the next village.

I reckon I would have resented her for all of it. Maybe not straight away, but eventually. Perhaps we would have lived in dumb bliss for a few years. But in my two hundred years of watching humanity, the one thing I've learnt is that falling in love is easy, but actually liking someone and being able to be around that same someone forever and ever… well, it takes a lot. It's exhausting and constantly challenging and I'm not that strong.

I think I loved her, or as much as someone can love someone else without actually knowing them at all. I know in my heart I would have ended up hating her though. I would have ended up taking all those years laid out so neatly in front of us and I would have ruined them, scarred them, and made them into a nightmare.

I still miss her though. I still wish I had said something. I can't help thinking about how it might have worked.

I never went back, not after I was turned into what I am now and what I've remained as ever since, so I have no idea what happened to her. I hope she lived a good life. I hope she died in her sleep, surrounded by lovely children (fine, and a lovely bastard of a husband too) after years of living a good life in a peaceful village, surrounded by sheep as far as the eye could see and a field with more than one cow in it.

This dream sucks.

***

I wake up and I immediately wish I hadn't. Nothing out of the ordinary, then.

It's very dark, uncomfortably dusty, and everything is very close to everything else. I find myself lying on an uneven and rocky surface, and I'm feeling half-dead and probably looking it too. Sitting up, I get my bearings, and a bit of my memory comes back to me.

We made it back to the tunnels—this cobbled-together, hastily-dug network of Amirah's doing—and I immediately found a corner to be left alone in. I didn't even see which way Amirah took Alma's body. Instead I took out my forearm, bit down hard, and drank my own blood. It doesn't taste good, and it makes me physically and mentally weaker with every drop I take from myself. But I passed out soon enough and that's the real endgame here.

But now I have to wake up, and though the dream is gone, the weakness doth remain. The whole thing is a cruel cycle of mocking torture and depreciating value.

Drinking blood takes effort, effort which is supposed to be offset tenfold by the blood being drunk, but in my case the blood being drunk is my own blood. I am quite literally like a snake eating its own tail. It'll be a while too before I've scraped up enough energy to drink again, and this thought sends my distant mood into the doldrums.

The world around me is dark and dimly lit by miner's lamps hanging from the ceiling, connected to each other by open wires. They hum gently, bringing a weak orange light to these underground passageways. As for these passageways, they are unnervingly narrow and apparently held up with intermittent wooden beams and occasional metal foundations. Never mind the dangers of an earthquake or a cave-in, these crude tunnels look like a loud sneeze could bring it all down on top of us. All of us.

I can scarcely believe it. Everyone's down here.

I'm up and walking now, shuffling along down this seemingly random and haphazard maze. Everyone who lives in the borough—or at least everyone in the borough who can fit, sit, or stand awkwardly to the side in these tunnels—is here. All of them. Goblins chitter, elves pass on by, a drake eyes me with suspicion, an elderly rat-man sits in quiet contemplation, a few flame demons have curled up in a bucket of water, steaming away peacefully, and here are some gnomes singing sombre campfire songs as they sit around a large candle. They're here. She did it. Amirah brought them all with her.

I'm shoved to the side as a pair of dwarves push past me. They're both carrying bundles of cloth in their arms and hurrying off somewhere, talking quickly about things they need and where to get them. I'm not really listening, and I don't bother following. Instead I slump to the ground and join everyone else.

We're all just sitting here. Some of us try for whispered conversations, a few can't help looking up nervously, but most huddle together and keep their heads low. Sitting opposite me, with their legs pulled up and arms wrapped around shins, is a banshee.

Long hair, gaunt white eyes, and skin as creamy as a newborn babe. And it's staring right at me. It doesn't blink, doesn't look away, and it is muttering something silently. The lips are moving ever so slightly but there's no sound.

"You want something?" I ask, trying to sound extra churlish to cover up how unnerved I am by those unblinking eyes. It is like two white voids staring back at me. And apparently the void knows all. My spine is literally tingling and every little hair on my body is standing at attention (because what everyone needs in times of alarm and danger is a spine that feels like jelly and tiny little pointless hairs all over your body that point upwards).

The banshee just keeps muttering under their breath. It may look like a young woman—a girl even, so small and vulnerable—but banshees are bad news. Heralds of Ill Fortune, some call them. I call them something else, which is far cruder and not at all poetic.

"What do you want!?" I snap nervously.

I suddenly know this banshee. From the very first time I woke up in Vampire City, to the day after the night of flames, and now here, sitting across from me as we all hide from whatever hellish wrath might be happening above us...every time something changes for the worse, the banshee is there. Watching me.

Well, I can't take it anymore. I can't take the banshee's judgemental eyes or accusing whispers. I can't take it! I lunge forward to grab their hair. I don't know what I'm doing or what I'm going to do. Like a child, I only want it to stop.

The banshee lithely ducks under my grasp and slips away down the tunnel, easily moving through the crowded passageways. It's gone. Whether it was running away from me or not, I don't really care. I'm just glad it's gone.

"Bad luck, that," someone says to me in a croaky, old voice. I turn around to see a croaky, old person looking at me. A mouldy old rat-man, who looks like he went a few rounds with Father Time and lost, is looking at me with tired and dry eyes.

"Bad luck?" I groan. "I guess that'd be keeping with the theme, at least."

"We make our own luck in this world," the old rat-man says.

"Piss off."

***

We've been down here a long time. Apparently, everyone's waiting to be told when it will be safe to return to the surface. I'm still sitting here in this narrow tunnel, bundled in with everyone else and shoulder to shoulder with a crusty old faun.

Maybe I should have gone looking for Amirah. I brought Alma here, after all. Or rather, Alma found me, and I found Amirah. But I haven't moved. I'm either sulking, hiding, or I'm lost. Or all of the above.

Amirah hasn't come looking for me though. A fact that leaves me feeling rather resentful, and I know it's selfish of me to feel this way so I'm also feeling guilty about that, which piles on top of the whole sulking, hiding, and lost situation. I'm really going through the wringer here.

"I know you."

I need to get my head straight. Re-focus. Take a mindful, slow, deep breath and start with one small step. Okay. Here it goes.

What happens next? No idea.

Okay! Let's try a slightly smaller first step.

What's happening now?

Hm. Still not much of an idea. Serat and his vampires will have regenerated by now, there's no doubt about that, but what they are doing is more of a mystery. Is Serat still the alpha of the group? Or are they fighting amongst themselves? Electing a new alpha the only way they know how: beating the hell out of each other until the last vampire standing can drink up all the blood and become the new big cheese. Or did Alma take the power? In that case, is there even any power left, because Alma is —

"Oi! I do know you!"

That's probably what is happening. It would certainly explain why no one's come to find us down here. They're too busy tearing each other apart, and when they're finally done with that, only then will they resume lording over us again, unless the whole Alma situation has scuppered —

"It is you!" Someone grabs me and turns me round, and suddenly there's a face in my face. It's not a pretty face, unfortunately. Big eyes, bigger nose and somehow, a mouth that makes the eyes and nose look small. A raspy voice, in a gob full of broken teeth, with cracked skin and attire so shabby it makes my own clothes look positively smart. *Eww* and *yuck* are the words that come to mind. Gremlins are the worst.

"You're that vampire!" The gremlin prods my chest with a bony finger. "The one that ain't like the rest of 'em! The one that lives with us lot!"

"If you could step back a smidgeon," I say through pursed lips as I try not to intake the stale odour of the gremlin's awful breath.

"Oi! Everyone!" the gremlin calls out. And I'm suddenly aware of many pairs of eyes, and other sets of eyes at that, suddenly looking in my direction. I've got a bad feeling about where this is probably going. "I've got him!" And the gremlin looks down on me, with a vicious little grin on its ugly, uneven face.

"Is someone looking for me?" I ask, trying to sound innocent.

"Yeah," the gremlin nods, and a few others push their way to where I am. They're a mish-mash of sub-mortals, but they all look hungry and mean. Here's that bad feeling again. "*We've* been looking for ye!"

The body of a gremlin is a thin, rickety thing, and if it were to stand up straight it would be just shy of my own height. But gremlins never stand up straight. I don't think they can, and I've never seen one try. Instead, they're hobbled and bowed. Their heads dip low, their back curls over, and their limbs are always bent.

"You should be up there," an orc growls menacingly. Orcs are not like gremlins. Orcs are taller than me, bristling with muscle, and despite their sickly green skin, they all look like super-jacked supermodels who have had a set of shark's teeth rammed into their mouths.

"Doing what?" I scoff back at the big lug, which probably isn't the smartest thing to do.

"Sorting it all out!" the gremlin spits at me from the side. "Obviously!"

"Leave him be, Ankis," the old faun, who I had completely forgotten about, intervenes on my behalf. "Nothing can be done for it now."

"Shove it, you old goat," Ankis the gremlin retorts.

"Why aren't you up there?" a selkie challenges me from across the passage. Her big, bulbous eyes bore into me. "Why aren't you doing something about all this?"

"Me?" I try to scoff again, but it comes out sounding weak. I'm feeling rather cornered here. Mob mentality is a powerful thing. "What can I do?" I squeak.

"You're a vampire, ain't ye?" Ankis shouts, angrily. "It's yer lot up there! Ye should be sorting this out! He's the reason we're down here!" This last claim is shouted to everyone else, and everyone is listening intently and now looking at me.

"I'm hardly the reason we're down here—" I try, but it's hopeless. I can't do anything. They've got me cornered.

There is nothing more single-mindedly steadfast than mob rule, especially if the mob is a frightened one.

"Course ye are!" the gremlin shouts, and this apparently is enough to win the argument. "It's who ye are. Now, get up there! Go on!"

A chorus of agreement pipes up. Suddenly hands are on me, pulling and shoving me down the passageway. I think I hear some disagreeing voices, but they're quickly drowned out by the rising crescendo of this miniature mob. I protest, rather lamely, but I can't fight against the sea that is now taking me away.

A little pixie, half the size of the palm of my hand, does appear in front of my face though. Her little insect wings have to beat ferociously to stay ahead of me.

"Don't worry," the little pixie says in a tiny, tinny squeak. She's beaming at me, all rosy-cheeked and bright-eyed. "We pixies don't blame you for any of this!" And she darts forward and hugs my cheek, and through a smile of bliss and loveliness she adds, "I'm sure everything will work out. I'm sure you'll be totally fine. Bye!"

And she flutters away. That was nice, I think. Completely useless and utterly unhelpful, of course. But still nice.

∗∗∗

The door slams shut behind me and I'm outside.

It's quiet. No. It's not quiet. It's silent. Actually, not silent. It's dead silent. There is neither the sound of birds twittering above nor the distant chattering of strangers. I ascend the narrow stairway and find myself back in the alleyway. Every step I take sounds loud and obtrusive. There isn't even any wind. Everything up here is dead.

The fog is gone though. The air still feels dusty and uncomfortable, but I can see as far as I have ever been able to see, and what I can see is a deserted, devastated, and decrepit city. So, apart from the whole deserted thing, the city is the same. At best, the buildings are in disrepair, and at worst, they're halfway to collapsing in on themselves. As for the roads, they are long and cracked, ridden with weeds, and strewn with rubbish.

As I walk through the city, feeling like a lone ant returning to an abandoned anthill, I come across the meagre signs that indicate there is still life here, or sub-mortal life anyway. Empty markets, rickety stalls, cobbled together shacks, and rubbish… rubbish everywhere.

I'm heading for where Serat's building used to be. I'm not sure what I'm going to find there, but I have a sneaking suspicion it's a good place to start. Start what? I have no idea, but a start of any kind is better than nothing.

Serat's building is where all the other vampires would have been when it went up, or at least in the vicinity anyway, so that's surely where the infighting would have started. When in doubt, follow the bodies. Another old vampire proverb. I can only hope the other lords in Vampire City don't follow it. Hopefully they'll be either too scared to move into the place that just exploded, or too worried their own place is about to explode. Just as likely, though, they're probably having a good laugh to themselves and waiting to see what happens next.

I'm right. I'm standing in front of where Serat's building once stood and there are vampire bodies here. They're not dead, of course, but they are terribly weak. Some of them still look a little *blown apart* but there are many others who look like dry, withered corpses. Of these, all of them have fresh bite wounds on their necks that are now gaping black holes into an empty interior. Some of them shake a little, often one will spasm with a shiver, and one or two even manage to make a mournful moaning sound. I couldn't care less. That sounds heartless, but I'm a vampire, so not caring is kind of my modus operandi, comprendo? (Languages have never been my strong suit.)

Wow. The building really was blown to smithereens. Even I, a dullard in the ways of the occult, can sense a faint background of magical energy lingering here. Whatever that witch taught Alma to brew up, it was a big bastard of a bomb. And as far as I can tell, it achieved nothing except the death of the one vampire who seemed different, the very same vampire who brewed the bomb itself.

I don't want to think about Alma. I don't want to think about how a vampire can die. *Focus on the now*, I tell myself, and so I start hunting around for vampires who look more recently drained. I want to find whoever the new boss is. Serat was coming back, but we stopped him in the underground car park, or rather Alma stopped him. So the vampires will have had free rein to fight amongst themselves.

I'm following the yellow brick road to the Emerald City. And by yellow brick road, I mean I'm following the tortured, blood-dry, and crippled temporary corpses of my kin, and by Emerald City, I mean whoever the new bastard is who *gone-done-the-drinking*.

The withered bodies of defeated vampires are becoming fewer and further apart as I follow the trail. I step over one unfortunate soul who was evidently beaten to a pulp before being drunk dry. I pass by another who had their head rammed into a postbox that is now bent out of shape, and there's a body that has been cracked open, and there's another who is now in several pieces, and finally there's a vampire who looks relatively unharmed, except they have a giant stone brick where their head used to be— oh, and a little puddle of dark red mush that has splattered outwards from the giant brick. I quickly pass this one by and then I find another temporary vampire's corpse and this one… this one I recognize.

Helisha looks like hell. Of course, she looked hell the last time I saw her, seeing as I had rammed a mapinguari's severed head on top of her own head. But that was a different kind of hell. Back in the underground car park, she looked more monster than vampire. Besides, we had been fighting at the time, so I didn't mind so much when I put her through hell.

But this is different. Here, she doesn't look like a monster. She looks like Helisha. Drained. Limp. Eyes sluggish and mouth barely able to get out a whisper, she has two fresh but hollow bite wounds on her neck, and her dead skin is pulled tight against her skeleton. She obviously regenerated after our fight, only to take part in yet another fight, this one between all the vampires of the borough competing for the top prize. She did pretty well to get this far, especially considering what I put her through beforehand.

"So," I say, though I am not sure what I should say next, so I settle for, "how are you?"

I know she's basically a petrified hundred-year-old corpse right now, but I get the distinct impression she's trying to roll her eyes and huff in my general direction.

"You look… awful." I keep talking, because it's all I've got, and for some reason I can't not say anything. Should I have kept walking on by? No. That'd be cruel. I can't help her though (I'm not sure I would, even if I could) and time is an issue here.

With every minute that passes by, the new big boss—whoever they are—gets stronger. With as many bodies as I've passed already, I suspect I'm already far too late to stop another vampire taking Serat's place.

Except none of this makes sense! How have these vampires been able to drink from one another? As it stands, Serat could drink from a vampire, and based on all the evidence I've been following, all of his crony vampires have managed it as well. Alma is the only one who has died. Maybe… just maybe… there was something to what she always insisted upon… maybe she wasn't a normal vampire…

"You, er, put up a good show, I see." Why the hell am I still here? Why am I still talking? Helisha isn't like me, and I'm not like her. We're two very different vampires. "Maybe another time, hey?" Could I sound any more like a condescending arsehole? I don't mean to be one, but I don't know how to articulate what I'm feeling right now. This is mostly because I don't actually know what I'm feeling right now, as I find myself standing in front of someone who fought, struggled, and lost in a game designed to make you fight and to keep you struggling only to abandon you when you inevitably lose. But more pertinently perhaps, I'm standing in front of someone who I don't hate, and I don't think she hates me. But because I don't know what I'm feeling, I can't say the right thing, and so, like every lost fool in this stupid, stupid world, instead of saying nothing I instead say the wrong thing. "Well, I hate to say I told you so."

If corpses could kill…

***

I leave Helisha behind.

I think I'm getting close now as the street opens up into a large city square. An old and once-majestic fountain, now covered in bird crap, sits in the middle and that's about it. Long ago there would have been tourists taking photos here, commuters bustling on by, and the occasional activist bellowing on about the end of the world. Of course, it's all empty now. Fast-food chains, brand outlets, and dodgy-looking souvenir shops would have surrounded this square, all of it lit up by bright advertising screens and flashing logos. The buildings are now abandoned, and the advertising boards have fallen down. There is a bit of green though, as there is throughout the city, where nature has started the long and arduous process of reclaiming the land. Weeds are breaking through.

There is only one more vampire body. It's dropped at the foot of the fountain, emptied and limp. It's Munstone. The snivelling pen-pusher has seemingly reached the limit of what pen pushing can achieve. And the vampire that dropped him is Serat. It was always going to be him, I acknowledge with an inward sigh. His vampires weren't drinking each other then. Serat was drinking them. I guess he is a special one, after all.

He looks renewed and revitalized. Drinking the blood of all your followers will do that to you, I suppose. Where Alma had left him a useless and powerless drained corpse, now he is standing before me proud and strong. His snake-like face contorts into a knowing grin, his eyes pierce my own, and he comes towards me slowly, looking every bit the predator eyeing up its next kill.

"I'm glad you're here, Caiden," he tells me, in a quite annoyingly jovial tone.

"I'm not." I barely resist the urge to turn tail and run.

Serat starts to walk in a wide circle around me. A fly flits across my vision. I should do something. I should try walking in a wide circle of my own, around him, so we'd be circling each other, each one trying to circle a bigger circle around the other. But I can't even try because my legs don't seem to want to move right now… which is worrying.

"I'm curious, what exactly were you hoping to find here?" Serat asks me. Another fly darts across his grinning face.

"Well." I sigh outwardly now. "I was hoping to find you, I suppose, or someone like you. Still weak though and ready to be defeated."

"And then what, Caiden?" The bastard smiles with a malevolent twinkle in his eye. "Would you overpower me? Would you then drink my blood?"

"Isn't that how it's supposed to work?" I ask, my voice teetering and my circling faltering. I barely manage to stay on my feet although I can't shake the feeling I'm on wobbly ground here.

"No," he laughs. "No, no, no, Caiden. That's not how this works." He stops and faces me. "How is your friend doing? After all, she left quite the mark." And he holds up his hand and shows me his own bite marks. They've scabbed over now, but still the skin looks mangled and unhealthy.

Does he know? Does he know she's dead?

"She's doing well enough," I tell him, keeping my face as expressionless as I can.

"Wrong," he says, resolutely. "Your friend is dead."

"We can't die!" I snap, losing any pretence of composure. So, to make amends, I add a little petulant flourish. "You… idiot." Hmm. Serat gives me an exasperated look. That didn't hit as hard as I would have liked it to.

"Not in the literal sense," he explains, starting to pace around me again. "But she may as well be dead. Indeed, she likely wishes for such a fate even now."

"What the hell are you talking about?"

"It's not a natural thing," he goes on. "For a vampire to drink the blood of another vampire. It is against the laws of nature."

"We're vampires," I scoff. "The laws of nature don't exactly apply."

Serat stops in front of me. His long black coat billows impressively in a small gust of wind, his eyes gleam with power, his body is in perfect condition, and I realise beyond doubt that I'm inferior to him in every way. I need to get the hell out of here.

"The laws of nature are entirely focused on survival. Whether that be survival of the fittest, survival of the most numerous, or survival of the sneakiest, it matters not. Nature is nothing but what survives."

It's an impressive little speech, so naturally I have to find a way to ruin it for him.

"Say that all again," I say. "But this time, say it in your best David Attenborough impression."

"Attenborough?" Serat laughs uproariously. "Now there's a demigod not to be trifled with."

Huh. You learn something new every day.

"But my point stands," Serat continues. "Nature is survival. Vampires drinking vampires is not survival."

"I don't know about that," I shake my head. "Seems to work for you."

"A normal vampire cannot digest what has already been digested," Serat explains, ignoring my snide remarks. "What has been absorbed cannot then be absorbed again. Unless…"

I sigh, and then I take the bait. "Unless what?"

"…one is no longer bound to the laws of nature." Serat looks intently at me. "I am no longer a creature of this world. I belong to a higher plain, a greater power, and what was once against my nature now comes easily to me. Do you understand?"

"Not even a little bit," I say, putting on a big grin because I know it will annoy him.

"You need to understand, Caiden!" Serat insists, a vein on his forehead starting to show. "Because once you understand, you will stay where you are and desist your useless attempts to rebel, to change, or to upend the system."

Shit. He thinks I blew his building up.

"Alma…" I start, before performing some mental gymnastics. "…isn't dead?" I recover.

"Like I said, she may as well be," Serat affirms. "She tried to own me. She tried to take from me. Now, she is lost, no more than a lowly sub-mortal in a higher plain. She'll never walk again, she'll never talk again, she will never be as she was."

"So, she's a vegetable? Couldn't you have just said that?" I groan, and then I try to annoy him some more by forcing a yawn, stretching my arms out and then placing my hands in my coat pockets. "I mean, do you always have to be so dramatic? So, go on then, what makes you so special? Why can you drink a vampire's blood and the rest of us can't?"

"I…" Serat takes a deep breath, aiming high for the drama. "…have been *touched*."

I don't say anything. I think he's waiting for me to say something. It feels like the wind has stopped too. Almost as if the whole world has stopped just to raise a suspicious eyebrow in Serat's general direction.

"Erm…" I finally say. "…is that a… a good thing? Are you okay?"

"Of course I'm okay!" Serat snaps at me, irritated.

"Look, you don't have to put up any walls, you know." I take my hands out my pockets and hold out my arms, beckoning him in for a hug, smiling all the while like the goading arsehole I am. "You don't have to be afraid, Serat. Tell me, who was it that touched you… and did they touch your—"

I was about to snigger. I was on the cusp of giggling. My belly was ready for a slice of chuckle jelly. But I'm cut off, quite literally. Serat leaps forward and wraps one hand around my neck. I can't fathom how strong he is, even as he crushes my windpipe and cracks the bones under his vice-like fingers.

"You treat this like it's a game," he spits in my face, his sudden rage like that of an animal, "and still you complain when the world treats you like a pawn!"

He throws me. As I'm flying through the air, I'm grateful for the momentary opportunity to breathe, but then I fall headfirst onto some hard concrete and now everything hurts again, and the wind is knocked from my chest.

"You, and everyone like you, can only ever hope to survive." Serat advances on me, taking his time, and he can take all the time he wants because I'm struggling with just getting back up, let alone fighting back. "You're a lower form of existence," the smug bastard continues. "You are nothing more than soil in the ground. Oil in the machine."

I gasp, feeling as if my lungs are about to shatter, as I stand up. But even this doesn't stop me from poking the bear. "And you're nothing but a two-bit thug who got lucky. You're a nobody on a high horse—"

For the second time, I'm cut off, although this time it's because Serat slams me down with all his strength. My whole body hits the ground with such force that I feel every bone, every muscle, every blood vessel, and every one of my ornamental organs either break, tear, pop, or shake.

"This is what you don't understand, Caiden," Serat explains. "I didn't fight my way to the top. It was given to me. All of what I am. My power, my strength, my ability to drink the blood of my kin. It was all given to me. You think this is a game, a mere contest to be fought and to which the winner is given charge of a borough." He grins insidiously down at me. "But this is not a game. This is not a contest. This is a system, and you have your place in it, and I have mine. It's as simple as this. I am touched and you are untouched. I have the power, and you are powerless." He leans forward, his vile satisfaction reaching a fever pitch. "And this is why your friend has been broken by the power she took from me."

"Bullshit," I manage, but it's a feeble protest. "You're spouting meaningless drivel!"

"And you're nothing but a worker ant, Caiden." Serat straightens back up. He's finished with me. "Worker ants work their whole life and then they die. This is what you are, except you can't die so you have to keep working. This, Caiden, is your place in the system. Stop trying to change the world, little ant. I *am* the world."

***

I don't want this to happen again. I put my hands up. One grapples with Serat's tight grip around my throat and the other desperately pushes on his jaw. But it's all for nothing. He's coming down regardless, his mouth opening and his fangs growing. His eyes turn a shade of blood red, becoming wild and filled with anticipation.

Three times. Three times now. When I arrived in Vampire City, when the night burned and Alma was taken, and now today, while the city is empty, and Alma's magic bomb accomplished nothing more than a temporary and fleeting chaos.

And each time it has ended like this, with me drained and any frail hope revealed to have been false all along. Order is restored, the status quo has returned, and Serat has power over all. It is how it is. He really is the world. He is this city.

I still struggle, despite the futility of it. For some strange reason, I find it easier to struggle against the inevitable rather than sitting back and accepting it. Serat barely notices anyway, and his fangs are almost touching my neck. My own bite wounds are ugly scabs that have been distorted and scratched. And in a moment, they're going to hurt like hell.

I'll see her again, at least—my long-lost milkmaid— and maybe in this dream I'll spend a lifetime with her in the village we grew up in. That would be nice. A complete lie, of course, though perhaps a nice lie is preferable to the depressing truth.

No. No, I don't want to see her again. Not like this. The dream is too fragile. Reality is too strong. I don't want this. I don't want to be this.

I won't let Serat drink from me. Not this time. Never again. I won't let him do it. I feel like I'm going to rip apart under all the effort I'm expending to resist him. Serat notices me now. He becomes angry, pushing harder against me, and I can feel my hands start to slip, my arms weaken, and slowly, so slowly, Serat's fangs touch my neck. Like I said… inevitable.

A small fist punches through the back of Serat's head and rips through his skull, exploding out of his face. If my eyes hadn't been splattered with his dark blood, I would probably never forget Serat's ruined visage for all eternity, for both good and bad reasons.

His body goes limp, and he falls sideways. He's still alive and he'll still be conscious, but without a brain there's nothing Serat can do in the real world. All he can do is lie on the ground and wait for it to grow back, which it will eventually, but not before I've had a long while to do some slicing and dicing of my own. Or will I?

Standing where Serat was only moments before is a small person with a small fist, and this small fist is doused in dark blood and bumpy bits of brain.

This small person looks haggard and completely insane. I can see their long fangs as their tongue licks dark blood from the tips of their small fingers. Their attire is torn in places, dirty all over, and parts of what was once a nice coat whip about wickedly in the sudden wind. The wind also catches the small person's hair, stirring and thrashing it about to make it appear like a furious fire in a burning furnace.

It's their eyes that really catch my attention though. Catch my attention and hold me tight. They're alive with madness. They are eyes that have seen what is beyond the edge of the map. Eyes that went through hell and came out the other side. And they're looking down at me and I'm not sure if I have been saved or if I am about to be damned. All I know for sure is one thing and one thing only: Alma's not dead.

Touched? Ha. What a load of rubbish.

***

Moments later, Amirah joins us and the three of us—Alma, Amirah, and me—stand in an awkward circle around the faceless and brainless body of Serat. The fountain nearby is still dry, the roads are still broken, and the buildings are all still abandoned, but right now, the world looks a very different place.

"Okay," I start. "First things first… How? What? When? Why? Okay—er, are you?" I direct these five admittedly short questions to Alma. The fifteen-year-old fourteen-year-old looks at me with those wild eyes and that perky little nose and for a moment I think she's going to rip through my own head as well. But she doesn't. Thankfully.

"I woke up," she tells me. "That's all."

"That was *not* all," Amirah interjects. "You were screaming, inconsolable, you almost caused a cave-in, and then you almost tore yourself in two!"

"Well, to be fair, that does sound like a normal teenager waking up," I offer, and I'm rewarded with an impatient and unimpressed glare from Amirah.

"I feel… different," Alma tries to explain, although she looks like she's still working it out for herself. "But I also feel… like me. I feel more like me than ever."

"Weird," I comment. "Do you feel like a vampire, then?"

"No," she growls.

"We all thought you were dead," Amirah says, and she comes forward and holds Alma in a comforting embrace. It's the kind of warm, inviting, and comforting embrace that I wish someone would give me.

"No. Not dead," I say. "Serat told me Alma would be lost, as in lost in her head, because a normal vampire isn't supposed to drink another vampire's blood, or something like that."

"Then how is she here?" Amirah asks, turning to me but keeping a protective arm over Alma's shoulders.

"Erm, well… I suppose… err…"

"It's okay to admit you don't know, Caiden."

"I don't know, Amirah," I admit with a shrug. "Maybe Serat was talking bullocks, with his head so far up his own arse he couldn't see his spiel for what it was."

"No." Alma speaks up. "He just didn't know. That's all."

"Doesn't know what?"

"About me." Alma smiles, and I can't help feeling a little unnerved by the way she's grinning.

PART 3

I've been having this weird feeling lately.

It's like the feeling on a rollercoaster, when you're going down the first drop and you're caught between two different sensations. The first is of being lighter than air, as if you could drift away with the faintest nudge. And the second feeling is of crushing force, holding you tightly in place.

They're polar opposites. One is aimless drifting and the other is trapped constraint. I could be busy, I might be bored, there might be something on my mind, or I could be thinking of nothing at all, but regardless, and with neither rhyme nor reason, sometimes I find myself sinking into this weird feeling of contradictions. It sucks. And there's no escape. I even experience it in my dreams.

Some people dream of flying. Others dream of falling. I dream of sinking.

Oh, yes. I'm still dreaming. A quick bite on the arm and I'm out for the count. It's weird. I always thought if things were to ever get better in Vampire City that I'd stop the whole biting-my-arm thing. Ironically, I do it more now than ever before. Almost on a daily basis. It's a habit. A bad one.

Over a month has passed since Alma punched through the back of Serat's head and ripped his face off, pulling it backwards through his skull. My coat and shirt—being the only ones I own—still sport the bloodstains from that fun little move, defying all efforts to scrub and clean. Incidentally, I can't believe it's taken me this long to realise this, but I finally understand why vampires wear black. It's to hide the bloodstains. Red shows up on every other colour, and red itself is garish and ugly to look at, so we all wear black. It's another way to hide.

Amirah is sitting with me. She's wearing workman jeans, a heavy jacket with a dozen deep pockets, and a hooded top underneath. Next to her, I look quite the regular bum. Hm, not quite a regular bum, actually. More like a desperately poor, beaten-down, dirty bum. My short coat is tatty, my black shirt is smelly, my trousers are torn in places, and my trainers were worn out a few years ago. At least the park is pretty, and the markets have returned to Duke's Borough, and everyone is trying to get back to some sort of normal.

There is hope though. An underlying hope that no one dares talk about. Something about tempting fate and best laid plans, I suppose. But there's no denying the facts. Serat's gone. Or rather, Serat's been cowed. He's just another lowly vampire now, waiting on the boss like the rest of us. All his talk about being special was only that… talk, and nothing has come of it. He had us all believing it though.

"Alma should be returning any day now," Amirah says, fidgeting with her fingers. She's not her usual composed self lately. She's like everyone else. Excited at the prospect of change for the better and also terrified of change for the worst.

"Maybe I should have been the one to go," I say, raising this subject for what feels like the umpteenth time. But I haven't been able to shake it, and such thoughts have dogged me this past month.

Standing over Serat's crippled body a month ago, there had been two vampires who could have drunk his blood and take for themselves the power he had taken from everyone else. But only one of the two did it. Alma was the one. Well, Alma stepped forward first and neither Amirah nor I challenged her.

"Alma's the one who beat Serat," Amirah points out.

"Yes." I nod. "But she's also fifteen years old and still convinced she's not something that she most emphatically is. And she came back too."

"You mean when she woke up?"

"Yes, after drinking from Serat, it was… what?… a day, tops, and she woke up from that weird state she was in." I sigh. "But Helisha beat Serat, Amirah. She beat him when it all went down between them all. I've seen the wounds and heard it from the bastard's own mouth. But when she tried to drink from him…"

"Oh, and that's why she's still…"

"Yeah."

"Shit."

"Yeah."

So, for Serat and Alma, drinking the blood of another vampire is possible. But for the only other vampire I know to have tried it on another vampire, it remains to this day, one month later, as good as a death sentence.

For a few moments, Amirah and I sit in cold silence and watch the world. Treepeople are standing around looking like trees, a dwarf is sunbathing in the green pasture, and some pug-ugly halflings are playing a game of football against a team of trolls. Based on the trolls' growling, whining, and feigning unfairness, it would seem the halflings are winning. There's a small group of elves, also in workmen gear like Amirah, and they're cleaning up some of the last vestiges of Serat's building, brushing out the grey dust, collecting up stony shrapnel, and working towards righting all the little wrongs that came about from a month ago.

I'm drawn away from my observations when I hear a beeping noise. It's an annoying, insistent sound that I immediately want to quell and destroy or at least banish to the deepest depths of hell.

"Oh," Amirah starts. "That's my beeper!"

"You have a beeper?" I say incredulously.

"Mm-hm." She pulls it out, mercifully stops the beeping, and reads the little message. "Ah, today's the day. Come on. We haven't much time."

Amirah gets up and starts walking out of the park. I follow out of habit more than anything else, what with Amirah being pretty much everybody's boss now, but I'm also curious.

"How do you have a beeper?"

"Found a bunch of them a couple years ago in one of the high-rise office buildings," she tells me. "Humans left a lot behind when they left this city to us. You should look around more."

"I don't need a beeper."

"They're useful, but I wish we had mobile phones."

"And I hate mobile phones."

"No, you don't." She laughs. "You hate the internet, remember."

"We should all hate the internet," I say, perhaps being a little petty. "It's why this city exists in the first place. Why does the world need to be so connected anyway?"

"No one ever said progress was a straight line," Amirah says.

"Well, it should be," I reply childishly. "Where are we going anyway?"

"To welcome our now boss, of course." Amirah smiles. Ah. Alma's coming back.

***

The two of us wait at the border of Duke's Borough on the road that links up with the freeway. We pass the time watching the freeway's daily goings-on, including a few scuffles, a chase or two, a rampaging horde, and a small group of refugees that have incredibly made it this far from the wall.

We have no lord, what with Serat being defeated and Alma (our prospective new lord) currently being away, so we let the new arrivals pass on by. No doubt a borough or two further along will snap them up.

I wonder what Alma's orders will be regarding such newbies. Pretty soon, or rather today according to Amirah's beeper, Alma will return from meeting with the other lords, her newfound partners so to speak, and I suppose they'll install her as the new vampire lord of Duke's Borough, sort of unofficially ratified. I'm sure she won't become like them though. She won't change. They won't change her. Alma's one of the good ones.

Amirah and I wait in peaceful silence, sitting on the roof's edge of what was once a truck stop diner, just off the freeway and at the end of a slip road. It's a bit of a desert here, with dry open spaces and the odd destitute sign of a city. The freeway's gone quiet too. A lull in the constant chaos, maybe. Or perhaps the calm before the storm. Right on cue, here comes a storm…

Amirah sees it first and points it out to me. I look up and squint. Making its slow way down the freeway, heading our way, is a big black horse.

Eventually, I can make out clearer details of the horse as it comes off the freeway and starts down the slip road heading for us, and this is when I realise it is not a horse at all. It's a big black unicorn, as dark as night and as fearsome as its size suggests. Its horn protrudes out of the top of its head, looking weathered but immovable, ancient but unstoppable, and its eyes glow and sparkle from deep within, as if a whole universe exists in each eyeball.

"Quite an entrance," Amirah muses, caught between being rather impressed and thoroughly intimidated. I don't blame her though. I'm as awed as she is, but I'm also sensing trouble. That trouble appears to be confirmed when the rider and her unicorn leave the slipway and approach us. Oh yeah, by the way, Alma's riding the terrifying unicorn.

Dressed in a long coat and black suit, with her hair looking a little on the wild side, her face is as stern as it has always been. Her little nose and chestnut-brown eyes snap out at me, even with all the dark blood.

Oh yeah, also, she's covered in blood. Give me a break, a lot's happening right now, and even more is being insinuated. Because it's dark blood. Vampire blood. The unicorn looks entirely unbothered by their rider's appearance, and incidentally that goes for the rider too.

Alma looks serious but calm, thoughtful but determined, angry but composed.

"Hello there," she greets us both, bringing her unicorn to a stop next to the diner under our dangling feet.

"Ah! Lord Alma!" I cough and splutter for some reason. "How nice of you to... well, actually, what are you doing? Because I don't think you're here to drop in."

"Alma?" Amirah asks, her eyes wide. She's scared. "Just... what?"

"Oh, you know, the usual." Alma sighs, looking a little exasperated. "Tried to change the world, the world bit back, and now I think I've doomed us all."

"Oh... well, as long as it isn't anything to worry about."

"How?" Amirah asks, still as wide-eyed as before. "Just... how?"

"Well, the other lords didn't take too kindly to some of my ideas," Alma says, rolling her eyes. "They're a bunch of old farts stuck in their ways."

"Tell me you didn't go full revolutionary on them," I groan.

"Look, all I suggested was the free movement between boroughs—"

"Oh. That's not too bad, I suppose."

"—and to level up the underclasses—"

"Hmm, that's pushing it."

"—and to bring forward a system of government that is both transparent and democratically voted for by every individual, which at all times will be answerable to the voting of said individuals—"

"We're falling off the edge here."

"—and for all vampires to relinquish the right of ownership by way of drinking blood."

"We're dead. We're all dead. You've doomed us all."

"It can't be that bad," Amirah tries, sounding more hopeful than confident.

"No. Caiden's right," Alma begrudgingly admits. "I think I've killed everyone in Duke's Borough."

✳✳✳

All good arguments start off with something being thrown. Throwing the first punch, as it were. The something being thrown is usually an insult, and it's usually a really nasty and personal one rather than an actual punch. But in this case, it's a car. Alma picks a car up and throws the tonne of metal rust and sharp jagged corners right at me. It hurts a lot, and then it hurts all over again when I'm squashed between the car and the wall of the truck stop diner.

I groan, I moan, then I start to growl a bit, but I end up grumbling, and after a few seconds of this, my body has put itself back together. I can walk again, I can talk again, so now I'm ready to partake in this particular argument.

"Don't ever call me that again," Alma warns me. Okay. Fine. I threw the first punch, so to speak, and it was an insult. An insult I'd rather not own up to. Even so, I still feel justified in what I said, especially considering what Alma has brought down upon us all. With all that said though, I am grateful Amirah has already left and therefore wasn't around to hear what I called Alma (it really was quite bad, and I hate myself for saying it, but I'm still not going to apologize). The elf left a couple minutes ago to gather everyone in Duke's Borough for an emergency meeting, which Alma and I will attend as well, but first things first... the argument.

"Or what?" I scowl at the teenage vampire covered in blood. She's off her unicorn and that's not just a metaphor for her mental state. Her unicorn's grazing in a nearby patch of grass. "You'll drink me dry, will you?" I say, and even I know this is unfair of me, but I've said it now so I've no choice but to go along with it and make it worse. "Just like Serat would."

"The fact you're still talking," Alma attests, "proves I'm nothing like Serat."

Well, she's not wrong there. "You're full of it," I say anyway.

"You think I don't know what I've done?" she snaps. "You think I don't realise how much danger I've put this borough in?"

"Oh, I think you know *now*," I reply, hot-headed. "But I also think you had your head up your arse when you went into that council and made all those demands! And only *now* do you realise how bloody stupid that was! I knew I should have come with you!"

"You're not the new lord, Caiden!" Alma reminds me, standing her ground. "The other lords wouldn't have let you stay. And besides, be honest with yourself, what the hell do you know anyway?"

"I know not to piss off every other lord in the city, Alma! By the gods, it was only supposed to be a meet-and-greet! All you had to do was shake their hands, play the part, and leave!"

"But I want things to change, Caiden!" she shouts. "Or are you only interested on being on top?"

"Of course, change is what we're all working towards." I don't believe that at all. "But acting so rashly isn't going to change anything! If anything, what you've done has only given them an excuse to squash us all. Because the last thing those bastard lords want is change!"

"So how else are we going to make this place better, hm?" Alma challenges me. "Go on. Spit it out. What's your big plan to save this place?"

Hm. Big plan? I've got nothing, so I guess I'll have to wing it. "We need time, Alma. Time to let things settle down. Time to introduce new ideas, slowly, over… time. You know, time to—"

"Bullshit."

"It's the only way," I insist.

"To change the system, you'd have us become a part of it?" Well, when she says it like that, it doesn't sound half as convincing as it did in my head. "Can't you hear how crazy that is?"

"We wouldn't be like them, Alma—"

"—we wouldn't have to be," she tells me. "We'd always need more time. There'd always be another compromise." She turns and heads back to her unicorn. "That's the system. That's how it works. No one ever said it was fair."

"Fair?" I actually laugh. I didn't mean to laugh but it came out of me unbidden. "I've spent years in this city and have nothing to show for it. That doesn't sound fair to me. You've been here a little over a year, and now—*somehow*—you're the one with all the power. You're the one actually making decisions for all of us. That isn't fair. And finally—*somehow*—you survived drinking another vampire's blood, Serat's blood no less, and yet Helisha tried it before you and she's still a petrified corpse. That really isn't fair either!"

"Helisha? You suddenly care about someone else, do you?"

"I don't," I say, far too quickly.

Alma eyes me a moment, then shrugs. "Honestly, I don't know why I survived," she tells me, pulling herself atop her unicorn. "And I don't know how Serat could do it either, but the other lords didn't mention anything about being touched."

"Then Serat really was telling lies."

"Apparently so."

"What about Helisha though?" I ask. "Why hasn't she come back from it, like you did?"

"I told you, I don't know, but…"

"But what?"

"Well, it sounds stupid, but… maybe she's not… strong enough."

"And you are?"

"Maybe." Alma sighs. She then gives her unicorn a little nudge and starts heading further into the borough. I follow along. There's an awkwardness between us. A few minutes ago, we were practically at each other's throats. Now, we're heading in the same direction.

"What will they come at us with?" I ask her, more to break the silence than me actually wanting to know. I really don't want to know at all.

"Everything."

"Why aren't they here now then?"

Alma replies by gesturing her blood-drenched self. "I think I slowed them down," she elaborates.

"I see." But then I add, in a dry-as-you-like tone, "So, you can finish them off when they get here. Can you be our knight in shining armour, Alma? Our chosen hero? Our saviour?"

"Don't mock me."

"Don't be humble," I counter. "If anyone can do it, it's you—apparently."

"Maybe we can beat them, when they eventually come," Alma says. "But not if I'm the only one fighting them. I barely got away as it is…"

I let the silence hang in the void between us for a shade too long. Long enough for doubt to creep in, which is why I spot Alma glancing at me nervously.

"I'll be there," I reassure her. "We all will." And the magnitude of this hits me. The reality of what is coming feels all too real. We're gearing up for a siege, we're impossibly outmatched, and the crux of it all is no one wanted it to be like this. "You haven't given us any other choice," I add bitterly, and as true as that is, I really didn't need to say it out loud. I can be such an arsehole sometimes.

***

They're getting ready upstairs. And by upstairs, I mean the ground floor, which puts me here, in the basement. The dark, damp, dingy, dank basement. I quite like it actually. I'm lying on the cold floor, surrounded by pipes that have long since rusted and machinery long since inactive, and I'm completely in the dark save for a thin beam of light breaking in through a small window at the top. And I'm lying beside Helisha. This is where we keep her.

Upstairs, I can hear them moving chairs, shifting desks, and organizing space for everyone in the borough to gather in the assembly hall. Shortly, I'll have to go up and join this gathering where I'll have to pretend mostly everyone in the hall isn't about to die a horrible and painful death.

This whole place used to be a school for all the kids who grew up in the local area. It would have been a short walk from their family homes, back when this city was still populated by humans. Now, though, we don't need schools. After all, the last thing the humans would want is a city-sized breeding pen, so it's snip-snip for everyone before their one-way ticket to Vampire City.

Bloody useless things, anyway. The only worthwhile schooling I ever got was which end of the sheep the food went in and which end the lambs came out, and I turned out alright. It was a simpler time, I suppose. Even so, poor little Patrick, son of the village idiot, still managed to muck it up. Gave us all a good laugh he did, and only later did we feel sorry for the sheep.

I turn on my side to look at her.

She's been this way ever since she tried to drink Serat's blood. I guess the bastard was at least partly right about this whole *vampires-drinking-vampires* thing. Evidently, it's something only the lords can get away with doing… and Alma, inexplicably. And no matter how many times I try to beat it out of him, Serat maintains there's nothing to be done for Helisha. I won't stop trying, of course, no matter how sore my knuckles get, but deep down I know Serat's right. Looking at her now, I can see it in her eyes.

She looks almost alive. Her skin has returned, her eyes are full, and her black hair is as shiny as it's always been. But she doesn't have the pretty silver sparkles which she used to paint onto her face, and I haven't put her hair up in buns the way she likes it. Her skin has returned, but it looks dry and uncared for, and her eyes might be full, but they stare blankly upwards into nothingness.

We wrapped her up in a thick cloth, more to help with carrying her than for any actual modesty. When you've been around as long as we vampires have, there's not much left that'll make us blush with embarrassment. The cloth is dusty, even though I bat at it once or twice a week, and it lays over her like sand dunes on a desert plain. To a layman seeing her like this, Helisha looks dead. To us in the know, she may as well be.

"You look nice," I tell her, keeping my voice as soft as possible, not wanting to disrupt the heavy silence of this cramped underground basement. "It's all about to kick off upstairs."

No reply, no response, not even a reaction. I wasn't expecting one, but still… it would have been nice. I sigh deeply, spend a few moments contemplating all possible ramifications of never ever getting up again, then I sigh again, and finally I get up.

****

The assembly hall is a large, cavernous room trying to be as boring as it can possibly be. Grey walls, square windows, a hard floor, and a slightly raised stage at one end are the only features of a giant brick-shaped room that once would have contained hundreds of bright young children eager to learn (or, if not eager, at least reluctantly present).

With smaller chairs in the inner circle, all the normal chairs behind them, and finally open spaces by the walls for those too big for a cushion, the whole setup puts me in mind of a senate hall from ancient times. Everyone will be facing inwards, no one will sit at the head of some non-existent table, no one will be seated higher than anyone else, and there are a good few hundred chairs waiting to be sat on. Admittedly, there are probably a couple thousand in Duke's Borough alone, but a few hundred similar-sized chairs is still a lot better than one solitary big chair with Serat's bum on it. As I come in, the hall is already nearly full.

It looks like close to half the borough has turned up for this emergency meeting. I have had to shove, squeeze, and barge my way through a crowd that extends out of the assembly hall and over the grounds outside. But I'm inside the hall now, perched on top of a radiator in one of the corners, watching over everyone and everything.

So, this is how the end begins. Well, I had always wondered…

Trolls and tree people surround the outside of the gathering, some of them a little hunched and others sitting more than a little uncomfortably. In front of these, I can see orcs, looking grumpy and mean in leather jackets and heavy boots, while elves act as marshals making sure everyone is seated and behaving peaceably (Amirah's instruction, no doubt).

There are a couple of dryads sitting together, some drakes as well, and a little further in there are dwarves keeping remarkably calm and patient (for dwarves, anyway, so they're still shouting and growling and some of them are drinking).

Twinkling lights that can only be pixies flit about above us all whilst goblins are seated nervously together, bunched up and eyeing everyone else with suspicion and fear. In front of them, there are excited gnomes and a dense, humanoid-shaped wind that can only be a sylph—an air spirit. I keep scanning the crowd and this time I spot a selkie, who looks a little lost without her fish stall on the market, and, from outside, a giant peering in through a window. It feels like the entire borough has come to this hall, bringing all the noise and confusion with it, though there must be several hundred more who can't fit inside and must instead settle for waiting outside.

There aren't any vampires here, though. Despite them now being Alma's vampires and no longer Serat's cronies, none have turned up to this meeting.

I almost don't see her at all—the banshee who stares at me. She's not a she, though. *It's* not a she! I have to remind myself of that. Banshees aren't like us. They're omens, dark and foreboding omens. As their legend goes, they appear because something bad is probably going to happen.

Well, this one wasted its time. No need for an omen when contemplating what we're up against. Maybe this banshee is here because this borough is as much its home as it is anyone else's. It's in the opposite corner to me, sitting atop a high shelf, and of course it is staring at me.

Those white eyes fix on me, unblinking, though its emaciated expression is one of blankness. Its large grey hoodie can't hide how its thin and frail body must cling to the shelf. Even so, it neither trembles nor wavers, reminding me of how insects can cling to a wall and remain perfectly still.

What is it about this banshee that dogs me? That hounds me throughout my time in this city? Perhaps I should face it. Right now, in this hall, I should push my way over and put an end to this creature's haunting obsession with me. Every time something happens—from the very beginning, through the fire and darkness, and now here—this banshee fixates on me. I should fix it now. Fix it so that this banshee never looks at me ever again.

Before my temper can completely unravel, Amirah comes forward into the centre of the hall and calls politely for quiet. Naturally, no one hears her, and everyone keeps talking, shouting, arguing, drinking, and shoving.

Alma sits close to Amirah. Having cleaned off the dark blood of our kin, she once again looks like a teenage girl. She wears a small workman's jacket, which is far too big for her; baggy cargo trousers; dirty trainers; and she's found her favourite T-shirt with the face of a cartoon cat on it, something she kept safe all this time. She looks every bit the castaway refugee.

Next to her, standing and struggling to be heard, Amirah looks every bit the beleaguered leader, wearing a long grey coat, smart trousers, and what looks like a battle axe holstered on her back. Just in case you're wondering, I'm still wearing the same black coat, grubby jeans, and shirt I usually wear on any given day.

"Oi!" I shout, loudly and angrily. It has to be loud enough so everyone can hear me, and it also has to be angry, which is always a good way to get the attention of frightened and confused people.

The hall falls silent, and I pass the floor to Amirah.

"Thank you," Amirah sighs. "Now, I'm sure you're all wondering why I've called this meeting—"

"Where's the borough's vampire?" someone calls out.

"Should we be in the tunnels?" another whines.

"Why are we listening to an elf, anyway?" This is a dwarf. Of course it's a dwarf. Despite all evidence to the contrary, as in Amirah filling the role of de facto leader for the past year, a dwarf will always argue against an elf.

"Shut up!"

"What are we doing here?"

"You shut up!"

"Get off me!"

"This is a waste of time!"

"Oi!" I was about to say, but Amirah beat me to it. Quick on the uptake, she is. And then she adds, meaningfully, "Thank you."

With everyone's raptured attention on her, Amirah takes the lead and speaks with a calm clarity. "You're all here because you have to hear what we've got to say. But first, before that, I'm going to tell you… to be ready. Just that. Be ready. What you're about to hear, and what we are all about to go through, is going to be difficult. Difficult and scary. So I'm letting you know now, the best way to deal with what's coming is to remain calm, to stay strong together, and to not panic. Okay? Okay. Alma?"

Amirah steps back and takes her seat as Alma stands up and comes forward. All eyes are on this young teenager. For a moment, I fear she's going to wilt and back down, but then she takes a deep breath and speaks loud enough for all to hear.

"I stood up for you," she tells us all. "I wanted more for you, for this borough, for us all… and I wanted to search for a way out, for me, for you, for anyone who wants it…"

"And?" a rather hopeful, but quite simple goblin asks, breaking the silence.

"Well…" Alma wavers a little, dropping her head, but after a moment she looks up and speaks clearly again. "…the vampire lords of the other boroughs in this city… well, they didn't agree."

"Ah well," a tree person sighs, its creaking voice reverberating through my very bones. "At least you tried." The oversized plant actually smiles, and I'm shocked to see a number of others smiling genially. How do they not get it? Why can't they see what's really happening? And how the hell can a tree person, of all creatures, not see the wood for the trees here?

"Yes, well," Alma says, holding her hands up as if half warning and half surrendering, "it's not quite that simple. You see, they took a… a more hostile response to my requests… in that… they are now… well… hostile… to us."

"What are yer sayin?" a dwarf barks brusquely, though I detect a few underlying nerves as well.

Amirah stands alongside Alma. "We are about to be attacked," the silver-haired elf says.

There are frightened whispers and gasps too, which all amounts to the tension in the hall going from nervous curiosity to butt-clenching fear.

"By whom, exactly?" the potion-selling, earth-like dryad enquires.

"Everyone," Amirah admits. "All the vampire lords, and everyone they command from their own boroughs. They want to destroy us. More to the point, they want to destroy what Alma tried to do. We pushed for a new way of doing things… so now the old way is pushing back."

Silence. Deep and terrified silence. The banshee is gone, but other than that, everyone has been stunned into inaction. Bizarrely, I find myself thrilled. I watch them all and I am fascinated by their more intimate reactions. The goblins look terrified and unstable, the dwarves look shell-shocked, while the orcs look overly-pumped and eager to fight. The elves listen carefully, the pixies group together, and the tree person looks like a tree. I don't think any of the trolls are keeping up with what's being said though, because they're just watching it all play out with their usual dumb faces. People-watching really can be quite thrilling, can't it?

Finally, the silence is broken, and it is broken by a timid-looking gnome. "Maybe they won't attack if we apologize first?"

I groan. It's the denial that astounds me.

Amirah smiles patiently, ready to respond in a calm and concise manner, explaining how apologizing is not only futile, but also ridiculous and embarrassing and probably just as damaging in the long term anyway. She would have said all of that, and it would have likely as not gone in one little gnomish ear and out the other (fear is nothing if not a set of blinkers on a horse), but Amirah doesn't get her chance to speak, because Alma steps forward.

"Apologize?" Her voice is low but also resounding and composed yet also teetering on the brink of madness. "Apologize for what? For finding ourselves on the dirty side of a city? Or for not being able to turn a blind eye? Why the hell should we apologize?"

"Because, young missy," one of the older dwarfs remarks, rather belligerently, "if ye haven't already noticed, *we're* the ones under *their* thumb, and they're about to press down."

"We are under them," Alma accepts, responding with her eyes hard and her voice harder. "But all that tells me is that when I push back, I'll have to push upwards. Not sideways and not at each other… and not down, on any who have even less… but up, always up, and the harder they push down, the harder I'll push up. It's that simple. I will not break, and because I will not break none of you will break either, and because we are unbreakable there is no limit to how hard we're going to push back!"

Actually, that was a pretty good speech.

✳✳✳

This is such a stupid room.

Even now, after all these years, I can still see the faded posters talking about discipline, good behaviour, and respect. There's a big whiteboard at the front with thin black lines cutting across it. Lines waiting to be written on, only for the written lines to be rubbed out to be ready for more lines, and so the never-ending punishment cycle continues.

This is the detention room. Not far away, the buzzing activity of the hall has spread outside, and also close by is the school's basement, where Helisha lies cold and alone and as good as dead. But here, in this room that stands alone on little raised foundations, a building of one room, is where I have come. I come here often.

This is where I keep Serat.

Alma relented and let me take him. I think she understands the hatred and the need for revenge I feel, because I think she feels it too, or at least she once did. Now, though, Alma's got bigger fish to fry. But I don't. What I do have is what I've always wanted. A weak and defeated Serat completely at my mercy. This is my endgame. This is my reward. This is what I've been working towards.

I wish it wasn't so underwhelming.

"How is he?" Alma comes forward. I was so preoccupied with my own thoughts I didn't even sense her come inside.

Serat is fine, relatively speaking. Actually, he's sulking. He looks a bit worse for wear, but his bruises and wounds have healed up as they would on any lowly vampire, and so now he's sulking, sitting in the corner, staring at the small desk in front of him… just sulking.

Alma joins me sitting on the big desk at the front of the room.

"Look at him," I tell her. "So pathetic."

"What did you expect?"

"For him to scream, curse my name, decry my superiority. You know, the standard revenge-is-a-dish-best-served-cold deal."

"And how's that supposed to make you feel?"

I let out a deprecating sigh. "Alma, I know all teenagers think they know everything and understand the world better than anyone, but don't try that mumbo-jumbo feely-crap on a two-hundred-year-old soulless abomination, okay."

"Caiden…"

"I thought I would feel better. Okay?"

We sit side by side on the big desk in silence for a while. Serat keeps on sulking, I feel lost, and Alma is waiting to say what she has come here to say. I can feel it. Something's on her mind and for some reason she's come to me with it.

"I miss my mum," she finally says. I inwardly groan. Why the hell is she coming to me with this?

"I'm… sure she misses you too," I say, cringing at how lame I sound.

"I'm going to get back to her," Alma says. "One day, I'll see her again."

"Maybe," I say, knowing full well there's no escaping Vampire City, and then I foolishly try to lighten the mood. "I wonder what your mum will make of having a vampire for a daughter."

"I'm *not* a vampire."

"Oh, yeah." I stumble over my words. "Sorry?" For some reason, it sounds like a question.

Alma shakes her head. "I know you think I'm crazy."

"Maybe misguided, a little lost, but not—"

"I know what I am." Alma cuts me off. "I'm Alma, a girl, a normal girl, and just because I don't look like that to you doesn't make it any less true."

"But you have fangs."

"So do you," she says. "But they didn't make you act like him." And she looks at Serat, who is refusing to look up at either of us. She's right. I'm not like the others. I'm different.

"What do you want from me, Alma?" I sigh. "I don't understand what you're feeling."

"But you, of all people—the black sheep of Duke's Borough!—can still believe me."

Can I? I honestly don't know what is happening to Alma. I've encountered vampires who have enjoyed being vampires, who have resented being vampires, who have been afraid of their own shadows, and vampires who have gone and lost their minds. But I've never come across a rational vampire that still believed they are not what they so evidently are.

But she's right. I can believe her. She's a black sheep, just like me, only she's found herself in a different field.

"I believe you," I hear myself saying. "I believe you are what you say you are, and what you feel you are."

"Thank you." Alma gives me a friendly little nudge. "You'll fight, then?"

Ooh. I feel my butt clench a little and my gut turn a little more.

"To change this city?" I groan. "To unseat abusive lords? To save the poor? To build a better future? Come on, Alma, that's fairy tale shit."

"You know it's the right thing to do."

"I know it's pointless."

"Then if you won't fight for what you know is right," Alma says as she stands up and faces me, "then you can fight instead for who you believe in."

She's pulled it around on me. Clever girl.

"Or stay here with him," she continues, "and hope one day you'll start feeling better."

For a non-existent heartbeat, there is a gaping chasm in front of me. And then I blink and there's Alma, sitting next to me again and waiting for my answer.

"Fine," I say, surprising myself. "I'll follow you—although I'm not sure how useful my contribution will be."

She sighs. I like to think with relief, but it sounded a little too sombre, and then she follows this sombreness up with, "It should be Amirah you're following, shouldn't it?"

"Amirah?"

"Back in the hall, and in the tunnels, she was so… good at leading," Alma says. I rather think it is this that was really on her mind. "I can't be like her," Alma continues.

"She is a good leader," I agree, "but Amirah's an elf. She can lead a horse to water, caring for it all the while, but she can't break the fence that keeps it penned in."

"And I can?"

"You literally blew the fence up, Alma." I feel myself smiling this time, "What Amirah does so well actually comes later, and the rest of us will always follow, but right now we need something else. We don't need a leader right now. We need someone to break our fences."

***

"She's powerful," I say. "I'm not sure she knows how to use it, but she's definitely very powerful. It's a shame Amirah doesn't have any power, really." I continue to talk in the darkness, sounding quite lazy as I prattle on. "I think she'd know what to do with it. Elves are good at knowing what to do. Hm. Maybe not. Actually, I think Amirah would know what she *should* do with it, but I don't think that's enough. Not in this city. Not right now. Alma will do what she *can* with it. Do you follow me? Do you understand the difference?"

No response. But I wasn't expecting any. It's enough that she's here with me, though, even if she's not hearing a word I say.

"I'm not sure what I should do though." I carry on. It's easy to talk with her in this place. Maybe it's got something to do with lying down or lying down on a stone floor that is hard and cold, or maybe, just maybe, it's because I'm not alone on this cold, hard basement floor. "I mean, I know I'm a vampire, so they can't kill me, and I know I've been here longer than Alma, so I know the city better, and I know everyone in the borough, mostly... kind of... enough of them, anyway. But what can I actually do?" I think a moment. "Whatever happens, it'll amount to a waste of time anyway. Nothing can stop them. We can stand against them, but we won't stay standing. They have all the power."

Helisha doesn't respond. She stares up into nothingness and I lie beside her, staring off into the distance too.

"Maybe I should stay here." I perk up. "With you."

Nothing. Not a dickybird.

"I wish it could have been like this before," I admit, even blushing a little. "I know I never showed any interest, and I know you were never interested either, but is that really so important? I liked you enough, and I think you didn't mind me... a long time ago anyway."

I look into Helisha's eyes, but all I see are two eyeballs, each with a black pupil and a green iris bordering it. Nothing else though. No movement behind the pupil and no glint to the green iris.

"Did I ever tell you about the milkmaid from my village?" I ask her, knowing full well I've never told anyone about the milkmaid. "It was back when I was human, obviously. I really liked her. She was the first time I wanted to be with someone, and not just for… well, you know what it is humans want. But I mean to properly be with her. For good."

I lie on my back, staring up at the dark ceiling above me. "Do the whole *happily ever after* thing with her. But I guess it was just hormones." I sigh, picking up a small, cracked stone from the floor and turning it over in my hand. "It probably was now I'm thinking about it. Still, isn't that how it starts? Your hormones click and that's it." I toss the stone above me, and it disappears into the dark of the room. "Bloody hell, I should have said something…"

The stone falls back to earth, and I catch it. "Like hello, that would have been a good place to start." I throw the stone up again and hear the tap as it touches the ceiling. "But I wasn't ready." Quickly catching the stone again, I send it straight back up. "So even if I had pushed myself into it, it would have ended badly. Right?" The stone knocks against the ceiling. "I wasn't ready for any of that stuff. It would have blown up in our faces straight away, or died a slow death, dragging us both down with it." I whip the stone back up into the darkness and hear it crack against the ceiling. "Doesn't stop me thinking about her, though," I huff, brushing little stones off my chest, barely aware of Helisha's vacant body lying next to mine.

And then it's like the dam has burst and something inside me suddenly needs to throw itself up. I'm finally saying out loud what I've been keeping silent all these years. But it's okay, because no one can hear me down here. No one that matters anyway.

"You know what really hurts? The possibility, however slim, that it might have actually worked. Maybe it could have been something really great. Something that would have lasted… Dammit, I wish I could remember her name. Well, it wasn't her name I was looking at." I can't help sniggering.

"I mean, she was pretty, of course," I continue, a little abashed. "But no more than most girls. There was just something about her. She was different, you know. I really should have gone for it, shouldn't I? But I was young. No. I was scared. And I know everyone's scared when they fall for someone, but I was also a coward. Still am, I suppose. Why else would I be down here with you? Yeah, I should have gone for it." I keep talking, and I don't think I could stop even if I wanted to. "It could have been the best thing ever. Something worth going for, even if it all went to hell in the end… I guess it was the best thing I never did… and you know what the funny thing is—it all went to hell anyway."

And just like that, I'm done. No more.

I don't want this anymore.

So here I go again on my own, as quickly as that, pulling up my sleeve and taking a bite, to feel something… something else… something that isn't real…something that isn't this.

So this is what it feels like to completely give up. I had always wondered… This would be a good time to start all over again.

The timing is as good as it'll ever be, the night is calling for it, and if I can just remember how to speak, I reckon I've as good a chance as any other boy here. The tavern is full of music and folk are dancing. The music may be a combination of barely rhythmic banging and frantic blowing, and the dancing is more like hopping with enthusiasm, but if this works then the night will be perfect.

She's here and if I can talk to her, I can tell her that, for some reason, I want to spend the rest of my life with her, that I want to wake up every morning with her next to me and that I want to give her everything she could ever need or want. I want to be the one she feels closest to. I want to spend my life with her, and I want to die an old man, having already held her close as she went first, because I don't ever want her to feel alone. She'll never be alone. I'll always be with her.

Maybe that's a bit much. I should start with hello first and then ask her what she likes to do for fun. All the other stuff can come later. But… but… but… whoever it was that said sorry is the hardest word clearly never had to say the first hello to the love of their life. There's always a but.

I wait a while, hanging near the back, and then a while becomes a little while longer. The tavern is loud and boisterous. It's the end of the harvesting season and this is when we can blow off steam, where we're supposed to relax and enjoy life. I'm doing none of those things, of course, and that's why no one notices me back here. Whilst everyone else laughs and drinks and plays games and drinks and flirts outrageously and drinks some more, I am stuck between trying and running.

She's over there, in the midst of it all, and she fits in so well. I would be the intruder. I'm the one who doesn't fit. It takes me a long time to do it. Almost the whole evening, in fact. But, finally, I do it. I walk out and leave. I was never going to talk to her. It was never in me. I'm just not that person. I guess I'll be alone forever, working on a farm, shearing the occasional sheep, growing old, and waiting to die.

The problem with starting over is you end up right where you started.

Out of the tavern and walking back home, there isn't a cloud in the night sky and so a blanket of stars is twinkling above me, carefree and pretty. And because everyone else in the village is currently in the village tavern, I decide these stars are twinkling only for me. A small consolation for my resigned mood.

It's oddly serene as I walk back to my family's farm. This is probably because I've spent the last few hours in a very small place with a lot of people trying to be as loud as they possibly can, but even so, the village feels peaceful tonight. I think I'll take the long way home.

It's almost pitch black out here. The trees hang over and block out the starlight, but I pay that no mind. I've walked this way all my life. I could do it blindfolded and it's so dark I might as well be. It's quiet too. But for the distant music and muffled laughter, it would be completely silent.

Maybe something will happen. Fate might yet bring us together. Chance could still entwine our lives. Maybe all we need is a bit of luck, and seeing as luck is a fool's game and the good Lord knows there's no greater fool than I… maybe…

I don't see the red eyes in the night until it's far too late. A beast? A wolf? Some ungodly creature? I don't suspect any of these. I just freeze. Just as I did earlier in the tavern, just as I have always done throughout my nineteen years on God's earth. I freeze. I panic. I think *Oh no!* and then it's happening, and the rest of my life is over and my new existence on this rock of a planet begins.

***

"You're even more pathetic than I imagined."

No one likes to wake up to that, least of all me. And yet I wake up from the most depressing dream (or, rather, the most depressing memory) feeling like I've been put through a mill, and this is what I hear. Munstone sits above me, perched on the stone steps leading up and out of the basement. His smart hair, plain face, and buttoned-up shirt look completely out of place in this dank basement.

"Oh, piss off," I respond, rather lamely I admit.

"Nothing I would rather do, Caiden, I can assure you of that." The distaste in his voice is clear, but why he's here is not. "Our oh-so-wise and oh-so-supreme leader sent me to find you," he informs me. "She wants to talk to us all… together… right now."

"Us?"

"All her vampires, Caiden," Munstone sighs, exasperated. "You're still a vampire, even if you don't like the rest of us."

"Oh. That is true." I push myself up, rub my face, then eyeball the smug prick. "It's true… I don't like any of you."

"We must attend," Munstone insists, although doggedly. He doesn't want to be here any more than I want him to be here. It's a chore, an errand, an assigned task, and he's doing it because that's what a vampire does when given a job by their head vampire.

"Or what?" I childishly retort.

"I couldn't possibly say, but Serat had his ways of keeping us in line." Munstone sounds ominous, even a little shaken himself. "It never ended well."

"No," I agree, moodily. "It didn't."

"What are you doing down *here* anyway?" he asks me, and I don't know whether it's intended or if it's simply the way his voice is, but he sounds so much like a smug, self-righteous, holier-than-thou bastard I almost whip round and charge at him. I don't. Instead, I pull my coat on and try to ruffle all the dust out of my hair.

"Nothing," I tell him. "And keeping Helisha company."

"Ah, yes." Munstone eyes Helisha with a curiosity-tinged antipathy. "Her."

"I thought you two were mates."

He shrugs. "We hung out together sometimes. I didn't much care for her though."

"You don't care about anything, do you?" I stand at the bottom of the stairs looking up at him. "You really are just a boot-licking arsehole, aren't you? That's all there is to you."

"Maybe," he says, icily. "But out of the three of us, I'd say I'm the one who has come out on top. After all, I'm not a rancid, piss-poor excuse of a vampire like you, and nor am I a dead weight, put away in some old basement to rot."

✳✳✳

We're meeting in a graveyard, which feels a bit cliché, but in these unpredictable and unstable times, the clichés are rather welcoming. Indeed, they're almost comforting.

The other vampires, of which there are probably three dozen, are all dotted around the graveyard, and all have somehow taken up stylish and dramatic poses. Whether it be crouching atop a mausoleum, standing with one foot on a gravestone, or simply puffing out their chests and pouting, they are all undoubtedly so very good at being cool vampires. All black attire, sullen looks, and sunken faces. It's called vampire fashion.

What a bunch of arsehats.

Luckily, there are heavy rain clouds hanging in the sky and so we are protected from the worst of the unpleasant sunlight. The dying grass crunches under my worn-out trainers, and the dew seeps into my socks and dampens my toes.

"Finally," Alma sighs, rather dramatically. She was sitting with her back against a grave but now, upon Munstone's and my arrival, she gets to her feet and stands in the middle of her apathetic congregation. In her workman's jacket, baggy trousers, and cartoon cat T-shirt, Alma looks like a lost little girl surrounded by angsty ne'er-do-wells (albeit very professional, black-suited ne'er-do-wells). "Now that we're all here,' she says, shooting me a sideways accusing glance, "we can begin."

I stand amongst the other vampires, not doing anything dramatic or stylish or morose. I stand here plainly, happy in the knowledge that my being here, and indeed my very existence, is annoying the hell out of every last one of them.

"Eager to begin, Alma," I contribute, in a rather smug tone to really ramp up the annoyance levels. I even flash a *smug git* grin to any vampire who looks my way in derision. None of them like me, obviously, but I also note none of them are showing any fondness for Alma either. Could it be I'm not the one they're annoyed about?

"Thanks, Caiden," Alma continues. "Now shut the hell up." Well, that put an end to my *smug git* grin. "I know what you're all thinking—"

"I doubt that," Munstone interrupts, a dangerous hint of rebellion in his voice. The other vampires perk up a bit, curious to see where this goes.

"Okay." Alma takes a deep breath. "Let's deal with this first. You all hate me. Don't you?"

"Well, you did blow us up." One of the vampires speaks up, and not unfairly either.

"And now the other lords are coming," another angrily contributes. "And if you thought Serat was bad, then you're in for a rude awakening."

"The head vampires will make an example of us," someone else says, and this also is not untrue. "They're going to tear this borough down, including everything and everyone in it."

"At least they can't kill us. Right, guys? Guys?" a rather slow-brained vampires asks.

"This is going to be vampire against vampire," a particularly dramatic (and spectacularly foreboding) vampire warns. She's wearing a midnight-black dress that flows as smoothly as her long black hair. "There are worse things than death that await the likes of our kind."

"Yes, there are," Alma agrees and then she tightens her fists. "And one of them is spending the rest of eternity like this...because you're all losers!"

Huh. That stopped everyone in their tracks. Curse us, attack us, dominate us, decry us, or even just blackmail us, any and all are perfectly fine and even expected. But to belittle us? Now that hurts.

"You're nothing. You're nobodies!" Alma really twists the knife, and this fifteen-year-old fourteen-year-old is not at all phased by those who surround her, who are all bigger than her, and who are all far older than she. But this is what she does. Amirah is the one who leads but Alma is the one who can push.

"In this city, you toe the line," she continues, "hoping you'll never have to do anything real or anything that matters. You even pretend you all want to be the head vampire… but none of you really want it. No. What you actually want is a head vampire to tell you what to do, to keep the status quo, to make everything alright, and to take away any doubt or indecision. You are all so pathetic. You're sheep!" She's walking amongst us now, eyeing each of us in turn. "If you had any dignity, you'd have walked away… but you don't see it like that. You only see it as this is how things are, and nothing's going to change so, you know, ah well, it is what it is. You hate me? Well, guess what… I hate what you are even more."

"You've doomed us all!" Munstone yelps, angry but also nervous. Very nervous.

"*We're* vampires!" Alma cries out, a hint of a teardrop in her eye and an echo of a crack in her voice. "We were doomed the moment we were bitten. Now we either spend the rest of eternity stretching out our damnation, telling ourselves we don't mind some bastard drinking us every day and this is just how it is so there's no point in trying… or we can change this city. We can make it work for everyone—*including ourselves!* Because if you're honest with yourself, if you're really honest, you'll admit how much you all hate being vampires."

There's a heavy silence as Alma returns to standing in the middle of our group. I shift a little uncomfortably, but that's nothing compared to the rest of my kin. Some of them stare with such hatred at Alma, others shake their heads, and a few look on the edge of tears. And into this the vampire in the midnight dress with the long flowing hair steps forward.

"What would you know?" she says, her tone filled with contempt. "All the time you've been here, you've never even claimed to be one of us. The girl vampire who insists she is not a vampire."

"…I find myself one of your kind," Alma replies, resentfully. "But this is not who I really am."

"And what—pray tell—are you, then?" The vampire puts on a show of mocking Alma. "Are you a vampire only for today? Maybe tomorrow you are a pixie? Or a troll?"

There is some laughter and, because laughing is a far easier and safer thing to do than to question one's own identity and purpose, the laughter grows. "Let me tell you what you are," the vampire in the midnight dress continues, growing in confidence. "You are a silly girl who does not understand the world. You see, if we are to be honest, I mean completely honest, this city actually does work—*for us.* And no one else matters. The pixies and the trolls and the elves and the goblins are supposed to be the dregs, the slaves, and the fools. They are there to make the vampire's world work. And work it does. But you are not one of us, so… you are not welcome!"

Alma takes the vampire's head off with one swipe. It flies across the graveyard and bounces off a stone slab. The body in the midnight dress falls into a clumsy sprawl. The other vampires are frozen in shock, stuck between wanting to overpower Alma and wanting to keep their heads. In this little gap of hesitation, I sidle up to her.

"You know," I say quietly, "I think Amirah is better at this whole leading a community thing."

"I'm not here to lead!" Alma exclaims loudly. "I'm here to change this goddamned city! And you will all stand with me!" In response to this, the vampires—some of them scared, others furious, and all of them incredibly tense— attack Alma, because be you scared, furious, or tense, your first response when backed into a corner is to attack, attack, attack. And I'm stuck right in the middle of it all. Poor me.

***

They all attack at once and Alma, her blood up and ready for anything, somehow meets them all head on. There are more of them but she's stronger by far. A swing puts one into the ground. A sharp kick sends another flying up into the air, only to come crashing down on a spikey metal fence. A shove sends a few more careering into the wall of a mausoleum which is reduced to rubble on top of them. But still they come. They haven't any choice. It's started now and it can't end. They have to see this through and hope someone gets lucky.

I'm sandwiched between them, then trampled over and trodden on and pushed aside. Funnily enough, my first instinct is to protect Alma but, after I finally manage to scramble up and look at her, I can see I'd be no help at all. For starters, I can't get to her. The mass of vampires surrounding her, crowding her, and trying to smother her is beyond me. It's like a giant scrum or a huddle and Alma's the ball. Be that as it may, I rather think Alma is managing on her own just fine.

Her eyes are burning red. Her fangs are out. She looks more monster than teenager. And she's taking everything they throw at her and sending it back with interest. Punches, scratches, kicks, grapples, Alma takes it all and responds in kind.

"Prick!"

I turn at the last moment to see a fist land squarely in my face. It sends me toppling backwards and I land awkwardly on the ground. Standing over me is Munstone, his face torn between desperation and anger. He must really hate me.

"What the hell are you doing?" I growl.

"This is all your fault!" he spits at me. "Why couldn't you just fit in?"

He's on top of me now, throwing punches but landing only a few of them. He's too angry, too emotional, and far too clumsy. I twist under him, push him off, then get to my feet.

"Piss off, Munstone," I say, dismissively.

"No!" he cries out, sounding more child than vampire.

He tackles me to the ground and for a short while we're tangled with each other. I punch him and he punches me. I push him and he holds me. And then he bites me. The bastard bites me. But he hasn't got the power Serat had. He's as weak as I am, but now I'm incensed at his attempt to control me, to lord himself over me, and to violate me in this way.

I surprise myself by literally tearing his face off. It's not pretty and it's not easy. Munstone does a lot of a screaming, as one would expect; I also do a lot of screaming, but of a different kind to Munstone's. I then pound what's left of his skull into mush. Screaming all the while, of course.

I eventually collapse next to Munstone's corpse, barely keeping myself up with an outstretched hand on the grass. He'll come back. They all will. But it'll be a long while before they do, so now it is quiet.

As I look around, I see dismembered bodies, twitching limbs, blood splatters, and, on the ground, a network of dark blood rivers trickling around gravestones, onto pavements, and pooling into almost black puddles. Alma's barely staying on her feet. She's covered once more in blood, although this time some of it is her own. It seems even a head vampire, with all the power that comes with such a position, is vulnerable if the attack is numerous enough. I don't quite know how she got away from the head vampires before, but if a few dozen lowly vampires brought her to near ruin, then eleven head vampires working together will make short work of her.

She stammers, dribbling a little, and then stumbles over her own feet. I should go to her, but I feel exhausted too, and it'll only be a moment or two anyway. We're vampires. We regenerate. Even now, I feel energy coming back to me, rejuvenating me and bringing me back from the dire state I put myself in.

Alma is taking a little longer, leaning against a tall statue of a broken angel. The angel's face is sad, and I have no idea why I pick this out, but I do. Alma groans painfully. She has wounds all over. Her coat is torn, her trousers ragged, and her T-shirt is so blood-stained the cartoon cat is hidden from view.

And here comes Serat. Weak, feeble, humbled Serat. A thin wreck of a vampire. And he's approaching Alma. She hasn't seen him. Her pain is too much for her to notice anything else.

So, Serat's hung back all this time, just waiting for the right moment. His hand is on her shoulder, his eyes are baleful and hungry, his fangs grow, and Alma realises far too late. She is at his mercy.

I should really do something about this, but I surprise myself when I realize I'm already running.

As Serat's fangs touch Alma's bare throat, I grab his slick black hair and yank him backwards. He falls away, crying pathetically as he goes.

"No…" He moans on the ground. "…no… please…"

I stand over him. He really is too pathetic. A merciful fate would be putting an end to him right now. But vampires don't get ends. So instead, and for the rest of time, Serat will have to settle for dreaded, unfulfilling mediocrity.

I kneel, open his jaw with one hand, and with my other I pull out his fangs. He struggles, he fights back, but Serat isn't used to fighting ugly or fighting desperate. He spent too long being the strongest boy in the gang and now he's forgotten what it takes to survive in one, if he ever knew to begin with.

His fangs will return, but they'll take a very long time to do so, and he'll never forget the humiliation, even if he does eventually forget the pain. And then I break his neck and pull his head off, just to keep him out of the way for the time being.

"Thank you," Alma stutters, her voice a cracked whisper.

"Don't mention it," I reply, putting on a half-hearted smile. "So… this all went terribly."

We stand together and look around at what surrounds us. Bloody vampire corpses torn limb-from-limb with smashed bones and their innards ripped asunder, thrown apart and torn into small pieces… It'll be a few days before they're back on their feet.

"I really screwed that up, didn't I?" It's the kind of question that leans very heavily towards wanting a positive and affirming answer.

"Yeah," I reply, not reading the cues. "But for what it's worth, you didn't stand a cat in hell's chance anyway."

"Thanks," Alma sighs.

"Honestly, would it have made any difference if they had joined you?"

"Us."

"Hm?"

"Joined us," Alma corrects me. "Would it have made any difference if they had joined us."

"Oh, right, yeah." I shrug. "Well, would it?"

"Probably not," she concedes.

"There are eleven head vampires, not including you…" I ponder ominously. "That's all the power of the city coming to squash our little borough flat." And then a thought occurs to me. "How did you get away?"

"Huh?"

"When you went to the council," I remind her, "you came back all bloody on your horse—"

"Unicorn."

"Fine," I say, exasperated. "You came back all bloody on your unicorn."

"Snowy."

"What?"

"That's her name."

"…Whose name?"

"My unicorn's!" Alma huffs, clearly her energy is finally starting to return. "My unicorn's name is Snowy."

"That…" I start incredulously. "…That great, big, terrifying—oh,   fine! YoucamebackallbloodyonyourunicorncalledSnowy. How? How did you escape eleven head vampires?"

"Only three of them turned up," Alma admits.

"Only… three of them?"

"And they weren't expecting it when I attacked."

"I see."

"Also, one of them had popped out for a quick break."

"Of course." I take a moment to breathe in deeply, and then I exhale like a foghorn spewing out a bunch of words. "And now eleven of the bastards are coming here, and they won't be surprised this time, and I doubt any of them will take a five-minute breather in the midst of crushing us all into fine powder!"

"Yeah," Alma sighs, not at all bothered by my outburst. She wipes the bloody remnants of her inherited vampire entourage from her face and then looks me dead in the eye. "Let's go find Amirah. We've work to do."

***

The borough is alive with activity. The kind of frenzied, panic-ridden, fast activity that presages an oncoming disaster. Shacks are being rebuilt into walls, rubble is piled high at intermittent points, and dwarves are fussing over tripwires and booby traps. The elves are directing everyone's efforts and Amirah is directing the elves. This is why she has little time for Alma and me, until we tell her what happened with our other vampires.

"You killed them all?" Amirah snaps, her eyes wide with incredulity. "They're all dead?!"

"Technically, vampires can't die," I remind her, and I'm rewarded with a scathingly impatient look.

"They're dead for now, but we had to kill them, Amirah," Alma insists.

"Why?" Amirah demands of us both.

"Because..." Alma starts and falters and trails off a bit before finishing lamely with, "well... they wouldn't do what I was telling them to."

"And they attacked first," I offer, trying to help but only adding to the weakness of our reasoning.

"You vampires!" Amirah breathes out, angrily. "You'll fight each other to the death a hundred times over before you realise it's not you getting killed. You're the only ones who get to come back!"

"Well, technically, we never actually die in the first place so—" I start explaining again, but then I see the way Amirah is looking at me again and I decide to stop explaining.

"You've still got us two, Amirah," Alma says.

"No," Amirah replies.

"Wait." I hesitate, stumbling a little over my speech. "You're not… kicking us out, are you? Can you do that? Can she do that?"

"There are three of you left," Amirah tells us.

"We're the only ones who walked out of that graveyard," I say.

"I know, but there's one vampire who didn't attend." Amirah eyes me. "Your new girlfriend."

"My… my new girlfriend?" And now I really do stumble over my words. "I haven't got a… oh… oh, I see… You're talking about Helisha, right?"

"I am. Problem?"

"Well, only that she's a vegetable."

"Amirah," Alma butts in. "I don't think Helisha is coming back."

"You came back," Amirah says. "So, look for a way to bring Helisha back. It's the least you can do."

"It's a waste of time," I complain.

"Caiden's right. We can do more here," Alma says, "like help with building the defences."

"We don't need either of you here! We're doing all that can be done here. Now you two need to do all that can be done to bring Helisha back."

"She'll be like the others," I whine. "She won't want to fight against the whole city just for our sakes."

"Maybe." Amirah nods. "But, then again, she might choose us. Whatever her choice, we owe her the chance to make it. Besides, we're going to need all the help we can get and last I checked, three vampires is better than two vampires."

I sigh, resigned to our task. "Your math checks out. Come on, Alma. Let's try to do the impossible… let's give my *girlfriend* a reason to care."

***

The basement is dark and cold. The old pipes are covered with the webs of long-dead spiders, and various forgotten machinery, all bulky and cumbersome, sits like ancient statues in an undiscovered tomb. Alma and I sit either side of Helisha, the tomb's occupant if you will, and we both shift nervously.

"Do you really think this will work?" Alma asks me, nerves creeping between her words.

"I don't think what I think really matters," I reply unhelpfully. "I just think we need to try it and whatever happens, well, we can take it from there. Sound good?"

"No, it doesn't sound good. It sounds like we have no idea what we're doing."

"We don't," I say. "But that's good, right? At least it proves we're trying something new, and if it goes bad then we don't do it again, and if it goes good, then we call it a win."

Alma nods, but I can see she's still very unsure about this. I understand her concerns. For someone who doesn't see herself as a vampire, she's about to do the most vampire thing ever. She's going to try and turn someone into a vampire. The unknown part? This particular someone is already a vampire. But whatever brought Alma back, whether it's something special or simply raw strength, maybe, just maybe, giving Helisha some of it will help bring her back too.

Alma lifts the tip of her pinkie to her fang and then with a faint pressure she pricks her finger. A tiny droplet of dark blood grows on her fingertip. It's a tiny morsel that no one could possibly miss. So what good could it possibly do? My doubts plague me, they harangue me, and yet I hold my breath in hope.

As Alma touches her finger to Helisha's dry mouth, the droplet of dark blood dribbles from tip to lip.

And nothing.

"Nothing," Alma sighs, dejected, letting out her own breath.

"Wait." I hold my breath. "Just… wait."

So, we wait. For a good few minutes. It feels like we're wasting our time. Or maybe not. Maybe it just needs a little more time. Who knows? I certainly don't. But the longer I sit here waiting, the more I want it to work. Pretty soon, it's more than just wanting it. I need this to work. It has to work. I can't quite bring myself to put it plainly, but I need Helisha to be more than this basement, more than lying here lifelessly, more than what she's become.

Helisha's chest starts to move. She's breathing! It's nothing more than a useless instinct from our old forgotten humanity, but right now it means everything. Helisha's coming back.

"Helisha? Helisha!" I lean over her, and Alma joins me.

"Are you okay?" Alma asks, urgently. "How do you feel?"

"Helisha!" I don't know whether to smile or panic, cry or laugh.

We never leave her side. Watching for any possible hint that she is, in fact, coming back. Was it all only false hope? A cruel reaction to Alma's blood that in the end signified nothing?

"Helisha," I plead to her blank eyes. "We need you. I need you." I surprise myself at how sincere I sound, and then I surprise myself again when I realize I sound sincere because I am sincere.

I suddenly feel desperate for Helisha to be back. I want her to be the way she was. I want her out of this basement, I want her fighting her battles, no matter how benign they may turn out to be, but more than anything I want her to be herself again, even if she ignores me, even if she hates me. I know, in my unbeating heart, that she shouldn't be here, in this basement, lying cold next to me.

"What more can we do, Caiden?" Alma asks me, but it doesn't sound like a question she's expecting any kind of answer to.

"I can stay," I reply, firm and decided. "I will stay. As long as it takes—"

Helisha's clenched fist shoots up and strikes me across my cheek. It hurts like hell and sends me up and away to land painfully in a sprawled heap some distance away. "Ow!" I angrily snap. "You bitch!"

Helisha sits up, gasping for air she doesn't need, but Alma's with her, holding her shoulders. "Are you okay? How are you feeling?"

"I feel fine," Helisha croaks, shaking Alma off. "I feel better than fine." She stands up and stretches, wobbling a little and looking rather like a newborn deer taking its first steps, but only for a moment.

I look up as I rub my sore cheek, and see Helisha standing over me, suddenly strong and proud, and I can't tell what she's thinking of me. Then she holds out her hand for me to take.

"Thank you, Caiden."

"For what?" I ask, dumbly.

"For giving up your time," she says, "with me."

I'm not exactly sure what she means by that. As I see it, there are two possible meanings. One is quite nice and simple and sweet, for all the time I spent accompanying her, but the other is rather tragic and lonely. I don't want to risk it turning out to be the latter, so I don't ask for clarification. Instead, I take her hand and let her pull me up to my feet.

"Did you really have to punch me though?"

"Yes. Yes, I did." And that's all I get.

***

We're sitting on the edge of a rooftop, dangling our legs over a rather dizzying drop, and passing the time watching the hustle and bustle below. Well, it's mostly bustle, what with all the defensive works and trap-laying, but there's more than a few goblins on those streets so there's bound to be a bit of hustle as well.

Helisha, Alma, and I left the basement and made our slow way up here. We walked streets with ramshackle blockades, we saw day-to-day tools and other common heavy things being fashioned into makeshift weapons, and we watched for a time as some taught others how to either hide or kill.

Up here, it's almost peaceful.

"You know we can't win this, right?" Helisha says, speaking plainly.

"We have to try."

"No, no." Helisha shakes her head, a little despondent maybe but still sounding relatively even keeled. "Don't give me that fairy tale bullshit."

"But we *can* try!" Alma insists.

"This isn't that," Helisha cuts her off. "There's no sword in a lake, no genius pulling a fix-it-all plan out of their arse, and no one's suddenly going to become super powerful and save us all in the last minute."

I find it very depressing how much Helisha sounds like me right now.

"I'm only saying it how it is," she finishes.

"If you want to leave," Alma says, "you can go. I won't stop you."

"If only it were that easy." Helisha shakes her head again. "No one can leave. There's a big *fuck you* wall around this city, remember? But I… well, I… I guess I don't want to go back to the way it was before."

I turn to her and for a moment Helisha and I share a look. It's a knowing look, a truthful look, a hurt look, and a resigned look. It's not a hate-to-say-I-told-you-so look, so I guess I must have matured at least a little bit.

"I'm staying," Helisha tells us both. "But I'm still going to say it how it is. We can't win this thing."

Alma doesn't respond, not even looking up, and yet I can't take my eyes off her. She looks so small and so much like a child, and then I remember she is a child. A fifteen-year-old fourteen-year-old who has brought the vengeful wrath of the metropolis down on our little corner of existence.

"Maybe it's not about winning," I hear myself saying. "Maybe that's not the point of all this."

"You're happy with losing?" Helisha asks in disbelief, but I'm looking at Alma and Alma is now looking at me.

"We've been losing in slow motion ever since we got here," I say. "At least this way, we get to lose for something that actually matters to us."

For a short while, none of us say anything more. We sit on the edge, watching the world below, and I use this time to try to comprehend what is about to happen. A lot of us are going to die, that much is apparent, but I get the unsettling feeling they will be the lucky ones. Whatever happens, this place will never be the same again.

✳✳✳

I can't believe I'm here again. In this squalid and rancid cesspit of a decrepit and dilapidated piss pot. I hate this place as much I hate this city and as much as I hate my life in this city. Still, got to hang your coat up somewhere. Home sweet home.

I have no idea what this room was in the before-times, back when humanity populated this city. Maybe it was a boring office in a building of boring offices, or maybe it was a tiny cheap flat in a building of cheap flats. But now it's just a square room. Abandoned and slowly falling apart like every other building in this forsaken metropolis. It's a squat building, square in shape and grey in colour, and there are others like me with their own square rooms here. Some goblins, a few nymphs, and a troll who sleeps in the basement.

I come here when even the rooftops feel too cold and when the streets become too much of a grind on my brain. This is a place that's supposed to be mine. I've claimed it. I even nailed a coat hook to the wall, upon which my tatty black coat hangs now. I still don't feel anything though.

"Nice place." Amirah is standing in the doorway.

"No, it isn't," I reply without inflection. I couldn't care less if this place blew up tomorrow, but even so I'm now embarrassed because Amirah has tracked me down and now knows what a poor excuse I have for a home (or the closest thing to a home anyway).

"Why are you here?" the curious silver-haired elf asks me. Her smart attire (the long grey coat and nice trousers) looks utterly out of place in this back-end hole.

"Weeell…" I drag out the word as I drop to all fours and search under a large cabinet. "Seeing as we're all getting put through the wringer soon, I figured now was as good a time as any… for this."

I sit up and show Amirah what I've recovered from the little hiding place under the big, dusty cabinet. It's a little glass bottle that fits snugly in the palm of my hand. From the look of it, anyone can tell that it's an old bottle. About two hundred years old, in fact, or rather that's how long it's been in my possession, and it's been corked shut for all that time.

"Is that blood?" Amirah asks me of the drops of red liquid inside my little glass bottle, her curiosity turning into something like morbid fascination.

"Not just any blood," I say, eyeing the little bottle with a combination of awe and fear. "Human blood," I tell the elf, and then I add quietly, "and not just any human blood." I stand up. "It's very old, but I've kept it fresh in this special little bottle."

"Special?"

"It's magic."

"Oh. But why keep it at all?"

"It's a keepsake, of sorts." I roll the bottle betwixt my fingers. "A curiosity I've often wondered about. A gift from a stranger, if you like."

"You're not making any sense."

I sigh. I'm actually glad Amirah has found me here. She's a wise head on calm shoulders, which makes her a welcome companion when you're teetering on the edge of a mental precipice. "Do you know what happens when a vampire drinks fresh human blood?" I ask her.

She shrugs. "They get a high?"

"Yes and no," I reply. "It's not quite as simple as that."

"Go on, then," she pushes me. "What happens when a vampire drinks human blood?"

"Not here," I say. "Not in this place."

We go up to the roof. It's a square roof because it's a square building, and because it's a boring building it's also a boring roof. But up here there's the expansive sky above us, some white clouds, and a cityscape (albeit an abandoned and ugly one) surrounding us. Up here, there is air to breathe and room to move.

"I'm cold," Amirah complains, "and it's very windy up here."

"I know." I smile. "It's nice, isn't it?"

She rolls her eyes, but I don't pay any attention. "Vampires don't need to drink blood to survive. Did you know that?"

"Yes!" she groans. "Everyone knows that. Everyone here, at least."

"So why the hell do we do it?" I laugh. "It's disgusting and inconvenient. Why bother at all?"

"It gives you energy, doesn't it?" Amirah follows me as I pace along the edge of the rooftop, though she stays safely away from the edge. "You drink someone's blood, and you take their lifeforce, or something like that."

"Yes and no."

"Stop saying that!" She reaches out and grabs my arm, pulling me back. "And tell me what you're going on about."

"This." I show her the little glass bottle again. The little glass bottle filled with a small mouthful of fresh, red blood. "This isn't just energy. It isn't only a high. It's so much more. It's everything. No. Actually, it's more than everything. It *is* someone."

"If you don't start making sense soon," Amirah scowls, eyeing me impatiently, "I'm going to push you off this roof."

"I can only tell you what it is, Amirah," I say to her. "I'm not sure you can fully understand though. It's… it's… it's literally taking someone. When I drink their blood, I am them."

"You become them?" she asks, dubiously.

"No. Not literally." I know I'm contradicting myself here, and stumbling terribly, but that's what happens when you try to explain something you've always taken for granted. "I feel them, I see everything inside of them, I experience what it is to be them, but I don't actually become them. It's like looking through their eyes," I continue, wistfully, "but only while I'm drinking their blood, and also it's not just their eyes."

I find myself back on the edge again, the tips of my worn-out trainers peeking over. "It's like I'm looking through them, deep down, and I know what they want, how they feel, and who they really are. It's like I am them but still me. It's intoxicating, it's mind-blowing, it's a thrill like nothing else."

"Is that what happened when Alma drank Serat?" Amirah asks.

"No, I don't think it's the same when a vampire drinks from a vampire. After all, the living dead are still, by definition, dead. But when we drink from a human… a living, breathing, heart-beating human… To be someone else, to feel what they feel, to understand the world how they understand the world, to want what they want and fear what they fear, even for the briefest of moments, is beyond anything I feel when I'm only me. Because vampires *are* dead things, Amirah. We're dead and when we drink blood, we feel alive, but only because it is someone else's life. That's why vampires drink blood," I finally finish, and breathe.

"You take what you can't create for yourself." Amirah speaks quietly, calmly, although I can tell she doesn't like what I've revealed to her.

"What else can we do?" I ask her, a tad hopeless.

"Even if you are left with nothing and no other option," Amirah responds, sternly, "that still doesn't justify doing something that makes you into a monster… into a killer."

"But I'm a vampire, Amirah," I sigh. "Vampires are the *original* monster. It's what we are. It's what we do."

"Alma's a vampire," Amirah counters. "But that's not what she is. It's not what she does. She chooses to be different."

"Alma is different," I pout.

"Alma's a kid," Amirah snaps.

"Then maybe we should put the kids in charge!" I whip round and glare at her. She looks so safe standing so far from the edge. I momentarily wonder what that's like, but I can't imagine standing anywhere other than where I'm standing now… above a concrete precipice.

Amirah sighs this time, and then she comes forward to sit by the edge of the rooftop near me, though she keeps herself away from the very edge. "Sit down," she says to me, making it sound like something between a request and an order. Whichever it really is, I find I don't care, because I'd quite like to sit down next to Amirah. So, I do.

"Whose blood is it, then?" Amirah asks me. I'm still holding the little glass bottle in my hand. I stare at it, and I am surprised by the sudden urge to drop it. To let it fall to the ground far below where it would smash into oblivion and its contents would be lost amongst the wild earth and tortured concrete of this city. But I would never do this. Never. Often forgotten, either kept in a pocket or left in a safe space, but always it has been here, even if unseen. I've always kept it with me over the years, like a lucky charm… or an unhealthy memento.

"Someone I once knew," I explain, "when I was human."

"Wow," Amirah says, a little breathlessly. Is she astonished? Impressed? Or does she find the whole thing rather strange? Even creepy? After all, I have been holding onto this little glass bottle for a very long time now. Perhaps too long. Even if I have gone decades without thinking about it, it has always been there.

"She was…" I begin, then I try again. "She could have been… might have been… someone I would have known. I guess it's… it's what I would have been, if I had fit in."

This is hard. Getting words like these out is hard. "The point is, if I drink this blood, for the few moments it takes me to actually consume it, I'll know her. I'll know what she thought, what she wanted… and who she wanted."

"A lost love, is it?" Amirah asks me, sounding a little distant.

"No," I reply, despondent. "Not on her part, anyway."

"And you have some of her blood?" There's a hint of a challenge in the elf's tone. Not unfairly, I suppose.

"It was a gift to me, actually," I say. "Alma's not the only one who's met a witch."

There's an awkward silence. I think Amirah's trying to be tactful, suddenly aware that I'm in too deep and I'm feeling things. Deep things (shudder). On the contrary though, I am waiting for her to tell me what to do. More precisely, I'm waiting for Amirah to tell me which of the two options before me is the right one. Drink or drop? As far as I am concerned, I have been thinking about this for far too long. It is the itch that I've carried on my back. The regret that won't fade away. Something about the path not trodden is the sweetest and most deadly.

"She was a milkmaid, in the village I grew up in," I begin. "If I could have had a future with her, if she could have felt the same way about me as I felt about her, that would be…" Well, this is awkward. I appear to be lost for words.

"Good?"

"Yes," I sigh drily. "It would feel good. But—"

"That would also mean you missed out on something wonderful."

"Yes," I sigh again, even drier this time. "Thank you, Amirah."

"Here to help," she says warmly, giving me a friendly little nudge.

"On the other hand," I continue, "if I drink this little mouthful of her blood only to learn she never once thought about me… and maybe she didn't even know me… I don't know if I want to know that. I think I'd rather live in ignorance."

Neither of us say anything. There's just us and a cold wind and a very high drop below us.

"Okay," Amirah says, slapping her knees. "Let's think about this. What would you gain from drinking that?"

But all I can do is resurrect the silence because I have no answer… then again, maybe that's exactly what I want from this. "An answer," I eventually reply. "Closure."

"Closure from what? This woman you loved?"

I shake my head, surprising myself. "It's not really about her." It isn't? After all this time spent yearning and moping! Sometimes I shock myself. "I mean, it is about her, but she's only one part of it. The point is it was all there. The girl, the village life, the future kids, and then the dying-of-old-age bit. It was all there for me to take. But I didn't. Instead, I ran away. And something else found me. A vampire found me. I hate what I am." This is the first time I've said it and not just felt it. "I hate who I am." And that's the second time.

Amirah takes the glass bottle from my hand and holds it up with her own fingers. She studies the blood inside, holding the bottle in front of her. For a few moments, the only thing keeping it from falling is the index and thumb of an elf, albeit an elf I realise I've grown to admire and respect. I trust her. She's a damn good leader.

"I don't think you're supposed to know," Amirah finally says, sounding sage and calm. "I don't think any of us are supposed to know such things. But I don't think you should let it go either. We should hold onto what might have been. If nothing else, it's a reminder of where you've come from and who you were."

She slips the little glass bottle into my inside coat pocket, where it rests snug and safe and where it is barely noticeable at all. As she leaves it there, her fingers come away and brush against my chest, taking a little longer than would be natural. Right where my heart would be, I think morosely.

I turn slowly, nervously, and our eyes meet. "What are you doing?" I ask her.

They really are beautiful eyes. Pearly white with black pupils, like all elves, but each elf's pupil is contained in a thin circle the colour of their hair. Amirah's circles are silver, and they twinkle, even gleam, as she meets my own eyes.

"Don't look too deeply into this," she tells me, her fingers still on my chest. "It's like you said though… we're about to go through the wringer." Her voice cracks a little, something I've never heard from her before. "And unlike you and Alma and Helisha, I won't be coming back if the worst should happen."

"Don't talk like that, Amirah. You'll be fine," I say without thinking. In the context of what has happened and what is surely about to happen, it's such a stupid thing to say.

"I don't need reassurance, Caiden," she insists, and she sounds like she almost believes it. "I've worked hard and I'm proud of what we're trying to do, so I wouldn't change anything—anything that I could change, at least. With all that said though…"

She trails off a little, faltering. Apparently lost for words. I guess it's my turn to help her out then.

"You're still shitting yourself?"

I'm rewarded with a genuine smile, so my crude attempt at light humour was worth it.

"Something like that," Amirah nods. Her fingers left my chest a little while ago and I find that I miss them. "You know, I never thanked you for saving me in the car park, when that Munstone creep caught me with a left hook."

"Oh, that. Well, it was nothing, really."

"You haven't asked me why I tracked you down here, to your little *nice place* that you claim isn't a nice place."

She's right. Not only have I not asked why Amirah appeared at my doorway unannounced a short while ago, but I also haven't thought about it one bit. I've been so wrapped up in myself, in my little glass bottle, it never occurred to me Amirah might have a reason of her own for coming to find me.

"Oh, sorry." I stumble a bit. "Erm, why are you here?"

Amirah brushes her fingers against my cheek and I'm suddenly very aware of how close we are, sitting next to each other on the edge of this roof. Her face is close to my face, a gentle breeze moves through her hair, her eyes are close to my eyes, and now I can feel her lips close to mine.

"Like I said, don't look into this," she warns. "I think, sometimes, it's okay to be with someone, if only for the comfort of being with someone."

"I'm someone?" I ask, sounding like a frightened schoolboy (and in some ways, I suppose that's exactly what I am).

"You don't need me, not like everyone else does," Amirah whispers, "and I don't need you."

I'm not sure where she's going with this, but I definitely feel my non-existent heartbeat *not* drumming harder than a drummer boy on a sugar rush.

"For a little while, I don't want to be needed, Caiden." There's that cracking voice again.

"I don't need you at all," I say, breathlessly, almost tasting her lips. Then it happens.

It's nice. A bit simple perhaps. But nice. And I don't think about her blood at all. Well, now I'm thinking about it a little bit, but give me a break, I'm still a cold-blooded vampire after all.

***

We don't do anything. For one thing, it's impossible for anything to be done between a vampire and an elf. She is a descendant of a deity, pure in soul and one with nature, and I'm an abomination of mankind and an anomaly of the natural world. Also, neither of us are really here for that.

We spend the night lying next to each other, in my nice place that isn't a nice place. It's nice to be near each other though. To be with someone for a while. As the sun begins to rise on the new day, Amirah rises wordlessly and quietly puts on her coat. I could say something, but I get the sense she doesn't want me to. I have nothing to say anyway. That's not to say that I want her to leave. In fact, I'd rather like it if she stayed, but our time is up and our short while together has come to an end.

Bleurgh. It's all too complicated, so I push it all out of mind and Amirah leaves without even a glance between us. Is she embarrassed? Does she feel guilty? Hell, does she even like me? Respect me? I don't know. It's too complicated, remember. Eventually, I rise too, although by the time I do the irritable sun has well and truly dawned the new day. It was about this time yesterday when Amirah and I were sitting in the park and Amirah's beeper announced Alma's imminent arrival. The eleven vampire lords, each a ruler of their own borough in this city, will surely have gathered their forces by now. It might be today, then.

***

Everyone's ready. Everything's prepared. The streets are mostly deserted, but there are things that look like roadblocks, and shabby-looking defensive walls too, and every so often a dwarf is ready to warn you of a hidden tripwire or a secret trap.

I make my way through these streets, having to climb over defences and follow (to the letter) the barked instructions from nearby dwarves, and it's not long before I reach headquarters, our base of operations, and what was once a rather depressing and mundane school assembly hall.

There's a rush of activity. Tools fashioned into weapons are stacked up against the wall. Garden forks have been sharpened, spades have been weighted, and hammers now have spiky bits instead of flat bits. Metal sheets and other scrap have been bent into armour and are being fitted onto traders and gardeners, be they old or young, tall or small. The only qualification seems to be if you can pick it up then you will fight with it.

"Do I get anything?" I ask Amirah, who looks rushed off her feet giving instructions, inspecting armour, offering reassurance, and seemingly being pulled in every which way but away.

"What?" She turns to me sharply, angry for the interruption. She makes no acknowledgement of last night at all.

"A weapon?" I suggest. "Or some armour? Some armour would be nice."

There's a troll who looks more like a tank, somehow standing in front of us with all that metal hanging off him, and a group of orcs are in the corner, looking like a heavy metal American football team, and they're jovially barging into one another. Elves are wearing chic plating whilst dwarves vehemently refuse any kind of armour (they'll go into battle completely nude, save for a discreet loincloth, as their forefathers have done for centuries, because honour and tradition and identity are more serious to them than losing a limb). I even spot some pixies fluttering past, each one wearing what looks like heavily-altered salt and pepper shakers.

And I'm suddenly struck by how hopeless it all is. It's like Helisha said, we can't win this thing. Heavy metal and American football can only do so much against a force that is genuinely immovable and completely unstoppable. And what good is a salt and pepper shaker against the insurmountable and indomitable forces of control and dominion anyway? Not much good at all, I'd wager.

As I watch them, however, I realise the armour isn't really for their safety at all. It's for their peace of mind. Without it, they wouldn't stand. Without it, there'd be no moment of jovial solace. And without it, no one would take them seriously. I think this is why I asked Amirah for my own.

"Why on earth do you need armour?" Amirah challenges me, herself in some rather shiny chic plating with her silver hair pinned back to be kept out of her face.

"Well, why not?" I reply, innocently.

"Why not?" she gasps, quite incredulous this time. "Because you can't die, Caiden! You don't need it."

"I still feel it though," I object.

"Sorry, but it's still a no." Amirah waves me away. "I'm afraid you're at the bottom of the list here."

"How about a weapon?"

"You're a vampire," the elf breathes out, exasperated. "You can just bite them. Now, go on. I'm very busy, seeing as we could be attacked at any moment!" She marches away, surrounded by her elven assistants with their various baying questions.

Amirah's right. We *could* be attacked at any moment. I wonder why we're not.

I leave the hall, leaving behind the blinkered helmets and the suffocating armour suits being strapped on so tightly. I suppose I'm better off without all that stuff. Even so, it would have been cool to wear something with spikes on it.

I find myself absentmindedly walking in the direction of the school basement. It is the lowly place where I idled away many hours with Helisha (or rather, a petrified Helisha). With this in mind, I turn sharply away and decide to go in search of either Alma or Helisha (an un-petrified Helisha). Preferably Alma though, because I'm pretty sure we're on good terms, but I'll take Helisha, even though I'm almost positive we are on awkward terms teetering on downright dislike on her part.

I think there's an understanding between us, an alliance of common goals if you will, but there's also a history of ideological clashing and, most recently, I jammed a severed mapinguari's garlic-infested head on top of her own. That kind of thing can really stay with someone.

Be that as it may, I'd like to be with my own kind, and I also want to know why in the twenty-four hours since Alma came back to us, dripping in dark blood atop a unicorn she's named Snowy, we still haven't heard a peep from the other boroughs.

The vampire lords will be coming. That much is certain. There's no way they could allow Alma's defiance to pass them by unsquashed. The only problem is… they should have already come and done said squashing. What could they be waiting for?

***

"Maybe they're waiting for an apology?" Helisha suggests, but from the derisive looks she gets from both Alma and me, she ends up shrugging defensively. "Hey, it's possible."

We're sitting inside the truck stop, next to the freeway, and we're all alone. Duke's Borough's very own lookout post.

Everyone else has taken up defensive positions further inside the borough. Amirah concluded we'd be stretched too thinly if we made a stand here, so we're going to let them have this bit uncontested. We'll make our stand further in. She's right, of course. It would be suicide to try to defend everything that belongs to us. Quicker suicide, anyway.

But such dangers hold no threat for the likes of us three, nothing permanent anyway, so we sit together around a dirty table, on the edge of the borough, and wait for the beginning of the end. We eat away the slow hours with stilted conversation and nervous checks on each other. Are we ready? What were the other lords like? What was being petrified like? Are those stains on your coat from Munstone? What do you think is going to happen?

All pointless conjecture and unimportant questions. But it helps to pass the time. I do feel, however, and I suspect the other two feel this too, that we could be doing more. What it is we could be doing, I have no idea, but I still feel quite wasteful sitting out here. The rest of the borough are shoring up for an assault they cannot withstand, the other boroughs are no doubt gathering to perform said assault, and the vampire lords are spearheading the whole thing. And us three are sitting here waiting for it all to kick off. There should be a way to be proactive, I think, without putting oneself into unimaginable and terrifying danger.

By my reckoning though, said unimaginable and terrifying danger is running late.

"Maybe they're arguing over who gets to go first," I make a guess, and then wince because of how uncomfortably likely this seems.

"How far is the closest borough?" Alma asks, quite out of the blue.

"Queen's Corner is a few miles that way," Helisha replies matter-of-factly.

"It's not direct though," I add. "You'd have to go through the city to get to Queen's Corner. Lots of corners and up and down bits. Lord's Landing, on the other hand, might be a good five miles away, but it's also a straight shot along the freeway so you'd get there long before you could reach Queen's Corner."

"How far can a scream travel?"

"Erm…" I start, and then I give up. "Why? Are you hearing screaming? Do you hear it?" Helisha shakes her head. "Oh, good. Then it's just the person in charge hearing the imaginary screaming."

"Not as far as Queen's Corner," Helisha replies to Alma, ignoring my sardonic wit.

"Well, depends who's screaming," I interject, suddenly sounding like an expert.

"Everyone," Alma says. "What if everyone was screaming?"

"In that case," I gulp, "I think we would hear it."

"Alma, what are you getting at?"

Instead of replying though, Alma gets up and heads outside. "Follow me," she tells us, and we both fall in behind her, eager to keep up.

We stand on the roof of the truck stop. The freeway's next to us, our own borough is behind us, and in front of us is the rest of Vampire City.

"Listen," Alma says.

We listen and we hear… nothing. Barely a gust of wind. It's a dead city.

"There's never much to listen to," I hastily put in, but I know I'm kidding myself and the other two know it too. It's usually quiet, of course, but if you really listen, and if there isn't anything close by distracting you, then you can hear the faint rumblings and the occasional bangs of our neighbouring boroughs. Not right now, though. It's almost as if they aren't there at all.

"And the freeway's empty," Helisha gasps. I suddenly realise how true this is. We've spent much of the morning at this truck stop, and yet I can't recall seeing any roaming bandits or borough recruitment teams (read: bandits with authority).

"What the hell's going on?" I wonder aloud, sounding more nervous than I would have ideally let on.

"We're about to find out," Alma says, pointing far down the freeway. And she's right. Because here they come.

⁂

Here *it* comes.

It's quite far away, so at first it only looks like a dark blob creeping towards us along the freeway. But as it gets closer—and it does come closer remarkably quickly—I see that it is not a dark blob. It's a spider. A fearsome, hairy dark spider, easily three times the size of the truck stop on which the three of us are still standing.

"Erm," I manage to say. "If anyone asks, none of us have ever killed a spider we found in the house, instead we've always picked them up and put them safely outside. Okay?"

"It's not the spider we've got to worry about," Alma says. And she's right.

Riding the spider, standing just behind the eight table-sized, jet-black eyeballs, is one of the eleven vampire lords. The huge spider comes down effortlessly off the freeway and is pulled to a stop in front of us via the reins held by the vampire riding it.

"Someone tell him this place doesn't do drive-thru," I say.

"He's on his own," Helisha points out, ignoring me. "Why is he on his own?"

He is one scary-looking bastard. His face is scarred. His uniform-like, black clothing is pulled ragged and torn in places. His hair is long and flat, stretching down to his waistline, and is a smoky grey in colour.

None of that stuff is really all that noticeable though. Not the scars on his face nor his weathered clothing. It is all just background to what is actually most striking about him. His eyes.

Bad guys have red eyes like the fires of hell, or dead eyes to serve as windows into their rotten souls. But this vampire lord has neither fire nor death in his eyes. I can't look away from them. They're horrifying.

They're scared.

Wide-open and panic-stricken, in fact. They look like eyes that have gazed upon the worst of all things and come away traumatized, terrified, and powerless. Perhaps they have seen such things. They are large and wet and unblinking. It's as if he wants to break down to either cry and run or curl up and shake. The rest of him is bloody terrifying, perfectly monstrous, and terribly evil, but his eyes convey the most terrible fear. It is a fear that will never leave, never lessen, and never let go of his very being. He is truly cursed by it and will never recover. Poor bugger.

I don't know why I think this. Why should I feel sorry for the one who is about to fill my immediate future with great pain and horrible prospects? I don't know. But I do. It's those eyes.

"Little one," the lord hisses at Alma, his voice crackling and serpent-like, and it echoes to us from atop the giant spider. This vampire lord is everything Serat wished he could have been. "Please… please… beg for your borough folk and come back to us."

He's not being condescending. I wish he was being condescending. Rather, he sounds completely genuine. He doesn't want to be here. He doesn't want to do what he's about to do. He wants Alma to make it right again. Yet his voice is filled with venom and hostility. There is no quavering voice. Only frightened eyes. It is an intensely unsettling combination to behold.

"Piss off," Alma responds antagonistically. I suddenly feel like she's spent too much time with me. My small influence on her has not gone unnoticed, especially not if Helisha's sideways dagger eyes are anything to go by.
I wish Amirah were here. Amirah would have done the right thing, but Alma's not Amirah, she's Alma… and Alma is, if nothing else, a pusher. She'll push for change, she'll push against any opposition, and as she so eloquently said herself, she'll push up and keep pushing up, and that's how she gets things to change. Amirah, for all her wisdom and leadership, could never push like Alma. The unfortunate thing with pushers, however, is that there's no half-measures and certainly no compromise when the going gets tough. And the going is about to get very, very tough.

"We warned you!" the lord decries. "Oh, how we warned you… but you leave us no choice… Why do you do this? Why will you not relent?"

One of the spider's tower-sized legs comes down and crushes a nearby building. It wasn't a big building, barely more than a large shed really, but now it's in pieces. For some unknown reason, I momentarily think of the people who built that small building. It was nothing special, but it would have taken days, maybe weeks, and they would have needed skills and knowledge and teamwork to finish the job. And the spider didn't even react when its leg obliterated the whole thing.

"Because you will not listen!" Alma cries back at him, standing with the wind in her face and looking like a school-aged David going up against an eight-legged Goliath. At her fearsome defiance, the vampire lord is overcome with an uncontainable rage. It is more than animalistic or beast-like. It's a personal rage. An emotional rage. A storm of unfathomable hurt with lightning bolts of savage hatred and deep thunderous rolls of desperate panic.

It's a toddler's tantrum.

"Petulant child!" the lord screams at Alma and, after a sharp tug of the reins, the spider responds. It screeches out a piercing bellow and brings truck-sized pincers down on the truck stop.

Helisha is already running as the roof crunches under the attack. A chunk of the rooftop is instantly turned to rubble and the rest is quickly following. I grab Alma's hand and pull her in the direction Helisha went.

The three of us leap Hollywood-style off the roof just as the spider swings a front leg that completely demolishes the building we were just standing on. The thing about Hollywood-style leaps though is the Hollywood-style *landing* is performed at a different time and after much careful preparation. Only later will the leap and the landing be stitched together in the editing phase.

So, we don't land like Hollywood action heroes. Instead, we land like the terrified, limb-flailing bags of bones that we are. It hurts. I think we all break a few bones. But by the time we're on our feet we've healed and we're running full pelt deeper into the borough, running away from the edge and away from a giant spider and a hysterical vampire lord.

Come to think of it, we really should have scarpered upon first sighting the giant spider with a terrifying lord on top of it. Ah well, we didn't make a very good lookout post.

***

For as long as I've been in Vampire City, and as far as I can tell for as long as Vampire City has *been* Vampire City, there have been twelve boroughs.

These are Duke's Borough, Queen's Corner, Lord's Landing, Marquess Marshes, Earl's End, Viscount Way, Baron's Bottom, The Prince District, Knight's Passage,

Gentleman's Gate, Esquire's Alley, and Dame's Devil. Of the twelve vampire lords who each have one of the above boroughs to rule over, eight have come to Duke's Borough on this grey and windy day. Eight lords. Where the other three are, I don't know, and I don't care. Eight is bad enough. Eight of the bastards. At least we've got Alma though. So, you know, that's one.

It's only the eight of them though. Eight individuals. Our various scouting parties (me, Alma, Helisha and some brave elves and pixies who volunteered) have scoured the borough and there's no one else. Only eight of them. No militia from their boroughs, no vampire cronies in tow. Just eight vampire lords, and their familiars.

It seems every vampire lord has an animal familiar, although such monstrosities are more devilish freaks than actual animals. I wonder why we never saw Serat's familiar, or even if he had one at all. I make a mental note to ask him when all this is over, once he's regenerated.

The fearsome hairy spider, the one the size of a large building, is the familiar of the vampire lord with the terrified eyes. His name is Derig and he was one of the three lords Alma met at their earlier gathering. The other two she met are here with Derig as well. They are Onaea and Nroat.

I spy Onaea first. She's straddling the neck of a drooling, muscle-ripped hyena. A hyena that happens to be the size of a full-grown elephant. Constantly cackling, with wild eyes and a mouth full of sharp, broken teeth (a mouth that seems to be permanently stuck open), it truly is a fearful sight to behold. Incidentally, the hyena looks rather scary as well. Onaea is clearly insane. She looks like a cross between the Mad Hatter and Slenderman, with dark bloodshot eyes missing their eyelids and bloody lips around a wide mouth.

Nroat is close by, and I eventually see him too. It seems the vampire lords are circling us and sizing us up, all while enjoying the anticipation of what is surely to come. Nroat walks whereas Onaea and Derig ride. Always at Nroat's side, flanking him and following him obediently, are his two dogs. Large black dogs, each one as big as I am, and each one looking like a vicious hunter and a mean killer. Nroat himself is tall and elegant, with a long face and tight cheekbones. I can tell just by the way he walks that he's a posh prick.

At first it is only these three, but we soon spot the others. Some come creeping into Duke's Borough, others stride in as if they own the place (which, as far they're concerned, they do), but a few come bulldozing in, wiping out everything in their path.

Now, are you ready for some incredibly pompous ancient vampire names that once, a very long time ago, would have meant something, but are now just names adopted by those who feel they deserve them? Good. Strap in. If you can't remember them though, don't worry, because getting stomped by one is much like getting stomped by any of the others. They are:

Derig of Priory Ford, Onaea of Dame's Devil and Nroat of Lord's Landing are joined by Atog of Earl's End, Liit of The Prince District, Deoitcl of Knight's Passage, Tacsitc from Queen's Corner, and Ricmeet heralding from Esquire's Alley.

Atog comes in riding his truck-sized dung beetle, an armour-plated behemoth that looks as unbreakable as it's rider. Deoitcl strides in side-by-side with his big, dark-haired lion, both of them far too proud in themselves to notice anything or anyone else.

At first, Helisha and I do not spot Tacsitc, but this is because she's lounging on the back of her cat, who comes meandering into Duke's Borough like a curious… well… cat. This specific cat however, which is of course black, is the size of a large house, so it's understandable why we couldn't spot Tacsitc lounging on its back. When we do spot her though, both Helisha and I skip a heartbeat, or at least it feels like we would skip a heartbeat if we did, in fact, have a heart.

Tacsitc is beautiful. No. That's not enough. It doesn't do her justice. She *is* beauty. This vampire lord is a dark-haired angel with perfect curves, perfect eyes, perfect lips, and perfect everything. What I would do to drink her blood… and by the thirsty look in my scouting companion's eyes, Helisha would do it too.

Liit blunders in riding a normal-sized (but still black) ostrich and proceeds to fall off when the big bird comes to a stop, yapping all the while (Liit the vampire lord, not the ostrich). Ricmeet is the last to arrive, having got lost several times and what with being weighed down carrying his own familiar: a small, black-and-white panda.

Derig, Onaea, Nroat, Atog, Liit, Deoitcl, Tacsitc and Ricmeet. They're here. They have come. And we are at their mercy.

✳✳✳

They're already attacking us. Without shedding a drop of blood, nor even hurling a cruel insult, they are attacking us. They attack us with their sheer presence alone. What hope do we have against such creatures? How can we possibly overcome such figures? These questions may as well be swords thrust into our sides.

As the lords pass by, circling inside our borough, their mere presence is enough to shake our courage, to unsteady our steadfastness, and yes, someone, somewhere, is starting to blub.

This is bad. I mean, I knew this was bad before, and I'm fairly sure everyone who can die today *will* die a horrible and painful death, but now it's even worse because now… now this might get embarrassing.

I pass through one of our street barricades, on the edge of our defences, whilst keeping track of three of the lords: Derig on his giant spider, Deoticl with his lion, and Atog on his beetle. The three of them are a couple blocks away from our lines, and they are watching us watching them, all while they make their slow way around us. But it is not at them I find myself looking, but at my own borough-kin.

An elf hunkers behind a makeshift wall, tense and ready to pounce. There's a dwarf hastily sketching a crude tattoo on her bare skin. It's a spider, a lion, and a beetle. In the ancient dwarven tradition, she will wear her enemies. Some armoured orcs are quietly psyching each other up, punching shoulders and knocking helmets. A dryad looks lost but also resigned to being lost, a few gnomes whisper prayers to each other, a goblin is rocking back and forth, and a drake is peering over the barricade, curious till the end.

None of them look especially ready to meet this threat. But then who could be ready for what's about to come? After all, nothing can stop what is about to happen. So, why exactly are we bothering again? Oh yeah. Principles. What a stupid thing to die for.

I leave the barricades behind and return to the city square. This is where our last stand will be, this is where Amirah and Alma direct the defences, and this is also where our best pieces are waiting to be deployed to wherever they will be needed most. Incidentally, this is also the same square in which Alma drank Serat's blood and started all this. It might be poetic to think this is where it will no doubt end—a hope-ends-where-hope-began kind of thing—but I see it more like a cruel jest.

"Report?" Amirah asks of me, looking tense and a little nervous. I am her soldier once more and nothing more, certainly no longer her night-time companion.

"They're still circling us." And that's my report.

"Why?" Amirah curses. "Why don't they just get it over with?"

"They're playing with us," I say. "They're bastards, remember? Trust me, they'll drag this out for as long as possible. I doubt they'll even attack today." At which point, of course, they attack.

✳✳✳

Amirah stays in the square. Alma, Helisha, and I, however, race towards the sound of crashing and screaming. The adrenaline is suddenly up, the fear is now electric rather than gnawing, and I want to beat the other two. It's so silly. So stupid. But there it is. I'm almost laughing. It's a race and the winner gets bragging rights.

I'm the first one there! A victorious wave of euphoria overwhelms me, leaving me feeling light-headed. Wait. No. That's not euphoria. That's the building right in front of me exploding in my face and blowing me back through the air. And exploding out of the building is Tacsitc's house-sized black cat (well and truly in kill mode). The stunning beauty that is Tacsitc herself stands atop her familiar's head, gripping onto a feline ear that is as big as she is.

"Go, Poppy!" Tacsitc shrills. "Kill the vermin rat!"

Her cat growls and it is like the deafening roar of a jet engine. But I'm still horizontal and seeing cartoon birds chirping around my head; also I think the lower half of me might have been ever so slightly pulverized by the debris, so what is essentially a loud meow doesn't really bother me. I sit up amidst rubble and dust just in time to see Alma launch herself into the air and, with one clenched fist, whack the side of the cat's face so hard the whole thing topples. Tacsitc shrieks in anger as she leaps off, rolling onto the ground.

Helisha is on her in seconds, but she's still too late. Tacsitc is a vampire lord, and she does two things very well: drink blood and steal energy. Whereas Helisha is a collared stiff. Helisha doesn't get to drink, and any strength she might have had was stolen every night by her own vampire lord, Serat the Bastard.

Helisha tries gallantly (or rather, not gallantly but more rage-fuelled madness) but Tacsitc blocks every swing, deflects every kick, and then goes on the attack. One. Two. And it's over. Helisha's got several broken bones, and she has been sent flying through the air to land, coincidentally, somewhat close to where I am still sitting.

"How goes the farm?" I call to her, in my best country farmer's voice. It's an old joke. So old I'm not sure where it comes from or even if it is, in fact, a joke. But it's better than being honest about our situation.

Helisha is honest, however, and that's why she screams in pain, then screams in anger, then screams for revenge before finally getting up and charging at Tacsitc, screaming all the while. It wasn't too long ago that Helisha would have fallen into line behind her attacker. But that time is over now. Realising the futility of one's ambitions and the finality of your ultimate fate can change a person and make them scream for revenge. I still can't feel my legs, otherwise I'm sure I'd be helping Helisha. I'm sure of it.

It's a scene of devastation. Thick, grey dust clouds hang over everything, and the usual roads and street paths are hidden under an uneven layer of broken bits of stone and cement that once formed a building. In the middle of it all, three vampires, two of whom are vampire lords, hash it out.

"Measly little toerag!" Tacsitc wails, infused with rage and looking every bit like a demonic (but still somehow pure and beautiful) angel. She grapples with Alma, but where Alma is weaker for her youth and inexperience, Helisha is there to make up for it.

Tacsitc is hurled onto the stone, only to grab Alma and fling her backwards, but Helisha steps up and grips the evil bitch tightly, throwing her down. Tacsitc turns unnaturally, smiling all the while, and twists Helisha's grip into one of her own. Her hands are over Helisha's face; her long, sharp fingernails start digging into her skull. Helisha's screaming again. Oh. Look. I'm wiggling some of my toes. That's a good sign. I'll be back up in no time.

"Helisha!" As I wiggle some toes, I hear Alma's war cry and then I see her come to the rescue. The fifteen-year-old fourteen-year-old tackles Tacsitc with such force it almost splits the beauty in two. In the immediate aftermath, the three of them lie amongst the ruins of the crumbled building, mentally catching their breath. And I wiggle another toe.

Maybe it's the excitement of the fight happening in front of me or the thrill of wiggling more than two toes, but it takes me until the last moment before I realise Poppy—Tacsitc's house-sized, mean-faced black cat—has snuck up behind me and is now looking down at me, and looking every bit like a big cat eyeing a very small and very crippled mouse. On the plus side, I am now wiggling my third toe.

"Hyarrr!!" A great war cry bellows towards me. Or, at least, it would have been a great war cry were it not for the squeaking and the voice breaking halfway through. As Poppy and I look to where the squeak came from, the effect of the attempted war cry is further diminished when we see who cried it.

A halfling comes bounding over the rubble, heading straight for me. Like all halflings, this one is halfway to everything. Halfway to normal height, halfway to a pleasant face, and halfway to general hygiene. This one appears to be holding above his head a giant ball of string. Yes. That's right. A giant ball of string. Where he got it, I have no idea.

"Have at thee, foul beast!" the halfling squeaks, then throws away the giant ball of string that is easily thrice the size of himself. Poppy, being a cat and therefore cursed with both single-mindedness and a very small mind, whips around and chases the bouncing ball of string.

"Take my hand." The halfling stands before me, all heroic-like, and holds out his tiny, dirty hand for me to grasp. "We must be away, if a new day we wish to see!"

I grip the halfling's hand, the halfling pulls with all his might, and then falls flat on his face next to me. But hey! A fourth toe is a-wiggling!

"Fool!" Tacsitc screeches. "You don't know what you've started!" She swipes Alma down. "And you will pay dearly." She grips Helisha by her throat. "You *must* pay dearly!"

"You've got to get me the hell away from her!" the halfling panics as he puts his face in my face. The idea of being a hero is gone, replaced with desperation and terror and… wait… he's not one of us! What with the big cat, the giant ball of string, and my legs sewing themselves back together, I hadn't noticed it until this very moment. This halfling is not from Duke's Borough. My vampire nose is tingling. His scent is all wrong. But if he's not from here, then where the hell is he from and what is he doing here?

"Chips!" the halfling blurts out after I've put these questions to him.

"What?" I exclaim, caught between looking perplexed at this halfling and watching in terror as Tacsitc beats down Alma and Helisha.

"It's my name! My name is Chips," Chips the halfling explains. "But there's no time for your other questions. You must convey me from this place!"

"Eh?"

"Carry me, henceforth!"

"Erm?"

"Get me the bloody hell away from her!"

"Why?" I instinctively ask. "What's so important about you?"

"Can't you tell? Don't you see?" Chips looks over his shoulder, exasperated and hopping from one hairy foot to the other. This little, honest-looking chap is about as terrified as one can be. "I'm one of hers!"

Ah. Chips the halfling is not from Duke's Borough. He is a subject of Queen's Corner, the borough of a certain stunningly beautiful vampire lord named Tacsitc. This explains Tacsitc's rage, and it also clarifies just how much danger we are all in. She is obviously chasing this runaway, this defector, this fleeing immigrant, and all for no greater reason than to save herself and her borough from embarrassment. We are in an exceedingly large amount of danger because Tacsitc is fighting for her pride.

I realise this just as Tacsitc hurls Helisha through a nearby wall and, based on the following smashing sounds, several other walls after the first one. Alma stands against her but it's hopeless. The vampire lord breaks the fifteen-year-old fourteen-year-old's leg in a few places. Then she breaks the other leg. And the arms. And probably the rib cage too. Ouch.

Alma's down, Helisha's missing, and I'm the one next to the poor halfling who is the target of all this destruction, and this is when Tacsitc spots Chips.

"You!" she spits in fury.

"Oh no!" Chips squeals.

Five toes are go. Time to run.

***

We can't lead Tacsitc back to the city square because most of Duke's Borough's defenders are waiting there. So, while we're running in exactly that direction, I wrack my brains for somewhere else to run to.

For a small fellow, Chips is showing me he can run with the best of them, though I'm hardly the best of them. It's probably down to the effect of the enraged, maniacal, but still somehow beautiful vampire lord who is chasing us with the kind of desperate wild energy usually reserved for serial killer clowns in horror movies.

Through one street, round a corner, we're just about clear when I grab Chips and pull him down a side alley.

"You can't hide from me!" Tacsitc shrieks after us, hot on our trail.

"We… can't…" Chips gasps, his little lungs sounding as if they're about to give up on him. "Hide… from… her…"

"Yes! I heard!" I snap back, irritably.

"Please tell me… you've got… a plan…"

"We just need to lose her," I shout in response. "There's a whole maze of side alleys down here so we can—oh bugger."

It's a dead end. We've hit a wall, quite literally in Chips' case, and there's no convenient window to slip through or ladder to climb up.

"Got you."

We both turn in unison to face Tacsitc. Holy moly, she is beautiful. Even now, as her eyes blaze with anger, with her nails all bloody and her fangs extended, I still can't look past how beautiful she is.

"No one leaves me," Tacsitc remonstrates Chips, her voice cruel and yet now teasing, playful, psychotic and… victorious. Hm. That would explain the teasing. "You're mine. You're all mine."

"Please!" Chips cries. "I'll go back. I'll be good. I won't run again."

"No." Tacsitc stands over him and her fingers stroke the little guy's cheek. "You won't."

I don't know what happens next.

One moment, I'm standing just to the side, waiting for this vampire lord to dismember her runaway subject (whilst also guiltily enjoying her alluring aroma) and in the next moment I'm grabbing something out of Chips' top pocket.

I have no idea what it is. I have no clue as to why I'm grabbing it. And I definitely cannot comprehend what I then do with the thing I've just taken and now hold in one hand.

I smash it into Tacsitc's chest—whatever *it* is—and she screams in agony. A dark-red light cascades from whatever it is I'm holding against her chest, and the same light seems to infect Tacsitc's body and move through her veins to cause her great pain. The one thing I know for sure however is that if I let go, if I stop what I'm doing, or even if I give just the slightest hint of relenting, then Tacsitc will have me. But doing what I'm doing now, I know I have her.

She screams. She wails. Her eyes grow larger. Her fangs shrink. Her body weakens and falls but still I press this thing against her chest until, finally, she explodes. Yeah. She explodes. Not in blood and guts though. But in light. Bright light that blinds me and then a shockwave hits me, shaking the very bricks in the walls around us.

And then she's gone.

"You killed her," Chips whispers, trembling behind me.

"No," I say. "She's just gone." I stand up, straightening myself, and look over my shoulder. "Vampires don't die."

"But, she—"

"You wouldn't have felt it," I explain, "but I felt her being taken away, presumably to be dropped somewhere... trust me, I can tell. I'm a vampire too. We have a kindred instinct, you might say."

I remember the thing in my hand. The thing I grabbed inexplicably from Chips' top pocket and with which I banished Tacsitc just by pressing it against her. I don't even know what it looks like.

So I look at it, resting as it is in the palm of my hand. It is the size of a tennis ball and as round as one too, but it is not a ball nor is it corporeal. It's... it's unlike anything I've ever seen, primarily because I'm not one hundred percent certain that I'm actually seeing it.

It's like when you spot something in the corner of your eye. At first, you're not sure if you saw anything at all, then you think you might have imagined it, or perhaps it was just a trick of the light, and then you eventually decide it was all just a brain fart on your part.

That's what this thing is like to look at, with the added complication that it's right in front of me and very much bang in the centre of my vision.

I should be seeing it clear as day, and while I can see that it is red, and glowing, and humming a bit, and pulsating ever so slightly, and that it is indeed round, I'm still not sure I'm actually seeing it. My eyes are relaying all the information but my brain's having trouble conceptualizing the data. This is most weird.

"Where did you get this?" I ask Chips, quite breathlessly.

"That is why I was sent here," Chips tells me, his voice weak but still filled with awe. "It is why I have come. It is my errand, my duty… my precious—"

"Alright! Alright!" I cut him off quickly. A halfling and his precious—during the end times, no less—is about the last thing we need in this forsaken city. But it isn't a small and unassuming piece of jewellery in the palm of my hand (nor is it a cease-and-desist letter from a lawyer). It is this strange, glowing red orb thing that has just banished a vampire lord.

"A witch entrusted it to me," Chips tells me, and my blood runs cold(er). "She told me I must only give it to someone who does not need it."

"Well, what bloody use is that?" I scoff, overcompensating for my colder blood. "Here. Take it back, then. I certainly don't want anything from a witch." I shove it into Chips' hands. "Why have you come out this way at all?"

"I came on the witch's errand, of course," he says. We walk out of the side alley, and I start heading back to the city square. I'm sure Alma and Helisha will make their way back there too, and they'd have healed up by now, but for some reason Chips is following me.

"She sent you here, did she? Well, go back to your witch, then," I say. "We don't need any magic. And you make sure to tell her that! We don't need any of her trickery or her whims! The last one blew us into the mess we're in now! We don't need it, and we don't want it. No good ever comes from magic."

"But she told me—"

"I don't care what she told you! I'm telling you to piss off, so piss off."

"But I can't not do what she's asked of me!" Chips whines. "She *is* a witch!"

"Look at it this way," I say, rounding on Chips, who almost walks straight into me. "Everyone here is, right now, stuck up a certain well-known creek without a paddle. We're all in need here, all of us, and it is the type of need of the most dire variety. *This*," I point at the red ball in Chips' hands, "is *not* a paddle! It's something from a witch, which means it's not here for us, it's here for whatever *she* wants! I don't trust it, even in this most dire of situations."

"How dire?" the halfling squeaks.

"Everyone here is about to die," I snarl. "Is that dire enough for you?"

"But this could save you—"

"Tacsitc doesn't die! They don't die! Vampires can't die! You know what they can do! What they always do! They come back! I felt her being moved, which means she will be coming back! This thing you've brought here is not a weapon… it's a sick joke."

A sick joke that didn't work on me. On touching Tacsitc's skin, it activated and banished her. But when I grabbed it, when I held it in my hand, it did not activate. I have no idea why.

"Vampires can't die."

"No, we can't."

"Which means you won't die either…"

"No, I won't… but even so… what's your point?"

"Vampires can't die, so you don't need this."

"But I don't want it!" I hurry my stride.

"But I'm giving it to you." And he's keeping pace with me.

"But I'm not taking it!"

"She told me not to take that into consideration."

"Well, I'm telling you to consider it!" I snap. "I don't want anything to do with whatever that thing is! Understand?"

"Yes."

"Then you'll take it away?"

"No."

"What are you going to do with it, then?"

"Give it to you."

"But I just—" I feel like pulling my hair out. If there can only be one rule in all the world, it is this: never mess with magic. It's completely limitless and totally beyond comprehension. "What even is it anyway?"

"She told me it was a power *to* all other powers," the halfling recalls, "and an end that cannot be reversed."

"O… kay," I sigh. "So, what is it?"

***

It's probably difficult to understand why I want nothing to do with this weird red orb that glows and pulsates. Indeed, it just saved me from the wrath of a very nasty (but oh so beautiful) vampire lord. Well, to understand, you have to look at the fine print.

First of all, Tacsitc isn't dead. I don't know where she is exactly, only that she is somewhere that is not here. This thing in my hand—a gift from a witch—banished Tacsitc from being where she was, but that doesn't necessarily mean it will stop her from returning to where she has previously been. Follow? Magic is very particular like this and not at all definitive. In not so many words, Tacsitc will be back. I feel it in my bones. My shaking bones.

Secondly, after the giving, magic often takes, and what it takes is usually far more than what it has given, and besides, what it usually gives isn't always what it appears to be. Still following?

Basically, I have no idea what exactly this orb can do, what it will do, what it has done, and what will happen to me if I use it. Just because it does one thing doesn't mean it's not doing something else. Case in point, how the hell did I know it was in Chips' pocket? And why did I instinctively press it against Tacsitc? It's in my head. I know it. The orb knows it. It's a deus ex machina, but who is it deus ex machina-ing for exactly? Me? The witch? Us? Them? Itself? Or is it really just a sick joke from an omnipotent witch looking for a laugh? A weapon that doesn't kill, a solution that only delays, and just another false hope.

It's all too much. It's all above my head. I want nothing to do with it! I shove the thing back into Chips' hands, forcing him to take it back. Still, Chips grips the orb tightly and follows me closely, resembling my very own miniature shadow as I walk into the city square.

Everyone's still here. A little nervous, still quite tense, and looking at me. I'm in no mood for staring contests so I stomp on by and find myself directed into what was once a fast-food restaurant.

Inside, the tables are dirty, the counter is empty, the walls are peeling, and yet still there are posters clinging on, showing off their latest burger (for the brand new low, low price of ninety-nine cents!) and there are fun cartoon characters on the posters, all with bizarre and unnatural smiles, dotted around the place and also stuck here for eternity. No wonder their smiles are so warped.

"We have to act now!" Alma demands of Amirah. They're both at odds with each other and I immediately regret walking into the middle of it.

Helisha sits off to the side, looking far worse for wear after her confrontation with Tacsitc. There are only a few others here too. Some elf marshals, a dwarf priest, and a dryad with a bag of potions. They all look very nervous and keen to stay in the background. I wish I could join them.

"I am acting now, Alma," Amirah retorts, stressed and starting to look it. Her elvish skin isn't quite so smooth, her eyes are looking a little strained, and her silver hair is a little frayed.

"You're running away!" Alma barks.

"It's the only option we have," Amirah counters.

"No." Alma is pacing, her blood is up. "We can attack."

"That's suicide!"

"Not if Helisha, Caiden and I move in first!" Alma argues. "It'll be the last thing those bastards are expecting."

"They're not expecting it, Alma, because it's suicide!" Amirah repeats.

She's not wrong. Helisha looks in no condition to lead a brave charge. Even with our vampiric healing abilities, she is taking a long while to recuperate. A very long while. Alma, on the other hand, looks like she would happily take on all seven remaining vampire lords. I, on the other *other* hand, have never been the sort to put my neck willingly on the chopping block, as it were. Without meaning to, I brush my fingers against the old bite wounds on my neck, the ones Serat gave me when I first arrived in Vampire City.

"Running will achieve nothing," Alma says. Again, and most unhelpfully, I don't think she's wrong.

"It will give some of us a greater chance to survive if we go now," Amirah says. "Some can hide, others can flee, and perhaps the lords will show mercy if they see we pose no threat—"

"So, you've made up your mind!" Alma growls. "We've lost. The resistance is done. The revolution never got off the ground. Is that it!?"

"Alma!" Amirah silences our own head vampire. "You did not see the condition we found you in." Hmm, so Alma and Helisha didn't heal up quite so quickly after their fight with Tacsitc as I thought. "You had both been so... it was... and it had only been one of them. If two of you cannot hope to stand against just one, what hope do the rest of us have?"

There is momentary silence. Everyone here waits and watches, holding our breath...

"You knew this would be difficult," Alma finally says, facing Amirah.

"I did." Amirah nods, turning away. "And I would still die for everyone in this borough, but I won't lead them into a battle they can't win. I'm going to give the order. Those of us who can't flee the borough will have to fall back to the tunnels."

"And do what?" Alma snaps. "Pray?"

"Yes," Amirah replies, unfazed.

It's only now that everyone in the small restaurant turns and notices I am here, accompanied as I am by a small, ugly halfling peeking around behind me.

"Caiden?" Helisha is surprised to see me.

"Are you alright?" Amirah asks reservedly.

"What took you so long?" Alma demands of me, rather brusquely.

Earlier, I had no idea why I put my hand in Chips' pockets nor why I pressed the strange red thingamabob against Tacsitc (that's what I'm calling it now, by the way— it just doesn't feel like an orb, even if that is the shape it has taken). But now I do know what I need to do.

I turn around to face Chips, with my back to everyone else in the restaurant, and I snatch the thingamabob from the halflings' grip and hide it inside my own tattered coat. I then shush Chips into secrecy. He nods, confused but also relieved I've finally accepted the thingamabob.

I spin back around and put on my best attempt at a genuine, disarming smile. By their suspicious looks, it's clearly a failed attempt.

"Hi, Helisha." I press on. "You look awful." At this, she shoots me a look, so I quickly move on. "I'm fine, thank you, Amirah. A little knocked and definitely tense around the shoulder region but, all things considered, I can't complain—especially considering how Helisha looks." Another look. Another hasty move onwards. "Alma, I'm afraid I took a little longer because I was looking after our new friend here."

"Is that a halfling behind you?" Helisha scoffs, not hiding her distaste. "You shouldn't have bothered with him, Caiden. Halflings aren't good for anything. They're a waste of space, even if that space is half-sized."

"Helisha, halflings may well be small, dirty, scummy, weird, mischievous, unhygienic, unhelpful, ill-mannered, quite ugly, untrustworthy, rather simple, and adorned in rags that I wouldn't give to a dog… but that doesn't mean they're not part of our society." Chips gives me a thankful thumbs up. "Or, rather, in the case of Chips here, not this society, but the society of our neighbouring borough, Queen's Corner."

"Eh?"

"How?"

"What?!"

"Yes, you heard me correctly," I smile, teasingly. "This grotty little fellow has come from Queen's Corner."

"Tacsitc's borough?" Amirah confirms, then looks at Chips. "She was after you, then. Why? Speak up!"

Nothing. Chips doesn't move. So, I shove him a bit. Then a bit more. Then I poke him until he finally squeaks into action.

"I… I came here to deliver—"

"This here is Chips!" I quickly interrupt loudly. "He ran here seeking asylum—*skip the whole witch thing*—and he needs asylum—*and don't tell them about the thingamabob*—because…" Again, Chips doesn't speak up, so I have to nudge him… again. "Tell them what you told me just before we got here."

"About my borough?"

"Yes."

"And all the other boroughs?"

"Yes."

"Oh… can't you tell them?" he whispers nervously.

"Oh, come on!" Alma bursts out. "If someone doesn't tell us soon, I'm going to—"

"We disobeyed!" Chips panics.

And the restaurant goes silent, so I give Chips yet another nudge and he continues. "Our lords told us about the changes called for by the new lord of Duke's Borough. They said it was outrageous and not to be tolerated. We… didn't agree."

"That's why the lords are here on their own," Amirah realises. "Because no one would follow them!"

"Well, most of us are hiding," Chips explains. "Some of us were found, and they… well… But the lords didn't want to waste any more time looking for us, so they left their own vampires behind to look for the rest of us, and they've come here by themselves to deal with you, and then they'll deal with the rest of us when they have the time later."

"Nowhere to run to now," Alma says, aiming her firm words squarely at Amirah.

"By the gods," Amirah whispers, shaken. "What have we done? We've doomed the whole city."

"Well, actually, there's something this witch gave me—" Chips starts without thinking, but I cut the halfling off by shoving my hand over his mouth.

"And this funny little halfling's the only one who got through!" I talk over him, and then I shush him again.

"We must attack!" Alma insists. "We have no choice now. All we can do is attack!"

"There may yet be a chance to withdraw," Amirah thinks aloud. "To save some of us, at least."

Before their argument can begin anew, Helisha stands up. She's staring at me, eyeing me with suspicion. "What have you got in your pocket?" And everyone turns to look at me again.

"What pocket?" I stumble, sounding dumb.

"Your inside pocket," Helisha says. "Your hand keeps going to it. What have you got in your nasty little pocket?"

"Nothing!" I say far too quickly. I'm obviously lying, and everyone can tell, but Amirah looks at me and I know what she's thinking.

It doesn't matter that she's got the wrong idea about what is currently in my inside pocket (what she thinks is in my pocket is actually safely hidden away again, under that big cabinet in that place I call my own). Her sympathy for my hang-up, however misplaced it is, is enough to get me out of this jam. What I'm trying to say is this… Amirah is a good person.

"He has nothing in his pocket." Amirah comes to my rescue. "Nothing more than dirt and grime. An elf can always tell."

Helisha eventually nods, accepting Amirah's air of authority, although I'm not sure my fellow vampire really believes it. Alma couldn't care less. All Alma cares about is taking the initiative, pushing the offensive, forcing the issue, and breaking down the enemy. But Amirah wants only to protect, to survive, to serve, and to do right by those in her charge. Helisha's still eyeing me suspiciously, so I decide to skip the details of Amirah and Alma's revived argument and slip outside, pulling Chips along with me.

"Why didn't you tell them—"

"Because they would use this thingamabob." I can't explain it right now because it's just a feeling I'm having. But it's a pressing feeling. A feeling that feels all too real. The others would use it because they need it, and the witch said to Chips…

Gods, I hate magic, and I hate witches, and I hate their games.

The square is a mishmash of tall, small, big, and spindly. Everyone sits together, and I notice how their cliques may be noticeable (orcs sit with orcs, dwarves with dwarves, tree people stand next to trees), but they're not quite so defined as one might expect. A day spent in each other's company has blurred the usual boundaries. If it wasn't for all the spikey weapons, heavy armour plates, thick blockades around the perimeter, and all the oil barrel fires, it would all look quite nice.

"Care to explain," Chips chirps in at my side, pumping himself up and putting on a face, "why is it you refrained from divulging such possession of a gift bestowed upon you that can wield the power to banish your enemies forthwith?"

"…What?"

The halfling sags again, giving up once more on the bravado. "Why didn't you tell them about the thingamabob?"

Ah yes. The thingamabob. Walking around the edge of the square, avoiding as many wandering eyes as possible, I take the thingamabob out of my pocket and hold it in my hand. It is a touch smaller than it was before. Hm. Magic is limitless, but it appears in this case that limitlessness is not limit-free.

"Because they need it."

"And you have it!" Chips squeaks. "So, why not help them?"

"Because they'll use it. Or they'll make me use it."

"Is that a… a bad thing?"

"Think about it," I sigh, only just realising it myself. "Why did the witch tell you to give it to someone who doesn't need it?"

"Who knows why magic-wielders do what they do?" Chips shrugs. "I just do what they tell me, so they don't turn me into anything."

"Give power to someone who needs it, or even just wants it, and they'll be sure to use it," I say. "But give power to someone who doesn't want it, doesn't need it, and would rather be without it, then you know what you've got?"

"What?"

"Someone who will really think before using it." I sigh. "Come on, I know what I have to do."

***

Tacsitc is gone. Where she has gone to, no scout can tell me, but the other vampire lords have gathered together.

They have retreated a little bit but still reside deep within Duke's Borough. No doubt Tacsitc's banishment has shaken them and the remaining seven of them seem to be in a quarrel. Luckily, from my vantage point, I can get a good idea of who is winning.

Atog is larger and louder than the others. I can hear the sound of his booming voice from up here where I secretly watch them. He is like a manifestation of a pit bull, but still tall enough to be head and shoulders above all the rest. His face is gnarly and grim, his attire heavy and dark, his hair dirty and unkempt. Of course, none of this is surprising considering his animal familiar is a dung beetle the size of a truck.

"I'm… I'm… here… finally…"

I turn round and, for a moment, I forget all about the vampire lords below us. Us! I can ascend a towering building such as this with ease, but by his red face, profuse sweating, and glazed eyes, this little halfling has found it a far more strenuous activity.

"You didn't have to follow me up the building, Chips!"

"Oh…" Chips takes a moment to breathe, sweat matting his untidy hair and his little legs wobbling like jelly. "…Thanks… for telling me now… right after I've… all the way… so many… stairs…"

I shake my head and turn back to watch the vampire lords quarrelling.

Atog remonstrates in front of the others. Derig, with his frightened eyes and frightening appearance, is staying atop his giant spider, but some of the others are closer. Liit looks to be panicking, Deoitcl pontificates seemingly in agreement, Ricmeet looks lost, Nroat hangs back, and Onaea wanders around the others, content to giggle to herself in her manic way.

"What… are they… doing?" Chips asks me, peering around me and looking down.

"Arguing," I reply unhelpfully.

"Are they going to attack?"

"Eventually."

"Why don't they attack now?"

"Because I banished one of them, remember?" I say. "They're nervous, and they've never been nervous before… so now is the perfect time."

"The perfect time for what?" Chips gasps. "Wait, what are you doing?"

"What does it look like I'm doing?" I say innocently. "…I'm going back down."

"But I've only just… it took me so long… my legs are… why… just… just why…"

I can't wait for a little halfling with even littler legs. I'd like to, of course. After all, it's always nice to go into a confrontation side-by-side with someone who can't run as fast as you, but I simply can't wait. The time is now. The lords are nervous. Amirah's right—attacking them is too risky. But Alma is also right—running won't achieve anything (if anything, it will only encourage our overlords). So, I'm going to do to them what they have been doing unto us. I'm going to scare them.

Minutes later, I step out of the building, and I stand in the middle of this deserted city street. Deserted, that is, but for seven angry and very cruel vampire lords. And a banshee.

It's watching me with its pale, creamy eyes. Peeking out from a side alley, apparently unseen by the others, the banshee crouches nervously. Its long fair hair doesn't look quite so fair anymore, and the grey hoodie hanging over its body is even more dirt-stained than before. I stop and stare for a moment. The banshee looks frightened, but not for itself. As the moment passes, the banshee slinks back down the alleyway and is gone from my sight.

"Oi!"

I snap back to reality and find myself faced with seven vampire lords surrounding me, all of whom look even angrier than they did before. All eyes on me. Hooray.

"Sorry," I stumble awkwardly. "I zoned out for a moment. What did you say?"

"I said," Atog barks while his eyes seemingly try to burn holes into my skull, "what's a pathetic whelp like yourself—a bloodless embarrassment to our kind, no less—doing stepping out in front of us?"

"Oh, I see." I try to sound nonchalant, because if anything could get under the skin of this lot, it would be a pathetic whelp like me acting neither anxious, interested, or excited for any of them. "This is why I'm here," I say before steam has a chance to shoot out their ears.

And I take out the thingamabob and show it to them. Just to show it to them, mind. I have no intention of actually using it, because it's ultimately useless, but they don't know that… I'm hoping.

"What?" Onaea squeals, her huge mouth dripping saliva and her wild eyes stung by what I now hold in my hand. "What is it? What does the fool bring? A shiny little bauble, for sure, but to what end? To what end?! Our end? No end? The fool's end? Yes! Yes! *Ha ha ha!* The fool's end! End the fool! End the fool!"

"Be quiet, you nattering crackbrain!" Nroat chastises Onaea before turning his long face in my direction. He looks down at me as if I'm a pile of poo on his pristine garden patio. "You seem to have in your possession an interesting item. One you have no doubt thieved somehow, for which you will presently be punished."

"It looks scary," Ricmeet whines. "I don't like the red. Someone make it stop. Make it go away!"

"Yes, yes, but what is it?" Liit asks, tilting her head and scrunching up her face as she scrutinizes my thingamabob. "Looks like a Christmas tree decoration. Where's the harm in that?"

Only Derig and Deoitcl hang back. Derig stays atop his giant spider, whilst Deoitcl seems content to let the others come toward me first, staying instead next to his big lion who sits and watches me with dark eyes.

"A pretty bauble maybe, but what use is it?" Atog, his huge bulk leading the others, is now several feet away from me. I should run. Every fibre in my being is telling me to run. But this is why I'm here. Because it's got to be me. Alma can only lose quickly, fighting a battle she can't hope to win, while Amirah's chosen path to retreat and survive is only doomed to lose slowly, but I can beat them. This can beat them. In a world of fights they always win and subjects forever at their heel, the one thing that can beat these bastards is what they cannot control. If they don't see through my bluff, they'll see a power they're not sure of. They'll see something they can't defeat through force, something they can't bring to its knees, and therefore something that defies their control. And they'll run. I hope.

"Turn away," I say, sounding more confident than I feel, "and never come back. Do you hear me?"

Silence. Complete silence. Some of them look dumbstruck, others look piqued, but Atog just looks angry.

"I don't know what you think you've got there, little fang," he says to me through clenched teeth, "but I assure you, it can't save you from the likes of us."

Oh dear.

"That…" I say, forcing a smile onto my face, "…is where you're wrong." Now I try to sound smug, but I fear a little squeak escapes me. "Seen Tacsitc lately, hmm?"

"Yes."

Wait. What?

"She's standing behind you."

Erm. Are they bluffing? Do I look round?

"*Ha ha ha!* Tacsitc looks none too pleased! None too pleased at all! Sent back to her home, she was! But back now! Back and happy!"

I really want to turn round. Maybe just a quick glance. But Tacsitc can't be standing behind me. She's banished! I banished her! What good is banishing someone if they're only going to turn up again a few hours later?

I turn round. Yep, she's there. Apparently, I only banished her as far as her own borough.

"Boo." She smiles, her blood red lips parting to show off her pearly white fangs.

Shit. Bluff definitively seen through.

***

Atog is the first to grab me and I instinctively turn round and slam the thingamabob against the side of his face. He screams in anger and agony, but I dare not flinch or pull away. Within seconds, the red light of the magical orb has travelled through Atog, overwhelming him before dying away. And Atog is gone, vanished, disappeared—not presently here—and the thingamabob, which I still hold in my hand, is a little smaller than it was moments ago, yet still it pulses with such power.

The seven remaining lords descend on me with vigour and violence, and they are joined by their animal familiars. It all amounts to a confusing mess of flying fists, swiping claws, angry shouting, and chaotic tumbling. This isn't how this was supposed to go.

I try to get away, which is exceedingly difficult when surrounded by seven of your kin who are far stronger than you are, as well as a spider the size of a large building, a crazed hyena the size of an elephant, large black dogs, a truck-sized beetle, an oversized black lion, and finally Poppy, Tacsitc's cat which is as big as a house. There's also an ostrich and a panda, though in fairness these two are not doing that much.

The concrete road beneath us cracks and shakes under the chaotic bundle that I find myself beneath. I lash out in any and all directions. I wave the thingamabob, trying to scare them away at the very least, but they show no fear. Why should they? It's barely more than an inconvenience to them.

I'm punched hard in the face, elbowed in the gut, kicked out from under my legs, picked up and swung around and released. I fly into a wall, breaking some bones, and I fall face first onto the ground below me, breaking my nose. I'm up in moments and my bones are healed, only to be broken again when the giant dung beetle charges into me. A wall falls over me, and then another wall and another wall, and finally a building drops down on us. Luckily, I roll under the beetle, so I'm not completely squashed—only a little bit squashed.

As the beetle smashes its way out of the rubble, I see my chance to escape. I see it, but I don't get the chance to take it. Onaea jumps on my back and pulls roughly at my face.

"A naughty vampire!" this insane psychopath cackles. "Should play nice with everyone else! A game only plays well if everyone plays nice!"

I shoulder her off, knocking her off balance, only for the posh prick Nroat to come forward, grip me by my throat, and lift me up into the air. Somehow, even as he holds me up, I still feel as if he's looking down at me. Where's my thingamabob? Ah, I can see it below me. I must have dropped it when Onaea jumped on my back. Bugger.

"Onaea's point is relevant," Nroat scoffs. "The game only works…" He squeezes my throat; the pain is unbearable, and I hear something inside of me crack. "…when all the little pieces *fall into line*."

He throws me down. A moment of lying on these fallen ruins might well be enough for my neck to regenerate (and to scoop up my thingamabob) but the pain is still here. Pain doesn't just stop, even if the cause of such pain is no longer present. It has taken me far too long to learn this. I try to run for it, but I'm immediately trapped again. They're just playing with me at this point.

Deoitcl prances around whilst his big dark lion circles me. Deoitcl's a foppish, all-style-no-substance kind of vampire. His big clothes and dramatic hair style would fit well into a particularly pretentious Shakespeare performance.

"Don't trouble yourself with thought, my dear," he mocks me, hopping around like a prancer on a stage. "Come away from your aspirations. Be well with your lot. Find a new passion to burn your frustrations with."

The lion pounces and bites down hard on my leg. I scream, which surprises me because in the past few minutes I had quite forgotten I had my own voice.

"Come away, pet. Come away," Deoitcl says in his oily voice, and his lion steps back, releasing me. The beast keeps its eyes on me though, no doubt eager to finish me off.

I watch my leg knit back together in moments, and then I look up to see I am surrounded. Seven vampire lords, and behind each one of them their own familiar, look down on me.

"What do we do with this one?" the cowardly Ricmeet, small and simple, asks the others.

"I don't know. Is he that important?" the idiot called Liit ponders aloud, his body as misshapen as his mind is underdeveloped.

"Shut up, you two," Nroat growls, and the both of them slink back. "You have a name, boy?"

"Caiden," I say. My voice croaks but I think I manage to get a decent amount of resentment and disrespect into my tone. I must have done because Nroat insults me as he strikes me across my face. The hit sends me back to the ground, spinning me round so I am face down. Perfect! I have the thingamabob in my hand. It got rid of Atog, even if just for a while, so maybe if I can even the odds a bit, I can still get out of this.

"But what *are* we going to do with him?" Ricmeet whines, coming forward again, panic-ridden and unable to keep silent.

"We're going to crush him," Tacsitc says.

"Separate him, also," Nroat adds.

"And cast the parts of him left to the farthest corners of the city!" Deoticl proclaims.

"Where your growth will be diminished tenfold," Derig says, his frightened eyes practically quivering but his rotten teeth grinning maliciously. "For the smaller the piece of you that is left, the longer it will take, and we will make you so small. I warned you. How I warned you."

"A severed leg remains, and in days you will return," Onaea whoops, "but a little finger and it'll be a year, a tiny toe and you can be sure it will be more."

"We will leave you so small. Smaller than a grain of sand."

"Too far apart to find yourself."

"Yes, yes, yes!" Onaea continues, excitedly. "Years it will take him to grow back! Years and years! Pain all the while! And all the while—pain!"

I notice even Ricmeet has become excited. "Yes, yes, we'll be free of him, then!"

And Liit joins in as well, "It serves him right. And I was just about to suggest crushing him, and pulling him apart, and then putting the bits of him in, erm, different bits, or parts, of the city. Yeah. Yeah, it's a good idea. A really good idea—of mine. My good idea."

One of them is right above me. I can feel their presence like a weight on my body. It's now or never. I grip the thingamabob tightly and turn fast.

Derig's frightened eyes are all I see, but I can feel the scarred vampire lord holding my wrist tightly, the thingamabob inches away from making contact with him.

"Don't you see?" Derig pleads with me. "This is the only way. The only way you'll learn. All is as it is, and all is as it will always be. You must understand this. You will understand this, after you return."

"Take a long time!" Onaea chuckles incessantly. "So long! Goodbye! Come back with a new head!" The chuckling stops and suddenly her madness becomes a burning rage. Her wicked face comes close to mine, and still my wrist is held by Derig, making the thingamabob useless. "A new head, you hear me! New thinking thoughts! Or don't come back at all!" A moment. I have absolutely no idea what Onaea's going to do next and I don't think she does either. As it happens, the moment passes and she bursts out laughing, dropping down and rolling around, completely unable to contain herself.

"Let us begin," Nroat commands, "and once Atog returns to us, we'll set about finishing this sorry little affair."

No. No, I can't let them do this. Not so easily, anyway. It's as if this is all just another day at the office for them. For me, it's terrifying and agonizing. I can't stand the idea of Alma being taken or even being torn apart like I'm about to be. And Helisha and Amirah, I want them to be okay too. I don't want them to suffer. Everyone else in the borough as well. I suppose I should feel bad for them too.

I really thought I could have scared the lords away. I thought the witch had given me the thingamabob for a reason. But it was all for nothing, and I'm about to pay for my total and utter failure.

The seven lords surround me, and they take hold of my appendages, my neck, and my torso. They lift me up so that they are standing, and I am held above the ground.

"No! Wait!" I'm embarrassed it's taken me this long to speak out loud. I'm even more embarrassed to hear how desperate I sound. "Please!"

But they're not listening. Some of them are laughing, others are directing orders, and a few growl with anticipation. And amidst it all, a little voice in my head points out to me that Tacsitc holds me at my neck, which means I'm staring up into her beautiful, terrifying, lustrous, horrifying face.

"Hmm," she whispers seductively in my ear. "No safe word for you."

Not all bad, then. Until, that is, they start pulling me apart. Today's word, children, is owwwwwwww.

****

A long time ago, I met a travelling witch. Or maybe she met me. It's very difficult to know where one stands with witches, wizards, warlocks, and the like. Anyway, the old crone gave me a little glass bottle and told me anything I put in the bottle would, quite literally, be timeless. I think I may have wasted such a gift, but on the other hand, I don't really see what else I could have done with it.

My arm and leg bones broke a while ago. My neck has clicked a few times. My spine is cracking. I can feel my skin tearing and my muscles ripping. I'm not thinking at all about that little glass bottle, hidden under a big cabinet, filled with barely a mouthful of a long-lost milkmaid's blood. Blood that is captured in time. Instead, I'm thinking about just how much being pulled apart really, really hurts.

And then it stops hurting. They suddenly let me go and I fall to the ground. Above me, the sun breaks through the grey clouds, allowing light to strike us. And as if heralding from the heavens themselves, Alma leaps across me astride Snowy, her terrifying jet-black unicorn. Her workman's jacket and baggy trousers billow magnificently in the rushing wind of her own charge. Even her T-shirt—on which stills remains some of the dried dark blood of our own kind—looks majestic and the cartoon cat is now somehow *heroically* proclaiming *I don't do mornings… or afternoons… or evenings.*

She circles round me, knocking over my attackers. Snowy the unicorn kicks out and sends the remaining vampire lords hurtling backwards. Deoitcl's lion leaps forward, teeth bared, but the unicorn smoothly turns to avoid the attack, following up with a hefty kick that puts the big cat down. The actual big cat—the one the size of a house—hisses loudly. Alma turns Snowy, kicks into a charge, and then jumps up. The jump is an impressive one. A very impressive one. It would have to be impressive, of course, for Snowy's horn to painfully poke the big black cat on the nose.

The startled kitty panics and jumps several hundred feet into the air, causing a small earthquake when it lands.

Then it runs away with its tail between its legs. Finally, Snowy faces off against Ricmeet and his ostrich. Ricmeet cowers in fear, dropping to his knees and curling up into himself, blubbering like a baby. As for his ostrich… well… it's a misconception that ostriches bury their heads in the sand to hide from danger, but apparently no one told Ricmeet's ostrich about this. I have never seen an ostrich bury its head in the sand, but I can now say I have seen an ostrich smash its head into a concrete road.

"Caiden!" Alma turns to me and holds out her hand. "Come with me if you want to get the hell out of here!" And I do. I really, really do.

Riding a unicorn, even as a backseat passenger as I am now, is a funny thing. All around you the world is rushing past. It is a messy collage of blurred buildings, momentary images and fleeting oddities. But what's funny is how distant it all feels from up on this unicorn.

Even as the hooves thunder across the road and as this fantastical beast jolts up and down, up and down, up and down, it is all happening as if from far away. I am neither deafened by the hooves against stone nor buffeted by the wind whipping by. I'm not even dizzy from the rough ride. I am in a bubble of pure contentment. I even feel safe.

I hardly notice the building-sized spider and house-sized cat charging after us, taking intermittent swipes at us which Snowy narrowly ducks under or hops over. I am unbothered by the chasing lion biting at our heels. I don't even mind when the huge hyena crashes into a building after it takes a corner too fast, causing bricks and mortar to drop down all around us like some hellish, metropolis rain.

It's all good where I am. Maybe it's the magic of the unicorn I'm riding. Or maybe it's because I'm holding onto Alma, and she's the one saving me from what would have been a terrible fate. Ever since I took her hand, actually, I've felt it. She might not be as wise as Amirah or as pragmatic as Helisha or as worldly-wise as I am (ahem) but she has something about her that none of us have. She's definitely a pusher, but now I realise she also leaves a sort of wake behind her, a wake that one can ride on.

And it is all good because we're away from them, our pursuers buried as they are under rubble and ruin. We've escaped. Alma gives a little kick and Snowy leaps into the air, jumps off a wall, then another wall, and we're climbing very high indeed. I can almost—*almost*—feel my blissful bubble about to pop, but then all is well as we land safe and sound on a rooftop overlooking the borough and the city beyond.

Alma slides off her unicorn with effortless elegance. I let gravity take hold and do what it does best.

"Are you okay?" Alma asks me.

I answer with a question of my own. "Do you ever like something, but then it stops, and you realise how horribly terrified you were the entire time?"

"I don't follow."

"No," I sigh, my entire body still lying flat on the rooftop. "You're too young, I suppose."

BOOP

"I guess that's what it does," Chips tells me. "It sends us back to places? Maybe?"

"Wow," I sigh. "So, this incredibly powerful gift from a witch, which you delivered to me with instructions to give to whomever didn't need it, can only send a terrifying and incredibly dangerous vampire lord, ooh, a few miles away…"

"Yes."

"So, it *is* useless. This is why magic should be avoided at all costs!"

We're in the square once again. Everyone is here, actually. Amirah's pulled everyone back and put us all on red alert (or redder alert). This, terrifyingly enough, seems to be it.

Using the thingamabob, I sent Atog back to his own borough, just as I sent Tacsitc back to Queen's Corner earlier. Chips is able to confirm this with his half-sense, which he shares with all the other halflings spread throughout Vampire City.

"We're all connected, see," Chips explained to me. "What us halflings lack in size, we make up for with a special bond we share. Our understanding, our knowledge, our thoughts, these can all be shared between all us halflings, but only through our half-sense."

"Why didn't your half-sense warn you about Tacsitc turning up a few hours ago, then?" I asked, bad-temperedly.

"I'm the only halfling from Queen's Corner who survived," Chips answered. Wow. Now I feel bad about sounding bad-tempered.

And so here we all are. Waiting for Atog to return and so initiate the vampire lords' siege in full. The afternoon grows late, the sky is dark and heavy (though it stubbornly refuses to rain) and no one is talking much.

Helisha is close by, Chips and I are hunkered down behind a barricade, and we are flanked by every kind of sub-mortal this place has to offer. Orcs in armour, elves rushing back and forth, bare-chested dwarves, nervous goblins, a particularly mean-looking faun, and so on and so forth. Everyone except for vampires (not counting Alma, Helisha, and me). Duke's Borough's own vampires eventually healed up after our graveyard tussle… and scarpered. Cowards and self-serving leeches, the lot of them.

Amirah is in the middle, sending out her elf marshals with new orders and receiving reports from those returning. Alma is with her too, but where Amirah is energetic and constantly moving, Alma is calm and patient. Waiting. Ready. I think to myself, if I could be like anyone, I would be like Alma… but only if someone like Amirah was close by at the same time.

"I just don't get it!" Chips pulls my focus back to reality. "Why give me the errand at all? Why send the gift at all? It doesn't make any sense."

"Like I said," I say through clenched teeth, "magic is a waste of time and should be avoided at all costs. It's just a plaything for those who don't have any rules to play by. A sick joke."

"But I risked my life!"

"What are you two moaning about?" Helisha calls over to us, her eyes filled with suspicion.

"Nothing!" I quickly say. Rolling her eyes, Helisha moves on, checking barricades, tightening armour, sharing tips on how to stab efficiently, and just generally keeping herself occupied.

"Why are you still hiding it?" Chips asks me once she's definitely out of earshot.

"Because the others would either use it or not use it," I reply, "and, as we've proven, using it is pointless and not using it is just as pointless."

"I don't follow."

"Don't you get it?" I growl, exasperated. "This gift, this magical orb, this thingamabob… it's an illusion, only a trick, it promises a weapon, but it doesn't *win anything*. Your witch was playing a nasty little trick on us. To use it is to be found hopelessly wanting, and to not use it is to hold onto something that has no worth."

"Right."

"You don't get it, do you?"

"No."

"That's fine too."

"Oh." Chips nods, although I'm not entirely convinced he's satisfied. "So, why did the witch want me to give it to someone who wouldn't need it? Why not give it to Alma and watch her fail spectacularly? Or why not give it to the elf and watch her run without hope?"

"I don't know," I sigh. After all, I'm just a normal guy, with no leadership responsibilities, no personal sense of ambition, and no burning desire to save the world and correct all injustices. Why *do* I have this useless power? "But the reason, whatever it is, doesn't change how useless it is. The best I can do with it..." I feel my hand in my pocket holding the thingamabob tightly. "...is delay the inevitable."

And speak of the devil, here comes the inevitable.

***

There are eight roads leading into the square. Some of them are main roads, others are smaller side roads, and a few of them branch out into other roads and streets almost immediately upon leaving the square. Regardless of their nature, there are eight roads leading into the square. And eight vampire lords. It's funny how the real world often fits together all snug and perfect like a puzzle.

"Don't let them see the whites of your eyes," an elf marshal says behind us, moving along our line. "If they get too close, move back." I would like to think I'm surrounded by those with enough common sense to move out of the way of a charging spider the size of a huge building. But, you never know, it doesn't hurt to offer a little reminder.

"We're all going to die, aren't we?" Chips suddenly says. He's wearing a loose-fitting helmet along with a rather shabby chest piece and holding what used to be a garden shovel. I don't see any point in lying to him. Besides, I don't think I have the willpower to lie even if I thought it would help.

"You all are, yes," I say.

Along each of the eight roads, a vampire lord advances. Derig on his giant spider, Atog marching in front of his truck-sized dung beetle, Onaea on the back of her crazed hyena, Ricmeet behind his ostrich, Liit ambling up alongside her panda, Nroat surrounded by his fearsome dogs, Tacsitc practically lounging on top of her house-sized cat Poppy, and finally Deoitcl, making a show of it all with his dark lion, all swagger and swank.

They stop not far from our defences. I wonder what they see. Do they see a squalid and irritating nuisance before them? Or do they see defiance? Are we even a problem to them? Might they even be enjoying this?

Or are we an appalling insult? Does our very existence throw their own concept of reality completely out of whack?

Whatever they truly think of us, just like the nature of the eight roads leading into the square, it really doesn't matter. They're coming for us regardless. Oh look, here they come now.

Derig comes first atop his giant spider.

Almost everyone on this planet has experienced the horrible terror of seeing a house spider scurry unnaturally quickly across a carpet. All those legs, moving too fast to see, and it's coming for you! Well, it turns out size really doesn't matter. Derig's spider is bigger than most office blocks yet still it comes at us faster than seemingly possible. Those massive legs crash through walls and knock aside obstacles without hindrance. The snarling fangs open up and a terrible screech deafens our ears. Here it is!

"Fire!" Amirah roars from behind us.

Dwarves are awesome. Of course, I don't particularly care for them. This is mostly because I've never bothered to get to know any of them. But right now, as a titanic hairy spider charges at me (and others, I suppose) I am absolutely convinced all dwarves are awesome. This is because, on Amirah's command, our dwarves fire their catapults, their ballistae, and some other strange mechanical contraptions that send spinning, flailing, and spikey missiles towards the humongous oncoming arachnid.

Balls of fire burst on the spider. Pointy things imbed themselves in its skin. A large bag is fired over the eight eyes and explodes, raining dust and rubble onto those great big black saucers. The spider screeches, Derig wails, and so an out-of-control, giant arachnid stumbles and squirms almost right above me. For a moment, a blissful moment, the spider looks dazed and frightened as it stumbles into an awkward retreat.

But that's all. It stumbles a bit, it squirms for a moment, and it goes back a few steps before now coming back with anger. Dwarves are useless. All they've done is piss it off! And now an oversized hyena is causing trouble.

I don't know what we thought would happen, or rather what we hoped would happen, or perhaps that should be what we prayed-to-any-deity-who-might-be-listening would make happen. Whichever it is, it was a bloody waste of time. These shabbily made blockades and barriers, and these walls made out of whatever could be found might disrupt a charging army but to these animals they prove no problem at all.

I look to my side and see Nroat's dogs are in amongst us. They bite and bark and pull down defenders, all the while skipping away from frightened attacks and clumsy swings. Onaea's hyena is ahead of me, picking up victims in its jaws and shaking them fervently. The dung beetle rams its way through defensive formations, a big lion is running us down, Poppy is playing with us, an ostrich is running around being completely useless and very loud, and there's also a panda. The panda isn't doing anything productive or helpful, but it's obviously still evil because the black-and-white bear has sat down and is idly munching through a fallen tree person.

The vampire lords themselves howl, cheer, whoop, and snarl as they direct their familiars, and they also get stuck in themselves. It's chaos. It's madness. It's hopeless. It's coming right at me!

"Ooooh!" Onaea cheers with wicked delight, her lidless and bloodshot eyes fixing on me. She leaps atop me, her wild hair resembling a burning firework, and she pins me flat to the ground. "You didn't want to play before—such a sourpuss! - but you'll have to play now! *Ha ha ha!* Oh, little vampire, I'll add your fangs to my own! To my own! To my own!"

She cackles insanely and I get a full, close-up view inside her unnaturally wide mouth. What I see turns my stomach, and that really is saying something. Fangs that are definitely not her own have been forced into her gums and up into the inside of her mouth. It's like a shark's mouth trying to outdo all the other shark mouths. It's a dentist's worst nightmare. Upon receiving the bill, it would be the patient's worst nightmare too.

"No!" I writhe, losing my mind. "No, thank you!" As if that might help.

"Don't be so silly!" Here's her anger again. Her wild madness switches instantly to inconsolable rage. She's in my face, her horrifically wide mouth inches from mine, her deranged eyes burning with hatred. "This is the game! And you're playing! You're playing! You're playing! You're playing!"

I shove the thingamabob inside her mouth. She instinctively bites down hard but it's too late. The thingamabob goes off.

Red light snakes its way under her skin and wraps around her body. Such terrible pain grips Onaea but still she won't let go. If she's going, she's apparently taking my arm with her. Just as I think I can't bear it any longer, the red light explodes out of her and blinds me.

My arm looks like it's been through a shredder. Moments later, as the blinding light fades away and my vision heals itself, I can see Onaea is gone, and my arm is just about finished pulling itself back together.

An elf marshal is thrown clear over the square, dwarves are being squashed underfoot, orcs are taking a beating, and Alma rides from one disaster to another. Her unicorn, Snowy, kicks and bites and Alma herself leaps off and pushes various lords away, snapping a few bones in two. Nroat's beastly hounds surround her and keep her pinned down, but it's not too long before each pup has been walloped, crippled, or thrown back.

"Unruly bitch!" Nroat snarls. The posh prick slaps Alma who is caught off balance by the sudden attack. Meanwhile, a part of my brain wonders how I could have heard Nroat's insult from so far away. Oh, I see. It's because I'm not far away. I'm running at him and I'm right next to him. Wait! I'm right next to him!

But he hasn't noticed me. Instead, he's standing over a fallen and stunned Alma, throwing down on her without mercy. I grab him and pull him back, desperately holding on, terrified of what he'll do to me were I to let go.

But it's Nroat who ends up wailing in wretched torment. The mystical red light of my thingamabob worms its way through him before erupting in explosive fashion. And Alma and I are alone, and the thingamabob in my hand is quite a bit smaller now. I'm not thinking about it though. I'm only looking down at Alma who is looking at the thingamabob in my hand and then she looks at me, her eyes wide with bewilderment and I think anger too.

"What the hell is that thing?" she manages to say pointedly.

There's no way to tell her everything right now, so I settle for something meaningless and unhelpful instead.

"My contribution. Don't get your hopes up."

As she gets to her feet, Alma looks like she's going to press me for more, but then we both remember there's a desperate battle being lost around us and so we turn our attention to bigger fish and head off in opposite directions.

I run, I scramble, I roll out of the way and as I straighten up, I find myself back to back with Helisha.

"What are we doing here?" she spits out, sweating and exasperated.

I groan. "Not you as well!"

"You and me." Helisha keeps going, ignoring me. "We're vampires. Old vampires! Shouldn't we be on the other side?"

As she says this, a spider's leg comes down between us. The ground beneath us cracks and we both roll away. Helisha's roll is expertly athletic and smooth, like that of a soldier's, whereas my roll starts off as a tumble going down before finishing with a desperate muddle to get back on my feet.

"Probably," I reply despondently, now running alongside Helisha, "but I guess we're just too damn honest!"

"Honest?!" she exclaims after we've found momentary shelter behind an upturned, rusted, burnt-out vehicle.

"We know the world has to change, don't we?" I elaborate. "The other side probably knows it too, deep down, *really* deep down, but you and I are the only ones who are facing up to it, because you got shit-canned and left to rot by the way the world is, and I…"

"You what?"

Yes. Quite. I what?

"…I found someone else to follow," I say, feeling very honest. And then the vehicle explodes and sends us hurtling apart from one another.

I land at a pair of six-digit, black-and-white panda claws. Looking up, I see the barely curious, overwhelmingly lazy eyes of a panda looking down at me.

It would be funny, even cute, if only the panda wasn't chewing on some fresh offal.

"Hello there." Ricmeet, the smallest vampire lord, bends down and peers at me with a strange, detached look in his eye. "Can I help you?"

"Are… are you serious?"

"I just don't want anyone to get unnecessarily hurt," Ricmeet says, and above him a dryad screams as they are thrown through the air to land somewhere beyond with a nasty crunching sound.

"You're useless!" I jump to my feet, suddenly enraged.

The evil I can understand, the greed is just how it is, the bullying and the hatred and the selfishness all comes with the package, but this…this is privileged ignorance. Worse! This is feigned good guy behaviour! "You're pathetic!" I scream in Ricmeet's shocked face, and even the panda looks up. "You're so incomprehensibly powerful and yet so utterly useless!"

"Well," Ricmeet shrugs weakly, "if you would only do as you're told—"

"So it's our fault? It's our own fault you're killing us!"

"…in a way, yes."

"Unbelievable!" I decry. "You actually believe that, don't you!?"

"Well, if your new lord hadn't tried to change anything, then we wouldn't be here, would we?" Ricmeet argues, glancing nervously to across the square where Alma is currently throwing aside a yapping hyena. "Besides," he continues, "what can I do? There's only one of me."

"Then do at least one thing!" I explode and punch Ricmeet across his cheek. It's a really strong punch, taking him off his feet, and he doesn't come back down. I only realise now I was holding the thingamabob in my hand, and upon being punched Ricmeet exploded in a sudden ball of light and disappeared.

The panda goes back to chewing.

***

It's over.

Our resolve has broken. The defences are down. We're running. Fleeing. Just trying to get away. I knew it would end like this. Even so, it stings the eyes to see it.

The sun is starting to come down, peeping through heavy clouds and drawing long shadows across the city, and only now does the sky break. A cascade of little raindrops falls to earth, seeming paltry and insignificant compared to the bodies strewn across the city square.

I can't tell who is who or what is what (although there's a big broken piece of bark that was probably a tree person).

Everything is stained in red. I have no idea where Alma, Amirah, Helisha, or Chips are. Amirah and Chips are probably dead, I think glumly. I should have done more. Could I have done more? I shake my head to rid me of this guilt and these questions. None of it matters now, anyway.

"I warned you."

I turn round and see Derig standing in front of me. His giant spider waits silently behind its lord. Derig's eyes look as strained and as terrified as before. His scars are especially sharp though, or maybe I'm just noticing them more. The vampire lord stands amidst the destruction he and his kin have wreaked. I reckon about half an hour has passed since Amirah shouted "Fire!".

"Oh, foolish one," Derig sighs. "You were all warned."

"You think we didn't know it would end like this?" I angrily reply. "We might be poor but we're not stupid!"

"Only a simpleton would defy the order of the city!" Derig spits back at me in fury, but his frightened eyes tell a different story.

"Only someone desperate enough would take on such a hopeless cause," I reply, or rather that's what I should have replied with. What I actually reply with isn't quite as poignant: "Piss off."

"You fool!" Derig spits again through broken teeth and scarred lips. "Nothing you have done today will change a thing! Everything is as it ever was, and everything is still as it ever will be!"

"Erm… what?" I ask. All that bluster, all those big words… I wonder just how frightened Derig really is.

"We warned you!" he berates me. "How we warned you! Can you not see how all have their place in this city? Is it not conducive to peace for all parties to adjudicate such alignments bestowed upon them amidst the ordering of society?"

Here's a pro tip from a veteran bullshitter: if it sounds overly indulgent and needlessly confusing, it's because the point they're trying to make is total bullshit. It's very difficult to argue against such bullshit though, because after all, the bullshitter making the argument is already eating bullshit. Some might try to reason with them, others might try to force them, and a few will simply ignore them, but I do none of these options. I am far too angry, much too weak, and right now there's a light inside me that thinks it is a flamethrower.

"I refer you to my earlier statement," I say as I turn away from him. "Piss off."

This utterly terrified and utterly terrifying lord rushes at me in a whirl of angry vengeance and childish petulance. His spider comes too, striding forwards, overtaking its master and stabbing its legs down in a clumsy attempt to squash me. I swerve to the side easily enough and duck when the creature tries to swipe me up with its fangs, but luckily the dreaded thing is far too large for any kind of accuracy. Or rather, I am far too small. It seems usual roles are presently reversed, and I am the tiny pest evading the clumsy, erratic stamping of this giant, hysterical bully.

Derig pays his spider no mind, not even looking at the trunk-like legs slamming down around us or the occasional thundering bite of fangs. He hits me and I stumble backwards precariously, only just righting myself in time to roll out the way of a descending spider leg. The ground where I had just been cracks and crunches under the heavy weight, but I have no time to breathe before Derig is on me again. He grips me, lifts me up, shakes me, and spits into my face.

"There is an order to our city!" he splutters, as if caught between a terrible rage and a terrifying fear. "If you cannot find your place within it, then you will be cast without! Torn asunder! Held apart! You cannot—you *must not*—be allowed to fester!"

His hands are on my face, he holds me down, and his fingers start to bore into my skull. The pain is horrible. I try to pull him off, but my hands around his hands are like dandelions against stone. How can I be this weak? He doesn't even notice me trying. He's not even flinching with the effort, yet here I am screaming with all my strength, as futile as it is.

No. I am not weak. It is not me that is so weak but him that is so strong. Derig is strong. Years spent hoarding the power of his borough, drinking his subjects dry, taking their own strength for his own has made him stronger than any vampire has any right to be.

Ouch. My skull appears to be cracking. The pain is indescribable, so I won't bother trying. I'll just keep screaming instead. Then the world erupts around us and for a few moments I don't know what is up or down, left or right, earth or sky, living or dead. I don't care though. I'm just happy because the pieces of my skull are clicking back into place.

I land hard but, relatively speaking, it is pleasant enough considering what my brain has just been through. I look up, dazed but present, and I realise that it was Derig's spider that saved me. The great big clumsy oafish arachnid basically trod on us. Too many legs and far too much adrenaline. As big as it is, I bet it's still got a normal-sized spider brain.

If I am dazed, however, then Derig is stupefied beyond all comprehension. He's sitting on his bottom not far from where I now stand up, and he has his legs sprawled out in front of him with a blank look on his face. He's had all his stuff knocked out of him and he doesn't know what to do now.

The spider is also clueless. It can't see us and whatever connection these beastly familiars hold with their lords has, for the moment at least, been stunned into silent nothingness. So, while the giant beast blunders off to the side, I walk over to Derig and this time it is I that looks down upon him.

"For all your power," I say, unable to hide the wry, somewhat spiteful smile on my face, "none of you know how to lose."

He just looks at me like a dumbfounded toddler, then touches his finger to his nose before holding it out in front of him. There's dark blood on the tip of his finger and, as I look now, I see a trickle of the stuff dribbling down from his nostril. I wonder how long it's been since Derig has seen his own blood. Perhaps this is even the first time.

"And if you don't know how to lose," I continue, "then you'll never understand what winning really is."

And with that, I press the thingamabob against Derig's face. He's too dumbstruck to defend himself and with a pop of light he's gone. Just like that. The spider, masterless and thoughtless, continues to blunder down an empty street, and I am alone.

***

It's worryingly small now. Shrivelled, even. I'm not sure how much the little chap's got left to give but I can't fathom it's much. It's kind of droopy as well and so it feels depressingly flimsy in my hand. I wonder if the witch had a way to recharge her gift. Probably not. I imagine she lost interest a while ago. Magic-wielders usually do.

The streets are oddly quiet. I use the word *oddly* because every now and then there's a scream, or a crash, or a crowd running in terror, or a building falling down. A few fires have broken out too. I've left the city square behind, but the bodies aren't disappearing. They're not as messy as they were in the square, but they're still about, dotted around the place. It's cold too. The wind is starting to pick up and it's blowing the rain into my face.

"I don't understand it." Liit wanders towards me. She looks as jumbled as her own brain undoubtedly is. "I just don't understand why we had to do all this."

"Yet you did it anyway?" I grumble.

"Well, yeah," Liit shrugs. "The others were doing it, so…"

"You're an idiot," I say, without fear or anger. I'm too tired and I don't want to waste the morsels that are left of my energy on someone who simply isn't worth it.

"Yeah." Liit shrugs again, and this time she's smiling. She knows she's an idiot, but she doesn't care. Why should she? She's got it all. I feel absolutely no sympathy for her.

"Here." I put on a smile, "catch!" And I toss the thingamabob to her. She lets out a little whoop of delight and happily catches the thingamabob. She even holds onto it while it sizzles in her hands and creeps under her skin. Then *poof* and she's gone.

"Idiot." I sigh as I bend down to pick up my flimsy, droopy thingamabob, which is now even smaller, barely bigger than a ping-pong ball.

***

I wander towards the entrance to Amirah's tunnel network. I am in no particular hurry though. The battle is lost. Nothing can be gained from trying to save anyone who might have initially gotten away. They're either running or hiding. If they're running, then they'll eventually be caught. After all, there's nowhere to run to in this city. And if they're hiding then good luck to them; if they can't hide, there's nothing I can do for them anyway.

I arrive at the side alley which leads to the narrow stairs that themselves lead down to the entrance to Amirah's tunnels but, bizarrely enough, I can't go any further. There's a dead cat in the way. The whole side alley is completely blocked off… by a giant dead black cat.

At some point, Poppy appears to have met her match. The place reeks of guts and sweat, the heat emanating from the big kitty corpse is almost overwhelming, and I haven't thought once about biting my arm and disappearing into my dreams. This is surprising to me, until a small voice points out I just did think about it. I shake the little voice away and start pulling on some cat fur.

I doubt anyone's ever tried to move a one-hundred-and-fifty-tonne kitty cat, so that would make me the first fool to try. And even though vampires are supposed to have some supernatural strength, I have been through a lot today and I'm all alone, so Poppy ain't budging.

To tell the truth, I have no idea what I'm doing. I have no idea why I'm trying to move this immovable pussycat.

What do I think I'm going to find? Yet still I try and am predictably met with resounding failure. Then the earth shifts under my feet. No. Not the earth. The pussycat! It's moving, sliding towards me, and I just barely regain my wits in time to step back and move out of the way.

The whole body moves, crunching over rubble and dragging over concrete, until the side alley is clear to enter. Alma comes around the side of the cat and stands in front of me. She's barely broken a sweat. She is, however, covered in dark blood, bruises, a few cuts, and the cartoon cat on her shirt has been ripped ragged.

"Hi." She nods to me in greeting.

I'm not sure what to say. I'm caught between the horror of our situation (which up until now, and with only myself to think about, I have been keeping at bay) and the delirious relief from seeing a familiar face. As per my usual, I settle on saying something that doesn't need to be said, that isn't funny, and that doesn't fit well with the atmosphere: "I loosened it up for you." I nod in the direction of Poppy.

Alma rolls her eyes. Then stops at the mouth of the alley. I come alongside and I too stop beside her. Tacsitc has been torn apart, her beauty no longer beautiful, and Deoitcl has been broken almost beyond recognition (as has his big lion), but it is Amirah we see, lying at the door of the tunnels (a door which is firmly closed). The elf with the hard face lies open and limp. Silver-circled eyes no longer cutting. Blood-stained hair no longer silver.

Helisha's dead too. Well, not dead. She is a vampire after all. But judging from Alma's account, it'll be a while before Helisha puts herself back together. It'll also be a good few hours before either Tacsitc or Deoitcl come back as well, probably even a whole day. Being not a vampire, however, there's no coming back for Amirah.

I seem to have missed a large chunk of the battle. Alma and Helisha went up against Tacsitc, Deoitcl, and Atog, and they held their own. While they managed to take down Atog, by the time Alma and Helisha had lost to the other two, Amirah had put most everyone in the tunnels. Except for herself.

I don't know why Amirah didn't save herself. Maybe she was caught, maybe she was making a stand, or perhaps she figured the only way to save everyone in the tunnels was to get rid of the vampires chasing them down. I don't know and we'll likely never know. But she stayed outside and somehow—*somehow*—she finished what Alma and Helisha started, but at the cost of her own life.

I should have been running to get here. Ooh, that there is a nasty little truth that will haunt me for the rest of time. I guess I'll just have to keep it at the back of my mind, with all the other nasty little truths I've collected over the years.

Alma and I pick up Amirah and take her inside. There are elves who eventually come forward and take over from us, carrying Amirah deeper into the tunnels that she designed. They have some time now and they tell us they'll use it to lie low and hunker down. It's all they can do. To just hope and pray the storm passes them by.

"It should have been her." Alma finally speaks. We've been sitting together in silence for some time now. What was once just a basement and is now the entranceway to Amirah's network of tunnels, is where we sit. So here we are sitting on this dusty floor, a single dim light bulb above us, and a closed door to an outside world of chaos and blood. Amirah's sanctuary.

"This is where I first saw her," Alma continues. "She was so good at it. Telling people where to go, helping direct the effort, managing all of them. She should have been the lord of Duke's Borough. She wouldn't have messed it up like I did. I doomed us all. I did this."

"She wouldn't have done anything," I say, perhaps cruelly so, but it's true. I turn to Alma, and I speak harshly but, I think, fairly. "There's nothing special about you, Alma. Nothing special about your blood. You just woke up quicker after your first time drinking, that's all, probably because you're so young and your blood is still… bubbly. Helisha would have come back, eventually, but when she drank Serat, she couldn't do it completely and he was able to drink her back when she passed out."

"Then Helisha should have been the new lord?"

"No. I mean, she could have been, but she would have been just another Serat, and so would I. Maybe not so cruel, maybe not so hard, but we wouldn't have done anything meaningful. Nothing outside what this city is, what it really is… We've been here too long. We're too entrenched. Too tired."

"Amirah, then," Alma gasps, holding her knees tightly against her chest, and here come the tears. "It should have been Amirah! She was a good leader!"

"But it could never have been Amirah!" I insist. "She might have been a good leader, but she was also an elf. She was too weak in a world designed to keep her weak."

"So it has to be a vampire?" Alma asks me, quietly.

"It has to be a vampire." I nod. "This broken world crushes rebellions and executes leaders. It's designed to do just that. It cannot be conquered. It can only be relinquished."

"What do I do now, Caiden?"

"You keep pushing, that's what you do, and you keep breaking fences and tearing down barriers," I tell her. "And you find good people to be leaders, and you find people who also want to change the world."

"In Vampire City?" She sighs, already defeated. "I already had all that. I pushed this city, I had Amirah too, and you and Helisha followed me, and so did most of the borough. But it still came to nothing!"

She kicks a bucket. At some point, I gather, she got up and started pacing. I'm still sitting though. And now it comes to me. The answer is so clear to me now. So obvious. And so fucking impossible.

"There's a big world out there," I say, and Alma is listening to me, "and if we can't change this city on the inside, then maybe we have to change the world beyond it, and we can be a light on dark corners, that kind of thing. And you know now… you know you need to push, and you know what it is to have good leaders, and you know people will follow you… and most importantly, you've lived in this city now, you've seen what it is really like, so you know this city *has to change*…"

"How the hell can I change the outside world from inside this city, Caiden? I'm trapped in here, same as you."

"I know you are!" And I'm starting to laugh, I can't help it. It's so hopeless. So perfectly designed. "That's what makes it so impossible! No one can get you out and no one will ever let you leave. It's completely impossible. A perfect trap. A rat race without a winner. Fresh air! If only we could breathe fresh air!"

"Yes. Fresh air. Let's go for a walk."

That isn't really what I meant, but I could still do with a walk.

The last two walking vampires in Duke's Borough walk along a deserted and partially destroyed high street. Evening is in full swing now. The sun is low in the sky, casting a deep but fractured orange light over the city. The shadows are dark and long and there is a heavy and sombre ambience that hangs over the dusk, although this might just be the lingering smell of rain mixing with the stench of rotting flesh.

"What is it, then?" Alma asks me, getting straight to the point. I don't blame her.

"A witch sent it to me," I explain, eyeing the small thingamabob in my hand, which I most recently used to get rid of the remains of Tacsitc and Deoitcl.

"A witch? To you?"

"Chips brought it," I tell her, and I wonder what's happened to the little tyke, and I feel yet more guilt for not thinking of him sooner. He's probably long dead.

"Well," Alma sighs, "what is it, then?"

"As far as I can tell, it's completely useless." I sigh back at her. "The first time I used it on Tacsitc, all it did was send her back to her own borough, Queen's Corner."

"And you've used it on the others?"

"Yes." I nod. "Derig, Onaea, Nroat, Liit, and Ricmeet, and now Tacsitc again and Deoitcl. And Atog much earlier, but he came back too."

"Yeah, I noticed." Alma breathes out deeply. "And all you had to do was touch them with it? Why doesn't it do anything to you when you hold it, then?"

"I have no idea, Alma," I admit, laughing at the complete absence of sense. "It's just a sick joke from a bored witch, remember."

"But you got all of them with it?"

"I did. For a while, at least," I moan. "They'll probably be back here soon."

Alma shakes her head. "We can still do something."

"Like what?"

"Like keep going," Alma insists, exasperated. "Amirah told me it would be a marathon, not a sprint."

"She was usually right," I accept.

"She was."

It's quite a nice moment, thinking about our departed friend, only to be ruined by a dung beetle's severed head, as big as a large motorbike, cannoning into us. Thrown through the air, it bowls me completely over and knocks the wind out of me. Sprawled out on the ground, I turn just in time to see Atog rush Alma.

He's angry, desperate, bloodied, and vengeful. His face is ragged, his eyes worn out, he's covered in blood, and his attire has been torn ragged.

"Piece of filth!" he roars in Alma's face. The much smaller vampire holds up her arms and tries to move out the way, but she's nowhere near quick enough nor strong enough. Atog throws her down with his immense strength and rains down hateful punch after hateful punch.

And I'm running. And incredibly I'm happy to be running. I want to do this. I have no regrets (I might have a few later, but that is a problem *for* later). I've got no plan, no idea, no hope, but still I'm running. What I find so incredible about this though is that I'm running towards Atog.

Atog's going to rip me limb from limb; I've no hope of doing anything except delaying Alma's beating. I simply can't save her. But still I'm here and I rugby-tackle the dude built like a rugby player. I may have country good looks and nice blond hair (and sparkling blue eyes) but I'm not exactly physically imposing, so this is only going to end one way.

Still, I catch Atog off guard and we crash to the ground. He growls in venomous rage and turns as lithely and speedily as an apex predator. *Whack!* My jaw barely stays connected to the rest of me. *Oof!* My gut turns to mush. *Crack!* Some of my bones are broken. I'm not sure which ones. Everything's a little fuzzy right now. *Smack!* That would be an advertising board I've just been slammed into. The slogan on it tells me how *Every Bit Helps* but right now, with my body feeling like a maraca, I could use a bit more.

"What do you want?!" Atog barks.

Alma's still on the ground and her body looks fragmented and crushed. She'll be a few minutes in the oven yet. But I can still just about stand. So, I do. And I face Atog.

"What do you want?!" Atog shouts again, demanding an answer. "What has all this achieved?!"

"Nothing," I admit. Maybe it could have been something. Perhaps somewhere in the future someone will look back and take inspiration from what we tried to do, but I doubt it. In all likelihood, this will just be another footnote in the long history of Vampire City. Certainly, right now, we've achieved less than nothing, because Duke's Borough will be punished for our insubordination.

"Then tell me," Atog persists. His face suddenly in my face. His eyes fixed on mine. His anger burning. "What did *you* want?"

I hold up my finger, asking for time to think of an answer, and to also delay the incoming beating. But what did I want? Change? I suppose so. Power? I wouldn't have said no. An easier life? That's arguably relative. Or was I just helping the poor and unfortunate? No. I spent years not helping them, so I'm not here because of them. So, why am I here?

"What do you want, little fang?" Atog asks again, gripping my throat. "Answer me!"

Well, I know what I don't want. I don't want to be *little fang*, but this doesn't feel like a big enough answer. And then it comes to me, and I know unequivocally why I am here and why I ran at Atog and why I tried to drag Poppy out the way and why I've stayed here and fought this entire time. "I want to feel better."

"So simple? So pathetic?"

"Following her made me feel better about myself. About everything."

"And now," Atog grins, his teeth yellow and his breath foul, "you will hurt tenfold!"

"I know," I sigh, "but I was hurting before, so… you know… at least now I'll feel better about it."

I try to move the thingamabob (which I really should have used earlier, but emotions and tiredness have played their part) up to Atog's face, but he grabs my wrist, breaks it, and then slaps the tiny, mystical red orb away. It rolls across the broken road and comes to a stop beside some rubble.

"No, no, no!" he laughs. "This is not the end for you," he tells me with insidious relish in his gravelly voice. "This is forever. This is *your* forever."

What follows is the worst beating I've ever taken. He kicks me, punches me, throws me, breaks me, and never lets me stop for air. Just when I think I'm completely numb, he finds a new way to hurt me. I taste my own dark blood in my mouth and cannot stop myself from swallowing it. For a few moments, I fade, and I can feel my dream state calling me, ready to take me away from all this. But he won't let me go. Every punch brings me back to the land of the living (or is that the living dead?).

This city street once boasted high-end shops alongside a constant parade of huge advertising paraphernalia, all of it haunting the bustling commuters and wealthy customers, but that was then, and this is now. Now this city street is only witness to a broken pavement, a cracked road, abandoned buildings, fallen adverts, and two vampires. One is a big vampire and the other is a smaller vampire, and the big vampire is beating down on the smaller vampire. Compare then to now and I'm not sure there is as much of a difference as one might initially think.

There is also a third vampire, fragile and miniature, laying crippled on the ground not so far away, but neither of the other two vampires are thinking of her right now. Atog's too caught up in his attack on me, and I'm too busy being attacked to spare Alma a thought.

Finally, mercifully, and perhaps inevitably, I land in a crumpled heap face down beside Alma, which reminds me she exists. Atog is coming, but he's taking his time now, apparently satisfied with his most recent throw. Alma turns her head slowly to look at me. Her chestnut brown eyes are bloodshot, her button nose is bloodied, yet despite it all she gives me a little smile.

"It's going to be alright," she tells me weakly.

This is absurd. There is no rhyme nor reason behind this statement. No logical thought process could possibly arrive at such a belief. Hope is one thing, but this is like buying a lottery ticket with your last penny. And yet I believe her. I don't know why. I just do. She brings it out of me. So it really is going to be alright.

"What do you want?" I hear myself asking her, but I don't recognize my own voice. It's too broken, too cracked, too small. I'm not sure why I ask this question either. Maybe my brain is a bit frazzled. Or maybe I just want Alma to give me something to help me through this. Maybe what I want isn't actually enough and I need someone like her. I guess, at the end of it all, I just want an answer that will justify all of this. Tall order, I know.

She smiles again. And then she laughs! Unable to keep it inside her, she has to endure the pain of her broken ribs and her tortured throat as she chokes up a laugh, before eventually replying, "I want to go home… I don't belong here… and I want to see my mum…"

And then it all falls into place.

That witch.

The one who gave Chips the thingamabob. She knew it would be like this, of course. And now I know why she wanted someone like me to wield her gift, and not someone like Alma or Amirah, and I know why the thingamabob didn't do anything to me when I touched it.

I roll onto my back. Atog is still coming but he's far away and even further from my thoughts. I look up and I want to stare up at the darkening sky, but all I see are two blank eyes staring down at me. I feel like I was expecting to see them though. It's the same kind of feeling I had when I pulled the thingamabob from Chips' pocket.

She looks too young to be what she is, but what she is isn't entirely clear, so maybe looks aren't all that helpful. Her gaunt white eyes stare down at me, her baby cream skin appears remarkably smooth and unblemished, and her long fair hair hangs over me, casting me in the kind of shadow one gets when lying under the canopy of a forest.

Her grey hoodie, which covers almost her entire body, is still just as dirty as it has ever been, but what I have never seen is what I am looking up at right now. She's smiling. This banshee that has haunted me ever since I dropped into Vampire City is smiling for the very first time. It's somehow creepy and heartwarming at the same time. But this time I'm not going to tell her to piss off. This time I'm not going to attack her. This time I'm not going to ignore her. This time I know what I need to do. So I smile back, I welcome her, I open up my mind, and I ask her to help.

The banshee brings her hand up and reveals she is holding the thingamabob. My thingamabob. This bad omen girl that has haunted me for years is now, with a smile shared between us, my little saviour. She was always an omen, but every time before this time, it was my own actions that made her into a bad one. Now, though, she's right on time. I wonder how such mysterious cosmic paths can lead us to where we need to be and how they guide us into becoming who we're supposed to become, and I am awed by the great unknown wonder that weaves such fates—Atog stamps on my groin. Admittedly, vampires don't have much need of that area, but it's still there and so it still really hurts when a fifteen-stone, muscle-ripped killer drives his boot into it.

My banshee flitters away, skipping speedily out of view, and Alma's still lying broken on the ground next to me. But I have the thingamabob now. My thingamabob.

"That little bauble won't save you, little fang." Atog grins down at me. "It just put me right back where I belong—here!" *I know*, I want to say, but then he kicks me again, in my chest this time, and I crumple in on myself with my back to Alma. "So, you are not the knight in shining armour," the big brute continues, kicking me in my stomach this time, "and this is no fairy tale ending!" This time his boot strikes me across my face and spins me round.

Through dark blood I see Alma watching me, her chestnut eyes reaching out for me. "You have nothing to gain," Atog growls before stamping on my side, breaking most of my ribs. "You have nothing to fight for!" Another stamp, breaking what's left of my rib cage (breathing is now quite difficult). "You have risked it all…" a hard kick to my spine, I think my back is broken but it's difficult to be sure right now, "…for nothing!"

"Not for nothing," I splutter, unable to move most of my body. I am lying sideways on the ground, staring at Alma, and she is staring at me.

"For *her*?" Atog scoffs, laughing loudly. "She's just another useless, pathetic little fang. Just like you!"

"No," I manage to say with blood in my mouth and my head breaking from within. "She's not… like me."

I take one almighty breath, and I do what I was always supposed to do. This is why the thingamabob was sent to me, because I'm the only one who wouldn't have attacked with it or run away with it. I'm the only one who could have come to this conclusion. She's ready now. She knows what she needs to do. And now someone from this city needs to put her there.

And I'm that someone. "She's not a fucking vampire!" I shout, then I cry with the effort to lift my arm, bringing my hand down on Alma's face and so pressing the thingamabob onto her skin. I wish I could say it beams with white, iridescent light and that all is well and Alma smiles in peaceful serenity. But no. It's the same red light infecting her skin. It's the same agonizing scream coming from her lips. And then darkness for a moment, and when the world returns to my vision, Alma is gone. "She's not a vampire," I whisper, and I fade with the last of my energy spent.

***

For a moment, I catch my breath. It's nice. I even have time to wipe the sweat from my brow. One has to appreciate the little things, especially when the big things are the ones currently hunting you down.

It's dark here. The night sky is a mesmerizing picture of twinkling stars over Vampire City, but their light doesn't quite reach this far down. This is a dark side alley. Just a nook and a cranny in which I have found momentary respite from the hunt. Even now though, I can hear them. Howling. Laughing. Calling my name.

"Caiden!" they cry. "Caiden! Come out and play!"

I'll have to get going in a moment, but for now, I pause, and I listen. The earphones are taped to my head (from prior experience, they often fell off whenever I started to run) and the song is telling me to *straighten up and fly right*. Out of all the CDs from the (full) 100-disc wallet I found nearly a year ago, this CD ranks somewhere in the middle. Still good. Not exactly me though.

For what feels like the umpteenth time throughout this past year, I thank whatever deity might be out there that I found this wallet next to an old Walkman. It really is my little reward.

Somewhere out there, in the big wide world, there's some schmuck who forgot to take his music collection with him when he and the rest of humanity abandoned this place, thus condemning this city to the likes of me… and them. And here they come.

I leap up, climb the back-alley fire escape, hop from one ledge to another, then slip on the edge of the rooftop and fall, squealing like a piglet, to land painfully on my back.

"They're coming."

I look up into the sardonic eyes of Helisha, her shiny black hair in little buns, her black attire more party than predator.

"As they are wont to do," I sigh, taking her offered hand and standing back up.

"Oh, come on." She smiles. "It's not as bad as it used to be."

"That's true," I nod. "In another year's time, I might even have a night off from being hunted down, brutally beaten, and, sometimes, torn apart."

"At least none of the lords bother with you anymore."

"Just their ever faithful, pawing underlings," I shoot her a look. "Speaking of which, how is it in Serat's new clubhouse?"

"He barely talks," Helisha tells me. "He barely even drinks from us anymore."

"He still owns you though," I point out.

"He owns you too," Helisha points out right back at me.

"Ah, yes," I huff. "Order is restored, and I am the black sheep of the blackest city in the world once again."

"What do you reckon she's doing now?" Helisha asks me, a little out of the blue, but then our conversations are quite infrequent now and often time-sensitive, so maybe I shouldn't be surprised. Still, the question catches me off guard.

"Hm? Oh. No idea," I say quickly.

"I wonder where she is." Helisha looks up at the small section of starry sky directly above the alley.

"Well, she's not here," I reply, glancing over my shoulder. They're coming closer. I'll have to get moving soon. "And that… is all that matters."

"You know," Helisha wonders aloud, "I've been thinking—"

"Think quickly, please," I say as I start to hear boots running across nearby streets.

"We can't even be sure your little trick worked," Helisha continues, unbothered by my pursuers.

"The thingamabob moved whoever it touched to wherever they belonged," I say. "That's why it only moved the lords back to their own boroughs. That's why it didn't move me anywhere."

"And you still think it sent Alma to her home? To her family?" Helisha asks me, with more than a hint of hope in her question.

"I do."

"Why?"

"Because that's where she belongs, on the outside," I say, in full faith (admittedly of the blind variety). "But one day, Helisha, she'll come back. She's a pusher, which is what we need right now," I insist, regurgitating the thoughts that have spun around in my head throughout this whole year. "But she also knows the value of a good leader, and the world will become caught in her wake, as we both were. She'll never stop finding a way to fix this rotten city, she might even find a cure for us, and then she'll come back, and she'll bring a new world with her. We just had to… get her out of the rat race first. Free her from a system designed to crush her."

"And after she changes the world, we live happily ever after, right?"

"Why not?" I smile, just as some of Serat's vampire cronies turn into the alley and spot me. "We might as well try," I say quickly, "and you never know, it might actually work."

"Go on, then. Run, Caiden," Helisha laughs.

And so I run, in blind faith and with headphones on.

THE END

About Robin Brown

Robin started writing as a young boy because his Dad's old computer could barely play Minesweeper. Despite purchasing a modern gaming computer to play Minesweeper today, it turns out Robin is terrible at it and doesn't understand the rules anyway, so he's taken up writing again.

He is over twelve thousand days old and lives somewhere in Manchester, England. He is genuinely not a hundred percent sure exactly where.